SUNSHINE AFTER THE RAIN

JESSICA REDLAND

Boldwood

First published in Great Britain in 2025 by Boldwood Books Ltd.

Copyright © Jessica Redland, 2025

Cover Design by Lizzie Gardiner

Cover Images: Adobe Stock and Shutterstock

A CIP catalogue record for this book is available from the British Library.

Paperback ISBN 978-1-83518-320-5

Large Print ISBN 978-1-83518-321-2

Hardback ISBN 978-1-83518-319-9

Ebook ISBN 978-1-83518-322-9

Kindle ISBN 978-1-83518-323-6

Audio CD ISBN 978-1-83518-314-4

MP3 CD ISBN 978-1-83518-315-1

Digital audio download ISBN 978-1-83518-318-2

This book is printed on certified sustainable paper. Boldwood Books is dedicated to putting sustainability at the heart of our business. For more information please visit https://www.boldwoodbooks.com/about-us/sustainability/

Boldwood Books Ltd, 23 Bowerdean Street, London, SW6 3TN

www.boldwoodbooks.com

To all the amazing people who have bought or borrowed my books, making it possible for me to write more, making it possible for me to write full-time, and making it possible for me to reach ten years as a published author. I cannot thank you enough for helping to turn the girl who read the books into the woman who writes them for a full decade. As long as you keep loving them, I hope to be able to keep writing them. To the next ten years with eternal gratitude... xx

AUTHOR'S NOTE

The Willowdale series is set around Derwent Water in the Lake District National Park – an area I know and love from many wonderful holidays. When I started writing the series, I had a burning question. Is it Derwent Water or Derwentwater? As it happens, there's no definitive agreement, with the versions being used interchangeably. I have chosen to consistently use the two-word spelling of Derwent Water because both Ordnance Survey and the National Trust use this. Neither version is incorrect.

There are also variations in spellings of fells and other places (e.g. Cat Bells and Friar's Crag), in which case I have gone with Ordnance Survey's spelling.

Please further note that, while I've used Keswick as an anchor for the fictional setting of Willowdale and do mention several real places in this series such as Carlisle and Ambleside, any businesses, farms and schools mentioned are fictional.

CAST OF RECURRING CHARACTERS
FOR SUNSHINE AFTER THE RAIN

There are several recurring characters across the Escape to the Lakes series. While I can add in backstory reminders as to who they are and their connections to other characters, I prefer to only do this when the information is relevant to the new story being told. I therefore thought readers might find this cast of recurring characters helpful. Please note that it only lists characters who have appeared in previous books. It does not include any characters appearing for the first time in this book as including them would give spoilers for the story about to unfold.

Rosie Jacobs
Owner of Willowdale Hall Riding Stables & Equestrian Centre at Willowdale Hall. Partner of Oliver

Oliver Cranleigh
Owner of Willowdale Hall. GP at a practice in Penrith. Partner of Rosie

Alice Jacobs
Rosie's mam. Lives in Horseshoe Cottage at Willowdale Hall with dogs Toffee and Chester

Xander Cranleigh
Rosie's dad. Hubert's cousin. Lives in Grasmere. Divorced with two grown-up children, Angelica and Evan. Good friends with Alice

Christian Wynterson
Oliver and Emma's dad. Retired science teacher. Lives in Pippinthwaite

Kathryn Cranleigh
Oliver's mum who died when he was twelve. Willowdale Hall has been in her family for generations

Hubert Cranleigh aka his Lordship
Former custodian of Willowdale Hall. Kathryn's husband and the man Oliver believed was his dad

Emma Wynterson
Oliver's half-sister. Partner of Killian. Lives in Pippinthwaite with her dad, Christian. Former Head of Sciences at Corbeck School in Carlisle. Now owns and runs My Alpaca Adventure – an alpaca-walking business at Willowdale Hall

Killian Buchanan
Groundsman at Willowdale Hall. Partner of Emma. Adoptive dad to his brother's children, Lyla and Elsa. Lives near Willowdale with his sister Aoife

Rachael Murphy
Emma's best friend. Head of Languages at Corbeck School in Carlisle

Autumn Laine
Rosie's best friend. Illustrator and aspiring author. Lives with partner Dane in Cotton-tail's Cottage in Willowdale

Dane Featherstone
Part-time chef at The White Willow and aspiring author. Member of Mountain Rescue. Father to grown-up son, Ellis. Lives with partner Autumn in Cotton-tail's Cottage in Willowdale

Kelly and Aled
Dane's aunt and uncle who own The White Willow. Parents to Felix and Maya

Maya and Jonah
Kelly and Aled's daughter and her fiancé. Live in Keswick. On the quiz team with Rosie, Autumn and Dane

Trudy Eccles
Retired teacher. Chair of the village hall committee. Lives in Pippinthwaite. Former owner of Cotton-tail's Cottage where Autumn and Dane live (belonged to her mum, Beatrice Eccles)

Robert 'Arnie' Mainprize
Landlord of The Hardy Herdwick in Willowdale. Host of the Thursday-night quiz

1

I picked up the empty tube of toothpaste and groaned. I'd already scraped my toothbrush along it several times to push out every last vestige of paste and it was time to admit defeat. Except I didn't have any spares – very unlike me to be so disorganised, although, with such a grim start to the New Year, it was hardly surprising something had slipped.

I'd spent Christmas and New Year in St Lucia and remembered a packet of miniature toiletries I'd been given on the flight home. I crouched down and rummaged in the various storage containers in the under-sink cupboard in the hope that I'd tossed it in there in case of emergencies.

'Yes!' I muttered, spotting the package. As I reached for it, I knocked over a can of body spray and my heart sank as I spotted it was one of Graeme's. He evidently hadn't checked the cupboard in his haste to clear out his stuff last night. I'd told him there was no rush – that he could come back another time or I could drop it off for him – but he'd seen no point in prolonging things. I could relate to that. When I'd made the decision to leave my husband,

Flynn, I'd felt that way too – had just wanted to pack up and leave.

Had Graeme left anything else? I couldn't see any more of his belongings in the cupboard but, body spray in my hand, I wandered across the hall into my bedroom and checked the drawer he used when he stayed over. A feeling of weariness overcame me as I closed the empty drawer. Slumping down on my bed, not caring that the towel swathed round me was wet, I sprayed the can and breathed in the scent of bergamot and sandalwood. I liked it but I didn't love it, which struck a chord with me because I'd liked but hadn't loved Graeme. It was right that it was over, but that didn't stop me feeling sad about it. I was going to miss his company.

I shivered and goose bumps broke out over my entire body. We were a third of the way into January and the central heating in my rented flat was on its last legs. Sitting still in a chilly room wrapped in a soggy towel with wet hair dripping down my back wasn't ideal, but I couldn't seem to muster the energy to haul myself up and get ready, especially when I had mixed feelings about how I'd be spending the day, or rather *where* I'd be spending it.

I was returning to Willowdale – the small village beside Derwent Water in the stunning Lake District National Park where I'd been raised and where my parents, Bruce and June, still lived – to celebrate my mum's eightieth birthday. I loved that part of the world so much but I rarely went back. It held so many painful memories that I had to psych myself up ahead of each visit and invariably returned to Newcastle feeling emotionally drained. Having Graeme accompanying me the last few times had helped deflect the standard question – *When are you coming home?* – but without him by my side today, I'd not only be asked that but there'd be a host of other questions about why we'd split up, none of which I wanted to answer. Too complicated.

I winced, realising I probably should have let my sister Georgia know that there'd be one less for the meal. I glanced at my phone charging by the bed and shook my head. I'd message her from the car instead, right before I set off – best way to avoid an interrogation.

Shivering again, I wished I could crawl under the duvet and give today a miss, but it wasn't an option. I had to go. My family had been supportive of my move to Newcastle-Upon-Tyne after I'd left Flynn. I think they understood why I needed to get away, but I was fairly sure they didn't understand why I'd stayed away. Sometimes I wasn't sure of that myself.

I looked round the bedroom and sighed heavily. It was the first flat I'd viewed that summer. Built in the 1980s, boxy and soulless, I'd only planned to stay for six months while I worked out what my life would look like without my family around me. Six and a half years later, I still hadn't moved flat and I hadn't moved on either.

My mobile ringing made me jump. Spotting Georgia's name on the screen, I hesitated. I knew why she was calling. She did it every time there was a family get-together. But if I spoke to her now, I'd have to tell her about Graeme. Better to ignore it. The ringing eventually stopped but started up again moments later. Georgia always did that and, if I didn't answer, she'd keep calling until I did. Rolling my eyes, I accepted her FaceTime request.

'You took your time,' she said, raising her eyebrows at me. 'I was beginning to think you were screening your calls and avoiding me.'

I pointed to my wet hair. 'I've just got out the shower. Didn't think you'd want me answering in the nip.'

'Too right!' She pulled a mock-disgusted face. 'Does this mean you're still coming?'

'Of course! You don't have to keep checking, you know.'

'Don't I? Because you've never dipped out before, have you, Mel?' she said, her tone teasing.

'Yeah, but I've always let you know. I've never just not shown up and there's no way I'd miss Mum's eightieth.'

'Good. I know Mum and Dad never visit you, but it doesn't mean they don't miss you.'

'I miss them too. It's just...'

Georgia nodded slowly. 'I get it. But it's been seven years, Mel. I know you can't put a timescale on grief, but you'll *never* come to terms with it if you keep hiding away.'

My shoulders sagged as another wave of weariness overcame me. 'I'm not hiding.'

She raised her eyebrows at me once more.

'Okay, maybe I was at first but this is my home now and I like it here.'

'You *like* it? Such a glowing endorsement. You should work for the tourist board. Come and visit Newcastle. You'll *like* it here.'

'You're hilarious.'

'I am, and I'm also honest. You *like* Newcastle but you don't *love* it. You *love* the Lakes.'

I opened my mouth to protest but I'd never been able to lie to Georgia. Newcastle-Upon-Tyne was a fantastic, vibrant city with loads to do and the people were so warm and friendly, but there was no getting away from the fact that it wasn't the Lake District. With each passing year, the yearning to return grew stronger but I wasn't sure I could do it.

'Were you just making sure I won't be a no-show or was there something else?' I asked, shivering once more as another droplet of water trickled down my back.

'So suspicious! There's no ulterior motive. A couple of Mum's friends have had to dip out due to illness and the Lakeside Inn want the final numbers so I thought I'd double-check that you and Graeme are still coming before I call them.'

'I'll be there, but Graeme won't be,' I said, trying to sound casual.

'No! Really? Is it work? I thought he'd booked the weekend off ages ago.'

Graeme was an Accident and Emergency doctor. He'd occasionally taken a raincheck on our plans due to work pressures, but he'd never have let me down for a significant event like this. Graeme had never let me down on anything that counted. I wore the crown for that.

'It's not work. It's me. We've split up.'

Georgia's eyes widened and her mouth dropped open. 'Why?'

'It wasn't working.'

'Since when?'

'Does it matter?'

'Yes! I'm your big sister and I had no idea you were having problems. I need the details.'

'Well, if you want me to be on time to Mum's party, you can't have them.'

She sighed. 'I'll get it out of you later. How did he take it?'

'Badly. Said a few harsh things.'

'Like what?'

'Seriously, Georgia, do you want me to get ready or not?'

'Okay, I'll let you go. We can dissect it over a bottle of wine tonight.'

'There's not that much to tell. We'll be done halfway down the first glass.'

She shook her head. 'Uh-uh! Not accepting that. You were together for two years, Mel! There are things to talk about.'

'Clock's ticking,' I said, tapping my bare wrist, my *nothing-to-see-here* mask firmly in place.

'See you soon,' she relented. 'Drive carefully.'

'Always do.'

We said our goodbyes and disconnected.

Dropping my phone on the bed, I returned to the bathroom and squeezed some cold water from my long dark hair. I reached for my hairbrush but I didn't use it, staring instead at my reflection in the mirror with a sigh. Georgia was right. Nobody walks away from a two-year relationship without feeling something. I hadn't. I really was sad that it had ended, but I also felt guilty because the sadness wasn't about the relationship being over – it was about my social life being over. What did that say about me? The thing is, I'd thought Graeme understood. I'd thought we were on the same page about what sort of relationship we had. Turned out we hadn't even been in the same book. So I wasn't only sad. I was also annoyed and frustrated that everything had changed and fearful of the emptiness that lay ahead. Especially when that meant even more time to think and remember and regret.

* * *

Half an hour later, I pulled out of my parking space and set off on the two-hour journey cross country to Willowdale. Driving in the city centre always put me on edge. I hated the volume of traffic, the pedestrians stepping out without looking, the food delivery drivers on their electric bikes jumping red lights and swerving onto the footpaths, the noise and general chaos. The moment I left the outskirts and reached the lush green countryside, that tension ebbed away.

I'd always strongly proclaimed that I wasn't a fan of city

centres, feeling hemmed in by the tall buildings and so many people, so my family had been right to question my choice of Newcastle but, at the time, it had felt logical. It took me away from home, but not ridiculously far. It was more convenient than Willowdale for my job as a conservation architect – a role specialising in the preservation of historic buildings – because I worked on more projects in the north-east than the north-west of the country. And the biggest pull had been that living in Newcastle would be completely different to life in Willowdale. I foolishly believed the contrast would make a fresh start easier.

I usually listened to the radio when I was driving and particularly enjoyed a local radio station which only played music from the seventies, eighties and nineties, evoking happy memories of my childhood, teens and twenties – a time before my world turned upside down and I lost everything.

'Welcome to Themed Thirty,' Ricky the DJ announced in a sing-song voice brimming with enthusiasm. 'You know how it works by now – I give you a theme and we play thirty minutes of songs selected by you. Today's theme of weather has been a popular one and we've had some brilliant suggestions in so far so keep those requests coming. I'm sure you'll agree there's only one song we could possibly use to kick off today's Themed Thirty. Alleluia!'

I smiled as 'It's Raining Men' by The Weather Girls started. I loved the Themed Thirty. Ricky typically mixed regularly played tracks with some almost-forgotten gems and the choices were always upbeat so perfect for singing along to.

He followed The Weather Girls with some brilliant choices. 'The Sun and the Rain' by Madness – a song I'd almost forgotten – followed by Crowded House's 'Weather With You' and 'Tsunami' by Manic Street Preachers. The three tracks transported me back in time to school, university and work respectively.

The next track – 'Sunshine on a Rainy Day' by Zoë – also took me back to my university days but conjured up a more vivid memory of holidaying in Tenerife with Georgia and her husband Mark in the year Flynn and I got engaged. The heavens had opened and the four of us had bundled into the nearest bar, completely missing the signs for karaoke that night – not our thing at all. By the time we realised, none of us fancied another drenching so we stayed put. After a while, fuelled by alcohol, Georgia and I decided to give it a go. 'Sunshine on a Rainy Day' was our prayer for the weather to improve, delivered with gusto but not necessarily the right notes. Neither of us have ever liked being centre of attention, but we let go of our inhibitions in a bar full of strangers and I'd always cherish that special memory of bouncing up and down on the stage with the woman who was my best friend as well as my sister.

My stomach lurched as my memories moved on because that hadn't been the only special moment that evening. Even though we'd been together for a little over a year, I'd never heard Flynn sing so was convinced the karaoke host had made a mistake by calling his name. But Flynn took my hand and kissed it before holding my gaze like some gallant knight in a fairy tale. I could still remember the tenderness in his beautiful green eyes as he whispered, *This is for you, Mel.*

Shuddering, I focused back on the radio, trying to push all thoughts of Flynn from my mind. At least Ricky wouldn't play the weather-related song Flynn had sung to me – not uplifting enough for Themed Thirty.

'Final Themed Thirty tune coming up,' Ricky announced a little later. 'I hesitated about including this one as it's a bit slower than usual but it's such an anthem, I'm sure you'll forgive me. Over to you, Mr Withers.'

My stomach lurched once more. He'd only gone and chosen the one song I couldn't listen to anymore because it wasn't Bill Withers I heard singing 'Ain't No Sunshine' – it was Flynn, looking directly at me, serenading me with a velvety smooth singing voice that I'd no idea he possessed.

I jabbed at the radio, changing station, my heart racing. Maybe I should start listening to podcasts in the car instead. Less chance of being floored like this.

2

Lakeside Inn – the venue for Mum's birthday celebrations – was a hotel and restaurant in Willowdale, just a two-minute walk from my parents' beloved home, Derwent Rise.

It was Mum's actual birthday today – a Saturday – and, not being a fan of late nights, she'd decided on a lunchtime hot buffet, asking guests to arrive by noon with an anticipated 5 p.m. finish. There were only a few spaces left in the car park when I pulled in at quarter to twelve. A cold blast of air made me gasp the moment I opened the car door. Shivering, I yanked it shut, wrapped my scarf round my neck and put my coat on.

As I crossed the car park, I could see into the large conservatory where we'd be eating. There were flowers on the tables and balloon bouquets dispersed around the room and I wondered whether I should have volunteered to arrive earlier to help set everything up, but Georgia hadn't asked me to. I grimaced as it struck me that Georgia's suggestion before Christmas that I stay at hers last night as well as tonight *to give plenty of time to get organised* had been her subtle way of asking for help. I was fifty-two years old. How had she not realised in over half a century shared on this planet that subtlety was completely lost on me? Hopefully she'd had some willing volunteers and hadn't needed to do everything by herself.

Laughter and loud chatter hit me before I even opened the side door and nervous butterflies swooped in my stomach as I stepped into the foyer. *Please let it go well.* Georgia had told me that the guest list was a mix of relatives and friends. The former nearly all lived in Cumbria and the latter mainly in Willowdale, Pippinthwaite – the next village over where Georgia and Mark lived – or in the nearby market town of Keswick.

There were several hooks on the wall so I hung up my coat and scarf as I peered through the glass doors into the bar, looking for my immediate family. Mark was talking to my Auntie Sue – Mum's younger sister – and I soon spotted Mark and Georgia's kids, Keira and Regan. I say kids, but Keira was twenty-six, married and expecting her second baby in the spring and Regan was twenty-four and living with his long-term boyfriend Clarke. Every time I saw my niece and nephew, I experienced a moment of surprise that they were grown adults and not the little children I remembered chasing each other round the garden or splashing in the lake.

They all looked deep in conversation and I didn't like to interrupt so I hovered by the coats, wringing my hands, trying to muster the businesswoman in me. She wasn't fazed by walking into a room full of people and striking up conversations with strangers, so entering a room consisting mostly of family and former neighbours should be a breeze. But it wasn't.

A couple I didn't recognise arrived, smiled politely, and removed their coats. They made a show of trying to get round me to hang them up – my cue that I couldn't loiter in the foyer forever. I apologised for being in their way, took a deep breath and pasted a smile on my face, steeling myself against the inevitable barrage of comments about my absence over the years.

Opening the door, I was immediately hit by a combination of heat emanating from a real fire mingled with the warmth of lots of bodies in a relatively small space. I eased my way through the bar, smiling and nodding but inwardly cringing as the predicted remarks came thick and fast. Several greetings of *Hello, stranger!* vied for popularity alongside *Long time, no see!* I caught whispers of *I was beginning to think she wasn't coming* and one of the villagers even said it to my face, accompanied by, 'Your mum's going to be so happy to see you at last,' the final two words spoken with great emphasis after a pause. Made me wonder what Mum had been saying to her friends about me.

Even though the comments were delivered light-heartedly (the whispers perhaps not so much), I couldn't help feeling judged.

'Auntie Mel!' Keira cried, approaching me with her arms out for a hug and rescuing me from a conversation with another villager about how long it had been since my last visit.

'Great to see you,' I said, hugging her. I stepped back and took in her baby bump. 'How are you feeling?'

'Really good. Did Mum tell you what we're having?'

'No, she wanted it to be your news.' Keira and Johnnie already had a two-year-old girl called Astrid. They hadn't wanted to find out the gender when they were expecting her and had intended on remaining in blissful ignorance with baby number two but curiosity had got the better of them.

Keira removed a scan photo from her handbag and passed it to me. 'Meet Astrid's little brother, Arlo.'

It would be customary to say something at that point – give my congratulations, tell her Arlo was a great name, comment on how cute it was that both siblings had names beginning with the same letter, say how lovely it was that they'd have a boy and a girl – but I had nothing. I stared at the baby photo, instantly transported back in time to when I'd held a scan photo of my own, almost an identical match to this one.

All the way through Keira's first pregnancy, I'd been convinced she was expecting a boy and had tried so hard to prepare myself for it. I'd almost cried with relief when Georgia rang me with the news that the proud parents had welcomed a baby girl into the world. But now they *were* having a boy and I needed to get my act together. Quickly.

'Are you all right?' Keira asked, looking at me with concern.

'Hot flush,' I said, pulling at the neckline of my dress with one hand as I handed back the photo. 'The joys of being a woman of a certain age. Congratulations. I'm so pleased for you all and I can't wait to meet baby Arlo.'

I wafted my neckline again and tucked my hair behind my ears. 'Sorry, Keira, I'm going to have to nip to the ladies' to cool off. I'll speak to you later.'

Without waiting for a response, I made a beeline for the toilets, relieved to find them deserted. I placed my hands either side of one of the sinks and braced my arms as I took several calming breaths. Raising my head to look in the mirror, I sighed. Hot flush? One glance at my paler-than-a-snowman's cheeks and there was no way Keira would have bought that. Hopefully she'd get distracted and forget about my reaction.

The door opened and Auntie Sue entered, permeating the room with her signature lily-of-the-valley fragrance. She smiled as soon as she saw me and drew me into a hug, kissing me on both cheeks.

'Lovely to see you, Mel. How are you doing?'

'Fine, thanks. You?'

'Wonderful. I swear that op has given me a new lease of life.'

I had no idea Auntie Sue had needed an operation. She'd likely assumed one of the family had told me, but they hadn't and, to be fair to them, I couldn't remember the last time I'd asked after my auntie. With no kids of her own, she'd always been really close to Georgia and me and I should have made more effort to stay in touch. One more thing to feel guilty about.

'That's great news,' I said. 'We must catch up properly later. Have you seen Mum?'

'She's in the conservatory with your dad and Georgia. The landlord just announced ten minutes until we can join them so, if you haven't already got yourself a drink, you might want to wait. There's drinks on the tables.'

'Thanks for the heads-up.'

Auntie Sue disappeared into a cubicle and I headed towards the conservatory in search of my parents and sister. The double doors were closed and there was an A3 sheet taped to one of them.

Welcome to June's 80th birthday
Please relax in the bar until called through.
Thank you!

There was a lovely photo of Mum on the sign. I hadn't seen it before but I recognised her surroundings as the back garden at Derwent Rise. Either side of the door were easels on which rested boards full of photos. The board on the left depicted Mum's first four decades and the one on the right showed the next four. All the photos were at jaunty angles and mounted on pretty patterned paper with floral stickers and swirls filling in the gaps. Guilt prodded me again. This was Georgia's work and it must have taken her hours to create. She'd said she was displaying a few photos but I hadn't imagined something as impressive as this. I could have helped if I'd known this was the plan, although perhaps I should have realised. It *was* Georgia, after all, and she never did things by halves, especially when it came to anything creative.

I peered through the glass, debating as to whether to go in or take heed of the sign. Directly opposite the door at the far side of the room was a long table and Mum was sitting on a chair pulled out at the end of it. Nearby was a small table holding a three-tier birthday cake. By the looks of it, Mum was directing Georgia on the angle to display the cake while also directing Dad on where to place a pair of giant silver balloons in the shape of an eight and zero. I smiled as I watched them. Mum did like everything to be just so. The interior of Derwent Rise was always immaculate with everything in its right place. When we were kids, Georgia and I used to wind her up by moving her ornaments a couple of centimetres and seeing if she'd notice. She never said anything, but they always moved back. We escalated our mischief with swapping ornaments around and, once more, they moved back with nothing said. Then I went and took it too far, swapping her favourite figurine of an Edwardian flower seller with the toilet brush. In my defence, the toilet brush was clean and dry, but Mum read me the riot act for that one and we never messed with her belongings again.

I slowly pressed down on the door handle and crept inside.

'But Mum! This is where it was at the start!'

Georgia normally had the patience of a saint so they must have been faffing with the cake for quite some time for her to sound so exasperated.

'It isn't,' Mum insisted.

'It is. Exactly.'

'Okay, it is, but it might have looked better from a different angle so it was worth a try.'

'How long have you two been bickering?' I asked, crossing the room, immediately kicking myself for such a negative opening statement. Couldn't I have gone for a straightforward *hello* or *happy birthday*?

'We're not bickering,' Mum said, her tone a little defensive. 'Just perfecting a few things. If you're going to do something, you should do it well. You know that.'

It was Mum's mantra for life and was the approach I took to my work. If only I'd managed to apply it to my personal life.

'Happy birthday, Mum!' I said as I bent down to hug her.

'Thank you, Melanie. Your lovely card arrived yesterday, but why didn't you save the postage and bring it today?'

'I wanted you to have something to open when you woke up this morning.'

'I see! That's okay, then. We were concerned it meant you weren't coming today.'

That sounded like a dig but I maintained my smile. 'I did write *look forward to celebrating with you* inside.'

She nodded but didn't respond, which I translated as *they're just words and it's actions that count*. Or was that my own guilt filling in the blanks?

'I've missed you!' Georgia launched herself at me and held me tightly.

'The guests will appear at any moment,' Dad said, so Georgia released me.

'Good to see you, Mel,' Dad said, giving me a quick hug. 'Let's get you over to the door, June.'

I stepped aside as Dad and Georgia helped Mum up from her chair.

'Can you put the chair back?' Dad asked me.

'Sure.' I pushed the chair back under the table and did a double take. Mum had linked her left arm through Georgia's and her right arm through Dad's. Since when had she needed help to walk? I caught Georgia's eyes, my eyebrows raised in question. She shook her head slightly and focused back on assisting Mum.

I watched, my stomach in knots, as Mum shuffled across the room, clinging onto my dad and sister. A few years ago, after struggling with severe back pain, Mum had been diagnosed with degenerative disc disease or DDD. Not actually a disease, despite the name, DDD was a condition where the discs between the vertebrae deteriorated over time, affecting a person's movement. Mum and Dad used to trek miles across the fells and I knew she'd stopped doing that the summer before last, but I had no idea her mobility had deteriorated to the point where she needed assistance from two people to cross a room. Why had nobody said anything? Another stab of guilt. Why hadn't I asked? Or, better still, why hadn't I visited more often to see for myself?

As the guests filtered in and were welcomed by my parents and Georgia at the door, I felt somewhat superfluous. They hadn't asked me to join them and it didn't feel right to include myself in the welcoming committee without an invitation. No way could I smile and laugh and give the impression that I was an important part of Mum's special day when I didn't feel as though I was. Their welcome hadn't been overly warm, although, to be fair to them, there hadn't been much time and they had been distracted. I kicked myself once more for not having the foresight to accept Georgia's invitation to stay at hers last night.

I glanced around the room at the rapidly filling tables. They were rectangular, each set up with between six and ten chairs. There hadn't been a seating plan outside so presumably guests would park themselves at a table appropriate to their group size and mingle after the buffet. The only reserved table was the large one where Mum had been sitting. I counted the chairs – nine plus a highchair, which had to be for Astrid. Mum and Dad plus Georgia's family made eight adults so the ninth chair was either for me or Auntie Sue. If I was meant to be sitting with my parents, surely they'd have said something, although when would they have had the time with me turning up at the eleventh hour?

The last time I'd felt this uncomfortably conspicuous was when I was aged eight and in the school Christmas nativity dressed as a snowman because there would, of course, have been heavy snow in the Middle East at the birth of Christ. I managed to trip over my own feet, face plant the manger, send the baby Jesus flying into the audience where it clobbered Toby Parkin's grandma on the head and broke her glasses. All the while I lay beached centre stage because my snowman costume was so round and padded that I couldn't get up. And every single moment was caught on camera and, even worse, on camcorder to be trotted out at every possible humiliation opportunity.

There were no dark corners in the conservatory for me to retreat into and the only escape routes were a fire exit on the far side, which would activate an alarm, or pushing through all the guests filing in. So I was stuck there, hovering awkwardly between tables, smiling and saying *hello* in between nibbling on a piece of loose skin round one of my fingernails and making it bleed.

'They haven't told you where to sit, have they?'

I turned at his gentle voice and smiled gratefully at my nephew Regan and his boyfriend Clarke.

'Is it that obvious?' I asked Regan as I hugged him.

'Gotta say, the helpless finger-chewing was a bit of a red flag.'

I glanced down woefully at my sore finger and tutted to myself before giving Clarke a hug, so grateful that they'd come to my rescue. I adored the pair of them. Although they were both country boys at heart, they enjoyed the occasional burst of city nightlife. Manchester's Canal Street was their favourite destination but Newcastle's Gay Village, also known as the Pink Triangle, came a close second. They always invited me to join them on a night out, which was sweet, but I usually politely declined, happier providing a bed for the night and a hearty breakfast in the morning. I'd joined them a few times to celebrate a birthday or other special occasion and it had been lovely but, like Mum, I just wasn't a late-night person. It seemed to take me a week to get over it, even if I wasn't drinking. I much preferred to be up with the lark and tucked up in bed by ten.

'You're sitting with us on Grandma's table,' Regan said.

'What about Auntie Sue?'

'She's with the other rellies.'

Mum was Auntie Sue's only remaining immediate family member but the pair of them had several cousins, most of whom were here today, so it made sense that Auntie Sue would join them.

Regan and Clarke led me to the reserved table.

'Anywhere in particular I should sit?' I asked, not wanting to make a faux pas by sitting in the wrong place.

'Grandma'll be in the centre facing her guests,' Regan said, 'and Granddad'll be next to her. Unless you want to feed Astrid, I'd suggest the opposite end to the highchair with us.'

'Facing the guests or back to them?' Clarke asked me.

'Definitely my back to them. I know they'll be talking about me but I'd rather not see it.'

'What they'll be talking about is how fabulous those boots are,' Clarke said, glancing down at my high-heeled purple ankle boots. 'They're divine. New purchase?'

'Especially for today.'

'Loving the accessories too.'

My hand immediately went to the matching purple pendant hanging over my charcoal-grey wool dress. I used to wear bright colours all the time but, when the colour unexpectedly left my world seven years ago, it left my wardrobe too. Now everything I wore was muted with only accent colours in my footwear and/or a piece of jewellery. Would colour ever fully return to my life?

Keira and Johnnie came over and Johnnie settled Astrid into the highchair while Keira retrieved some toys and a juice bottle from an enormous changing bag. I glanced round the room while they were getting themselves settled. The decorations were peach, silver and cream and Mum was wearing the same colours. I wondered if she'd chosen her outfit then matched the decorations to it or whether it had been the other way round. I probably should have known. It was easy to rule myself out of organising things because I didn't live locally, but I could have asked questions. I could have been part of this.

Mark appeared shortly after and gave me a hug as he sat down beside me and finally Mum, Dad and Georgia joined us. There were bottles of red, white and rosé wine on the table, pitchers of water and a jug of fresh orange. I reached for the latter and filled my glass. I'd accepted Georgia's invitation to stay at hers tonight and was meant to be leaving my car here overnight so I could have a drink but, with a strong flight urge kicking in, I wanted to keep my options open. I might drive back to Newcastle tonight instead.

Once everyone was settled, Dad tapped his knife against his glass, hushing the guests as he rose to his feet. I expected a quick welcome and a happy birthday toast to Mum, but it was a proper speech. He shared that they'd met at work but it had taken him a whopping eighteen months to pluck up the courage to ask her out and how grateful he was that his dithering hadn't lost her. He talked about how happy Mum made him and how proud he was to be by her side celebrating her eightieth birthday. Dad wasn't one for public speaking or declarations of feelings and he had me tearing up. It was funny how I just thought of them as my parents rather than a couple still deeply in love after sixty years together.

When he finished, Mum rose and spoke about how wonderful Dad was and how grateful she was for the beautiful family they'd raised.

'Doesn't the room look gorgeous?' she said, sweeping her gaze from left to right. 'This is all thanks to my eldest daughter, Georgia.' She looked down affectionately at my sister seated beside her. 'She booked the venue, organised the invitations, sorted out the decorations and the cake and even took me shopping for my outfit so I have a thank you gift for you, my angel.'

Dad produced a stunning bouquet of flowers and Georgia hugged my parents and thanked them for the gift before sitting back down, her cheeks glowing. It was then back to Dad who raised a toast to Mum, instigated a chorus of 'Happy Birthday to You', and declared the buffet open in the function room next door.

I smiled, lifted my glass and sang along with everyone else but it was a struggle to get the words out over the lump in my throat. It was right that Mum had acknowledged Georgia for organising her party. I didn't expect or deserve a mention because I'd done nothing, but it hurt that she hadn't mentioned me by name at any point during her speech. When she'd talked about her *beautiful family*, she'd specifically name-checked Georgia and Mark. She'd named her grandchildren and their partners and her great-grandchild. She mentioned *my beloved sister Susanna*, blowing a kiss to Auntie Sue, and named their cousins. Yet she hadn't mentioned me. I hoped it was an oversight rather than a deliberate slight. It could be that she'd thought the blanket term of *my beautiful family* was enough to cover us all, but why use that and then name every single family member present except for me? Even Arlo was mentioned and we wouldn't get to meet him until March.

Hopefully I'd been the only one to notice and we could forget about it, but when the guests started moving out for the buffet, I felt Regan's and Clarke's eyes on me. Regan placed his hand over mine.

'Are you all right?' he asked.

'Of course!' My voice sounded strained as it forced past the growing lump in my throat. 'Why wouldn't I be?'

He squeezed my hand. 'It won't have been deliberate.'

'If it was, I deserve it.'

'No, you don't,' the pair of them chorused.

I looked from Regan's eyes to Clarke's, my own filling with tears. 'Don't be nice to me. It'll tip me over the edge.' I drew a deep breath. 'So, how are the plans going for your side hustle?'

They'd met at art college, bonded over a shared passion for Victorian design, and now both worked for Clarke's family's business – Darrowby's Auction House & Removals, known locally as just Darrowby's. Most of their work was on the auction side of the business, undertaking house clearances, valuing items and running auctions. They loved it and had no intention of leaving but they were steadily building a side business capitalising on their artistic talents by designing Victorian-inspired textiles.

As I listened to them enthusiastically updating me on their business plans, my melancholy lifted momentarily but, when we returned from the buffet a little later, it came back. Everything had looked and smelled delicious, but I had no appetite for it and struggled to eat the few items I'd added to my plate. Looking down the table at my family chatting and laughing, I had the sensation of being on the edge of everything. There were updates on things I knew nothing about and in-jokes which made me very aware of how much of an outsider I'd become. Nobody had pushed me out. It was all on me. I hadn't just removed myself from my family physically by moving across the country to Newcastle. I'd removed myself emotionally. If Mum not mentioning me in her speech had been deliberate, that was all on me too.

3

As soon as Dad and Georgia helped her across the room to greet her guests, I'd been worried about Mum. When I'd noticed her gripping tightly to the table during her speech, that concern had deepened, but it was how the afternoon played out that made me realise how much her mobility had deteriorated since I last visited.

Mum loved socialising and I'd long admired her ability to circulate at events, ensuring she spoke to everyone. This afternoon she'd barely left her chair, allowing guests to come to her for a catch-up, sometimes prompted by Georgia. The only time she moved was to visit the ladies' and she'd clung to Georgia's arm as she crossed the room then. Without Dad to support her on the other side, it was clear to me how unsteady Mum was on her feet. I'd wanted to jump up and help but I'd noticed Dad watching intently, looking poised to rush over if needed, and concluded that Mum was trying to draw as little attention as possible to her mobility issues by just having Georgia's assistance.

I wanted to speak to my parents to find out how bad things really were, but this wasn't the time or place. Guests might overhear and it would likely dampen Mum's spirits on her special day. Any chance of a general catch-up with my parents was a struggle as, every time the chairs around them were vacated, someone else slipped in for a chat and I thought it would be rude to plonk myself down beside them and join in with someone else's conversation. Not that I had the confidence to do that unless the conversation was work-based.

By 4 p.m. I'd accepted that I wasn't going to get any time with my parents and, if I wanted to find out how Mum was doing, I'd need to make another trip over to Willowdale. I'd spoken to all our relatives and several of my parents' friends and was feeling exhausted from batting away the questions about when I was coming home. I needed to be where people weren't so I grabbed my coat and scarf and set off on a walk through the village. With sunset imminent, the light was fading but it wouldn't be fully dark for a while yet.

Wandering along the footpath, I passed The White Willow on the right – a café by day and bistro by evening during the peak season. I'd never been inside as it had only opened a couple of years ago but Mum and Dad were regulars. Their next-door neighbours, Aled and Kelly, owned it but as they'd only moved to the village after buying the café, I'd never met them myself. The outside lights were off, signalling that it was closed for the day, but I could see a couple of staff inside stacking chairs on the tables and cleaning the floor.

I passed houses on the left and right. Derwent Rise was five doors down from The White Willow. Warm white lantern lights strung across the front of my parents' home and fairy lights draped around a couple of potted shrubs either side of the door made it look really inviting. My parents loved their house so much. With stunning views across Derwent Water, it was hardly surprising – if a bit morbid – that they'd both said the only way they'd ever leave their home was in a coffin.

Reaching Willowdale Marina on the left, I paused by the entrance. If I kept walking, I'd hit a few patches without footpaths. Walking on the road in the dark wearing black clothes wasn't the best idea but I wasn't ready to return to the Lakeside Inn just yet. The metal barrier was down so vehicles couldn't get through but there was room to walk around it. I knew the owner and didn't think he'd mind if I cut through and wandered down to the lakeside.

I passed the buildings and headed down a slope to the pebbly beach. Several small motor boats and sailing boats were moored to a wooden pier in front of me. There was a smaller jetty at the other end of the beach with nothing moored to it. Several kayaks were hauled up on the beach in front of metal trolleys full of kayaks and canoes. Georgia and I had learned how to paddle both types of craft when we were kids and I had so many happy memories of splashing about on the water with my sister and our friends, playing tig, racing each other and doing challenges, as well as learning the safety and skills side of things.

The biting cold wind whipped my hair across my face and took my breath away. The lake was choppy but the sound of the water slapping against the beach was both mesmerising and comforting. Closing my eyes, I breathed in several deep lungfuls of fresh air, trying to quieten the battle inside my head.

Standing here beside the lake, even in the cold and darkness, I felt a sense of belonging. I never had and never would fall out of love with the Lake District. I still thought of it as home even though I hadn't lived here for years. I liked and appreciated Newcastle but my heart would remain forever in Willowdale with the lake, the fells, my favourite old building – Willowdale Hall – and, of course, my family who I loved and missed so much.

The positive memories of my home weren't only from my childhood. I'd had forty-five years of happiness here until that one terrible day when my whole world fell apart, the sunshine disappeared, and the black clouds arrived. The black clouds which rained down on me, and rained, and rained, and rained. If six and a half years living somewhere else hadn't brought the sunshine back, would it ever return? Would I be better off coming back here? Even if those dark clouds didn't disappear, at least I'd be with my family and not out on a limb, especially now that Graeme was no longer part of my life.

I opened my eyes and looked at the dark silhouettes of trees across the lake. Was I strong enough to come back knowing that Flynn was still here?

* * *

'I was worried you'd left.'

The picnic bench outside The White Willow creaked and shifted as Georgia stepped up onto the seat and sat down beside me on the table top a little later.

'I thought about it,' I admitted.

'Nowhere to sit over the road?' she asked, gazing in the direction of the Lakeside Inn diagonally opposite us.

'I didn't look. I went for a walk to the marina and decided to park myself here for a bit before returning to the party.'

'It's bitter out here,' she said, zipping her coat up higher, her breath hanging in the air. 'Aren't you freezing?'

'Can't feel my extremities anymore.'

We sat in silence for several minutes. A couple of cars passed, as did a teenager walking a dog, but he was too engrossed by his phone to pay any attention to us.

'Why didn't you say anything?' I asked eventually.

'About what?'

'Mum's mobility.'

'It's not really an over-the-phone conversation.'

'But I had no idea it was so bad. Why did nobody warn me?'

Georgia exhaled, long and slow. 'Dad wanted to give you a heads-up but I said...'

'You said what?' I asked when she didn't finish the sentence.

'I said you'd already run away to Newcastle and we didn't need to give you another reason to stay there, burying your head in the sand.'

She said the words gently but they felt like a punch to the stomach.

'Is that what you think I've been doing all these years?'

'Isn't it?'

'Of course not!'

'Then what *have* you been doing, Mel?'

'Having a fresh start.'

She blew on her hands and rubbed them together. 'How's that working out for you?'

When I didn't respond, she continued. 'What's Newcastle got that Willowdale hasn't? New job? Beautiful home? Relationship? Friends?'

'That's not fair.'

'Maybe not, but it's the truth. You're doing the same job you did before you left, you're still renting the first soulless flat you found, you've dumped Graeme and I'm pretty sure he was the only friend you made in the whole time you've been there.'

'Not true.' Actually, scarily accurate but it made my life sound like a disaster. 'I have got other friends.'

'Who?'

'Liz.'

'Liz?' She placed her fingers against her temples, the deep-thinking gesture exaggerated. 'Oh yeah, I remember Liz. Wasn't she the woman in your building who you went jogging with for six months before she moved back to Edinburgh and never contacted you again?'

I'd hoped she wouldn't remember that sad indictment on my ability to create a new life in Newcastle.

'Elspeth?' I suggested.

'A client in her nineties who invited you for afternoon tea as a thank you.'

Why did Georgia have such an exceptional memory?

'Hashtag friendship goals,' she said, nudging me playfully in the side and lightening the mood.

I laughed as I nudged her back. 'Don't ever use hashtag in a sentence like that again.'

'Why not? Hashtag down with the kids.'

'Oh, my God! Stop!'

We sat in silence for a couple more minutes until Georgia shivered from head to foot and clambered down from the picnic bench. 'I need warmth. You must too. Come inside and have a drink with me.'

'I might just say goodbye and drive home.'

'No, Mel, don't go. Stay at mine tonight as planned. In fact, stay longer. Join us for Sunday lunch tomorrow. It'll be less chaotic.'

I hesitated, torn between the desire to run and the knowledge that the only thing awaiting me on the other side of the country was loneliness.

'Who's coming?'

'Just the immediate family, although Regan and Clarke need to eat and shoot. They're preparing for a big auction next week so it'll be lively while we eat and calm once they're gone. You'll be able to talk to Mum and Dad properly then.'

'I'm not sure they'll want me there. Only family member not name-checked in Mum's speech.'

She grimaced. 'I was hoping you hadn't noticed that. Please don't hold it against Mum. It won't have been deliberate. She was looking forward to seeing you today.'

'So much that she didn't speak to me all afternoon.' I sighed as I slipped down from the bench. 'I had a longer conversation with the young lass serving behind the bar than I did with my own mother on her eightieth birthday. And it's not like I didn't try. I shuffled along the table several times, but...' I shook my head. 'Never mind. I brought it on myself. Come on. Let's get you inside before you turn blue.'

We crossed the road and entered Lakeside Inn's car park. Passing my car, I had to fight hard against the temptation to slip my hand inside my bag, retrieve my car keys and get out of here. At least the party was almost over. Even though Mum was in her element at gatherings like this, after five hours of pretty much non-stop chatter I knew she'd be ready to return to Derwent Rise, get out of her party clothes and switch off. There was therefore no danger of the evening continuing back at theirs. I could do this!

It was 4.50 p.m. by the time we returned to the conservatory and there'd been a mass exodus. A few members of staff were clearing tables and another one was handing over a large cardboard box to Dad, presumably containing what was left of Mum's birthday cake. Mum had changed tables and was now sitting with Auntie Sue. Their cousins had either left or moved into the bar and they'd been joined by a few of Mum's friends from the village who had full glasses of drink as though they were settled in for the evening. The rest of the guests were clearly preparing to leave, downing the last of their drinks or pulling on coats, ready to brave the elements.

'You *are* still here!' Mum exclaimed. 'I haven't seen you in ages. Sue and I thought you must have left.'

I could imagine how that conversation had gone – *She never sticks around, Sue. Always cancelling or rushing off.* And if it had gone like that, I deserved it.

'I wouldn't go without saying goodbye.' I pulled out a chair and sat down beside her. 'Have you enjoyed your day?'

She smiled at me. 'It's been wonderful. I think I managed to speak to most people, although it's not easy when you've got so many guests and don't want to offend anyone.'

The intense way she held my gaze made me wonder if there was an apology in there somewhere. I'd like to think there was. I'd found so much about today really tough and not being able to engage my own mum in conversation had been hurtful. But it was her special day, she'd enjoyed it, and that was the important thing here.

'That's what you get for being so popular,' I said, smiling back at her.

'Are you heading back to Newcastle tonight?' Auntie Sue asked.

'I haven't had anything to drink so...' I was about to say *I might as well*, but I caught Mum's expression. She looked sad. All day I'd been very aware of feeling on the outside of my family and out of date with what was going on, particularly with regards to Mum's health, and leaving tonight wasn't going to change that. But if I stuck around tomorrow, I could find out. It couldn't be any harder than today had been.

'...I could go back,' I continued, 'but I told Georgia I'd stay at hers and that's what I'm doing. In fact, she's invited me to stay for lunch tomorrow so I'm doing that, assuming that's okay with you, Mum.'

Mum's expressions always revealed what she was thinking

and that revelation had definitely taken her by surprise. Made two of us!

'Oh! Yes, of course!' she gushed. 'It'll be lovely to spend some time with you. I wanted to talk to you earlier but people kept appearing.'

'I know. It's all right. As I say, that's what you get for being so popular. Everyone wants a piece of you so I'm sticking around to get my time with you.'

I didn't want to prolong my stay but I needed to. I used to be so close to my parents but it felt like there was a wall between us now and only I could bring it down. I was worried about Mum and wanted to know what was really going on with her health and the only way anyone was going to give me the full story was if I put in more effort to be part of this family. The only problem was that getting my relationship with my parents back on track meant I needed to spend a lot more time in Willowdale. Doing so might fix things with them, but at what cost? Might it break me even more?

4

'Home time, I think,' Mum announced shortly after. 'It's been lovely but I'm ready for a rest now.'

Georgia fetched Mum's coat and scarf and, after Mum said her goodbyes, helped her into it. Mark was the designated driver and offered to drive her the exceptionally short distance to Derwent Rise but Mum insisted on walking, saying she'd spent nearly all afternoon stuck indoors on her backside and was craving some fresh air and exercise. She might well have craved it but her body didn't. My stomach churned as I watched her shuffle slowly across the car park, over the road and along the path to the bottom of Derwent Rise's drive. It struck me how small and frail she looked sandwiched between Dad and Mark. The three of them paused for quite some time before setting off up the drive.

'I wish she'd accepted the lift from Mark,' I muttered to Georgia.

'Me too, but it must be hard losing your independence like that.'

I was about to ask more but the rest of the family joined us.

'Astrid's getting crotchety so we're going to make tracks,' Keira said. 'See you both tomorrow.'

'Should we start loading the car?' Regan asked.

With a stack of gifts, flowers, balloons and the cake to carry, we'd agreed that it made more sense to load up Mark's car than do loads of trips over the road so Regan, Clarke, Georgia and I set to work clearing everything from the conservatory. The boys had already said goodbye to my parents so they headed off once the car was packed. Mark returned and drove his car across to the house and Georgia and I followed on foot, helping him to unload.

'Thanks for bringing everything over,' Dad said as he placed the giant eight and zero balloons in the corner of the lounge. 'I'd offer you a cup of tea but your mum's gone for a lie down and I don't want to disturb her.'

'We understand,' Georgia said. 'It's been a long day so we'll leave you to relax.'

We both hugged Dad and then I followed Georgia and Mark back to Pippinthwaite in my car. Mark carried Georgia's flowers and a bouquet of balloons inside then headed into Keswick to pick up a takeaway.

'I'm shattered,' Georgia said, kicking off her shoes in the hall. 'I'm dying to quiz you about Graeme but I'm craving a bath. Would you mind if I abandon you?'

'Please do. Happy to delay or, even better, forget about my interrogation.'

She shook her head, laughing. 'Delay? Yes. Forget? No chance.'

Georgia disappeared upstairs and I went into the lounge and flicked on the television but I couldn't find anything to hold my interest so I switched it off and sat in silence. I felt as though I was approaching another crossroads in my life, this time with three routes. The first involved staying in Newcastle and returning to life as it had been before Graeme – not a particularly appealing choice because it had been pretty bleak. A second one involved staying in Newcastle but coming back to Willowdale far more often. And the third route... I shuddered. Was I strong enough to even consider coming home for good?

'That feels better,' Georgia said, appearing in a fluffy dressing gown and slippers a bit later. 'Sorry about that. So, tell me about Graeme.'

But the sound of Mark's car pulling onto the drive thankfully put paid to that.

'You're not off the hook,' she said, heading into the kitchen. 'We'll discuss this later.'

Tiredness had taken hold of us all and the conversation over food was stilted. Afterwards, Georgia declared she had a headache and needed an early night so I was off the hook after all. I joined Mark in the lounge to watch a crime drama but I soon lost track of what was happening thanks to all the options spinning round in my head.

When the programme finished, I went upstairs to bed. I was usually a good sleeper but I couldn't settle. The bed in Georgia's spare room was incredibly comfortable, the temperature was spot on and it was wonderfully peaceful and quiet... except in my mind. No matter how hard I tried to relax, I could not switch off. I kept picturing Mum being helped across the conservatory and, later, across the road and worrying about how much I didn't know about her health. I kept thinking about how little contact I had with everyone except Georgia and how much I missed being a part of a close family – both emotionally and physically. I imagined my life back in Newcastle without Graeme and tried to weigh up which would be the most difficult – being lonely and cut off in Newcastle, or being back in Willowdale with my family but surrounded by painful memories and at risk of bumping into Flynn.

In the early hours, with no conclusion reached, I gave up fighting sleep and crept downstairs to make a hot chocolate.

'What are you doing up at half two?' Georgia asked, shuffling into the kitchen-diner in her slippers and dressing gown and yawning.

The kettle clicked off and I poured boiling water over the contents from an instant sachet.

'Mind too active,' I said. 'Want one?'

'Go on, then.'

I handed her the mug I'd just stirred and tipped the contents of another sachet into a fresh mug for me.

'Sorry if I woke you,' I said as I joined her at the large table. 'I tried to be quiet.'

'I was already awake.' She stirred her drink. 'It's not quite the same as a bottle of wine, but how about you tell me about Graeme over a hot chocolate instead?'

'There's nothing to tell.'

'Last I heard, you were talking about moving in together and now you've split up. There's definitely a story there.'

There was no way Georgia was going to let this one go. Nobody had mentioned Graeme's absence at Mum's party – and I couldn't decide if I was relieved or hurt by that – but it was bound to crop up over the Sunday roast and it would be better to have my sister on my side batting away questions rather than leading the charge.

'I never lied to Graeme,' I said. 'Right from the start, I was clear with him that I wasn't looking for anything serious and he swore he wasn't either. It seems my definition of *not serious* and his vastly differed because he asked me to marry him.'

'He did what?' she cried, eyes wide. 'When?'

'While we were in St Lucia. Just before New Year.'

'Oh, my God! No! What was he thinking?'

I sighed heavily, shaking my head. 'Exactly.'

'I'm so sorry, Mel.' She grimaced. 'That's shocking timing. Did you have any idea it was coming?'

'Not a clue. I don't know what possessed him. I'd never expressed any desire to get married again and we certainly hadn't talked about a long-term future together.'

Georgia wrinkled her nose. 'But you were moving in with him. Wouldn't that suggest long-term?'

'Moving in was meant to be a practical thing and temporary. I thought I'd told you that.'

When Georgia shook her head and looked at me blankly, I continued.

'The heating's knackered and the kitchen's falling apart so the landlord's getting his team in to do a big refurb next month. In theory, I could stay at the flat and have them work round me but it'll be too noisy to work – not to mention the mess. He offered to put me up in a B&B but that's no good either. I need a big room with natural light and you know how much I like peace and quiet when I'm working. So Graeme suggested I stay at his, which would have been perfect if he hadn't stupidly taken my acceptance of his kind offer as some sort of commitment to spending the rest of my life with him.'

'Not good. Urgh! I can't believe he proposed to you while you were away. I'd have credited him with more sensitivity than that.'

'Me too. You can probably imagine my reaction. What was even worse was that he didn't get why I was so annoyed.'

'You're kidding!'

'Apparently he'd have expected a negative reaction if he'd proposed on New Year's Eve or New Year's Day but he couldn't see why the thirtieth was an issue.'

Georgia winced again. 'I'm so sorry.'

'Me too. I still can't get my head around why he did it. I liked Graeme but that's not the same as being in love with someone. I'd never told him I loved him and he'd never said it to me either. If he had, we'd have had a serious conversation a long time ago and it would have been over then. Asking me to marry him was left field enough, but asking me while we were away just beggars belief. He *knows* why I go away for Christmas and New Year. He *knows* how difficult that time of year is for me. What would possess him to think that proposing then would be a good idea?'

I shook my head, reliving the excruciating moment when it happened. We'd had a delicious evening meal and were walking back to our room. The swimming pools were lit by pretty spotlights and surrounded by beautiful plants and water features and it looked really romantic. I'd made a passing comment about that and, next moment, Graeme dipped down onto one knee and whipped out a ring.

'Did you actually split up while you were away?' Georgia asked.

'Yeah. I tried to let him down lightly, saying I wasn't ready for marriage but he managed to add a big *yet* to the end of that. He was full of reassurances that there was no rush to set a date and I knew there and then that it had to be the end for us. There would *never* be a good time to set a date because I didn't want to marry him and never would. I could never give him what he wanted or what he deserved and he could never be right for me because proposing when he did showed how little he understood me.'

'You said he didn't take it well,' Georgia prompted.

'He was okay with me in St Lucia. He was embarrassed but managed to make a joke out of being relieved that he hadn't been brave enough to propose in the restaurant in front of everyone like he'd originally intended. He moved into another room and we still spent time together. It was a little strained but I did think we might manage to salvage some sort of friendship. We got home, had some time apart, and arranged for him to come round on Friday night to collect his things and it was awful. He was in a really argumentative mood and demanded to know why I'd said no. I was as gentle as I could with him but I mentioned the inappropriateness of the date and he just didn't get it. He told me I'd led him on, wasted his time, ruined his life. Nice stuff like that.'

Cold-hearted and *frigid bitch* had been thrown in for good measure. That hurt. It wasn't true, but I could see why he'd said those things. I'd held him at a distance, showed affection but not love, kept things from him.

'I'm sorry you've been through all that. Bet you wish you could have spent yesterday curled up in bed eating chocolate instead of feeling like an outsider at Mum's birthday party.'

'I never said I felt like an outsider.'

'Your mouth might not have but your eyes did. The smiles and polite conversation didn't fool me. You looked lost.'

Lost. It was the perfect word for how I felt right now. How I'd felt for the past seven years. I was fifty-two. I should have everything sussed by now but I'd never felt less in control of my life.

'I haven't been burying my head in the sand,' I said, referencing our earlier conversation outside The White Willow.

'I shouldn't have said that.'

'No, it's fine. I can see why you would. But you were right about the other part. I *did* run away to Newcastle. I had to. You do understand why, don't you?'

She gently placed her hand on my forearm. 'You know I do, and I think it probably was the right thing for you at the time. It's just that...' She paused and sighed, shaking her head. '...I'm not convinced it's right for you anymore, especially now that you've split up with Graeme. How about taking that as a sign that it's time to come home?'

I placed my hand over hers. 'I've been thinking about it all day, but I'm not convinced I can do it.'

She nodded vigorously, eyes wide. 'You can! I'm not saying it'll be easy, but I'll be here for you. You've got so many people here who love you and want to see more of you. Please come back to us.'

I knew how happy I'd make Georgia if I agreed to return, but this was a huge decision and not one I could make in one day.

'I'll keep thinking about it,' I said, my voice soft. 'I can't promise you more than that.'

She gave me a weak smile. 'I suppose thinking about it's better than a firm no.'

'You won't say anything to Mum and Dad in the meantime? If they knew I was thinking about it but decided to stay in Newcastle, I'm not sure they'd forgive me. I already feel like I'm such a disappointment.'

'You're not. I just think that, like all of us, they're struggling to understand why you've stayed away. They understood you leaving – they really did – and they might have continued that way if you'd...' She lowered her eyes as she tailed off.

'If I'd come back to visit more often,' I finished for her.

'A few more phone calls even?' she suggested.

'I kept meaning to but...' I shook my head. 'Anyway, I want to try to fix it but I'm going to need your help because I can't do it on my own. I've already made that mistake.'

She pushed her chair back and wrapped her arms round me. 'You're never on your own. You can count on me always.'

The only response I could give was to squeeze her tighter. I might have distanced myself from everyone physically and emotionally but Georgia had refused to let me go and I couldn't be more grateful. Her constant messages, phone calls and Face-Time requests as well as the intermittent trips to Newcastle – *I need some new clothes* or *I'd love to see that show at the theatre* – had been a lifeline for me and I'm not sure how I'd have made it this far without her.

Although I hadn't made a decision about my future home, I had finally admitted to myself that running away hadn't been the answer. But when the question was *how do you get over the death of your eighteen-year-old son and the subsequent end of your marriage*, was there actually an answer?

5

There was a joint of beef in the oven and Georgia, Mark and I had just finished preparing the vegetables when Dad rang on Sunday morning to say that the celebrations had taken it out of Mum so they were going to stay at home and give her a chance to rest.

'You'll still stay, won't you?' Georgia asked, looking at me with sad puppy-dog eyes.

I could hardly abandon them when we'd just prepared a mountain of food so I stayed for lunch and was glad I did. Keira and Regan had the same close sibling relationship as Georgia and me, full of affectionate teasing and the ability to tell it as it is without causing offence. Observing the banter between them over lunch, with Clarke as referee, was lovely but it was another reminder of how much I'd missed by leaving. It was also a reminder of who was missing. Growing up, Noah had been as close to his cousins as they were to each other. When Regan discovered he was attracted to other boys, Noah was the first person he told and, when Noah realised he wanted to be more than friends with our neighbour Jessie, it was Keira he turned to for advice. If Noah was here today, would the three of them still be as close? Would he be joining in the ribbing like he used to? I'd like to think he would.

Experiencing that same feeling I'd had at Mum's eightieth of being out of touch with what was going on with my family, I waited for a pause in the conversation and asked Regan and Clarke about their approaching auction.

'It's all from one house clearance and completely out of the blue,' Regan said. 'The client passed away at the cracking age of 101. He had no living relatives so he left instructions in his will that we were to do the house clearance with the profits split between five local charities.'

'It took weeks to go through everything,' Clarke continued. 'He lived in this enormous Victorian mansion and it was like stepping back in time. A few mod cons had been added for comfort but, other than that, it had barely changed. The things we found! Completely in our element, we were.'

Between them, they described some of the items – valuable paintings, clocks, vases, dinner sets and even clothing.

'One of my favourite finds was a Penny-farthing,' Regan said. 'It looked to be in good working condition so Clarke dared me to ride it.' He clapped his hand to his heart. 'I've never been so scared in my whole life. It's so high.'

The pair of them were in fits of giggles as they described Regan's attempts at riding the old-fashioned bicycle with the enormous front wheel and tiny back one.

'Did you have a go too, Clarke?' I asked.

'God, no! I had a really bad fall off a regular bike when I was ten – broke several bones – and I've never been on one since so no way was I attempting that beast. Regan's the cyclist, not that he does that much these days.'

I was surprised to hear that because Regan had been heavily into mountain-biking. He and Noah had spent many a weekend exploring the local trails.

'You don't get up to Whinlatter Forest anymore?' I asked.

Regan shuffled in his chair, looking uncomfortable. 'It's not the same without...' He tailed off, his shoulders sagging.

'Without Noah?' I asked, my throat burning.

'Sorry.'

'Don't be sorry,' I said, gently. 'I get it. When you've always done something with somebody and they're not there anymore, it's... it's not the same, exactly as you say.'

There was a moment's silence and it struck me how little we talked about Noah as a family. Why was that? Was it because I didn't tend to talk about him and they were taking my lead, not wanting to upset me? That wasn't fair on them.

'If Noah was here, I bet he'd have wanted a go on that Penny-farthing,' I said.

Regan smiled, but his eyes were glistening. 'He'd probably have wanted me to source another one and do races.'

'And you'd have tried to sabotage each other,' Keira added, her voice full of affection. 'Do you remember that time when he stole one of your pedals so you stole his seat?'

Suddenly the table was alive with conversation and laughter as memories were shared of the tricks the three of them used to play on each other. I lapped up the ones I hadn't heard before and joined in with others. It was wonderful but it was also an eye-opener to something I couldn't believe I hadn't thought of before – how much my family had been affected by losing Noah. I'd been so angry, so lost, so wrapped up in my own world that I hadn't paused to think that Georgia and Mark had lost their only nephew, Keira and Regan had lost their cousin and close friend, and my parents had lost their grandson. He'd been such an important part of all their lives and they should have been able to grieve for their loss with me and share their happy memories but I hadn't let them. How can you help others through their grief when you've bottled your own up?

6

The following day, I phoned home to check Mum was fully recovered. She spent most of the call updating me on conversations she'd had with her friends at the party, several of whom I didn't even know, but at least she seemed keen to chat to me. The call was about to end when she said, 'We didn't get to talk about Graeme on Saturday. What happened?'

Surprised at the sudden detour, I rolled out a standard excuse, 'We wanted different things.'

'Oh! What was it you wanted? Flynn?'

My stomach lurched. 'Flynn? Why would you say that?'

'Because it's true, isn't it? He's your magnet.'

'He's my what?'

There was a scrabbling sound and the next voice I heard was Dad's. 'Hi, Mel, yes, we're sorry to hear about Graeme. Are you all right?'

'I'm fine. It was for the best.'

'Good. Well, these things happen. We need to go. We're meeting friends at The White Willow. Speak soon.'

And before I could say goodbye, he'd disconnected the call,

leaving me staring at my phone, flummoxed. I wanted Flynn? He was my magnet? What was that all about?

A fortnight passed and, even though it occupied most of my waking thoughts – and many of my sleeping ones too – I still hadn't made a decision about moving or staying, despite daily memes and GIFs arriving from Georgia begging me to return to Willowdale.

There was one week left of January and the bitterly cold snap which had started before Mum's eightieth was expected to continue into February. My landlord had brought round a couple of electric heaters to compensate for the poor heating but they were only effective in warming the immediate space around them so I'd spent a lot of time working from my bed wearing several layers, a hat, scarf and fingerless gloves.

I hadn't heard anything from Graeme, not that I'd expected to as he'd made it abundantly clear what he thought of me. With my social life gone, I'd worked solidly but had got myself so far ahead that there was nothing left for me to do this weekend.

Convinced it would be warmer outside than in the flat, I ventured into the city centre. There was nothing I needed and I wasn't a big fan of shopping anyway, but I did enjoy a spot of window-shopping. What I hadn't considered was that most of the high street shop windows would be plastered with sale signs and little else to catch my eye.

I was debating whether to return to the flat when a large group of men walked past, shouting to each other and laughing. Presumably they were on a stag do as they were all wearing matching elf outfits except for one who was dressed in a Santa suit. It was an odd costume choice for a month after Christmas but it was a crowd-pleaser, drawing smiles and laughter. Despite my low mood, even I couldn't help smiling.

I used to love Christmas and New Year. My family had always made a big fuss of both and, although Flynn's childhood Christmases had been lower-key than mine, he'd fully embraced our game-playing tradition, enthusiastically joining in with charades, pin the nose on Rudolph, a selection box treasure hunt, Pictionary and a whole host more. So much love. So much hilarity. I remembered being doubled up with laughter during the last treasure hunt when Flynn and Noah spotted the largest selection box at the same time and play-wrestled each other for it, only for Keira to swoop in and steal it from them both. Watching them chase her round the garden, calling her a cheat, I'd thought about how blessed I was to have such a wonderful husband, son and family and how life surely couldn't get any better than that. I could never have known that just a week later, Noah would be dead and that, by the summer, I'd have left my husband, my home, and my beloved family and moved to the other side of the country.

Nobody had questioned my decision to go to Mexico the following Christmas. They understood my need for space at a difficult time. Georgia had offered to accompany me and I'd considered it, but it was something I needed to do by myself. Everything about that first festive period abroad felt alien – being away on my own, waking up in a hotel room on Christmas Day, the hot weather and bright blue skies – but it served its purpose. Without being surrounded by the traditions and trimmings of a typical British family Christmas and without my family and our party games, I was able to convince myself that it was just a regular holiday and I wasn't really spending Christmas Day all alone after losing the two people I loved most in the world. Well, most of the time. During the day, there was plenty to distract me but the evenings were hard. I'd return to my room after my meal and, as my bedroom door closed behind me, I had the sense of being enclosed in a prison cell. I hadn't technically lost my freedom but it felt as though I had. The idea of living my life without my son and husband was so bleak.

I'd stayed away for New Year too. Mum, Dad and Georgia had all tried to talk me out of that, saying I shouldn't be alone on the first anniversary of Noah's death. They'd suggested everything from a memorial event to a quiet day together but I couldn't face any of it. I wanted to be away from the memories. Was it the right decision? To this day, I still wasn't sure. I might have been more than five thousand miles away from the place where the tragedy took place, but the distance provided no escape from the memories. I'd stayed in my room on New Year's Day, curled up on my side on top of the bed, clinging onto Noah's favourite hoodie, aching from the emptiness in my heart.

Going away just before Christmas and returning after New Year had become *my thing* after that. With working freelance, I rarely took time off so it was a good opportunity to try to relax and recharge my batteries. Graeme had joined me last year and this year, although this year had, of course, been a disaster.

The stag do had disappeared from sight but, as I looked around me, it struck me how many couples, families and groups of friends there were and an overwhelming feeling of loneliness engulfed me. *What am I doing here? Why do I insist on staying?*

Georgia's recent words about my move to Newcastle came back to me – *How's that working out for you?* Bit of a disaster, truth be told. I'd honestly thought it would be easier to deal with what happened when I was somewhere else but I think it might have been harder. Instead of solving my problems, I'd exacerbated them and added a whole pile of new ones into the mix, including damaging my relationship with my parents.

It was too loud here, too busy. Wanting a place to sit down and think, I pushed open the door of a nearby café but a wall of chatter hit me and I closed it again, shaking my head. If I wanted peace and quiet, I knew where to go instead.

Fifteen minutes later, I was standing beside the statue of Queen Victoria outside Newcastle Cathedral and gazing up at the impressive Lantern Tower. Mum was a Christian and a regular member of the congregation at Willowdale Methodist Church. Georgia and I had attended Sunday School when we were little but hadn't continued as teens. Mum had been disappointed but had said it was our decision to make and perhaps the church would call us back later in life. It hadn't done in terms of religion but the buildings had certainly captivated me. I'd been inside the cathedral several times studying the architecture and I'd taken the tour up the tower, taking in the views across the city. At the time, I remembered thinking that they were impressive but city views didn't speak to my soul like the views from the fells back home.

I stepped through the north porch and breathed in the peace and serenity. There were several visitors milling around, taking photos, looking up at the roof, reading information and speaking in hushed tones. Just ahead of me was a table with tea lights on it. After making a contactless donation, I lit a candle in remembrance of Noah and watched it burning for several minutes. I slowly passed through the nave and into the quire area where I slipped into one of the traditional wooden choir stalls. Bowing my head, I closed my eyes and thought about the crossroads I was at. I pictured my bedroom at the flat – the white flatpack furniture which was falling apart, the faded curtains which were an inch too short for the windows and the chipped mirror on the dressing table. It couldn't have been more of a contrast to The Bothy – my former family home between Willowdale and Whinlatter Forest –

which had been beautifully and tastefully decorated. But, like choosing Newcastle city centre over the countryside, I'd signed the rental contract on the flat because it was nothing like The Bothy or Derwent Rise. I'd invested in a decent bed, desk and bookshelves but I hadn't bought any pictures or cushions or anything to try to make the flat homely because it wasn't home and the truth was it never would be. Home was Willowdale. Home was my family. And it was time to return to them.

7

Across the rest of the weekend and the start of the following week, all I could think about was moving home. The idea still scared me but I felt lighter having made the decision. Well, almost made it. There was one more thing I wanted to do – have a proper walk around Willowdale during daylight hours and see what my gut told me then. It was Georgia's birthday on Thursday and we were going out for the evening. Although she'd be at work during the day, she'd already said I was welcome to drive over earlier and work from her house if that was more convenient for me. It would give me the perfect opportunity to take that walk without telling anyone.

I drove over to Willowdale after lunch and parked on the road between the community centre and The Hardy Herdwick – the village pub and our destination for Georgia's birthday night out. It was cool but thankfully not freezing like it had been last week. The sun was low in the pale blue cloud-free sky and dazzling me so I needed my sunglasses on. My eyes had always been really sensitive to the sun and Georgia used to tease me for being a poser wearing shades in winter but I could barely keep my eyes open without them.

I followed the path to the village centre where it curved round to the right with Lakeside Inn on one side and the giant willow tree on the other. As I passed Derwent Rise, I spotted Dad's car on the drive and wondered if I should drop in to say hello. They were taking Georgia out for a birthday meal on Saturday so wouldn't be joining us at the pub tonight. I probably should make an effort to see them but, if I popped in, I'd do it on the way back.

My walk continued past the marina and out of the village. Derwent Water was on my left but I wouldn't be able to see it again until some way past Willowdale Hall. Trees of various species, some deciduous and others evergreen, flanked me on either side of the road. Shafts of gentle light filtered between the branches and a light wind teased the ends of my hair.

With every step, I felt lighter, more relaxed. How many times must I have walked along here over the years? Whether I was walking to the lakeside, hiking up Cat Bells or doing a full circuit of Derwent Water, there was one stop I always made – Willowdale Hall. The manor house itself was set so far back from the gates that it couldn't be seen from the road. As a young girl, I'd often pressed my head against the railings, willing the trees to temporarily turn invisible so I could see the beautiful building beyond them.

Reaching Willowdale Hall, I couldn't resist pressing my face against the gates once more. The wrought iron felt icy cold against my cheeks, making me gasp, so I didn't stay there for long. I continued further along the track past the estate grounds. Derwent Water came into view again and I followed a track down to one of several wooden jetties around the lake.

There was nobody on the jetty or the pebble beach beside it so

I picked up a stone and attempted to skim it, only managing a pathetic two bounces. Flynn and Noah had been the experts, always winding each other up about who was the best. I smiled as I recalled the pair of them on this very beach. The water had been really calm and Noah – age twelve or thirteen at the time – had managed an impressive twelve bounces. When it was Flynn's turn, Noah was determined not to be beaten and had tried every trick he could think of to distract his dad – fake-sneezing loudly, tickling his ears with a twig he'd found on the ground and even hurling a dead slug at him. I'd completely forgotten about that until now.

I skimmed another stone – three bounces this time – then hugged my arms across my chest. I'd fled to escape the bad memories but doing so had taken me away from the happy memories like this. This was how I wanted to remember my son – fun-loving, mischievous and loving life. This was where I needed to be.

* * *

When I walked back through Willowdale, there was no car on the drive at Derwent Rise. Dad never put the car in the garage so its absence meant nobody was home. Probably just as well because it felt right for Georgia to be the first person I told about my decision to return.

I managed ninety minutes of work at Georgia's before she arrived back from work.

'Happy birthday!' I cried, jumping up to give her a hug.

She opened up her gift – a handbag she'd fallen in love with on a visit to Newcastle last year but which she'd refused to treat herself to, saying it was too expensive. She hugged it to her chest, beaming at me.

'I can't believe you went back for it! Thank you so much.'

'You loved it so I was always going to get you it. So, how was the library?'

'Busy. We've started running Story Craft on a Thursday afternoon where we read babies and toddlers a picture book and they create some of the characters or scenes from the story using painted hands and feet.'

'Sounds messy.'

'It is, but it's fun and the stories are always so heartwarming. I love children's books.'

'You love *all* books.'

Our parents had been voracious readers so books had always been a big thing in our family. While Georgia took after Mum in devouring fiction, I followed in Dad's footsteps with a love of non-fiction, especially anything historical. From being a little girl, Georgia had wanted to work in a library. We'd visited the one in Keswick every Saturday where she took forever to select her books. Some of the librarians let her stamp the return date on the books she borrowed and she still maintained that the best Christmas present she'd ever been given was a set of library cards and a stamp. In her teens, she'd developed a particular interest in rare and first editions and now, alongside her library role, she was the book expert at Darrowby's.

'So, are you excited about the quiz tonight?' Georgia asked, tucking her dark hair behind her ears as she peeked into the slow cooker which had been teasing me with the delicious aroma of honey and garlic chicken.

'Erm...'

She laughed. 'Daft question for someone who hates quizzes.'

'It's not that I hate them. I'm just no good at them. I know a considerable amount about a few niche subjects which don't typically come up on quizzes.'

'You've got some music and film knowledge.'

'*Some* being the operative word. Mid-eighties to early-noughties, if that. But I promise to try my best and not let you down.'

'You could never let me down,' she said, her expression serious, and then she laughed once more. 'That's Mark's job. That man has an uncanny ability to present wrong answers with such conviction that nobody likes to challenge him. Right, I'm off upstairs to get showered before he gets home.'

She left the kitchen and I returned to my laptop to sneak in another thirty minutes of work before I got changed.

* * *

Quiz night was clearly popular as The Hardy Herdwick was packed.

'How long is it since you've been in here?' Georgia asked as we grabbed a table with Keira while Mark and Johnnie went to the bar to get the drinks in.

'A decade? Maybe more?' It had been several years before Noah died. Flynn and I used to love coming here. It was the place where we met so it had always been special to us, but we both got so busy with work that we'd stopped finding the time. 'It hasn't changed much.'

In some ways, that felt reassuring. The walls were painted a different colour but everything else was so familiar from the dark wood furniture to the pictures of Herdwick sheep all over the walls to the soft toy sheep beside the optics. There was a real fire burning, taking me back to how much Flynn and I had especially loved coming here on a winter's evening to relax with a drink in front of the crackling fire. We'd been so happy back then. If Noah hadn't died, we likely still would be.

Regan and Clarke joined us just after Mark and Johnnie

returned with the drinks, wishing Georgia a happy birthday and giving her hugs. Mark returned to the bar for their drinks and then we all toasted to Georgia's fifty-fifth birthday.

'Thank you,' she said, smiling round the group. 'I couldn't think of a better way to spend my birthday or better people to spend it with. But you know what will make it the best birthday ever? If we actually win for once.'

'You haven't won before?' I asked, surprised.

'Second's the best we've come,' she said. 'We're usually somewhere in the middle.'

It was on the tip of my tongue to ask why they kept coming if they never won, but I reminded myself that my sister had never been competitive. She didn't mind being at the bottom as long as she felt she'd done her best and I had to applaud her for that. It was a much more relaxed way to approach life instead of wanting to be the best at everything like I always did. When you lived your life the way I did, failures were so much more catastrophic and I'd had plenty of those.

A young woman approached the table clutching several sheets of paper and a pot of pens. 'Are you quizzing tonight?' she asked.

Following an enthusiastic chorus of *Yes, Connie*, she placed an answer sheet and a pen on the table.

'Please forgive the picture round. Arnie made one too many Christmas ones and decided he might as well use it tonight.'

I smiled at the quiz name which Regan added to the top of the page – Tequila Mockingbird. Nobody needed to explain the name choice to me. Harper Lee's *To Kill a Mockingbird* was my sister's all-time favourite book and I loved how they'd blended that with a drinks reference.

Regan removed a staple from the corner of the answer sheet

and placed a second page down on the table with a declaration of, 'Seasonally inappropriate picture round.'

I stared at the small photographs of scenes from Christmas films. I recognised a few obvious ones from *Elf*, *It's a Wonderful Life* and *Love Actually* but nothing else looked familiar. Although...

'That's *Die Hard*,' I exclaimed. 'That's not a Christmas film.'

Regan and Clarke both stared at me, their expressions incredulous.

'Take that back!' Clarke said, clapping his hand to his chest in mock indignation.

'Why? It's an action film.'

'Set on Christmas Eve at a Christmas party,' Regan stated, shaking his head.

'You've started something now,' Georgia warned and, sure enough, Regan and Clarke presented an argument as to why *Die Hard* was not only a Christmas film but the best Christmas film ever. I wasn't convinced by the latter, although I hadn't watched enough Christmas films to offer a winner myself, but I had to concede that it did have Christmas all over it and wasn't sure why I hadn't thought about that before.

'I can't believe you haven't heard the debate about it,' Keira said. 'It's been all over the socials for years. There are stacks of reels about it on TikTok.'

I shrugged apologetically. 'I don't really do the socials and I definitely don't do TikTok.'

'Speaking of which, I loved your post on TikTok earlier,' Keira told her brother and Clarke. 'And how many followers? I'm in awe.'

I was the one in awe as I listened to them discussing the enormous social media presence Regan and Clarke had built up for both Darrowby's and their textiles business. They showed me some of their recent posts which were funny and imaginative. I'd missed out on so much by not being more present in their lives, but that was going to change.

A buzz from a microphone interrupted us, followed by a man's deep voice announcing, 'Five-minute warning, quizzers, five-minute warning.'

'That's Arnie,' Georgia told me. 'He's the landlord.'

I vaguely recalled her telling me that the pub had changed hands but I couldn't remember how long ago that had been. The past seven years had blurred into each other.

The quiz got underway and, sure enough, my niche knowledge of historical buildings was no help whatsoever. I knew a couple of easy general knowledge questions and one of the music ones but the others got the answers quicker than me so I sat back, enjoying my drink and soaking in the atmosphere.

It was lovely observing the banter between Georgia, Mark and their kids but soon my mind drifted. If things had been different, would Flynn, Noah and I have joined Georgia and her family for weekly quiz nights? Maybe we'd have made our own team and there'd have been some family rivalry – Waters family versus the Crofts. Noah might have had a girlfriend who joined us. He might still have been with Jessie – perhaps engaged or even married. I glanced across at Keira on the other side of the table – older than Noah by only seventeen months – and felt a tidal wave of grief threatening to pull me under as I noticed her hands resting on her baby bump. Noah and Jessie could have had children by now. My grandchildren. Throat burning, tears blurring my vision, I had to get out but without alerting Georgia that something was wrong. I'd been to the ladies' less than ten minutes ago and had made a trip to the bar on my return so the only thing I could think of was to fake a coughing fit. With one hand over my mouth, I tapped my chest, rolled my eyes at Georgia and pointed out the window. She nodded, indicating her understanding, and I dashed outside.

The temperature had plummeted from earlier and the cold air stabbed at me, taking my breath away, freezing my nose, cheeks and fingers. I wished I'd grabbed my coat but it had never entered my head in my haste to escape. I paced up and down at the side of the pub, clenching and unclenching my fists, a scream welling up inside me. I often thought about Noah in the present day – how old he'd be and what he might be doing with his life – but none of those thoughts had been so strong, so vivid as the vision I'd had just now. I'd clearly pictured him sitting beside Jessie, hands entwined, happy together – the future he should have had.

I slumped against the wall, swiping away a couple of escapee tears as I tried to pull myself together. I'd barely shed any tears for years and this wasn't the time to release the floodgates. Tonight was my sister's birthday and she deserved to enjoy it without any drama from me. But I wasn't feeling strong enough to go inside yet. *Just a couple more minutes.*

8

'Are you all right?' Georgia whispered when I returned to the group. The concern in her eyes suggested I might look a wreck. Quick thinking was needed.

'Choked on my own breath,' I said. 'My eyes were streaming. Has my mascara run?'

'A bit.' She rubbed at my cheek with her fingers. 'Sorted. Although your eyes are a bit red.'

'My nose probably is too. There's a heavy frost out there now.'

I was saved from any further conversation by Arnie asking another question. I didn't hear it so I sat back, heart still pounding, as Clarke and Keira debated the answer.

'We're halfway through,' Arnie announced. 'Connie will come round to collect your answers and give you a new sheet for the second half. We'll start again in twenty minutes.'

'There's some people I want you to meet,' Georgia said, standing up. 'Bring a business card with you. You're going to love this.'

Intrigued, I removed a card from my purse and followed her to the other side of the pub where we joined a table of three men and three women I didn't know, all of whom looked younger than us. They were evidently quiz regulars but not very good at it judging from their team name – The Numpties – and the banter exchanged with Georgia.

'This is my sister, Mel,' Georgia said. 'This is Maya and her fiancé Jonah. Maya is Kelly and Aled's daughter.'

I knew Mum and Dad's next-door neighbours had a son who still lived with them, but I hadn't realised they also had a daughter.

'This is Maya's cousin Dane who's in Mountain Rescue with Mark, and his partner Autumn,' Georgia continued, moving round the table. 'You remember Beatrice Eccles? They own her house.'

'Cotton-tail's Cottage? Aw, I love that place. I remember going inside once when I was younger and it was like a shrine to Beatrix Potter.'

Autumn and Dane both nodded, smiling.

'We rented it from her daughter, Trudy, for a while before we bought it but one of the conditions of renting it out was to clear out all the memorabilia.'

'You might remember me mentioning it,' Georgia said. 'Darrowby's handled the sale of some of it about a year ago.'

'I do remember,' I said, nodding. 'Weren't there some books in it?'

'Several first editions and rare copies. Gosh, what an honour that was.' Georgia's eyes were shining and she'd clearly drifted off into happy memories.

'Sorry,' she said, evidently realising we were all staring at her. 'I haven't finished the introductions. This is Rosie and her partner Oliver Cranleigh.'

She hadn't given anyone else's surname and, from the way she was grinning at me, I knew she'd done it deliberately with Oliver.

'Cranleigh,' I repeated, wondering how I knew that name. 'Oh! As in the Cranleighs who own Willowdale Hall?'

Oliver nodded. 'Good to meet you, Mel.'

'And you but, oh, my God! Willowdale Hall? I've been obsessed with that place since I was a little. I used to drag Georgia out on our bikes and we'd stop by the gates and stare into the grounds.' I started laughing. 'That makes me sound really creepy. It was the building. I promise I wasn't stalking your family. Old buildings are my deepest passion.'

'Georgia told us,' Rosie said. 'She says you're a conservation architect and you work on projects in this area.'

'That's right.' I knitted my eyebrows at Georgia, confused as to why she'd been talking about me.

'She hasn't joined the dots yet,' Georgia said, placing her arm round my shoulder. 'Mel, you'll be interested to hear that Oliver and Rosie are starting a major redevelopment programme at Willowdale Hall and they need a conservation architect to help them turn the hall into part home, part holiday accommodation without losing the character and history. So I thought the three of you might like to get together for a chat.'

I clapped a shaking hand across my mouth, eyes wide, hardly able to believe I was hearing this. A true business professional would have been calm and collected but I was completely incapable. This was the project of my dreams.

'I think she's in shock,' Georgia told them. 'Happy shock, though.'

'Very happy. I can hardly speak. Yes, please, I'd love to talk to you about your plans. Name the date and I can show you my portfolio and client testimonials and...' I paused to draw a breath. 'Apologies. Very excited here.'

'We obviously can't offer you the project until we've talked and seen your work,' Rosie said, 'but I'm loving your enthusiasm.

We both love Willowdale Hall very much and it's important to us to work with someone who feels the same.'

Oliver nodded his head. 'Have you ever been inside, Mel?'

'I wish! No. I've never even seen the outside up close.'

'So you love it even though you've never seen it?' Rosie asked.

'The closest I came was a boat trip on the lake. I've seen some old photographs but what makes me fall in love with a place isn't just the bricks or stones – it's the history. I'm fascinated by the Beatrix Potter connection and how the hall was used in both wars. That background is what gives a place a heart and when a building gets restored, I'm all about getting that heart warm and beating again. That probably sounds corny.'

'I love that,' Autumn said. 'It's not corny at all.'

Arnie gave us a ten-minute warning which had Jonah and Maya jumping up to get another round of drinks in.

'All my details are on here,' I said, handing my business card to Oliver. 'Call or email me when you're ready to meet and let me know if you'd like anything from me in the meantime. I can send you links to my work and client testimonials if you like.'

They both shook my hand and said they'd be in touch very soon. I said goodbye to the group and returned to our table with Georgia. A short while ago, I'd needed to squash down a squeal of grief but now I needed to keep a lid on a squeal of excitement. What a turnaround.

'Willowdale Hall!' I said as we sat down once more. 'I can't believe it! Thank you.'

'I didn't do anything.'

'You got me an in. That's huge.'

She shrugged. 'I was in The White Willow last week and Rosie and Oliver were at the next table. I overheard them saying they really needed to get their act together and start searching for an architect if they were going to have any hope of refurbishing the hall this year, so I butted in and told them I happened to know the perfect woman for the job who I could introduce them to tonight.'

I put my arm round her waist and rested my head on her shoulder. 'I thought it was your birthday. How come I'm getting the best gift ever? Or at least the chance of one.'

'Because you deserve something to light that smile and make your eyes sparkle again,' she said, her voice cracking.

I changed position, hugging her tightly. Did I deserve that? I wasn't so sure. Did I need it? A hundred per cent. Even in that brief conversation with Oliver and Rosie just now, I'd felt more alive than I had in a very long time. I wanted to light my sister's smile and make her eyes sparkle too and I knew how to do it. I had been planning to save my news until we got back to Georgia's but I couldn't imagine a better time than right now.

'I do have another birthday gift for you,' I said when I released her.

'You can't have! You've already spoilt me.'

'I know, but it's something you've wanted for a lot longer than you've wanted that handbag.'

'Colin Firth in his Mr Darcy days?' she asked.

'I *am* here,' Mark said, attempting to look indignant.

'It won't be here immediately and it'll be too big to wrap,' I added.

She shrugged. 'You know I'm rubbish at guessing games.'

'It's something I wasn't sure I'd be able to give you but I think I'm ready to now.'

Georgia gasped, her eyes widening. 'Is it... is it you? Are you coming home?' The words were hesitant, as though she feared it was an impossibility.

I nodded. 'I think it's time.'

I thought she might squeal but she pulled me into another

hug and I stroked her back as I felt her tears soaking into my jumper.

'You've made me cry on my birthday,' she said, rummaging in her new handbag for a packet of tissues moments later. 'But I'll let you off. You've just given me the best gift ever.'

'Even better than Colin Firth's Mr Darcy?' Mark asked.

'A million times better.'

Georgia's reaction – and that of everyone else – made me feel warm and fuzzy inside, but that familiar stab of guilt was there too. Georgia and I had been so close, always doing so much together, and I'd moved away without even discussing it with her. I should never have done that but leaving had been the only thing I could think of to do at the time to not only save myself but to save her because I was so angry with everyone. It had already lost me my husband and I'd been terrified that it might lose me my sister too.

9

I'd intended on driving back to Newcastle first thing on Friday morning but I was still buzzing from meeting Oliver and Rosie at the quiz and the possibility of working on Willowdale Hall. When Georgia suggested breakfast at The White Willow before I hit the road, I accepted without hesitation.

'You're thinking about Willowdale Hall, aren't you?' she said after we'd placed our orders. 'I can tell because your eyes are shining and you haven't stopped smiling all morning.'

My smile widened. 'Tell me it wasn't a dream.'

'It was real.'

'I'm trying not to get my hopes up as I'm sure they'll want to talk to other conservation architects, but we're talking Willowdale Hall here. How long have I been obsessed with that place?'

'Only for forever. Remember when you built a replica of the hall out of Lego?'

'I still have it in a box somewhere, although I think it might be in several pieces now. I've got stacks of drawings too.'

I'd filled so many sketch pads with drawings of the outside from different angles, imagining the parts that weren't in photographs. For some of my interior designs, I'd returned the hall to how I'd imagined it would have been in its heyday and, in others, I'd modernised it into a variety of alternative uses including a luxury hotel, a spa, a hospital and a school. I looked forward to hearing about the vision Oliver and Rosie had for its future, particularly as it sounded like they intended on living there themselves. A dual-purpose design would be interesting to work on.

'If you get the job – which I *know* you will – how will it impact on your other projects?' Georgia asked.

'It shouldn't be a problem as I've always juggled my workload.'

'And what about moving back here when most of your projects are in the north-east?'

'Are you trying to put me off?' I asked, my tone teasing.

'No! Never! Just being practical.'

'It'll be fine. I covered the north-east when I lived here before – just means further to travel when I'm needed on site.'

'I'm beyond excited you're coming home, but...' A shadow crossed Georgia's face, stirring the butterflies in my stomach.

I shook my head. 'I don't want to talk about Flynn.'

Our drinks arrived, pausing our conversation, but Georgia clearly wasn't ready to let it go.

'The last thing I want to do is make you doubt your decision to return, but have you thought about what you'll say when you see him?'

'I don't intend on seeing him.'

'Maybe not intentionally, but you're bound to bump into him at some point, probably sooner rather than later.'

I stirred my latte, keeping my eyes down, but Georgia gripped onto my hand, stopping me from moving.

'Mel! Please look at me.'

I raised my eyes, sighing heavily.

'You won't be able to avoid him forever. This isn't a big place.'

'I don't want to think about it,' I muttered, feeling like a petulant child. 'I mean it, Georgia. Conversation's over.'

But as I drove back to Newcastle, seeing Flynn again was all I could think about. I pictured his dark curls, the tenderness in his green eyes and his dazzling smile. And then I pictured the hurt and confusion when I left and I shook my head, trying to dislodge it from my mind. I hated that I'd hurt him when he was already in pain but, if I'd stayed, I'd have only hurt him more.

* * *

By the time I arrived back at the flat, I felt weary and my head was pounding. Unable to face diving straight into work, I made a strong coffee and stood in the kitchen, resting my back against the chipped worktop, sipping on my drink and trying to empty my mind.

Georgia had shared something unexpected while we were in The White Willow – that Mark had stayed in touch with Flynn and the pair of them met up for drinks at least once a month. I was still reeling from that revelation.

'I thought it best you know now,' Georgia had said, her wary expression suggesting she had no idea how I'd take that news. 'Gives you a chance to get your head round it before you move back. If you need to, that is. Might not bother you.'

I'd given my usual copout response of, 'I don't want to talk about him,' and rapidly changed the subject by admiring the décor of The White Willow. But it *did* bother me. A lot. And I knew it was totally unreasonable of me to think that way. From the moment I'd introduced them, Mark and Flynn hit it off and soon developed a strong friendship. We often went out as a foursome and holidayed together before and after the kids came along. Neither of them had siblings and it was as though they'd found the brother they'd always wanted.

When Flynn and I separated, I never asked or expected any of my family to cut him out of their lives. When we divorced, I told them all that I didn't expect anyone to take sides but I did have one important request. If they did speak to Flynn or even meet up with him, I didn't want to know about it. Our marriage had ended badly and the only way I was going to be able to get through it was if I severed every tie to him. I therefore understood why Georgia had kept Mark and Flynn's ongoing friendship from me.

'I know you said we weren't to pick sides but I was always going to be Team Mel,' she'd said. 'I've exchanged pleasantries with him if I've bumped into him but I've never joined him and Mark on a night out.'

'I wouldn't have been angry with you if you had.'

'I know. But I would. I'd have felt disloyal.'

She shouldn't have had to make that decision. The four of us had been a tight friendship group. Just because Flynn and I had divorced, it didn't mean Georgia and Mark had to divorce him too. I'd just assumed that, over time, they would have done. When he'd met up with Mark, had Flynn asked after me? Had they talked about me?

Earlier in The White Willow, I'd been adamant that I didn't want Georgia to tell me anything about Flynn but now my mind was alive with questions. Where did he live? Had he managed to build another successful business? Had he returned to general construction or was he still doing restoration? I'd loved running a business with Flynn. I'd heard many disastrous stories about couples clashing and strong relationships ending when they tried to work together but, for us, joining forces professionally had strengthened an already solid relationship. We'd made a great team and the business had thrived. When we split up and I reverted to working on my own, I'd struggled at first. I hadn't realised how much of a sounding board Flynn had become and there'd been a period where I'd floundered, battling with my self-belief.

My thoughts drifted away from work and onto Flynn's personal life. Was he seeing someone, perhaps even remarried? Had he had more children? And was it wrong of me to hope that the answer to those questions was a resounding no?

'Nothing to do with you,' I muttered, tutting at myself for heading down that road.

I tipped the coffee dregs into the sink and dumped my mug beside it. I'd allowed my ex-husband far too much headspace and I really couldn't go there because, even though I was determined to make the move, I still wasn't 100 per cent sure about my return to Willowdale and I didn't want thoughts about Flynn to panic me.

Hoping that losing myself in my work would silence the questions, I wandered over to my desk and plonked myself down on the chair. My heart pounded when I clicked onto my emails and spotted Rosie's name among the list of unread messages.

To: Melanie Finton
From: Rosie Jacobs
Date: 31 January
Subject: Meeting to discuss Willowdale Hall

Hi Melanie

It was lovely meeting you last night and congratulations on coming third in the quiz. We were third too – from the bottom! Oliver and I were inspired by the love and passion you clearly have for Willowdale Hall and we're excited to meet you to discuss your work and our plans for the future of the estate.

Oliver's a GP and I run the riding stables so the best time to catch us both is a Sunday afternoon. If Sundays don't suit, I'm sure we can work something out. I look forward to hearing back from you and hopefully to working together this year.

Best wishes, Rosie

Talk about going from down in the dumps to high as a kite in the space of thirty seconds. My hands were shaking as I typed in a reply.

To: Rosie Jacobs
From: Melanie Finton
Date: 31 January
RE: Meeting to discuss Willowdale Hall

Hi Rosie

It was lovely to meet you too. I wish I could take some credit for third place at the quiz but, sadly, I contributed nothing! Congratulations on your place. It would be a lifelong dream for me to work on Willowdale Hall. Georgia and I were just talking earlier about how I built the hall out of Lego when I was younger. I'll have to see if I can piece it back together to show you. Sundays are good for me. Is this coming Sunday too soon for you?

All the best, Mel

A reply came back a few minutes later confirming they were free and suggesting I meet them at the hall at 3 p.m. I accepted immediately and sat there, shaking my head, stunned at the potential opportunity ahead of me. Working on Willowdale Hall would be the highlight of my career. What if I stuffed up the interview?

'You've got this!' I said, my voice strong. I'd dreamed of this since I was a little girl and there was no way I was going to throw it away. I always had a portfolio of work ready to show prospective clients and I had tonight and all day tomorrow to update it. Loads of time.

10

A fortnight later, Georgia, Regan, Clarke and I placed the last few boxes from the small Darrowby's removals lorry onto the drive outside Willowdale Hall.

'Sorry for abandoning you,' Regan said. 'I hoped we'd have had time to get it all inside for you.'

'Gosh, don't apologise. You two have been absolute superstars today and it's not your fault we got stuck in traffic. Have a lovely meal and thanks again for everything.'

Regan and Clarke clambered into the cab and waved as they drove off down the gravel drive, leaving Georgia and me both standing with our hands on our hips, looking at the pile of boxes.

'Nearly there,' she said. 'How about we move everything inside first and then tackle the stairs?'

'How about you get home to your lovely husband? It's Valentine's Day. You should be doing something romantic together.'

She rolled her eyes at me. 'We haven't done something romantic on Valentine's Day since we had the kids so don't you worry about that. We'll go out for a meal later in the week when the restaurants aren't heaving with couples feeling pressured into going out.'

'Ooh, you cynic!'

She lifted up a box. 'I prefer realist. Come on, slacker. Let's get this lot shifted.'

'Okay, but I just need a moment to take it all in. I still can't believe I'm here.' I stepped back from the boxes and looked up at Willowdale Hall.

Georgia put the box down and joined me. 'I knew you'd get the job.'

My meeting with Oliver and Rosie couldn't have gone better. I loved their vision for the future of the hall, they loved my work, and it felt for all of us like a match made in heaven. They advised me that they already had a local builder on board – Dougie Standish – and asked if I knew him. Relieved that it wasn't Flynn they'd taken on, I told them that, although I hadn't worked with him myself, I had met Dougie on a couple of occasions and knew he had a good reputation.

I'd anticipated a delay of several days while Oliver and Rosie made their decision so was surprised and thrilled when they announced there and then that they wanted me for the project.

Everything happened really quickly after that. We signed contracts and I told my landlord I was leaving. As he needed me to move out anyway for the planned refurbishment, it was all very easy. Finding somewhere to rent in the Willowdale area had proved somewhat more problematic. I needed somewhere with great light and plenty of space to work and nothing seemed to fit the bill. Georgia offered me a room in her house but the spare bedrooms weren't big enough to double up as office space and the kitchen table wasn't practical when I'd need to keep clearing it for meals. I was thinking I might need to temporarily stay at Georgia's and rent some office space when Oliver offered the perfect solution – to move into the hall.

'It's not like we don't have enough room,' he'd said when he rang me with the proposal. 'You can have two rooms – more if you need them – and you might find that living here helps you get a stronger feel for the building and how it could work as a home and holiday accommodation.'

So that's how I'd ended up moving my belongings across today in preparation for starting my dream job on Monday.

Georgia and I were carrying the last couple of boxes inside when Rosie appeared with her two dogs, Toffee and Chester. Toffee was a reddish-gold cocker spaniel which she co-owned with her mum, Alice, who lived in Horseshoe Cottage near the riding stables. Chester was a much larger dog, although not a dissimilar colour to Toffee. A Hungarian Vizsla, he'd belonged to her former boss, Hubert Cranleigh, who'd died at the start of last year following a riding accident. Georgia had told me that Oliver, Rosie and Alice were all lovely but they had a chequered family history which she was sure they'd share with me as they got to know me. Sounded intriguing.

'Welcome to your new home,' Rosie said.

I placed my box down in the large entrance hall and stroked Toffee, who was circling round my legs, while Chester offered a paw to Georgia. 'I can't thank you enough for letting me stay here.'

'It's our pleasure. How else could we make sure you work sixteen hours a day, seven days a week?'

'You laugh as you say that,' Georgia said, 'but if I know my sister, that won't be far from the truth.'

I shrugged my shoulders. 'Guilty. I can't help it. I love what I do and I get so absorbed in the research that the hours slip by.

You get just as engrossed when you're reading or valuing old books.'

Georgia smiled and admitted it was true.

'I'm the same when I'm at the stables,' Rosie said. 'We're all lucky we've found the thing we love. So many people don't find theirs or they have a thing they dream of but it's unattainable for whatever reason. So, how can I help? Do these need to go upstairs?'

Rosie took the dogs into the kitchen for some food and, while they were eating, returned to help carry the last of the boxes up the stairs.

'What have you got in here?' she asked, shaking out her arms as she placed it down in the corner of my bedroom. 'Weights?'

'Books,' Georgia answered for me, wiping her forehead with the back of her hand. 'Nearly all the boxes are books. History books, architecture books, books on the history of architecture. Plus there's the occasional lighter respite of a box packed full of boots.'

Rosie raised her eyebrows at me. 'Boots?'

'I have a slight footwear addiction,' I admitted. 'I love boots, particularly brightly coloured ankle boots.'

'Which she hardly ever wears because she never goes out.'

'Georgia!'

'It's true! But that's going to change now you're back home. Quiz night every Thursday for a start.'

'But I couldn't answer any of the questions so I can't help you win. Why would you want me on your team?'

'Because it's not about the winning. It's about being with you. We need to make up for lost time.'

Tears glistened in her eyes and I felt another rush of guilt at how much I'd hurt my sister by moving away. She'd never let on but there'd been a few comments recently which had opened my eyes. I'd make it up to her. I'd make it up to them all. Even Flynn at some point but it would take a while to build up to that because I'd hurt him the deepest.

11

When I woke up on Saturday morning, I lay under my duvet for several minutes listening to Willowdale Hall breathing. Georgia laughed at me when I told her I could hear old buildings breathe, which was rich from somebody who talked to books. I loved the phrase *if walls could talk*. I wish! The things these walls must have seen – the good times and bad, the joy and the pain.

I usually struggled with sleep the first night in a new place but I'd slept so well last night. It probably helped that the bed was familiar. When Flynn and I separated, I didn't want anything from the house. It would hurt too much to have all the reminders of family life around me so I'd told Flynn he could have everything. I'd already taken what I needed – my clothes, books and the contents of my office. The flat in Newcastle had only been sparsely furnished so I'd splashed out on a few essentials which were now in my temporary home. The bed had been too heavy for me to reassemble on my own so, when Oliver arrived back from work last night, he and Rosie had assisted me. They'd also offered to help me unpack my books onto the shelves but I'd told them I'd do it myself across the weekend. I didn't want to impose on their already generous hospitality.

I'd be on my own for most of today. Being a Saturday, it was Rosie's busiest day for riding lessons and Oliver was running a morning surgery then meeting his dad for a hike. I'd expressed surprise at that as I'd thought Hubert Cranleigh was Oliver's dad but they'd told me it was a recent discovery and a long story which they'd share over a bottle of wine one evening.

I'd been given free rein of the ground and first floor of the hall, told I could open any door and explore, although Oliver had suggested I avoid the top floor for now due to several rotten floor-boards and the cellar because the door was sticky and they'd hate me to get trapped down there on my own. I would need to see both but there was plenty of time to do that and just exploring the ground and first floor would keep me busy for a long time.

A Jack-and-Jill bathroom connected my new office and bedroom so I showered and dressed. Heading downstairs to make a coffee, I ran my fingers along the walls, wondering what secrets they kept. Places like this were full of them and I suspected that the discovery that Hubert Cranleigh wasn't Oliver's biological father was simply the latest in a long history of whispers, scandal and secrets.

The ten-year-old me would have been beside herself with excitement if she'd known that the grown-up me would one day get to look around Willowdale Hall, but she'd never have believed that I'd also get to live and work here. It was hard to pinpoint exactly what it was about the estate that had captured my heart at such a young age. Was it the mystery of a building that couldn't be seen from the road? Was it because it was by far the biggest house in the area? Or was it because I'd already fallen in love with history and this was a wonderful example right on my doorstep? When I'd first seen Willowdale Hall from that boat on

Derwent Water, it had been even grander and more imposing than I'd imagined and now here I was inside with access to nearly all the rooms. Talk about a dream come true.

During my tour of the hall as part of my interview, Oliver and Rosie had told me that they mainly lived between three rooms – the library in the west wing and the kitchen and their bedroom in the east wing. In the enormous kitchen, they'd pointed out the obvious – that it was dated, in a state of disrepair and in need of a major overhaul. Their bedroom was above the kitchen and Oliver told me he'd moved into it as a teenager and it hadn't been decorated since way before that. I could see why he'd chosen it. It had a stunning view over the garden and the lake and was so big that it could have a sleeping/dressing area as well as a section devoted to relaxing or studying without looking cluttered. Oliver and Rosie spoke very matter-of-factly about the kitchen and bedroom but their demeanours completely changed when they showed me the library and it wasn't difficult to see why. It was dated and needed a few repairs here and there but, unlike the rest of the rooms in the house, the library felt warm and loved and that's where I headed first with my coffee.

I opened the door and leaned against the frame, hands cradled round my mug, taking it all in. Floor-to-ceiling shelves ran all around the room, the higher shelves accessed by a ladder on a rail. A pair of sofas and an armchair were positioned round a fireplace to my left and there was a shabby chic writing desk and chaise longue on the right – pieces which I absolutely loved and which gave a real sense of history to the room.

Stepping inside and closing the door behind me, I turned right and worked my way round the library, running my fingers over the oak shelving, the desk and the threadbare fabric on the chaise longue. When I reached the other side, I smiled at the candlestick, picturing the sparkle in Rosie's eyes when she'd tipped it to one side and, with a click, the bookcase had rotated by 180 degrees to reveal a secret miniature library inside. I tipped the candlestick now, opening the hidden door and stepped inside the room where Oliver's mum, Kathryn, had loved to read.

I lowered myself onto one of the two high-backed armchairs, switched on the standard lamp between them, placed my mug on a coaster on the coffee table and breathed in and out slowly while I gathered my thoughts. Their plan was to convert the east wing into their living space and the west wing into holiday accommodation and that didn't make sense to me when the library was the only room to which they both clearly had an emotional attachment. Something like this could be recreated in their home but it wouldn't be the same because it wouldn't hold the precious memories Oliver had of his mum being in here. He'd talked about her loving baking and the kitchen being her pride and joy but it was obvious to me that the strongest and happiest memories he had of Kathryn were in the library. And why build a new secret room when there was already a fabulous one right here?

After I finished my drink, I explored the rest of the ground floor in the west wing, moved up to the first floor then returned to the library to pull together some thoughts on how they could keep the library within their living accommodation.

I was still at the desk when I heard voices and was shocked to see it was already half five. I'd been so absorbed in my work that I'd been oblivious to darkness falling. Moments later, the door opened and Oliver and Rosie appeared, both red-cheeked from a day in the cold.

'Aren't you chilly?' Oliver asked, rubbing his hands together as he headed towards the fireplace.

'Layers and these.' I held up my hands to show off my fingerless gloves. I'd worked in so many old properties over the years, many of which were empty with no functioning heating, that I came prepared. A long-sleeved thermal T-shirt was the perfect base layer, topped with wool or fleece tops and a down-filled gilet; all ideal material for trapping heat. I also usually carried a chargeable hand warmer in my coat pocket.

The dogs lay down on the rug in front of the fire while Rosie scrunched up some newspaper and soon the room was aglow with the flames. They left the dogs with me while they went to get changed – Rosie out of her riding gear and Oliver out of his muddy hiking clothes – and said they'd be back shortly to find out how my day had gone. That should give me just enough time to finish off the sketches I wanted to show them.

The room was warming nicely and, by the time Oliver and Rosie returned, I'd shed my gilet and gloves and moved to the rug to stroke Toffee and Chester.

'So, how's your day been?' Rosie asked, handing me a mug of tea.

'Fantastic. I completely lost track of time and nearly missed my lunch. This place! Honestly, I can't thank you enough for letting me be part of your plans.'

'I spy a notepad,' Rosie said, nodding towards my sketchbook. 'Have you been working already? You were meant to be settling in.'

'I couldn't help myself. So many ideas I didn't want to lose and I've got something major I want to run by you, although I can wait until later if you'd rather relax.'

'Sounds intriguing,' Oliver said. 'Fire away.'

Oliver and Rosie were sitting together on one of the two-seater sofas and I felt a little unprofessional sitting cross-legged on the floor so I moved onto the sofa opposite them and placed my sketchbook on the empty seat beside me.

'The plan we discussed was to convert the west wing into holiday accommodation. What's the reasoning for that?'

They exchanged looks and shrugs.

'We thought it would be easiest,' Oliver said.

'There's no emotional connection to the east wing?' I wanted to check I hadn't missed anything.

Rosie glanced at Oliver and he shook his head.

'So it's a practical thing with the kitchen and your bedroom already being there?'

'And because it's smaller than the west wing,' Oliver said. 'It seemed the logical choice.'

'It *is* the logical choice,' I agreed, 'and probably the easier conversion but I think you'd both regret it because it would mean losing the library. This room's really special and it's obvious it means a lot to both of you, so I was thinking you could convert the whole of the east wing and part of this wing into holiday accommodation but keep everything from the library and beyond for yourselves. There's already external access through the room at the end so that could become your entrance porch and kitchen/diner...'

I moved to the armchair so I was closer and flipped open my sketchbook, showing them my rough drawings on how the west wing could be configured into their private space. I watched their expressions carefully and could tell that keeping the library was a huge hit, but a shadow crossed Oliver's face when I mentioned upstairs so I closed the sketchbook and sat forward, my brows knitted.

'There's something about the space above us that makes you sad,' I said to Oliver. 'It's not going to work as your living quarters, is it?'

Rosie placed her hand on Oliver's thigh and her sympathetic expression as she looked at him told me I'd hit the nail on the head.

'Do you want to tell Mel now?' she asked him.

'You don't need to tell me anything you don't want to,' I said, my voice reassuring. 'We could make the ground floor your living space and convert upstairs into guest accommodation, or we can stick to the original plan. I just get the impression that this room is really important to you both and I'd love to find a way to keep it for you.'

Oliver's gaze travelled round the room and he nodded slowly. 'I would like to keep this room if we can and kudos to you that you've picked up on that, but you're right about the upstairs. It holds bad memories for me, past and present.'

'Understood. This has to be what's right for you both.'

'It *is* a good moment to give you an insight into the family history,' Oliver said. 'We were going to tell you anyway and I'd rather you get the truth from us than a variation of it from the rumour mill...'

Between them, Oliver and Rosie shared an unexpected and tragic tale of their past. Hubert Cranleigh – the man who Oliver had believed was his dad until shortly before Hubert's death at the start of last year – had been a womaniser and an abuser. Kathryn had found comfort, friendship and, in time, reignited love with her ex-boyfriend Christian. Oliver had been the result of that relationship, although they'd kept it secret, fearful for the repercussions if Hubert found out. When Oliver was twelve, Kathryn had finally decided enough was enough and she was going to leave Hubert for Christian but was struck down by a short, fatal illness before she had the chance. Oliver was left alone in the hall with a man he hated and no idea that they weren't blood relatives. He moved to the furthest bedroom in the east wing to put as much physical distance as he could between them and they lived separate lives until Oliver escaped to university aged eighteen. The next time he returned to the hall was after Hubert's riding accident.

Finding out that Hubert Cranleigh wasn't his biological father wasn't the only unexpected discovery for them last year. Rosie's mum, Alice, had been the victim of a hit and run on the road into the village a couple of years after Kathryn died – a horrendous incident I remembered from when Noah was a baby. Alice's physical injuries had healed but her mental ones hadn't and she'd struggled to leave the safety of the estate. The police had never caught the driver but, during a storm a couple of weeks after Hubert died, a tree came down on top of the boat house behind the hall. Hidden inside was the vehicle which had struck Alice. For nearly two decades, Alice had believed it was out of kindness that Hubert had let her and Rosie stay in Horseshoe Cottage and had placed a temporary manager at the riding stables until Rosie had finished school and could take over. Evidently it was a combination of guilt and fear of being caught – or perhaps just the latter.

It was a heartbreaking story of loss and deception but it was also a tale of hope and second chances. Oliver and Rosie had been a couple for a while during their teens but their relationship had ended badly. His return to the hall under difficult circumstances had brought them back together and had also saved the hall. Oliver had wanted to sell it but Rosie had presented him with a vision of how it could be financially viable as a business.

Oliver and Rosie's relationship and an exciting new future for Willowdale Hall weren't the only second chances. Alice and Rosie's dad, Xander, had been reunited following the funeral. Alice had always believed that Xander – who was Hubert's cousin – had abandoned her when he learned that she was pregnant with Rosie. She hadn't told Rosie the identity of her father, wanting to protect her from the rejection. Following the funeral, it emerged that Xander hadn't actually known about Rosie and had only left because he'd been led to believe that Alice wanted nothing to do with him.

Finding the car in the boat house and discovering that a man she'd considered a friend had been responsible for her accident had understandably been extremely traumatic for Alice. She had a breakdown and spent some time in a care facility, determined to regain control of her life. Xander had been and still was an incredible support to her. The pair had steadily become closer but had been adamant they were just friends but, over Christmas, they'd admitted that they were a couple, much to Rosie's delight. Xander had two children from a previous marriage, one of whom had a child and another on the way, and Rosie was loving getting to know her extended family.

A further second chance had been for Oliver and his biological father. Christian had been Oliver's favourite teacher at school and a mentor to him for many years afterwards, but they'd lost touch. When Oliver discovered his true parentage, he'd reconnected with Christian and they now had a really strong relationship. Christian had a daughter, Emma, from a relationship before Kathryn, and the half-siblings had met for the first time in the summer. Emma now ran an alpaca-walking business in the grounds, which sounded wonderful. I couldn't wait to meet her and her herd of seven alpacas.

'Apologies for throwing a million names at you and so much information,' Rosie said. 'I promise there won't be a test tomorrow on our dysfunctional family tree.'

'I don't know if I should admit it, but I'd probably ace it if there was. I have a thing for retaining names and dates. Georgia often says I have filing cabinets instead of a brain. Thanks for sharing that with me. A lot of the projects I work on are changes of ownership but, when the owners are staying, it really helps to understand the family history and what the place means to them.'

Rosie had produced a bottle of wine partway through our conversation and I paused while she topped up my glass.

'After what you've told me, I can definitely see why you'd be reluctant to convert the west wing bedrooms into your living quarters,' I said. 'Bad memories can be difficult to handle, but I can't help thinking that the whole estate held bad memories for you, Oliver. You've overcome those to the point where you're totally in love with this place and are about to invest heavily in it to secure its future and let others enjoy it. I'm guessing there are good memories here too which have made it easier to find your peace with the estate. I understand you not having positive memories from upstairs, but they are just rooms, which means they can be changed. When you change the furniture and décor, a room can become unrecognisable and, once it looks completely different, it feels different too and those bad memories fade with new happier ones taking over.'

Realising I was in danger of sounding like I was making a sales pitch when it really made no difference to me which part of the hall they kept as their own, I shrugged apologetically. 'And that's the last I'm going to say on the subject. Completely up to you what you do. I'll continue to explore and you can let me know whatever you decide.'

'Thanks, Mel,' Oliver said. 'And don't worry that you've over-stepped because you haven't. We're comfortable with you challenging us on anything about the build. You're the expert and you'll be much better at stepping back and seeing things we're too close to. We'll come back to you when we've had a chance to talk it through.'

* * *

I sat on my bed several hours later, reflecting on everything I'd learned from Oliver and Rosie across the evening. They had a vision of Willowdale Hall becoming a place of sanctuary and healing but it sounded to me like it already had been for both of them, for Rosie's parents, for Oliver's dad Christian and for Oliver's half-sister Emma. Granted, many bad things had happened here but those involved had recovered and were in a happy place now.

Could Willowdale Hall be the place to heal me?

12

I hadn't thought it would be possible for me to fall more in love with Willowdale Hall but it seemed it was. With only a few items of furniture looking lost within the large rooms, neither my bedroom nor my office in the corner of the west wing could be labelled 'homely' but, to me, they already felt like home. Oliver had invited me to use furniture from other rooms and had helped me relocate a pair of armchairs and a nest of occasional tables from one of the downstairs sitting rooms into my bedroom. The material covering the chairs was way past its best but they were still really comfortable and a couple of cosy throws and a pair of scatter cushions from a shop in Keswick soon transformed them.

Oliver and Rosie had been so welcoming and already felt like friends rather than clients. I'd been invited for Sunday dinner with Rosie's parents, Alice and Xander, and had also met Oliver's dad, Christian, along with the seven alpacas he was looking after for Emma this week. It was the local half-term break and she'd gone on holiday with her partner, Killian – the groundsman for the estate – and his family so I looked forward to meeting the pair of them when they returned to work.

I hadn't seen my parents since moving here because they were also away. Keira and Johnnie had booked a holiday cottage in Northumberland for a week and invited my parents to join them. With Astrid not yet attending school, they didn't need to go away during school holidays but it had been a last-minute thing fitting around other staff holidays. Their absence worked well for me, giving me a week of settling into Willowdale Hall and finding my stride with my new project without worrying about how to rebuild my damaged relationship with my parents. I'd hoped to drop in after my interview to tell them in person that I was moving back to Willowdale but they'd been away for a long week-end. We'd played telephone tag for a week and, when I eventually caught Mum on the phone and gave her the news, I don't think it sank in that I was actually moving home. She seemed convinced that I was just taking on a project here and, after going round in circles, I gave up and figured we could talk properly after their holiday when I was in situ.

Tonight, I was joining Tequila Mockingbird at The Hardy Herdwick quiz night and, while I was looking forward to it, I'd told Georgia I hoped she wasn't expecting me to replace Keira and Johnnie's collective brain power.

Rosie was meeting Autumn and Dane in the pub an hour before the quiz started so she'd invited me to join them. Although Oliver had been on their team on the night of Georgia's birthday, he wasn't a regular team member, usually playing squash with a colleague on a Thursday night and staying over at his house near Penrith.

We set off towards the village, chatting about how we'd spent the day. Rosie stopped as we reached the estate boundary and pointed to the other side of the road.

'That's where Hubert Cranleigh hit Mam and left her for dead.'

'Wow! I remember hearing about it at the time but I hadn't realised it was quite so close to the estate. Did they question him back then?'

'Yes, because of how near it was, but he had a strong alibi which placed him out of the area at the time of the accident.'

We set off walking once more.

'It must be hard passing the place where it happened every time you leave the estate.'

'Mam couldn't do it. Every time she passed that spot, she experienced terrifying flashbacks. What's weird is that, in the same storm that brought down the tree on the boat house, the tree which marked the spot also came down so there's not such a visual reminder anymore. I think that's really helped Mam with her recovery.'

I still couldn't quite get over what I'd learned about Hubert Cranleigh. 'Who drives into a person and flees from the scene?'

'The theory was that she'd been hit by a drunk driver and they were either oblivious because of that or they thought they'd hit an animal. We'll never know for sure because it was after his Lordship died that we found the car and pieced it together. I like to think there was a small element of humanity buried inside him somewhere and he would have stopped if he'd realised he'd hit a person.'

We continued for several paces in silence.

'If Hubert Cranleigh hadn't had his riding accident and was still alive when you found his car and made the connections, what do you think you'd have done?'

'Gosh, there's a question! What I'd have wanted to do and what I'd probably have done are a bit different. I'd have wanted to jump in his car and drive it straight at him so he could experience Mam's fear and pain for himself.'

'Understandable.'

'But what I think I'd have done is demand to know what really happened. Was he definitely drunk? Did he know he'd hit a person? Why didn't he stop? Why did he hide the car? At what point did he realise it was Mam he'd hit? What was the real motivation for making it possible for us to stay in the cottage? So many questions but I'll never get the answers and I've had to make my peace with that.'

'Do you think you'd feel any better if you had the answers?'

She contemplated for a moment. 'I don't know. Possibly not. The answers I got might have been worse than the not knowing. What if he'd been aware that he'd hit her, stopped the car, saw it was Mam and she was in a bad way, and ran off so she couldn't identify him if she came round? Would I want to know that about him? I prefer to think of him as someone who did a bad thing – a very bad thing – and did what he could to make amends by letting us keep our home and jobs. You know that phrase *ignorance is bliss*? In this case, I think it really is.'

It was interesting to hear Rosie's take on the issue. After Noah died, I'd wanted answers badly. Why had my boy been taken from me when he had his whole future ahead of him? I'd lashed out at everyone as I tried to find those answers, that explanation, that reason, because there *had* to be one. But every unanswered question fuelled the anger inside of me. There had to be somebody to blame. His friends, his girlfriend, his teachers, his dad. Anyone. Everyone.

I never got to the bottom of it and that anger and frustration was still there, eating away at me during quiet moments. So I avoided them, immersing myself into my work and research with more vigour than ever before. Would those questions eventually fade away or would they burst forth, refusing to be silenced? My biggest fear right now was that my first sighting of Flynn might be the trigger for that explosion.

'Slight subject change,' Rosie announced, breaking into my thoughts. 'Oliver and I have been talking about the conversion and we agree with you that it makes far more sense for us to live in the west wing and keep the library.'

'Really? You've laid the ghosts to rest?'

'Maybe not quite yet. What you said about the bedrooms just being rooms which can be changed in look and feel makes a lot of sense. The memories in Oliver's head are stronger than anything he conjures up by standing in his old bedroom, his mum's or Hubert's so he thinks that he would be okay to make those rooms part of our home. But we'd never considered our home just being on one level and we quite like that idea, so we wondered if you could walk us through your vision for each of the west wing options.'

'I'll smarten up my sketches tomorrow, add some more detail, and I can run through them whenever you like.'

'Awesome. I can't wait to see them.'

With perfect timing, we passed the lane where Autumn and Dane lived just as they appeared, so we paused and waited for them to join us. I remembered Beatrice Eccles living in the furthest of the three cottages and wondered what it looked like inside now that it was free from all the Beatrix Potter memorabilia.

Even though the quiz wouldn't start for another hour, it was already busy in the pub. The warmth from the real fire hugged me like an old friend as I slipped off my coat and scarf.

'We've got some big news,' Autumn announced, 'so the drinks are on us.'

I smiled as Rosie glanced down at Autumn's hand, presumably seeking out an engagement ring, but there wasn't one, so either that wasn't the news or there'd been a proposal with ring-shopping to follow.

Rosie and I grabbed a table and were soon joined by Autumn and Dane with four champagne flutes and an ice bucket containing a bottle of prosecco. The pair of them couldn't stop smiling as they poured and passed round the drinks. Beside me, Rosie looked fit to burst in anticipation of their news.

'We've secured a six-book publishing deal for Dane's books,' Autumn announced, her eyes sparkling. 'Dane's words, my illustrations, first book to be out for Christmas next year.'

'Oh, wow, that's amazing!' Rosie cried. 'Congratulations.'

I added my congratulations as we clinked our glasses together and took a sip of the bubbles.

'Was that what the video call with your agent was about?' Rosie asked.

'Yes,' Dane said. 'We thought it was going to be an update on her pitches to publishers but it was actually to tell us there'd been a bidding war and she wanted to check we agreed with her on the best deal.'

'I burst into tears!' Autumn said. 'It was so unexpected. We were geared up to hear a list of rejections although, looking back, she'd probably have put that in an email rather than a video call.'

'What sort of books are they?' I asked.

'Picture books featuring an animal mountain rescue team, inspired by Dane's real-life rescues. There was a risk that a publisher might want Dane's stories with their own illustrator's pictures but our agent, Lena, loved the partnership of a real-life couple and thought publishers would too, which thankfully they did.'

At my request, Autumn showed me some examples of the illustrations on her phone as well as some of the verses Dane had written. The pair of them were extremely talented.

'I'm so impressed,' I told them. 'Georgia knows lots of authors, some successful and some who are really struggling, and I've heard all sorts of stories from her about how difficult it can be to get a publishing deal.'

'We've been very lucky,' Dane said. 'You need to get the right story on the right person's desk at the right time and that's a lot of stars to align.'

'What about the books you wrote?' Rosie asked Autumn.

'You write too?' I asked, my eyes wide. 'Also children's books?'

'Yes, featuring the fairies and woodland animals who live in Derwentside Dell.'

My breath caught. Derwentside Dell? How magical did that sound?

'I don't know if you've explored out the back of the hall yet,' Rosie said, 'but there's an avenue of willow trees by the lakeside. That's the inspiration.'

Between the three of them, they told me how Autumn used to be an illustrator for a greetings cards company but had lost her creative sparkle. She and Rosie were long-term penpals but had never actually met until Rosie invited her to stay, suggesting there'd be no better place to recover her mojo than walking in the footsteps of Beatrix Potter. Autumn fell in love with Willowdale and with Dane and renewed her passion for drawing.

'Lena loved both series,' Autumn said, 'but we decided it would be best to lead with Dane's as we both had an involvement in that. Once we've signed the contract, she'll go back out with my series and some standalone books of Dane's.'

I loved how collaborative the process had been. Even though Rosie hadn't written the words or drawn any of the illustrations, she'd been instrumental in it all coming together from the invite for Autumn to stay through to the suggestion she add fairies into her tales. I was used to working on my own and I functioned effectively that way but there was something so special about working with likeminded people whose questions and suggestions could spark moments of brilliance.

Listening to Rosie, Autumn and Dane right now took me back to the excitement I'd felt working with Flynn. He was a talented builder and joiner who'd been working on new-build houses when I met him but, as the years passed, he found the work repetitive and lacking in challenge. He'd become increasingly interested in the old buildings I worked on and was eager for some hands-on experience to develop his skills. I had a word with Billy, the building contractor on one of my projects, and he offered Flynn some unpaid work experience in exchange for training him. With my support, Flynn dropped some hours on his regular job and the risk paid off. He showed such a passion for restoration as well as proving himself a quick and skilled learner that he was taken on full-time the moment Billy had a position and he quickly worked his way up to the number two in the business. Billy and Flynn recommended me to their clients and I returned the favour.

When Billy retired, Flynn bought the business and his first major change was taking me on as his partner, offering a fuller service to clients. I taught Flynn a lot but I also learned so much from him. I got such a buzz from working alongside someone as passionate about restoration as me, tossing around ideas, debating differences of opinion and working together to deliver quality projects. I'd missed that so much when our partnership dissolved. There'd been a few occasions when I'd felt a buzz since then by working with a particularly knowledgeable client or engaging building contractor, but those moments were short-lived and not nearly as exciting as they'd been with Flynn. Everything had been better working with him, but I'd blown it. I'd always been the fiery one and that fire had taken hold and burned everything around it.

Realising I'd zoned out for a moment, I focused back on what Autumn and Dane were saying about what would happen next in the process. It all sounded very exciting.

'I'll definitely want copies for my great-niece,' I said. 'She'll be four when the first one comes out.'

Thanking me for the support, Autumn apologised for hogging the conversation and asked me how I was settling into Willowdale Hall. I was waxing lyrical about how it was better than I'd ever dreamed when the door opened and Mark entered the pub. There was still half an hour before the quiz so presumably he and Georgia had come early for a drink. But it wasn't Georgia he was with.

The words stuck in my throat and I paused mid-sentence, heart racing, stomach churning as I stared at Mark's companion. And suddenly I was back to the day nearly thirty years ago when I first laid eyes on him in this very pub.

13

THIRTY YEARS AGO

Birthdays had always been a big thing in our family. No matter what day of the week it was, it had to be celebrated. Occasionally a night out was deferred until the weekend but a fuss was still made.

I didn't feel like celebrating my twenty-third birthday. A meal out or a few drinks at The Hardy Herdwick didn't really cut it when I should have been spending my birthday in Thailand with my boyfriend. Except Rowan Hawkins wasn't my boyfriend anymore – he was back with his ex and she was in Thailand with him right now.

I hadn't fallen in love with Rowan but I thought I'd miss his friendship when we broke up. The only thing I'd actually missed was the dream of Thailand. I'd spent hours poring over guide-books and brochures, planning out the holiday of a lifetime, but somebody else was doing it in my place, which was why I'd declared that I'd rather forget about my birthday this year. Which, of course, Georgia wouldn't accept.

'We'll make it small,' she'd eventually conceded. 'Just you, me and a few drinks at the pub.'

I was still living with Mum and Dad but Georgia and Mark had been renting a small house together in Keswick for the past two years. He dropped her off at Derwent Rise so we could walk round to The Hardy Herdwick together.

'Still feeling down?' Georgia asked, linking her arm through mine, as we set off down the drive after she'd said hello to our parents.

'A bit.'

'Missing Rowan?'

'Nope. It's the holiday I miss.'

'There'll be other holidays. You can go to Thailand with a friend or a future boyfriend.'

'I know and I'll get over it, but I should have been spending today at an elephant sanctuary. A day at work and a few drinks in the local isn't quite the same so I can't help feeling a little grumpy.'

'I get it. I'd be miffed too.'

'I'll let my birthday slip by quietly this year and maybe I'll spend it in Thailand next year or the year after.'

She squeezed my arm. 'That's the spirit.'

We arrived at the pub and, as we stepped inside, I jumped at a chorus of *Surprise!* Several tables on one side of the pub were filled with friends and family members and there was a large Dumbo helium balloon standing on the floor. Mark was there so he'd evidently dropped Georgia off then driven round to the pub before we got here. The door opened behind us and Mum and Dad appeared.

'When it comes to birthdays, you know we never do understated in this family,' Georgia said, hugging me.

As I joined the group, a drink was thrust into my hand followed by a gift bag containing a stack of elephant-themed items including a pair of silver stud earrings, a soft toy, a bar of soap, a notebook and a candle. Soon after, one of the staff appeared with the most amazing birthday cake of an elephant bathing in a bubble bath.

'You couldn't travel to bathe an elephant so we brought a bathing elephant to you,' Georgia said after everyone sang the birthday song to me.

I'd genuinely thought that being surrounded by people was the last thing I wanted today but it was the best gift Georgia could have given me. The bag of presents and the cake were amazing but knowing that I had friends and family who cared enough to come out on a Wednesday night to cheer me up was priceless. I didn't care that I didn't have a boyfriend and it didn't matter that I'd never been in love. It would hopefully happen to me one day when I least expected it.

The door opened and a group of eight men and one woman of varying ages from maybe mid-twenties to late-fifties made their way to the bar. One of the younger men caught my eye and I found my heart pounding – a reaction I'd never had at first sight before.

'What are you looking... Oh! No need to answer that,' Georgia said. 'Not bad at all.'

'I wasn't looking at him.'

'You keep telling yourself that.'

He was tall and broad with dark brown curly hair and a five o'clock shadow, but what really captivated me was his smile. It was so warm and friendly and I found myself wanting to be the person who made him smile like that.

'I like his smile,' I conceded, feeling my cheeks burning. This wasn't like me at all.

At that moment, he glanced in my direction and his eyes rested on mine. His smile widened and I looked behind me, convinced he couldn't possibly be smiling at me and must know one of my friends. But there was nobody looking in his direction. When I returned my gaze, he nodded and raised his glass towards me before returning his attention to his companions who were all toasting to the retirement of the oldest group member.

They pulled a couple of tables together at the other side of the pub and he sat down directly in my eyeline. As the evening progressed, we kept catching each other's eye.

'Just go up to him and introduce yourself,' Georgia whispered.

'In front of our parents? Are you having a laugh?'

They left a little later and Georgia repeated her suggestion.

'Would you infiltrate a group of that size and introduce yourself?' I asked.

'No. Far too intimidating.'

'Then why would you expect me to do it?'

'Fair point. But what if he leaves without you even saying hello?'

That thought actually made me feel a little nauseous, but what could I do? What if I walked up to the group and it turned out that the woman was his wife or girlfriend? Or what if his wife or girlfriend wasn't there but one of the men was related to her? Or what if there wasn't a wife or girlfriend but he wasn't interested in me, only smiling at me because I was smiling at him and it was the polite thing to do?

My group got smaller, as did his, but it was still too scary to walk up to his table. I nipped to the toilets and hoped that, if he was interested, he'd do the same and we could speak in the corridor. I even hung around for a couple of minutes but there was no sign of him. Returning to my friends, my heart sank as I spotted one of the bar staff clearing the empty glasses from his table. He'd gone and I'd lost my opportunity.

It was past nine but, with it being mid-week and everyone having work the next day, nobody was up for a late night. The last of our group finished their drinks and said goodbye, leaving Georgia, Mark and me to pack up my gifts while one of the staff wrapped the remnants of my birthday cake in some foil.

'We'll drop you home,' Mark said.

'No need. It's out of your way and, besides, I could do with the fresh air.'

'But you have stuff to carry,' Georgia protested.

'A gift bag, a balloon and some cake. I think I can manage. In fact...' I removed the soft elephant from the bag, placed the balloon weight at the bottom, added my cake package to it, and rested Edgar the elephant on the top. 'Now I only have one bag.'

'Okay, I'll let you off. At least it isn't dark yet.'

'Benefit of being born on the longest day of the year.' I hugged my sister and Mark, thanking them for organising an amazing evening and pulling me out of my slump.

We headed outside together. Mark had parked in front of the nearby village hall so I placed the bag by my feet and waited on the corner to wave them off. I picked up the bag once more but the addition of the balloon weight and the cake had evidently been too heavy for the ribbon handles and they ripped through the paper. I cursed under my breath as the bag dropped to the ground and Edgar the elephant made a bid for freedom, rolling away from me.

I reached out for it and stopped as a voice said, 'Here, let me.'

Heart pounding, I looked up into a pair of stunning green eyes and that dazzling smile.

'I thought you'd gone,' I said, my voice sounding husky.

'I had, but I forgot something so I came back.'

'Oh! I didn't see anything on your table but they might have it behind the bar.'

That smile! It was doing the funniest things to my insides,

making them feel like golden syrup being swirled around with a spoon.

'It wasn't an item,' he said. 'It was...' He still had Edgar in his hands and was squidging him as though he was nervous. 'I'm not very good at stuff like this. I erm... the thing I forgot... it was, erm... It was you. I mean, to say hello to you.' He held Edgar over his face. 'God! That sounded so much better in my head. Sorry.'

I placed my hands over his and lowered them and the elephant, touched by his show of vulnerability.

'I think you're doing a pretty good job at it, actually. Was it just the hello you forgot? Because hi.'

His smile returned. 'Hi. I forgot an introduction too. I'm Flynn.'

'Mel. Good to meet you. So that's a hello and an introduction. Anything else?'

'To ask if you'd like to go out for a drink with me sometime.'

'I'd like that a lot. And as it's still early and we're stood right next to a pub, I'm thinking *sometime* could be now. What do you reckon?'

'Is it your birthday today?'

I glanced at the balloon. 'What could possibly have given it away?'

He laughed. 'It'd be rude not to offer you a birthday drink.' He seemed to realise that he was still holding my soft toy. 'And it'd be rude not to return your elephant too.'

His fingers grazed mine as he passed me the toy and my heart raced faster as a zip of electricity shot through my body.

'I'm spotting a theme,' he added, picking up the broken bag for me. 'Are elephants your thing?'

'There's a story behind that...'

* * *

Georgia had met Mark five years ago when she was twenty-one and I vividly remembered her bursting into my bedroom after their first date, giddy with excitement as she told me she'd met the man she was going to marry. She'd been right about that – the big day was coming up a week on Saturday.

On several occasions over the years, I'd asked Georgia how she could possibly have known with such certainty that Mark was right for her after only one date and she'd smiled and said it was for the same reason I could say with absolute certainty that the latest boyfriend I'd dumped wasn't for me. You just knew.

I wished Georgia still lived at home as it would have been my turn to burst into her bedroom and declare that I now understood what she'd been talking about the night she met Mark because the same thing had just happened to me.

14

PRESENT DAY

It was nearly thirty years since the first time I saw Flynn and six since the last, yet somehow he still held the ability to make my heart race and my insides turn to liquid. What was he doing here? Surely Georgia hadn't been tactless enough to invite him to reconnect with me between questions on tonight's quiz. No, she'd never do that to me. She knew how difficult it would be for me to see Flynn again. I anticipated she'd keep pushing me to meet him, but she'd never ambush me like this.

'Are you okay?'

I was vaguely aware of Autumn speaking to me but I couldn't tear my gaze away from Flynn. His hair was longer and the curls on the top were unruly. It would be driving him mad but he hated going to the barber's. I used to have to drag him into town and plonk him down in the chair when I could no longer bear the sighs of frustration as he swatted the curls from his eyes. The beard was new and it suited him. I'd always thought it would and had encouraged him on several occasions to give one a try but he'd always shaved it off within a week, saying he looked too much like his dad and granddad. Perhaps the trend over recent years for beards on younger men had changed his mind.

'Mel?'

Someone lightly touched my arm – Rosie presumably – bringing my attention back to my companions.

'Yes, fine. Sorry. Where were we?'

'Rosie was telling us about making their home in the west wing,' Dane said.

The conversation resumed but I couldn't relax. Any moment now, Mark and Flynn would get their drinks, turn around and spot me. I couldn't do it. I'd known it was inevitable that our paths would cross at some point but I wasn't ready for it to happen this soon.

'I'm really sorry, but I've got a splitting headache.' I scrunched my nose as I pressed two fingers against the gap between my eyebrows. 'I think I'm going to head back to the hall.'

'Do you want me to walk you back?' Rosie asked, looking concerned.

'No. It's not a migraine or anything like that but I think it'll get worse with the noise when the quiz starts. I'll get some fresh air and an early night and I'll be fine by the morning.'

Pulling on my coat and grabbing my scarf, I congratulated Autumn and Dane once more on their exciting news, all the while praying the bartender would slow down because, any moment now, Mark and Flynn were going to turn.

I hitched my handbag onto my shoulder and headed towards the door, straight into Flynn's path.

'Mel?' He stopped short, spilling his pint over his hands.

It was overwhelming enough seeing him here – the place we'd met and fallen in love, the place we'd spent so many wonderful hours together over the years – but there was no way I could have a conversation with him.

'I didn't know you'd—'

'Sorry,' I mumbled, shaking my head at him. 'I can't.'

I hastened outside, praying he wouldn't follow me. Even before Georgia had mentioned it, I'd known I wouldn't be able to avoid Flynn forever, but I'd been here for less than a week and hadn't expected to encounter him quite so soon. Wincing, I realised I hadn't even acknowledged Mark, which was so rude of me. I also felt a little immature for letting my feelings overcome me like that and storming out. The door opened and I prepared to rush off but it was Mark who called my name.

'I'm so sorry,' he said, walking towards me. 'I didn't think you'd be here already.'

'Drinks with Rosie and her friends.'

He grimaced. 'I should have thought. It was meant to be one quick drink and he'd be gone before you got here.'

'Did he know I was joining you for the quiz?'

'Yes, so he suggested the Lakeside Inn instead, but I thought we had time and... well, clearly we didn't.'

'It's not your fault. It was going to happen sooner or later. I'd have preferred later.'

'It could be the perfect chance to get it over with.'

I started shaking my head vigorously before Mark even finished his sentence. 'I'm not ready. Moving back here is a lot for me and I can only handle one thing at a time.'

Mark nodded solemnly. 'I get it. Sorry, Mel. I shouldn't have—'

'It's fine. As you say, you weren't expecting me to be here. Tell Georgia I'll call her tomorrow.'

'Don't go! We'll take our drinks into the beer garden. You don't have to see Flynn.'

'No need. I've got some stuff to think about. Tell Flynn...' I paused. What was the message? 'Tell him I know we probably do need to talk at some point but not yet.'

'Any idea when?' he asked gently.

'Too soon to say.' I tapped the side of my head. 'Lots going on up here. See you soon, yeah?'

'Okay.'

As I walked away, I had a sense of being watched. I was pretty sure it was Flynn looking out of the window but I wasn't going to turn around. If I made eye contact with him, I wasn't sure I was strong enough to keep walking away and I had to do that. I'd break if I didn't.

15

On Saturday morning, I dressed warmly, pulled on my wellies and made my way over to Casa Alpaca – the area near the estate entrance where the alpacas were kept. Rosie had told me that it would be Emma's first day back at work after her holidays and I was eager to meet her as, from what Oliver and Rosie told me, she sounded like somebody I was going to really like.

There'd been a heavy frost overnight and the ground crunched satisfyingly beneath my feet. My breath hung in the air and my nose and cheeks tingled from the bite of the chilly early morning. The trees surrounding the hall looked picture-postcard beautiful with a layer of frost clinging to the branches. There wasn't any snow forecast but I hoped I'd one day see the estate covered in snow as, if it looked this stunning on a frosty morning, I could imagine it looking magical under a blanket of snow.

Casa Alpaca was approached down a lane with neatly cut hedges either side, their branches twinkling with the frost. Parked at the end of the lane, facing me, was a small van with the back doors open. A woman with long dark hair beneath a yellow bobble hat was unloading some straw bales. She looked up and smiled as I approached.

'Are you Emma?' I asked.

'I am. You must be Mel.'

'That's me. Architect in residence.'

She laughed at that. 'I'm so excited that they're kickstarting the refurb. It's such a stunning place. Deserves some care and attention.'

'I completely agree. I've been in love with the hall pretty much my whole life so I keep having to pinch myself that I've got this opportunity.' I nodded towards the bales. 'Can I help you with anything? I was keen to meet you but I don't want to stop you working.'

'You can give me a hand carrying these through if you don't mind.'

She closed the van doors and opened the gate. I was a little disappointed not to see any alpacas.

'The herd are at the other side of the paddock,' she said, as though reading my mind. 'I wanted to get this fresh bedding down before I call them in for their breakfast.'

I followed Emma's directions to pile up the bales in a wooden storage cupboard, leaving one out to distribute in what she called the Paca Shack – a large wooden structure with stable doors at either end. She told me the alpacas were fed inside it but might also bed down, especially in the colder weather. The floor had already been cleared of the old straw and swept.

'I met your dad last week and he said you were away in Northumberland,' I said as we scattered straw across the floor. 'Did you have a good holiday?'

'It was amazing, thanks. I went with my partner, Killian, his two girls, his sister and his mum. He's the groundsman here so you'll meet him soon, but he's not in this weekend.'

'Big family holiday,' I said.

'It was, and I'll admit to being a teeny bit nervous about going away with everyone. Killian and I have only been together for four months, but it honestly couldn't have gone better. I properly feel like part of the family now and we're already talking about going away again together in the summer.'

'Sounds lovely.'

'It really was, although I missed the Magnificent Seven, of course. I got my dad to send me photos and videos so I could get my alpaca fix. Do you want to meet them?'

'I'd love to.'

Bedding finished, Emma poured some pellets into a bucket.

'Have you ever met an alpaca before?'

'Until I came here, I'd never even seen one. Your dad said you wouldn't mind if he did the intros, but it didn't feel right when I hadn't met you so I said I'd wait till you returned.'

'I wouldn't have minded, but I'm pleased to have the honour. I get such a kick out of introducing them to new people.'

After hanging up a couple of nets of hay from ceiling hooks in the shack and pouring more pellets into a feeding trough outside, Emma gave me a short briefing on where the alpacas liked to be stroked and where to avoid. Then she grabbed the bucket of feed and took me through a holding pen into a pasture, shaking the bucket and whistling. It didn't take long for the alpacas to appear from the far end, a light grey one leading the way.

'That's Barbara,' Emma told me. 'She's the boss lady. Check out the swagger on her. I've had fun filming her and adding songs to the videos. Remind me to show you the one of her strutting to "Saturday Night Fever". It's my favourite. Guaranteed mood-lifter.'

I smiled as I studied Barbara's approach. She really did strut rather than walk.

Emma rattled off the other names – white alpacas called Florence and Bianca and two light fawn-coloured ones called Charmaine and Camella.

'The dark brown one's Jolene and the one at the back is Maud. She's got a grey fleece like Barbara but it's a different shade called rose grey. Isn't it pretty?'

'They're all pretty.'

They were very close so Emma shook the bucket again and led them through the holding pen to the feeding trough where they all dipped their heads and started munching.

'They're fluffier than I expected.'

Emma nodded. 'Their fleeces are really soft – great for keeping them warm in the winter as well as making fantastic wool. They get sheared when we get warm weather but we'll keep most of the fluffiness on their heads.'

She told me that there weren't any customer walks booked in for today as she wanted to spend her first day back settling in and giving her undivided attention to the herd, but she would still be taking them out for a walk and I was welcome to join her. I didn't need asking twice. Charmaine apparently refused to walk on afternoons so, after they'd eaten, Emma added halters and attached leads to Charmaine, Florence and Bianca, telling me that there were friendship groups within the herd and those three had a really strong bond.

I felt a little apprehensive as Emma handed me Charmaine's lead. We were a family of animal lovers but none of us had ever had pets so I'd never even walked a dog before, but I needn't have been concerned. The three of them sauntered along the drive with no need for direction.

'They've walked the route so often that they know where they're heading,' Emma said. 'They'll occasionally pull you over to a hedge so they can have a scratch, which is fine, and they might stop to eat the grass but there's an area we use round the back of the house so a gentle tug on the lead will keep them on track. They do know where their official feeding stop is, but they like to try it on sometimes.'

'Have you always had alpacas?' I asked.

'I've always loved them but, this time last year, I was a teacher and alpacas definitely weren't on my radar...'

As we walked the three alpacas, Emma told me how her fiancé at the time – Grayson – had secured a tenancy on one of Beatrix Potter's farms near Coniston and she'd made the decision to leave teaching to help him run the farm. The previous owner had told her about some research she'd done into alpaca walks around the farm, which immediately captured Emma's interest. The Magnificent Seven were a herd in need of rescue but, as she was about to start some building work on the farm to prepare for their arrival, Grayson dropped the bombshell that he didn't want the alpacas at the farm and he didn't want her there either.

'I was devastated at the time but it's funny how a bit of time and distance can give you a fresh perspective. Grayson was an awful partner – all take and no give – and I didn't realise it at the time. I wasted a lot of years on him, but I needed to go through that to get where I am today with my alpacas, this stunning place as my office, and Killian. I've also got an amazing half-brother who I didn't know existed and I finally have a great relationship with my dad, which is something I'd never expected. So, toxic as it was with Grayson, I wouldn't change my time with him for the world because of where it led me.'

It was a really healthy way of looking at the darkness and she presented it with such gusto. Would I ever be able to do that? Our circumstances were different and clearly there would never be a positive from losing my son, but could there be a time when I saw my divorce from Flynn as a positive thing which had propelled me to a better place? I couldn't imagine that I would. I'd already had nearly seven years of time and distance and no positives had emerged then so I doubted they ever would. Probably because there weren't any. Emma's relationship had been toxic but ours had been incredible. She'd wasted years on Grayson but every moment I'd spent with Flynn had been precious. Then tragedy struck and I went into self-destruct mode.

We'd reached the back of the hall. The lawn stretched out ahead of us but there was a rougher grassy area alongside some old sheds which was where we paused for the alpacas to graze.

'I loved teaching,' Emma continued, the leads for Florence and Bianca held loosely in her hands, 'but I love this even more. I still get to use my teaching skills but in a different context and without any of the stress. I can't tell you how much better I feel working with animals and spending my days outdoors. If things had been different and I'd set up my business at the farm as planned, it would have been special and I'd have loved it, but not on this level.' She closed her eyes momentarily and breathed in deeply before opening them and smiling at me. 'It's so restful here. I can't get enough of it. I know you've only been here a week, but can you feel it?'

'There's definitely something special about the estate.'

I was conscious that I hadn't really answered her question but my answer wouldn't be straightforward so it was easier to avoid it. Emma was clearly an open person and, while she hadn't gone into much detail about Grayson or given any insight into why she'd previously had a bad relationship with her dad, she'd shared enough to let me in. I couldn't reciprocate. I hadn't told Rosie and Oliver about Noah so I certainly wasn't ready to open up to someone I'd only just met, no matter how much I already liked her.

'Your dad said you're originally from Willowdale,' I said,

feeling it was time for a subject change. 'I'm wondering if we were at school together.'

Emma shared that she was forty-eight with an October birthday, making her five school years behind me, but we didn't remember each other from primary school. By the time Emma started senior school, I'd have been in the sixth form and our paths wouldn't have crossed, but she'd moved to Ambleside by then anyway.

'Do your family still live in Willowdale?' Emma asked as we set off walking once more.

'They do. My parents still live in the house I was raised in – Derwent Rise near The White Willow. My sister and her husband live in Pippinthwaite and their kids are grown up now and live with their partners in Keswick.'

I tensed, sensing what the next question would be – *Do you have kids?* I hated that question. A few years ago, a client had asked me it and, as we hadn't been talking about children or families at the time, it completely threw me off guard and I just blurted it out. *I had a son but he died when he was eighteen. Drug overdose.* I'll never forget the way in which her empathetic expression turned to shock as I added those final two words. She didn't voice it but I knew she was making judgements about Noah – bad boy, irresponsible, out of control – and judging me as a terrible parent without knowing anything about either of us. She never asked me anything personal after that, our meetings remaining strictly business, and I never answered that question with honesty again. *Do you have kids? No.* Followed swiftly by a change of subject so they couldn't ask me to expand. From what I'd learned about Emma so far, I couldn't imagine her being judgemental like that client, but I wasn't prepared to risk it and the best way to do that was to go to my happy place – a conversation about my work.

'I'm loving Oliver and Rosie's vision of Willowdale Hall being somewhere for people to relax, find their happy and, if they need it, to heal. I can see exactly how walking the alpacas fits in to that. I'm really enjoying this.'

'Isn't it great? Just being with the alpacas is calming in itself, but these surroundings take it to another level. You'll fully see what I mean when we get down to the lake.'

We walked along a pathway between trees with glimpses of Derwent Water through the branches on our right before descending a slope onto a pebble beach. The lead tightened as Charmaine tugged me towards the lake's edge.

'She's fine to go in,' Emma said, and I noticed that Florence and Bianca had already entered the water. 'Florence will probably lie down in a minute.'

Next moment, she did, and she started humming too. I glanced at Emma, surprised by the sound.

'Your face,' she said, laughing. 'That's her telling us how happy she is. Isn't it gorgeous?'

It truly was. I stood there taking in the view as Emma snapped a few photos of the alpacas against the wintry backdrop of snowy fells. The lake was ever so still, acting as a perfect mirror of its surroundings. I took some photos of Emma with the alpacas on her phone which she appreciated, telling me that she usually only appeared on the social media accounts in selfie form. She took several of me with the alpacas on my phone which I'd show to the family later.

With the alpacas enjoying their time in the lake and Florence providing us with background 'music', it was the perfect opportunity to get Emma's thoughts on the hall conversion as, being new to the estate, she'd view it differently from Oliver and Alice who'd spent most of their lives here and Rosie who'd lived her entire life here.

'Do you mind me quizzing you about the hall?' I asked. 'Imagine you don't know the area but you've come across Willowdale Hall online and you're thinking of booking one of the apartments. What would you expect from a holiday here?'

'Luxury,' she said, without missing a beat. 'It's a grand manor house set in large grounds so I'd expect the rooms to complement that. I'd want all the mod cons – coffee machine, microwave, powerful shower and so on – but I'd still want to feel that I was in an old building so I'd expect the colours, fabrics and furniture to reflect that. I'd want to know something about the history of my apartment and maybe have some throwbacks to that. For example, if it was originally the library, I'd expect to be told that and for there to be a small library of books. If it's a room where Beatrix Potter slept or drew, I'd *definitely* want to know all about that and maybe have an old desk with some art supplies set up on it.'

Florence rose from the water, shook herself off, and we set off back across the beach and up the slope. So far Emma hadn't said anything I hadn't expected or already considered myself, but I encouraged her to keep going as conversations like this could sometimes unearth a gem or two.

'I love that Oliver and Rosie want to open up the estate to the public with woodland trails and a café. It deserves to be seen and loved and it'll hopefully bring more customers for me, but I'm wondering if inviting the public in fully aligns to the vision of the residential guests being able to completely relax. If I came here wanting to get away from everything, I don't think I'd want the grounds to be swarming with people.'

And there was the gem.

'That's a really good point. Obviously the gates would be closed and locked at the end of the afternoon so there'd only be overnight guests in the grounds during the evenings, but I hear you about daytime. What if we made part of the grounds exclusive to guests? Would that work?'

'It's a fair compromise. If I was staying somewhere like this, I'd want to imagine it's my home – if only for a few days – so the more that can be done to make it feel like that, the better.'

Another gem. Any holiday was a chance to escape but a holiday in an old manor house was a chance to escape to a bygone time.

'I love that,' I said. 'And I can see how that fits with the relaxing and finding your happy vibe. Thanks, Emma. That was really helpful.'

'You're welcome. And speaking of relaxing, I hope you'll get some time to do that while you're here. I can imagine it's harder to switch off when you're living on site.'

'I'm not great at switching off from work anyway,' I admitted. 'It's so much harder when your job's also your passion. If I'm not doing actual work on an evening, I'm most likely found with my head buried in a history or design book, but I am making a special effort to take breaks and explore the grounds. I'm an early riser so seeking you out this morning was my way of not spending the whole weekend working.'

'But then you asked me work-related questions,' Emma said, laughing.

I grimaced. 'I can't help myself.'

'I completely get it. When I'm not here, I'm often still working. There's all the admin to do, customer queries and the socials. I'm also building up a range of merchandise and I do the illustrations for those so, believe me, I know how easy it is for work to take over.'

As we made our way back to Casa Alpaca, Emma told me more about her illustrations. She also shared the story of how the

Magnificent Seven had been rescued and ended up at Willowdale Hall, which all sounded very dramatic and stressful.

'They love it here, though,' she said as she opened the gate. 'I'm so proud of how well they've settled in and taken to their walks.'

Emma removed their halters and leads and the trio had a drink and a munch on the hay hanging up in the shack.

'I'll walk the others later,' she told me as she hung up the halters and leads. 'I want to check the perimeter fence and clean the water trough first. You're welcome to stay longer.'

I appreciated the invite but I'd decided to check out Keswick market so I told her I'd head off. 'Thanks for letting me join you on your walk. That's set up my day perfectly.'

'I enjoyed the company. Don't work too hard. It is the weekend, after all.'

'I'll try not to.'

'The first walk of the day is at ten so, if you're ever at a loose end first thing, you're welcome to stop by for a chat, although be warned that I'll probably thrust a rake and shovel at you and ask you to get scooping.'

'I'd be happy to help.'

'Excellent. Could be the first step in finding you a work-life balance while you're here. We'll soon have you all relaxed and any wounds healed.'

'No wounds to heal,' I said, 'but I hear you about relaxing. I'll try my best.'

We said our goodbyes and I thrust my gloved hands into my coat pockets as I strode down the lane, kicking at a frost-covered stick. *No wounds to heal?* If only!

16

I returned to the hall intending on having a coffee before heading into town but I felt on edge, my parting words to Emma swirling round in my mind. My wounds were so deep that I couldn't imagine them ever healing and it was fair enough that I hadn't shared that with a woman I'd only just met, especially when she was the half-sister of my new client. But why tell her an outright lie? There were so many other things I could have said in response. *Sounds perfect* or *I'll look forward to the hall working its magic.* Anything but a declaration that I had no wounds to heal. Willowdale was a small village and Emma was bound to find out about Noah at some point. What would she think of me then? Who loses their son and declares they have no wounds to heal?

While the coffee machine whirred and filled my mug, I stared out of the kitchen window, eager to focus on something nice in the hope of quietening the noise in my head. The lawn sparkled in the winter sun and I loved how unspoilt it was, stretching out into the distance to the trees and the lake beyond. I thought about what Autumn and Rosie had told me about the willow tree avenue which had inspired the setting of Autumn's books. That would undoubtedly look beautiful with the frost clinging to the branches. I couldn't see the willows from here but I felt compelled to see if they were as spectacular as I imagined. Leaving my mug on the machine, I pulled my wellies and layers back on and left by the side door. I wasn't sure exactly where the willow trees were but if I followed the edge of the lake, I'd happen upon them.

My breath caught when I found Derwentside Dell and I could immediately see why Autumn had been so inspired. The trees had been planted in two rows creating a walkway between their droopy branches, which followed the curve of the lake before rising up a slope. The outer branches sparkled with the frost and there were sprinkles of frost along the walkway where the branches weren't dense enough to shelter the ground. The dappled light from the low sun created an ethereal feeling and I smiled at the thought of Autumn's fairies and woodland animals dancing in the shafts of sunlight.

Autumn had probably visited Derwentside Dell during all weathers to capture the light and the colours for her illustrations, but I took some photos from outside and under the arches to share with her, just in case this particular morning presented something she hadn't previously captured. There was enough space to walk all the way through the willow avenue, although I had to duck occasionally to avoid getting my hat snagged on the branches.

The lake continued in a curve towards a two-storey boat house which had to be where Hubert Cranleigh's car had been hidden. What a shocking situation that was. I slipped my phone into my pocket and pulled my gloves back on as I crunched my way across the lawn towards the structure.

Much as I loved beautiful big old properties like Willowdale Hall, tiny structures like this could just as easily capture my imagination. I'd always been fascinated by Bridge House in Ambleside – one of the Lake District's most recognisable and smallest buildings. Now under the care of The National Trust, the tiny seventeenth-century two-roomed house on a bridge over Stock Beck had originally been an apple store for nearby Ambleside Hall, specifically built on a bridge to avoid land tax. It had changed purpose many times over, being used as a counting house for the nearby mills, a tearoom, a cobbler's, a chair maker's and even home to a family of eight. The latter particularly sparked my imagination, wondering how two adults and six children had lived in such a tiny space – way smaller than the boat house in front of me.

Oliver and Rosie hadn't said anything about their plans for the boat house. There was no sign of the tree which fell down on the roof last year but the damage from it hadn't been repaired. Perhaps that was an indication that they were planning to have it pulled down. I could understand why they might want to but, in my opinion, it would be a travesty to destroy it. I walked round to the other side on which the tree had landed, grimacing at the gaping hole in the roof. The double wooden doors onto the lawn were buckled and hanging off, and I knew without looking that there'd be some water damage inside as a result of a year's exposure to the elements, but the rest of the building appeared to be in good condition.

I whipped my phone out and took several photos as my mind whirred. There was such a demand these days for unique holiday destinations, the quirkier the better. Rooms in lighthouses, windmills, treehouses, shepherd's huts, underground bunkers and so on were let for a premium. Refurbishing the boat house as luxury accommodation for two would require a minimal outlay, relatively speaking within the scope of the whole project, but would bring in a speedy high return.

A dog brushing past my legs made me jump. 'Chester? Where did you spring from?'

Moments later, his partner-in-crime Toffee appeared with Alice not far behind. On Tuesday, Rosie had invited me to join her and Alice for lunch at Horseshoe Cottage. When Rosie returned to the stables, I'd stayed for another hour. Alice was so warm and friendly, just like her daughter, and I'd loved spending time with her.

I waved at Alice and she waved back, which was a good sign as I was acutely conscious of being beside the boat house and unaware of her feelings towards the building now.

'Exploring the grounds?' she asked, smiling as she came closer.

'Autumn and Rosie told me about the willow tree avenue so I wanted to take a look at it, and then I spotted the boat house.'

She looked past me towards the building, her head cocked onto one side. What must she be thinking right now looking at the building where Hubert Cranleigh had hidden his car for all those years?

'It's looking a bit sad and sorry with that hole in the roof and the doors hanging loose,' she said eventually, turning her gaze back to me. 'Did Rosie tell you what happened in the storm? I told her she could.'

'Yes. She wanted me to hear it from her rather than someone else. I'm so sorry. Finding the car must have been really difficult for you.'

'At the time, it was horrendous, but that tree coming down saved me. They say you sometimes have to hit rock bottom before you can make your way up again and that was certainly true for me. I had a breakdown that day but it was the start of my recovery.'

She wandered over to the boat house and ran her hand down

the stonework. 'It's still a beautiful structure, even in its sorry state.'

'I think so, and the location is incredible. Those views! I was just thinking that it could be refurbished and make a fantastic unique escape, but I wasn't sure how that proposal would go down after what happened.'

'I think it's a wonderful idea.' She turned to face me, smiling warmly. 'Even the things that seem the most broken can be fixed with enough time, love and will. A bit like me.' She glanced back towards the boat house once more. 'What would it look like if you breathed new life into it?'

'Modern. The stone would remain, tying it in with the house, but it would be wood at the back and glass at the front and sides – one-way privacy glass so guests can enjoy the beauty surrounding them but nobody else can see inside.' I could already picture it so vividly, even down to the wood and fabrics I'd choose.

'Imagine lying in bed and being able to see across the lake ahead of you and having a skylight to the stars above you,' I said. 'It's my idea of heaven. For a bit more space, it could have a wrap-around deck with solar lighting and a fire pit. All very romantic.'

'It sounds perfect.'

'Do you think Oliver and Rosie would be interested?'

'With my blessing, they would be. They wanted to pull it down last year but I asked them to leave it. I knew that, when I felt well enough to come back home, part of my recovery would be to stand on the road where I was hit and to see the boat house again.'

'You seem comfortable being here.'

'I wasn't the first time I came here after my breakdown. Even though the car was long gone, I could still vividly picture that moment when they pulled off the tarpaulin and how scared I was when I saw the green man.'

'Green man?'

'Rosie didn't mention it? It was raining heavily the night I was struck by the car and that same type of torrential rain triggered terrible PTSD episodes. I couldn't fully remember the accident but I often mentioned my fear of the green man. We had no idea who or what it was but it turned out to be a toy dangling from the rear-view mirror which had somehow lodged in my mind – probably the last thing I saw before I blacked out.'

'That's so scary, Alice. I'm so sorry you went through all that.'

'Me too, and not just for me. Rosie was only fourteen when it happened so she had to grow up fast to take care of me and the stables. What she went through must have been incredibly upsetting and frustrating for her but she just got on with it and never once lost her patience.'

'You've got a good one there,' I said, having already seen those positive traits in Rosie in the short time I'd known her.

'Haven't I just? She gave up so much for me. Thank goodness the universe has rewarded her for it with Oliver back in her life and Willowdale Hall as her forever home.'

'Have you ever wanted to live in the hall?'

Alice shook her head. 'They've asked me but I love Horseshoe Cottage. It was my sanctuary when I was pregnant and my parents threw me out, and it's remained my happy place ever since. I barely left the estate for a couple of decades but I can do that now and every time gets easier. I think that's partly because I know I've got the safety of my little cottage to return to.'

Chester and Toffee had been chasing each other round the garden but they both flopped beside Alice, panting.

'Time for a warm-up in front of the fire,' she said, smiling at the dogs. 'Lovely bumping into you, Mel, and do definitely share your ideas for this place with Rosie and Oliver with my blessing.'

'Thank you. The last thing I'd ever have wanted to do was cause you any distress.'

'I've made my peace with this place. The boat house didn't cause my accident and the car didn't either. Hubert Cranleigh made a choice to drive under the influence that day and he made a choice to cover it up. This is simply an innocent building where he hid the evidence and it doesn't deserve to be destroyed because of someone else's bad choices.'

Alice set off across the lawn with Chester and Toffee, leaving me outside the boat house mulling over her words. *The boat house didn't cause my accident... simply an innocent building.* She'd visited the boat house to aid her recovery and I'd seen with my own eyes the warmth she felt towards the building, heard it in her voice, felt it in her excitement about my proposal. If I'd stayed, would I have eventually felt that way about The Bothy – our family home? Flynn had urged me to give it time but it hurt too much. I couldn't concentrate on my work, I couldn't sleep, I couldn't be there. And so I left. I left our home behind, my marriage, my life and thought that a characterless 1980s flat with no resemblance whatsoever to The Bothy would ease the pain. How wrong I'd been. The reality was that, because my rented flat was so very different, I thought about and missed my beautiful home even more.

By the time I returned to the kitchen my coffee was cold so I made a fresh mug and took it up to my bedroom. Was Flynn still living in The Bothy? He'd bought me out as part of the divorce settlement so presumably he'd either sold up or remortgaged. Another prod of guilt that I'd left him to it all on his own. I'd packed up my clothes and my office and moved out, leaving him to pack up or sell everything else. From wedding gifts to kitchenware to the artwork we'd carefully chosen together, I'd walked away from our home as though it meant nothing to me. As though he meant nothing to me. I shouldn't have done that. I shouldn't have done a lot of things but they'd felt right at the time. I'd been thinking a lot lately about the phrase *act in haste, repent at leisure* and how applicable it was for me.

Inspired by Alice's courage to visit the places that evoked memories of a traumatic time, I had an urge to jump in my car and drive to The Bothy but what if Flynn was still living there and he saw me? I hadn't been anywhere near prepared for seeing him in the pub on Thursday and that hadn't changed in the space of two days.

An online search would reveal whether our house had been sold and, if it had, maybe I would drive over and take a look. Moments later, I found my answer. The Bothy *had* sold but only four years ago so Flynn must have remortgaged to release enough equity to buy me out. My stomach churned at the prospect of causing him any financial difficulties on top of everything else in my haste to get closure. That meant he'd stayed there for three years after Noah died. What must that have been like?

The details online were accompanied by what had presumably been the photographs used during the sale. A picture of the outside of The Bothy was the lead photo and the site indicated it was one of twelve. We'd been the first owners of the four-bedroom barn conversion on a farm between Willowdale and Whinlatter Forest, moving in when Noah was five. Whinlatter Close – a development of three barns called The Bothy, The Byre and The Stables – had been a side project Flynn was working on for a friend, Angus, whose dad owned the farm. Angus fancied himself as a property developer and had insisted on project managing the development himself, despite having no building experience. Costs escalated and he couldn't raise any more funds so the whole project was on the verge of collapse when Flynn and I offered him a lifeline. We'd always had a dream of building our own home but, even if we'd found some land, we were some years away from being able to afford to build what we wanted. The barn conversion could be a stepping stone to that – a property we could never have afforded fully refurbished but which we could buy as a shell from Angus, giving him an injection of capital to finish the other two barns while we financed our own refurbishment. It wasn't going to generate Angus the financial return he'd hoped for but it was the only option he had so he'd gratefully accepted our offer.

While The Bothy wasn't the dream home we hoped to one day build ourselves, it was a special place and the three of us had been really happy there. Flynn and I had hoped to have a brother or sister for Noah but it never happened for us despite tests showing that there was no physical reason why it shouldn't. It was disappointing but we knew how lucky we were to have one child already when there were so many couples who wanted children and couldn't have them, so we accepted that was how it was and embraced life as a small family.

When Noah was eight, there was the first change of ownership in the three barn conversions with an older couple moving out of The Byre next door to us and a family of four moving in. Trent was a year older than Noah and Jessie a year younger. The three of them spent stacks of time together and Flynn and I soon became good friends with their parents, Guy and Helen. We'd get together for barbeques, nights out and even had a few weekends away. When Noah was sixteen and Jessie fifteen, they realised they felt more for each other than friendship. They made such an adorable couple and I secretly hoped that their relationship would last and our two families would be united through marriage one day.

I clicked onto the next photograph. The kitchen looked exactly how I'd left it, as did the lounge, but my nerves got the better of me and I closed the laptop and sank back into my chair. I wasn't sure I could face looking at any photos of Noah's room. I often saw it when I closed my eyes and, try as I might to conjure up happy memories of him in there, all I could picture was Noah the day I found him. The day my world turned black.

I stared at the closed laptop and sighed heavily. What the hell was I doing? Seven years had passed since Noah died and I hadn't moved forward at all. This was no way to live my life and the worst part about it was that I knew Noah would be furious with me for my behaviour. If I didn't get a grip, I could end up like Alice with her past trauma trapping her for two decades. Visiting the places associated with her pain had helped her with her recovery. Could that work for me?

Feeling as though there was no time like the present, I grabbed my bag, power-walked down the hall and ran down the stairs, a fire burning in my belly to finally take control of my life.

I made it out of Willowdale and even took the turning towards Whinlatter Forest but the fire had fizzled out by then. I stopped the car by the side of the road and put my hazards on as I dropped my head to my chest. I couldn't do it. Even though I knew Flynn had sold The Bothy so wouldn't be there, and even though Noah's bedroom had been at the back of the house so I wouldn't be able to see into it, it was still too much.

Several cars passed me and a couple of the drivers beeped their horns. I was in the way and at risk of causing an accident so I pulled away, turned the car round as soon as I could safely do so, and returned to Willowdale Hall.

Alice had said it had been difficult to visit the boat house at first. I *would* go back to The Bothy one day but it was far too soon to attempt it now. What I needed to focus on was the reason behind my decision to return to Willowdale in the first place – spending time with my parents, particularly my mum. They'd be returning from their holiday this afternoon and we'd all been invited to Georgia's for Sunday lunch tomorrow. Should I go all formal with a declaration of *we need to talk* or should I go for the more casual approach: *I don't suppose you're around one morning this week for a cuppa and a catch-up?* Maybe it was better to play it by ear depending on how they reacted around me. I was glad we were meeting at Georgia's house rather than Mum and Dad's. Neutral territory would be better for initiating the peace process. Although my parents weren't the only ones with whom I needed to make peace. Georgia had messaged and called several times following my unexpected encounter with Flynn before quiz night. I'd responded to her messages, reassuring her I was fine, but I hadn't spoken to her and I knew she'd be annoyed with me about that. I was annoyed with me. None of this was Georgia's fault. Or Flynn's. As with everything that had happened after Noah died, this was all on me.

17

Georgia had asked everyone to be at hers for noon so I turned up at ten with a large bouquet of flowers as well as the usual *thanks for lunch* bottle of wine.

'What are these for?' she asked as I followed her into the kitchen. 'And why are you so early?'

'Same answer for both questions – to apologise for ignoring your messages.'

'So you were ignoring me. I knew it!' She gave me a stern look. 'You do realise your punishment will be to eat all your broccoli.'

'No! Anything but that!'

'I don't get what it is with you and broccoli.'

'It's the texture. It's like having a mouthful of tiny trees.' I shuddered at the thought. 'I'll have a double portion of cauliflower. Just don't make me eat the trees.'

She laughed. 'Fifty-two years old and still a child.'

I stuck out my tongue.

'And the only reason you're offering to eat double cauliflower is because it's cauliflower cheese so only part-vegetable.'

I grinned at her. 'Guilty.'

She reached a vase down from the top of a cupboard and filled it with water then unwrapped the flowers and started snipping off the stem ends.

'I know you don't want to talk about him, but you know I'm going to ask anyway. How was it seeing him again?'

'I don't know. For a moment, I was transported back thirty years to the night of my twenty-third birthday.'

She put the scissors down and held my gaze, a smile playing on her lips. 'The night the two of you met.'

'Yes.'

'The night you fell in love.'

I raised my eyebrows at her, patently aware of where this was heading.

'The night you knew you'd met the person you'd be with forever and ever till death do you part.' She winced, presumably registering the inappropriateness of her words. It was, after all, death that had parted us – just not each other's.

'Sorry. That was careless of me.'

'It's okay.'

I gave her a weak smile and she sighed as she picked up the scissors once more and continued snipping. I could sense her brain working overtime connecting the dots in the conversation we'd just had.

'I remember that night well. Your expression every time you looked over at him, it was as though you were...' She frowned, evidently searching for the right word. 'Enchanted. That's it! You were enchanted by him.'

'I was.'

'So, if on Thursday you found yourself transported back to the night you met, does that mean you still have feelings for him?'

Georgia was too clever for her own good. I shrugged. 'I don't know what I feel anymore. About him. About anything.'

She raised her hand in the air. 'Willing volunteer to help you work through it all. Mr Pino and Mr Grigio are offering their assistance too.'

I couldn't help laughing. Georgia always had known how to lift me.

'We'll see,' I said. 'Can I start on the veg for you? Anything except the tiny trees.'

She directed me to a bag of potatoes and I started peeling while she finished arranging the flowers.

'I did a thing yesterday,' I said after I'd peeled a few spuds. 'I decided to visit The Bothy but I bottled it when I got close.'

Georgia looked puzzled. 'You do realise Flynn doesn't live there anymore?'

'I wasn't looking for Flynn. I'd already looked it up online. I'd never have gone if I thought he was still there. Do you know why he didn't sell up straightaway? Actually, no, don't answer that. I don't want to know.'

'I couldn't tell you even if you wanted me to. He might have spoken to Mark about it but, like I told you, I haven't spent any time with him. But I do know where he lives now. Do you want to know that?'

I shook my head vigorously. 'Definitely not.'

'So if you weren't going to The Bothy to see Flynn, what was the reason?'

'I thought it might help if I went back there.'

'Help what?' She narrowed her eyes at me and, as I saw the realisation hit, she put her peeler down and gathered me into her arms. 'You're not okay, are you?'

I gratefully sank into her embrace. 'Not really.'

'Why didn't you say anything?' she asked when I released her.

I ran my hands into my hair and sighed heavily. 'Remember what you said to me outside The White Willow at Mum's eightieth? That I'd run away to Newcastle and buried my head in the sand. I later admitted that I had run away but was adamant that you were wrong about the other part. You weren't.'

I let my hands drop with another heavy sigh. 'I haven't come to terms with any of it. Haven't moved on at all. If anything, I think I might have regressed.'

'Oh, Mel.'

'I thought that visiting The Bothy might—'

'Panic over!' Mark called from the hall, stopping me mid-flow. 'I have gravy granules.'

'We'll talk later,' Georgia whispered, giving my arm a gentle squeeze.

'My hero,' she called to Mark. 'Mel's here.'

'Yeah, spotted her car.' He joined us in the kitchen, said hello to me, and handed a paper shopping bag over to Georgia before asking what his next task would be.

The mood had been heavy with my confession but Mark's return, with the addition of some music, lifted the atmosphere considerably. As the three of us finished preparing the meal together, I had flashbacks to so many happy times preparing food in this kitchen, in the kitchen in The Bothy and at Derwent Rise. Our family had always worked as a team to prepare meals, typically accompanied by laughter, music and even dance, and I'd pushed that away for years. What had I been thinking? The point was that I hadn't been. I'd needed to get out.

And now I wanted to be back in.

Everyone arrived within two minutes of each other, punctuality being another family thing. It was loud and chaotic with so many people appearing at once, calling out greetings, dishing out hugs and, before long, we were sitting down to eat.

Mum, Dad, Keira and Johnnie kept us entertained across the meal as they told us all about their holiday. It seemed that Mum had agreed to hire a mobility scooter for the duration of their break.

'You were adamant you'd never go on a scooter,' Georgia declared. 'Said they were for old people who can't walk.'

'Yes, well, I accepted that perhaps I do fall into that category now and I could either embrace it or miss out on all the lovely trips Keira had planned.'

'It did take her a while to get used to it,' Dad said, smiling, which prompted several stories of crashing into lampposts, bins and close encounters with pedestrians once she felt confident enough to travel at speed. I could imagine how hard it must have been for someone like Mum to admit that she needed a scooter as it meant accepting that the ability to walk without pain – something that, like most of us, she'd previously taken for granted – had gone. It undoubtedly hurt more as she'd always been so fit. Together, my parents had bagged all the Wainwrights – the 214 peaks in the Lake District National Park which the fell walker, author and illustrator Alfred Wainwright included in his pictorial guides – with their favourite fells summitted several times. They'd also completed the seventy-three miles of the Cumbria Way as well as the Coast to Coast walk which was nearly three times the distance at 197 miles. To go from that to barely being able to walk at all couldn't be easy so it was no wonder she'd rebelled against a mobility scooter although, of course, I'd missed all of that because I hadn't been here.

'We've got gifts for everyone,' Mum announced after we'd passed round coffees.

I had wondered what was in the large gift bags Dad had parked in the corner of the room. Regan unwrapped a beautifully intricate driftwood candle holder and a pair of church candles which he and Clarke said would be perfect in their lounge. The gift for Mark and Georgia was even bigger – a large glass hurricane candle holder nestled on a driftwood base.

'Aw, you shouldn't have,' Georgia said, admiring it. 'It's gorgeous. I know where that's going.'

'We thought it would fit the space perfectly,' Mum said.

I felt all eyes on me as I was handed a small paper bag. I reached inside and removed a box of shortbread, hoping my face didn't convey my disappointment. It wasn't the gift itself – I loved shortbread – but what I felt it symbolised. It was an afterthought gift or a token gesture for someone they didn't know and it hurt as much as not getting name-checked in Mum's birthday speech.

'This won't last me long,' I said, smiling at them.

'I know it's not a big box but—' Mum started and I clapped my hand to my mouth, grimacing.

'I didn't mean it won't last me long because there isn't much of it. I meant because I love shortbread and can eat a whole box in one sitting. It's great. Thank you very much.'

An awkward silence settled round the table, thankfully broken by Astrid banging her sippy cup on her tray in a clear demand to be released from her highchair. Everyone moved into the lounge and, after about an hour, Keira announced that it was time to head home. Regan, Clarke, Mum and Dad said they'd make tracks too, so there was a mass exodus.

Despite still feeling wounded by what I felt was a clear message in the holiday gifts, I was determined to make an effort.

'Can I visit you one day next week?' I asked, following my parents out to the car.

They stopped, both frowning at me.

'What for?' Dad asked.

'Nothing specific. Just a catch-up now that I've moved back here.'

They exchanged looks and I didn't miss Mum widening her

eyes at Dad in a way which suggested it was a no and it was up to him to convey that to me.

'Can we come back to you on that?' Dad asked, sounding flustered. 'We're only just back from holiday and there's lots to do. We don't know what our plans are.'

'Yeah, that's fine.' It was hard not to sound hurt. 'Just give me a call or text me when you're free. I can be really flexible with my time – morning, afternoon or evening.'

'We'll give it some thought later. Come on, June, let's get you in the car where it's warm. Sorry, Mel, but we can't squeeze past you.'

Biting back a sigh, I moved out of their way and retreated into the kitchen, feeling I needed to be somewhere where people weren't. Would it have killed them to have said an enthusiastic yes and suggested firming up the date later? Talk about making me feel unwanted!

While Georgia and Mark stayed outside, presumably waving everyone off, I wiped the placemats and coasters and cleared glasses from the table.

'You superstar, Mel,' Georgia exclaimed when she joined me. 'I'm loving having a cleaning pixie.'

'It was no bother. I like to make myself useful. Where's Mark?'

'He forgot to get fuel while he was out earlier so he's gone to the petrol station.' She straightened up a couple of the chairs then leaned on the back of one of them, her head cocked onto one side.

'I know how it looks,' she said, her voice gentle. 'They could have positioned things better.'

I didn't need to ask her what she was referring to. 'You don't have to explain anything.'

'I do. I couldn't say anything in front of the kids, but there's a reason why they gave me the gift they did. Mum and Dad came over on New Year's Eve. Mum was in a lot of pain but she'd lost her patience with Dad for telling her to sit down and rest all the time so she'd claimed she was fine when she wasn't. The pain made her even more unsteady on her feet. I had a lovely hurricane candle on the window ledge over there.' She pointed to the side window in the dining area. 'Mum got up to get a glass of water, Dad went to help her and she snapped at him, saying she was quite capable of managing the short distance to the sink. Except she wasn't and she fell. She grabbed at the window ledge to save herself and managed to knock the candle to the floor and it smashed to smithereens.'

I winced. 'Was she okay?'

'Grabbing the ledge kept her upright but she badly bruised her leg and arm. She kept saying she'd replace the candle and I said there was no need. I was more concerned about her than an ornament. They obviously spotted that one on holiday and decided it was the ideal replacement.'

'It's beautiful.'

'It is. As for Regan and Clarke, that was a moving-in gift.'

'But they moved in together eighteen months ago.'

'And Mum and Dad never got them a gift. They said they wanted to get something special and hadn't seen anything suitable until now. We assumed they'd forgotten and would never have said anything but they'd obviously still been looking. I overheard them apologising to the boys for it being so late.'

'I *am* happy with my shortbread,' I said, feeling bad now that I knew the story behind the other gifts, 'but I couldn't help feeling like a point was being made.'

'I get it, but I think a lot of that's in your head. You think you've damaged your relationship with Mum and Dad but I say it's only a little bit bruised.'

'I suppose.'

'Another thing to bear in mind is that you don't actually have a home at the moment so gifts like ours would be a little redundant for you.'

I shook my head at her. 'Urgh, I hate it that you're so reasonable. It's a fair point and, even if I did have a home, I guess they don't know what my taste is anymore, although I am trying to be part of their lives again. Not that it got me anywhere.'

Georgia's brows knitted. 'Yeah, that was strange. Maybe Mum's in more pain than she's letting on again and Dad was just focused on getting her home.'

'I hope you're right – not about Mum being in pain, of course, but about Dad being distracted – because that lack of enthusiasm about seeing me hurt way more than any token gift ever could.'

'This past year or so hasn't been easy for either of them with Mum's health and I think their patience has been stretched to the limit. Baby steps. You'll get there.'

'I hope so.'

'Going back to that thing you told me you nearly did yesterday,' she said, setting the dishwasher away. 'I think visiting The Bothy would be a good step in helping you dig your head out of the sand, but I don't think you should do it alone. When you're ready, we'll do it together. And whatever else you need to do to move forward, I hope you know that I'll be right by your side every step of the way. We'll get through this together.'

I hugged her, touched by her kindness. 'I'd really appreciate that because I haven't had much success tackling it on my own.'

'Cup of tea before you head off?' she asked.

'That'd be great.'

'You've got this. Baby steps with the parents and baby steps for this. We could call it Operation Ostrich.'

I rolled my eyes at her. 'I'm not convinced it needs a name.'

'What about a hashtag? Ooh! Hashtag be less ostrich.'

'Stop! Please don't ever say that again.'

'But it's genius.'

'It's certainly something.'

Watching Georgia preparing the drinks, I thanked my lucky stars that I'd been blessed with such a wonderful sister. She was such a calming influence, always able to step back and look at an issue from several perspectives. Weirdly, that was second nature to me when it came to my job but it somehow didn't translate into my personal life. If only it did, I might never have left. My relationship with my parents wouldn't be bruised. I'd still be with Flynn.

If only.

18

Returning to Willowdale Hall after Sunday lunch at Georgia's, I poked my head round the library door to let Oliver and Rosie know I was back. Alice and Xander were with them.

'Just the person!' Rosie said, inviting me to join them. 'Mum has just been telling me about your brilliant suggestion to turn the boat house into a luxury retreat.'

'But I'm bound to have missed some of it out,' Alice added. 'You tell them what you told me, Mel.'

'You like the idea?' I asked.

'We love it,' Oliver said, giving me that fizz of excitement I always got when a client enthused about an idea.

'In that case, I did some rough sketches last night so let me grab those. It's always easier to explain when there's something to look at.'

I returned minutes later with my iPad and sketchbook and ran through what I'd drawn, showing the photos I'd taken of the boat house on my iPad to compare what was there now and what it could become. My cheeks glowed with the compliments about the quality of my sketches, the attention to detail in such a short space of time and the proposal itself.

'It's a big thumbs up from us,' Rosie said. 'I reckon we should get the plans submitted to the LPA as soon as possible, get it sorted and get it earning.'

Oliver nodded his agreement. 'I can't imagine there'll be a problem with approval and this would be a great way of getting some income in to invest in the rest of the build.'

The LPA was the Local Planning Authority whose role it was to approve (or refuse) plans to build something new, make a major change to an existing building or change a building's use. Oliver and Rosie already had a designated contact who they'd spoken to last year when they first made the decision to develop the estate. He hadn't anticipated any problems in principle with the planned redevelopment, which was good news. Having worked with many different LPAs and planning officers over the years, I knew that what we'd be proposing for the boat house would be straightforward and unlikely to trigger any objections. As there was nothing Oliver, Rosie, Alice or Xander wanted to change about my proposals, my next step was to contact our builder, Dougie Standish, to run them by him before submitting them to the LPA.

'Could be tricky to fit in, Mel,' Dougie said when I called him the following day. 'I wasn't expecting to start work on the inside of the hall until the back end of the year and we're stacked up.'

'It won't need a huge team. Is there no way you can shift a few things around?'

He sighed and tutted but eventually conceded that he might be able to squeeze something in. He needed a few days before he could confirm it for definite so I couldn't do anything except get the plans into as good a shape as possible and wait.

Dougie wasn't the only one I was waiting on. Mum and Dad

hadn't come back to me following my request to meet up one day this week. I'd been determined not to pester them but, by mid-morning on Wednesday and still no word, I rang them on their landline. There was no answer so I left a message. When there was still no word by late afternoon, I sent Dad a text.

TO DAD

> Hope you've settled back in OK after your hols. How's your week shaping up? My diary is starting to fill up so I wondered if you have a day that's best. Can make it next week if you prefer x

A response came back an hour later.

FROM DAD

Will come back to you later

I noted the absence of a kiss but knew better than to read anything into it. Dad had been a reluctant convert to using a mobile phone and lamented that he still preferred life without one. Whenever he sent texts, he used as few words as possible, never used emojis and didn't include kisses – not even in messages to Mum.

I rang their landline on Thursday morning and got the answerphone again but didn't leave a message. By Friday morning, I was extremely frustrated. They'd had plenty of time to settle back in and I'd already given them the opportunity to pick next week if this one didn't suit. How could I try to rebuild our relationship if they weren't willing to spend any time with me other than when the whole family were around? Phone calls weren't working and neither were texts so more direct action was clearly needed. I pulled my coat on and set off to theirs, my footsteps fuelled by anger.

'Mel?' Dad stood in the doorway of Derwent Rise, frowning at me. 'What are you doing here?'

'You never came back to me so I thought I'd come to you.' I could hear the accusation in my words and winced inwardly. This wasn't a great start.

'It's not a good time. We're going out shortly.'

I wasn't going to be fobbed off again. 'Anywhere exciting?'

He hesitated for a moment. 'Not really.'

'Then you won't be in a rush to get there.'

Dad had left sufficient room for me to step into the hall without having to shove past him, so that's what I did, reassuring him, 'I won't keep you long.'

Mum was in the lounge with her Kindle resting on her knee. She must have heard my voice as she was looking in my direction expectantly, her brow furrowed.

'I'm sorry for turning up unannounced,' I said, adrenaline pumping through me that I was about to give my parents a piece of my mind – something I'd never done. 'I know that me moving away and staying away has hurt you and I know I've been shockingly bad at coming back to visit or even keeping in regular contact. I have reasons but reasons are just excuses and... anyway, I'm back here now and I know I have a lot of making up to do, but how can I be expected to do that if you refuse to even see me? You said you'd—'

Dad held up his hand to stop me mid-flow. 'Not everything is about you,' he said, his voice strong.

'I know that, and I'm trying to make this about you two, but you have to let me try. I had no idea about your pain or your mobility, Mum, and seeing you at your eightieth was a massive eye-opener for me. I realised how much I'd missed out on by not being around – by not being part of this family anymore. And then when you mentioned everyone in your speech – including

Arlo who isn't even born yet – but didn't mention me, I felt the full force of being on the outside. And I get that. I did that to myself and I can't change it but I can try to show how sorry I am.'

My voice had got higher and more garbled but I was thrown by them both just staring at me, open-mouthed, not saying anything, and the nerves had taken over. I paused for breath but the adrenaline flowed from me and my voice came out unsteady.

'I don't want to make an issue of what happened at your birthday because I do understand why you did it. I know it's not something we're going to be able to resolve over one cup of tea but I do desperately want to make amends. Me asking to see you this week was meant to be the starting point and I really thought you'd at least give me a chance to try.'

I'd completely run out of steam and my legs felt wobbly. I wanted to sit down but I could hardly do that now after I'd barged in without invitation and let rip.

'I'm sorry. I wasn't meant to blurt all that out.'

'I think you'd better sit down,' Dad said.

'Are you sure?'

He nodded solemnly and I sank gratefully into the armchair as he sat on the sofa beside Mum.

'That was quite a speech,' Mum said. 'There's a lot to discuss but we really don't have the time to do that now. There's a good reason why your dad didn't come back to you with a date this week and I can assure you it's nothing to do with not wanting to see you. We *do* want to spend time with you and, yes, we're hurt but we're not clueless or selfish or anything else you might be thinking. We know you wouldn't have stayed away or cut yourself off unless you needed to and, looking back, we could have done a lot more to help you through your pain at the time, so please don't think for one minute that you're the only one who has amends to make. We do too.'

'So why couldn't we meet this week?' I asked when the explanation didn't seem to be forthcoming.

'While we were on holiday, I...' Mum paused and took hold of Dad's hand, looking at him beseechingly.

'Your mum found a lump in her breast,' Dad said, squeezing Mum's hand.

My stomach lurched and I wrung my hands, fear preventing me from forming any words.

'The not-very-exciting place we're going to shortly is the hospital for a scan,' Dad continued. 'We didn't want to say anything to any of you as we don't want to scare anyone unnecessarily if it's nothing sinister.'

'Did your doctor say anything?' My voice sounded like it was coming from a distance.

'She could feel the lump but she can't give any sort of diagnosis just from that, but we'll know soon enough.'

'I can't believe I barged in here and lectured you when you're dealing with that. I'm so sorry.'

I was furious with myself for letting the fiery side of me take over. Dad had said he'd be in touch and I should have accepted that but I'd let my overactive imagination take over, fuelled by paranoia over the birthday speech and the holiday gift. Even though Georgia had explained the story behind the gifts, and she and Regan had separately said that the speech would not have been intentional, both incidents had obviously been niggling at me.

'I'll let you get ready for the hospital,' I said, rising from the chair. 'Any chance we can pretend I was never here, you never heard my pathetic little rant, and we can start over again when you're ready?'

Mum gave me a weak smile and it struck me how pale she

was. Her eyes were watery with dark circles below them. She didn't look at all well.

'The rant, as you call it, won't be forgotten,' she said, 'because I think you needed to say it and we needed to hear it. As I said, there's a lot to discuss but there's one thing I need to pick up on now and then we have to get going.'

She glanced at Dad and he nodded.

'I can't apologise enough for not naming you in my birthday speech. It was my intention to mention you all and I hadn't realised I'd missed you out until your dad pointed it out afterwards.'

'We figured that if you'd noticed, you'd have said something to Georgia,' Dad said, 'and she'd have mentioned it to us, but nothing was said so we assumed – hoped – you hadn't realised.'

I didn't know what to say. It seemed so unimportant now when Mum could have breast cancer.

'I'd better let you get ready,' I said. 'I'm so sorry you've found a lump, Mum. You will let me know what they say at the hospital?'

'We will. And can you not say anything to Georgia in the meantime? We'll tell her, but we'd rather do that face to face if it's bad news.'

I nearly said, *I'm sure it won't be*, but it would be such a throw-away comment when none of us could be sure of anything.

'I hope it's positive news.'

'So do we.' Mum beckoned me over. 'I could use a hug.'

Dad stood up so that I could take his place to hug Mum. If twisting round caused her any pain, she didn't show it and I was grateful for the tightness of her hold.

'We'll let you know what they say at the hospital,' Dad said as he walked me to the door. 'But it might not be immediately. Good or bad, we'll need time to take it in.'

'Whenever you're ready. I'm sorry again for barging in today.'

'And I'm sorry that it looked like I was fobbing you off. I was so focused on your mum that I didn't pause to think about how you might be feeling.'

'It's not important, given Mum's news.'

'It is, because *you're* important and we haven't made you feel that way recently. Whatever happens today, we'll definitely have some time together next week.'

'Okay. I hope it goes well today.'

'Whatever comes our way, we'll deal with it.'

Dad hugged me and I wished I could have held him for longer because I'd just noticed how shattered he looked too. With Dad being so fit and agile and having a youthful face, it was easy to forget that he was four years older than Mum.

I paused at the bottom of their drive, looking back at the house my parents loved and where I'd had such a happy childhood. When I left Flynn, Mum and Dad insisted I stay with them instead of being on my own in a B&B. Even though I knew it came from a place of love and concern, being constantly asked if I was all right was too stifling. There were photos of Noah everywhere and they lit a scented candle in his memory every night. My logical mind told me that everyone grieved differently and this was their way, but it was too much for me. I was struggling to deal with my own grief and certainly couldn't support them with theirs. My strongest memories of Derwent Rise were therefore those dark days before I moved to Newcastle. I wished I'd declined their offer to stay. If I had, maybe I'd have come back and visited more often – perhaps even stayed with my parents instead of at Georgia's – because I wouldn't have associated Derwent Rise with one of my lowest points.

I hoped beyond hope that Mum's lump wasn't cancerous. She already had so much back pain to deal with and I feared she wouldn't be able to cope with chemotherapy or radiotherapy or whatever course of treatment was needed.

A stiff drink would be very welcome right now but we were still some way off lunchtime. Did pubs even serve alcohol at this time of the day? It wasn't the answer even if they did, but a strong coffee and a cake at The White Willow might give some much-needed comfort.

It was reasonably busy inside the café. Most customers seemed to be enjoying scones or cakes and a few were tucking into breakfast. A member of staff directed me to a table for two tucked round a corner and ran through the specials. There was a huge selection of tray bakes and sponge cakes behind a glass counter and I was particularly drawn to the white chocolate and raspberry cake.

Eating on my own didn't bother me but I always felt conspicuous during that period between placing the order and waiting for it to arrive, and reading took that feeling away. It also stopped me from thinking about things I didn't want to think about. Because I hadn't expected to come here, I didn't have a book with me. Eager for a distraction, I looked round at the décor, thinking about whether I'd have done anything different if I'd been refurbishing the café and concluding that I wouldn't have.

Thankfully service was efficient and my espresso and cake arrived. As I placed the first delicious forkful into my mouth, the door opened and a woman walked in and requested a table for two. A man joined her moments later and I swallowed the cake a little too quickly, grabbing my drink to wash it down before I started coughing and he looked over. Of all the days our paths could have crossed again, why did today have to be the one?

19

I slid lower on my chair, cringing inwardly. Trying to make myself look smaller was hardly going to stop Flynn seeing me if he looked in my direction. That thought didn't make me straighten back up, though. *Please don't pick a table near me!* Fortunately they headed towards a table by the window at the other side of the café.

The woman was wearing a smart pale blue wool coat over jeans and, when she removed her coat, she had a tailored blouse underneath. Very smart. Probably about my age, she was very attractive with a shiny blonde bob and stylish glasses.

Flynn sat down with his back to me, so I was able to relax and sit upright once more. They ordered quickly and were soon deep in conversation. Eating my cake on autopilot, I couldn't tear my eyes away. Whatever Flynn was saying to her made her laugh a lot. He used to make me laugh a lot too and I missed that so much.

My cake and espresso were long gone and I was ready to leave but doing so would mean walking past his table, so I ordered a hot chocolate and prayed Flynn and his companion would hurry up and leave soon. They didn't.

Despite watching them for forty minutes, I still couldn't decide what the relationship was. If they weren't together, I suspected she wanted them to be. The way she kept smiling at him and tucking her hair behind her ear seemed a bit flirty. Was she Flynn's type? I knew he preferred brunettes, but a couple of his girlfriends before me had been blonde so that didn't prove anything. The thought of Flynn having a wife or girlfriend didn't sit comfortably with me and I knew it was totally unfair of me to feel that way. I'd chosen to end it so I had no right to feel jealous of him being with someone else but, the more I speculated on their relationship, the more nauseous I felt.

Our marriage had ended for a reason. Instead of turning to each other for support after we lost Noah, we turned against each other. Or rather I turned against Flynn. But as I tried to conjure up those dark times in an effort to eradicate the little green monster inside me, all I could recall were happy memories – the night we met in The Hardy Herdwick, our first date after that, when he proposed, our wedding day, when I took a positive pregnancy test, the day Noah was born. We'd had our moments like any couple – mainly bickering over stupid things like me piling my crockery up beside the dishwasher instead of loading it inside, and the way he draped his discarded clothes over a chair in the bedroom instead of putting them in the laundry basket – but we'd never argued over anything major until Noah's death. That tragedy blew a great big gaping chasm between us which got wider and wider until I couldn't see there ever being a way of us making it back to the same side.

Flynn leaned back in his chair with his clasped hands at the back of his head – a gesture I recognised from when he was about to announce something, like a big decision or a grand idea or… I gasped and my heart started pounding. He'd done that before he proposed to me. Surely late morning in a café was not the place for a romantic proposal. He put his hands down and I held my breath, waiting for him to get down on one knee or to take her hand across the table or for her to look shocked, but the conversation continued with laughter and nodding on both sides before Flynn gestured for the bill. Not a proposal then. Phew! And I knew I had no right to feel relieved but I couldn't help it.

My head was aching and I rested my elbows on the table, burying my head in my hands while I took several deep breaths. Out of the corner of my eye, I saw Flynn settling the bill then the pair of them left. My shoulders sagged and I sat there for a few minutes waiting for the tension to fully leave my body. By the time I'd paid my bill and zipped up my coat, it felt safe to go outside. Even if they'd paused to finish off a conversation, Flynn and his companion should be long gone. But the moment I stepped outside, a man rose from one of the picnic benches.

'Hello, Mel,' Flynn said.

My stomach dropped to the ground and, even though I wanted to run, I couldn't seem to make my feet move.

'Aren't you going to at least acknowledge me?' he asked, his tone teasing, a gentle smile on his lips.

'I didn't think you'd seen me.'

'I spotted you before we even went inside. I wanted to come over and say hello but I was with a client so it didn't feel appropriate. Better to wait out here for you.'

I hated the relief flowing through me that his companion was a client and not his wife or girlfriend but, next moment, I glanced down at his hand and he was wearing a wedding band so clearly he was married. That sinking sensation was back.

'Can we talk, Mel?'

'Erm, now's not a good time.' After what had happened with my parents, it couldn't be worse.

'That's fair enough. You weren't expecting to see me today. When would be a good time for you?'

'I'm not sure. There's some stuff I'm dealing with at the moment.'

'Anything I can help with?' He sighed and shook his head. 'Sorry. Old habits die hard.'

'What do you want to talk about?'

'Whatever we need to talk about to make this work for both of us.'

'This?' I asked, my heart pounding. What did that mean? Us? No, there was no way he meant that.

'You returning to Willowdale. Me still being local.'

Of course. Why would I have thought he could possibly mean us?

'We've already bumped into each other twice in eight days,' he continued, 'so I suspect it'll keep happening. I don't want you feeling uncomfortable or like you have to avoid places in case I'm there.'

I stared at him, wondering how he could be so considerate after how I'd treated him. But he'd always been the calm, reasonable one – the yin to my yang. It was one of the reasons our relationship had been so good.

'What do you think?' he prompted when I didn't respond.

'Erm, yeah. Maybe.'

'I hear you're working on the Willowdale Hall project.'

'How did you—'

'I saw Dougie Standish and he mentioned it. Congratulations.'

I felt relief that he hadn't heard it from Mark. I didn't want to think they'd been discussing me. 'Thank you. I still have to keep pinching myself that it's really happening.'

'I can well imagine. How many times did we fantasise about working on the hall together one day? It's amazing that one of us has had that dream come true. I'm so chuffed for you, Mel.'

He genuinely looked and sounded delighted when he could so easily have been bitter about it. Not that bitter was Flynn's style. He could have been angry with me for being so rude to him in the pub last week, but that wasn't his way either. Mum often referred to Flynn as *a gentle giant* and it suited him well. He always had been – and clearly still was – a kind and thoughtful man who tried to put others at ease.

'I need to get back to work,' I said.

'At the hall?'

'Yes.'

'Can I give you a lift?'

'I could do with the fresh air. Headache. It'll clear it.'

'You're sure? If I drive you, you'll be able to get some paracetamol sooner.'

Thoughtful yet again.

'I'm sure. So, I'll, erm...'

He pressed a piece of paper into my hand and the touch of his fingers against my palm made my insides fizz.

'My contact details if you do want to talk.' He clasped his hands behind his head and I waited, heart pounding, for his big announcement.

'I've missed you,' he said, his eyes full of sadness, his voice tender. 'I can't tell you how good it is to see you again.'

How was I supposed to respond to that?

He lowered his arms and smiled. 'I didn't mean to blurt that out. Sorry. Forget I said it. I think we should meet and clear the air, but it's your call. Hopefully see you sometime soon.'

As he walked away, he thrust his hands into his pockets and lowered his head. He'd missed me? I hadn't seen that coming and he was absolutely right that he shouldn't have said it. He was a married man! But I'd be lying to myself if I didn't acknowledge how good it felt to hear it. I just didn't understand how he could feel that way about me after how badly it ended.

None of us live forever and, sooner or later, we'll all shuffle off this mortal coil. When that day comes, all we can do is hope that we've lived a long, fulfilled and happy life. Sadly, some lives aren't nearly long enough. My mum's dad died in his forties before I was born. A devoted Christian all her life, my grandma used to say that Granddad was such a lovely, kind man that God needed him in heaven as an angel. I wasn't convinced of the logic behind it but if believing that brought her some comfort, who was I to judge? The only strong belief I had was that bereavements in this day and age should happen according to generation – fully supportive of the saying that *no parent should have to bury their child.* To outlive your child wasn't right. It went against the natural order of things, threw the world off its axis. And my world had never realigned when it happened to me. I wasn't sure it ever would.

20

SEVEN YEARS AGO

Sudden unexpected death. That's what the police and medical ambulance crew called Noah's passing. Pretty much summed it up. A post-mortem had to be carried out and, much as it broke my heart to think of it happening to my boy, my need for an explanation helped avert my mind from the medical procedure and kept me focused on the answers coming my way. Had he been ill and not told us? Did he have some sort of medical condition we hadn't been aware of?

When the phone call came through from the coroner, Dr Coates, I put it on speaker and placed my phone between Flynn and me on the sofa.

'Heart failure?' I said, glancing at Flynn beside me who looked equally surprised. 'That can't be right.'

Eighteen-year-olds who exercised and ate well didn't just drop down dead of a heart attack. Unless it was congenital.

'Was there something wrong with his heart?' Flynn asked, his voice husky.

'No. In this case, your son's heart failure was the result of amphetamines.'

Beside me, Flynn did a sharp intake of breath but I hadn't quite taken in what the coroner had said.

'Amphetamines?' I repeated, the word sounding alien to me. 'You mean drugs?'

'Yes.'

'But Noah doesn't do drugs.'

Silence.

'He doesn't!' I insisted. 'He's really anti-drugs. Tell him, Flynn.'

'Could there be a mistake in the report?' Flynn asked.

'No mistake. I'm sorry.'

Dr Coates finished running through his findings and I felt numb as I disconnected the call and sank back on the sofa. Amphetamines? Speed? It made no sense. Noah was a good kid with nice friends. He'd had a few drunken nights out, like most kids his age, but drugs? He just wouldn't.

'Drugs?' I murmured, staring questioningly at Flynn, but he shook his head slowly, confusion clear on his face.

Feeling restless, I wandered into the kitchen and boiled the kettle on autopilot, a stream of questions in my head. Why had he taken drugs? How didn't we know about it? Had it been his first time or was this a regular thing? Where'd he got them from? Who'd done this to my son? I took two mugs of coffee through to the lounge but Flynn wasn't there. I called his name but there was no answer. There was no sign of him downstairs but I could hear faint noises upstairs.

'Flynn?'

The noises were coming from Noah's bedroom and my stomach clenched. I'd only been in there once since the day I found him and I'd had to rush out and slam the door behind me because all I could picture was my beloved son on the floor, slumped against the side of the bed, lifeless. But now my husband was in there and he needed me. Swallowing back my fear, I edged nearer Noah's room on shaky legs, desperately trying to push that terrifying final vision from my mind and focus instead on Flynn.

He was sitting on our son's bed, head bowed, the small red teddy bear Noah had loved as a baby clutched between his hands. His shoulders shook as he sobbed, his anguished cries echoing round the room. I ran to him and knelt in front of him, cradling my hands in his.

'Drugs?' he whispered, his eyes red as he looked into mine. 'I don't understand.'

'I don't either,' I whispered back and, at that moment, the red mist came down. Somebody had given drugs to my innocent young boy. They'd killed him and they needed to pay for it.

'But I'm going to find out,' I said, my voice strong and determined as I squeezed Flynn's hands and rose to my feet.

'How?'

But I didn't respond because I'd just put two pieces of the puzzle together. I hadn't realised it until now but Noah's girlfriend Jessie hadn't been round to see us. Helen and Guy had but not her and was it any wonder? She'd been at the New Year's Eve party with Noah so she clearly knew something and couldn't face us because of it.

I shot out of the house and ran over to The Byre, anger fuelling me to bang on the door knocker way more times than was necessary.

Helen answered the door, frowning. 'Mel? What's going—'

But I didn't let her finish the sentence, stepping into the large entrance foyer. 'Where is she?'

'Who?'

'Jessie, of course!'

'Mel, I think you should calm down.'

'Calm down? Really? I've just found out that my son died of heart failure from taking speed. Would you calm down if that was Trent?'

'Oh, my God, Mel! I'm so sorry. Drugs? I had no idea Noah was—'

'Neither did we but I suspect your daughter did.' I strode to the foot of their stairs and shouted her name.

'Why would Jessie know anything?' Helen asked, looking perplexed.

Jessie appeared on the stairs, clocked me and stopped.

'Jessie, honey, can you just come downstairs for a minute?' Helen said, her voice gentle.

Jessie looked afraid and I reminded myself that she was still only sixteen, her seventeenth birthday not being until April, and me standing in her house yelling her name had to be pretty terrifying, especially when she was grieving.

'I need to ask you about the party,' I said, trying to keep my voice light but not succeeding.

She stayed where she was on the stairs. 'What party?'

I bit back a tut. 'The New Year's Eve party.'

'I wasn't there.'

'Of course you were! You went with Noah.'

'I didn't.'

'Don't lie to me!'

Helen glared at me, her body stiff, her arms crossed. 'She's *not* lying and I don't appreciate you speaking to my daughter like that.'

I glared back. 'Noah said they were going together.'

'Then you need to look a bit closer to home and ask your son if...' Helen gasped, her eyes wide. 'I can't believe I just said that. I'm so sorry.'

I barely registered her slip. I'd come here wanting answers and now I had even more questions.

'Why didn't you go to the party?' I demanded of Jessie.

She was gripping onto the banister, looking close to tears. 'Because I'm not his girlfriend.' She closed her eyes for a moment, her voice weak as she corrected her tense. '*Wasn't* his girlfriend.'

Not his girlfriend? Was she winding me up?

'Since when?' I demanded.

'Since November.'

'That's a lie! Noah would have told me.'

'Mel!' Helen snapped, but I ignored her.

'Why did it end?'

Jessie shrugged, which inflamed me further.

'There has to be a reason. Bloody hell, Jessie, you were together for two years and friends before that.'

'I think you'd better go,' Helen said, attempting to shoo me towards the door.

'I'm not going without a straight answer.' I sidestepped her and stared up at Jessie. 'If you weren't at this party with him, who was?'

'I don't know.'

'I don't buy it. You must know something.'

'That's enough!' Helen shouted. 'You need to go, Mel. Jessie, go back to your room.'

'You must know something!' I cried.

Helen was physically pushing me towards the door now.

'He must have got the drugs at the party,' I called up to Jessie. 'I need to know who gave him them. You must know who he was hanging around with.'

She shook her head. 'I don't. We went to a Halloween party. He was hanging out with some kids there who I'd never seen before and they weren't good. It might have been them but I don't know who they are or where they live. I don't know anything.'

'She's told you everything she knows.' Helen opened the door.

'Did you know they'd split up?' I asked.

'I found out recently.'

'And you didn't think to say anything to me?'

'Goodbye, Mel.'

I'd thought we were friends – close friends – but there was no warmth in Helen's voice. No words of comfort. Just a door slammed behind me.

I turned and stared at their house, trying to absorb what I'd just learned. Noah and Jessie had split up in November, he'd lied about going to the New Year's Eve party with her and he'd started hanging round with some wrong 'uns. They had to be the ones who'd given him the drugs, but who the hell were they?

His phone! It hadn't been in his jeans pocket or by his bed but it had to be in his room somewhere and it would surely give me answers. I raced back to The Bothy and took the stairs two at a time. Flynn was still sitting on Noah's bed but he'd stopped crying and the red teddy was on the duvet beside him.

'We need to find his phone,' I said, taking my phone out of my pocket and dialling Noah's number. It rang out but I couldn't hear it ringing in the bedroom. It could be on silent but it was more likely to be out of charge. I hung up before it connected to his voicemail message, unsure what hearing his voice would do to me.

'Why do we need his phone?' Flynn asked, his voice weary.

'Jessie says they split up in November and he was hanging out with some bad kids. I need to know who they are.'

'Why?'

'Because I need to know which one of them gave him drugs.'

'Why?' he repeated.

I flashed my eyes at him. 'Do you really need to ask?'

I opened Noah's bedside drawers one at a time and rummaged through them. I moved over to his bookshelves and shifted a few things around, blowing my hair out of my face in exasperation.

'Are you just going to watch me?' I snapped.

'No.'

I assumed that meant he was going to help, but he left the room instead. Fuming with him, I pulled the bed out to see if the phone had been knocked underneath. It hadn't. The more I searched the room, the more frenzied I became, yanking clothes off hangers, tipping out the contents of his drawers until the room looked like it had been ransacked by a burglar.

His old school PE bag from primary school was at the back of the top shelf in his wardrobe. There'd be no reason whatsoever for him to put his phone in there but I pulled apart the string fastening anyway and tipped the contents onto the floor. I shook out each item – polo shirt, shorts, plimsolls – and gasped as a small plastic bag containing three white tablets fell from one of the plimsolls. I closed my fist around the bag and shut my eyes tightly. I hadn't wanted to believe what Dr Coates said but here was the evidence hidden inside a plimsoll pushed to the back of my son's wardrobe.

Opening my eyes, I unfurled my fist and stared at the tablets. I raised my gaze to look round the trashed room, my eyes finally resting on the red teddy lying on the duvet. How had my baby boy become a drug user? Under my roof. Without me having any idea about it.

* * *

From that day, I was like a woman possessed. I *had* to know what had happened and why. I needed to speak to his friends and, with a date arranged for the funeral, I had a valid reason for contacting them but, without his phone, I had no way of getting in touch. He'd always cycled to their houses so I only had a vague idea of where they lived – no exact addresses. Social media might have been an option but he'd never shown any interest in Facebook – joked it was for old people like me – and I wasn't on any of the apps he used, so the only route I could think of was school.

I made an appointment with the principal and was shocked to discover that, after the summer break between his first and second year, Noah had returned to sixth form quiet and withdrawn. Across the autumn term, his attendance had slipped and his grades had dropped.

'Why's this the first I'm hearing of it?' I demanded.

'We've sent you several emails. Let me see.' He clicked into something on his computer and rattled off a series of dates on which I'd allegedly been contacted.

'I haven't received any of those. Are you sure you have the right email address?' It was fruitless me asking that as I'd had enough emails from school then sixth form over the years to know they had the correct details.

'Is there any chance Noah could have accessed your email account and deleted them?' the principal asked.

'He'd never do that!' I declared vehemently. 'He's not the sort to...' I tailed off. I didn't know what sort he was anymore. He'd split up with Jessie without telling me, was hanging around with some lads I didn't know and taking drugs. Why should it even be a surprise to hear that he was dropping out of college too?

'I'm sorry to be the bearer of bad news at what I can imagine is already an incredibly difficult time,' he said. 'Is there anything else we can do for you?'

'I, erm... I wondered if I could speak to his friends. I wanted to let them know the date of the funeral and ask them about the party he was at on New Year's Eve. He was...' I couldn't bring myself to say *taking drugs* when the principal presumably already had a low opinion of Noah from his poor record. 'Erm... his phone's missing and I wondered if he might have given it to one of them.'

'His friends will be in lessons at the moment but if you can let me know their names, I'll see what I can find out.'

I removed a piece of paper from my handbag and handed it to him, having noted down their names before I set off in case my mind went blank once I got here.

A couple of days later, I received a call from the principal with the news that Noah's friends had been spoken to but the message was the same from all of them – Noah had pulled away from them across the summer and they'd barely spoken to him when the new academic year began. Another thing I didn't know about my son.

None of it made sense and the only person who could give an explanation was lying in the chapel of rest at Trenham & Sons Funeral Directors.

I was so angry all of the time – angry that Noah was gone, angry about the cause of his death, angry that I had no idea what was going on in my son's life, angry that he hadn't confided in me about any of it, and angry at Flynn. So very angry at Flynn. Because Flynn didn't need answers like I did. He'd wanted to know the cause of death but that was enough for him.

'I don't see where it'll get us,' he told me after pleading with me for the umpteenth time to let it go. 'It's not going to bring Noah back so what's the point?'

'How can you say that?' I cried. 'The point is we'll know who's responsible for our son's death.'

'Who? There's no who. There's a what and we know the answer to that already.'

'But somebody gave him the drugs.'

'Do you really think you're going to find out who that is? Every question you've asked so far has only triggered more questions. Where's it going to end? This isn't doing you any good, Mel. You're going to have to let this one go.'

If only I could have.

21

The day of Noah's funeral arrived. It was dark and wet with storm clouds gathering – the perfect metaphor for my mood. My parents and Flynn's, Maggie and Keith, had gathered at The Bothy so the six of us could travel together in a funeral limousine behind the hearse. I shuddered as I watched the two vehicles pulling into Whinlatter Close. Flynn went to the door and Maggie joined me by the window, putting her arm round my shoulder as the drivers navigated the turning circle outside our house.

'It's not the right way round,' she said, her voice shaky with emotion. '*No parent should have to bury their child.*'

That damn phrase. I'd heard it so many times since Noah died, said it repeatedly myself, but it didn't bring any comfort. Was it even meant to? I suppose it was a shared declaration that it felt wrong, but feeling wrong didn't mean it wasn't happening. I couldn't force any words past the lump in my throat so I rested my head against Maggie's to convey that I'd heard and agreed.

Nobody spoke during the journey to the crematorium, which was a good thing as I really didn't want to make small talk. There was a sizeable crowd gathered outside but I lowered my eyes as the car pulled up, not wishing to make eye contact with anyone. I wasn't strong enough to see their pain while drowning in my own.

The service began and I barely registered anything the celebrant said. During the eulogy, there were intermittent ripples of laughter, presumably in response to the childhood anecdotes we'd shared and it struck me how inappropriate it was to laugh at a funeral. Why had we shared humorous stories when there was nothing funny about any of this? With every passing minute, I became more tightly wound. I turned around at one point and cast my gaze across the mourners. There were several teenagers here, some of whom I recognised as the friends who claimed to have been ditched over the summer, and others who were strangers to me. Had one of them given Noah the drugs? Had one of his former friends done it and the alleged falling out over the summer had been a lie to deflect any suspicion?

Outside, the mourners gathered to look at the floral tributes and chat. I spotted Guy talking to Jan and Colin – our elderly neighbours who lived in The Stables – and the red mist came down once more as I marched up to him.

'Helen and Jessie not with you?' I demanded.

Guy visibly squirmed. 'Erm, Jessie was too upset to come so Helen stayed with her.'

'Upset? Is that because she's feeling guilty for her part in this?'

'She wasn't there, Mel. She ended things with Noah in November.'

'Yeah, and that'll have broken his heart. Probably made him do what he did.' I knew it was a low blow, laying the blame on Jessie, and clearly Guy thought so too.

He took a step closer to me, his voice low. 'She ended it because he'd changed. Your son's drug habit had *nothing* to do with Jessie so don't even think about spreading rumours that it did.'

I winced at the word *habit*. Nobody knew I'd found those pills in Noah's bedroom – not even Flynn – so what right did Guy have to suggest it was habitual rather than a fatal one-off?

'Don't bother coming back to the pub,' I said, my tone harsh. 'We don't need your keeping-up-appearances sympathy.'

* * *

'I'm going to bed,' I said, heading for the stairs as soon as Flynn and I returned to The Bothy after the wake.

'It's only seven.'

'It's been a long day.'

'You haven't eaten anything,' Flynn called after me.

'I'm not hungry.'

In the bedroom I'd only got as far as removing my jacket when the door opened.

'We need to talk,' Flynn said.

'Not now. I'm tired.'

'So am I, but this can't wait. What's going on with you?' His tone was gentle but it did nothing to soothe me.

I tossed my jacket onto the bed and stared at him, incredulous. 'What's going on with me? You're seriously asking me that? It was our son's funeral today in case you didn't notice and I hated every single minute of it because it shouldn't have happened. *That's* what's going on with me.'

'You don't need to shout and you know that's not what I'm talking about. I'm worried about you, Mel. This obsession with finding out what happened isn't helping anything.'

'It's helping me.'

'How? You've fallen out with Helen and Guy and had a go at

Jessie. You've trashed Noah's room. You even shouted at his friends and accused them of being drug dealers in the middle of the wake.'

'Caused a scene, did I? Embarrassed everyone there?'

I hadn't been able to help myself. I saw them and I kept telling myself that it wasn't the time or the place but a few glasses of wine later and it felt like the only time and place I'd get the opportunity to speak to them. Except I hadn't spoken. I'd yelled accusations at them.

'I didn't say that,' Flynn said, his voice still gentle. 'You say it's helping you. Can I ask how?'

'I need answers.'

'We have answers.'

'No, we don't. How can you be so accepting of this?'

'It's not about accepting it. It's about drawing a line and knowing that, even if we did find the person who gave him the drugs, it wouldn't make a difference. Noah would still have taken the drugs and he'd still be dead. So why torture ourselves further when we're already going through hell?'

'You don't understand.'

'I'm trying to.' He sat down on the edge of the bed and patted the duvet beside him. 'Please talk to me. Help me understand.'

Deep down, I knew that I needed to sit down, hold Flynn, and let the grief pour out in tears, but I couldn't seem to.

'Someone knows something,' I said, my voice sounding cold and distant.

'Mel. Please. Sit down and talk to me.'

I removed my necklace – a delicate silver chain from Noah for my fortieth birthday – and turned my back against Flynn as I gently placed it inside my jewellery box, fighting hard not to unleash the cruel words circling round my mind. *You obviously don't care. If you cared, you'd want answers. What sort of father doesn't want to know who killed his son?*

I heard him rise from the bed and cross the bedroom, stopping near me. I thought he was going to touch me, although I prayed he wouldn't because I felt so tense I knew I'd shake him off.

'Mel? Please look at me.'

Reluctantly, I shuffled round and tilted my head to meet his gaze.

'Why don't we get away for a bit?' he said, his voice soft.

'On holiday?' I asked, shocked he could even suggest such a thing.

'Not a holiday. Just some time off to go somewhere on our own. A remote Scottish island, perhaps. Somewhere we can relax and find some peace.'

'We've cremated our only child today and you want to go on holiday? What's wrong with you?'

'It wouldn't be like that,' he insisted. 'I just think we need some space from all this.'

I wasn't listening to him. I heard *holiday* and a montage of all our family holidays filled my mind – sunshine, laughter, love. How could he possibly think a holiday was appropriate right now? Had he ticked off *funeral* on a list of things to do and now it was the *resume life* part? Resume life, take a holiday, return world to axis.

Then out it all came – everything I'd tried to keep buried. I accused Flynn of not caring and never loving our son or me, of being more concerned about keeping up appearances than finding answers. As I ranted and raged at him, a little voice in my head was telling me I'd got it all wrong but there was an angrier louder voice refusing to listen. I shouted, paced, gesticulated and Flynn just stood there, letting me pour it all out. He didn't get angry, he didn't try to defend himself and I took that as proof that he really didn't care.

When I finally ran out of steam, Flynn reached his arms out as though to draw me into a hug but I backed away, hissing that I didn't want him to touch me. That I never wanted him to touch me again. I'd never seen him look so hurt. Mumbling something about needing some fresh air, he left the room and, moments later, I heard the front door slam and his car start.

I dashed to the window and watched him pull out of the close. It tore me apart that I'd hurt him like that. Those words had been cruel, designed to sting, and they'd certainly done that and, at that moment, I knew that if I stayed it would happen again. And again. And again. Because I needed to lash out at someone. I needed someone to pay for taking my only child away from me. Flynn wasn't to blame but my anger would find a way to turn on him. So I needed to leave too. It would only be for a while – just until I found my answers and the red mist lifted.

It wouldn't be forever.

22

SIX AND A HALF YEARS AGO

The evening following Noah's funeral had been the start of the end for Flynn and me. One night away turned into three but the time apart didn't resolve anything. The anger still burned inside me.

I knew I couldn't hide from Flynn forever. We ran a business together and our clients had been extremely understanding but we had to return to work. *To normality.* It was a phrase I'd heard a lot from my parents and from Georgia. Normality? Nothing about my life would ever be normal again.

I might have physically returned to The Bothy and to Flynn but I never did emotionally. We didn't talk about me leaving. We didn't talk about much at all, although that wasn't for want of trying on Flynn's part. I had no idea how to be around him anymore, resentment towards him constantly bubbling beneath the surface. I was irritable all the time, picking fights over anything and everything. Flynn wouldn't bite, which angered me even more. How could he be so calm? How could he possibly be taking all of this in his stride instead of stomping about in a rage demanding answers?

Even work – my absolute passion – didn't excite me. I spent hours sitting in front of my drawing board or at my computer just staring into space, trying to make sense of what had happened and why it had happened to us.

I became convinced that Jessie knew more than she was letting on. She and Noah had been best friends for several years before they became a couple and I'd spent enough time around them to know they told each other everything. I'd always loved seeing them deep in conversation. It warmed my heart that he had someone special to whom he was comfortable chatting for hours.

Flynn was out on site each day, but my work was predominantly home-based. My office was at the front of The Bothy in one of the spare bedrooms and I became fixated on Jessie's movements to and from The Byre. She was in her first year of sixth form and none of the students had lessons on Wednesday afternoons. Jessie cycled home at lunchtime and, with Helen and Guy out at work, she was in the house on her own. It was the perfect opportunity to have a word.

The first time, a few weeks after Noah's funeral, I was really polite. *I'm so sorry to ask you again but sometimes we just need a bit of space to focus. I don't suppose you've thought of anything else that would help me understand what happened to Noah.* She didn't. She was sorry. She'd let me know if anything came to mind.

The following week, I'd made a few careless mistakes with my work which had been humiliating as well as costing a lot of time to resolve. I *never* made mistakes so I wasn't in the best frame of mind when I rapped on the knocker at The Byre. Jessie's face fell when she saw it was me. *There's nothing else to tell you.* So I told her exactly what I thought of that. She slammed the door in my face.

I was on tenterhooks that evening, expecting Helen or Guy to pound on our door and demand that I stop harassing their daughter. When they didn't, I concluded she couldn't have told them which, to my mind, confirmed my belief that Jessie knew more than she was letting on.

The Wednesday after, I tried again. I was so driven by my need to find answers that I never paused to think about how unreasonable my behaviour was or how it might be affecting Jessie. She shouted from the entrance hall that she wasn't going to answer the door and I'd better leave or she'd call the police. Not at all intimidated by her threat, I pushed open the letterbox.

'You *have* to know something, Jessie. You two were inseparable. Noah *must* have told you what was going on with him.'

Next minute, she yanked open the door, almost trapping my fingers in the letterbox.

'You really want to know what was going on with him?' she demanded.

Her hair was wild, her pale cheeks tearstained, and I knew I'd gone too far, but how could I walk away when her question was so loaded? She clearly knew something.

'Yes!' I cried. 'I need to know.'

'It was you! He felt invisible around you and Flynn. The pair of you spent all your time working and, if you weren't working, you were discussing work or you were talking about building your dream home. Did you ever include him in that? Ask him what he wanted? No! And do you know how that made him feel? Like he didn't matter. Like you couldn't wait for him to move out so you could get the perfect home without him.'

'It wasn't like—'

But Jessie was on a roll, her voice getting stronger and louder. 'He didn't have siblings and do you know what he thought about that? That you'd never really wanted kids and he'd been a mistake.'

A look of horror crossed her face, as though she realised she'd just crossed a line. Her voice softened. 'I loved Noah and he loved me. When he was struggling, I could always bring him round but, at some point over the summer, I stopped being enough. I don't know why. He never told me and now he never will. That's it. That's all I know. Please don't come back. I can't do this. I really can't.'

She closed the door and I stood outside for several minutes, reeling. Could there be any truth in that? Surely not! But I had a montage playing in my mind of numerous occasions when Noah had walked into the lounge or kitchen-diner where Flynn and I were deep in conversation, and had walked out again. Times when he'd asked what we were doing that evening or weekend and we'd told him we were working. Had he really felt pushed away?

If he had, that wasn't fair on us. Everything we'd ever done was for Noah. He'd been the centre of our world and we'd given him so much of our time. As he'd hit his teens, he'd wanted to spend more time with his friends and less with us – usual teenager behaviour – but we'd still talked regularly. Except... if we'd properly done that, wouldn't I have known he'd lost touch with his friends, split up with his girlfriend, was bunking off college and dropping grades? Had Jessie spoken the truth?

I was sitting in the dark when Flynn returned home from work.

'Jessie thinks we neglected Noah,' I said.

'You scared the life out of me!' he cried, flicking the light switch. 'Why are you sitting in the dark?'

'Did you not hear what I just said? Jessie thinks we neglected Noah.'

'I thought you were going to leave Jessie alone.'

I stared at him, unable to comprehend how he could be more

concerned about why I was sitting in the dark and why I was pestering Jessie than he was about what she'd said. My befuddled mind joined some dots and told me that it was because Flynn knew it was true and that he'd been the one to neglect our son, so I hurled that at him but all he did was roll out his usual patter about letting it go.

Days rolled into weeks with Flynn and I barely speaking to each other and then came the breaking point. I woke up early one morning in June to find the bed empty. I could hear noises along the hall, like furniture being moved. I crept along the landing and found Flynn kneeling on the floor of Noah's bedroom, picking up his clothes and folding them into bin bags.

'What the hell are you doing?' I demanded.

He twisted round, his cheeks wet with tears. 'It's time.'

'To hell it is!' I stormed over to him and tried to wrestle the bin bag out of his hand but he gripped it tightly.

'It's been nearly six months,' he said. 'I know you keep saying you're not ready, but this isn't healthy for either of us.'

'So it's your decision, is it? You get the final say?'

'I'm doing this for you.'

'If you were doing it for me, you wouldn't be doing it at all.'

Noah's favourite hoodie was draped over his bed and I grabbed it before Flynn had a chance to stuff it in a bin bag. 'You're not throwing this out.'

Flynn tied the handles on the bin bag he'd been filling and placed it beside several others before looking up at me.

'I'm not throwing any of it out.'

'Then what are you doing?'

'I'm bagging it up and putting it somewhere safe until we're ready to sort through it properly.'

'Why?'

'Because no matter how much I wish it wasn't true, Noah isn't coming back. Because I'm scared that, if I don't do something about it now, six months will turn into six years. And because it feels disrespectful to leave his room in a mess when he was one of the few teens in this world who actually kept a tidy room.'

He gave me a weak smile at the feeble joke. As I stood there clutching Noah's hoodie to my chest, I felt like I was at a cross-roads where what I said or did next would have a profound effect on our lives going forward. Flynn was in pain. I could see it in every movement, hear it in every word, feel it emanating from him, and I knew that my obsessive search for answers had made things worse for him. Deep down, I knew he was right about so many things. We *did* need to empty Noah's room. We needed to redecorate and repurpose it and, in fact, moving house might even be an option. I found it too hard to spend time in Noah's room and, as a result, our beautiful home no longer felt like a sanctuary. Flynn was also right that I needed to let go and accept that I was never going to find out why Noah took those drugs or who gave him them. Deep down I knew this. Very deep down. But the red mist still lingered close to the surface.

Noah really had been *one of the few teens in this world who actually kept a tidy room* and it had been a standing joke in our family. *Are you sure you're a teenager? Have you got a cleaning pixie hidden under your bed?* I could have responded with a smile right now. I could have even made a joke – *Have you found the cleaning pixie yet?* If I had, I'd have broken that tension between us. We might have laughed together, shared some anecdotes, talked, cried, hugged and somehow found a way through this. But that wasn't the road I chose to take. I was in self-destruct mode. My world was still spinning off its axis and I might as well blow the whole thing up.

'I can't do this,' I said.

'I know. That's why I'm doing it.'

'Not the room. This. Us. It's not working.'

I didn't know where those words had come from. I hadn't planned on ending things. Or had I? I'd repeatedly acknowledged to myself that we couldn't go on like this. *Something* had to happen. Was separating that thing?

Flynn stared at me for a moment, his eyes full of sorrow. 'We'll get through it. It's just going to take some time.'

'I think we're beyond that.'

He shook his head. 'You can't mean that.'

'I do.'

'Mel! No!' He took a couple of steps towards me but I backed away.

'I'll book into a B&B.'

'Can't we talk?'

'What difference will it make? You're so calm and I'm so angry and I can't... It's just... This is killing me, Flynn. I need some space.'

He swallowed hard. 'And after you've had some space?'

I lowered my eyes. I couldn't give him an answer. Well, not the one I suspected he wanted to hear. I needed to think. I needed to breathe. I couldn't do either while Flynn was around.

'I love you,' he said. 'Always have, always will. That's never going to change.'

Did I feel the same somewhere under the pain and anger? At that moment, I wasn't sure.

'I should go,' I whispered.

'Don't.'

Raising my eyes to his nearly broke me. 'I have to.'

Tears trailed down his cheeks. 'Then I'd better let you, but don't forget what I just said. I meant every word of it.'

Flynn walked towards the door, then paused. 'I hope you find the answers you need, Mel. And when you do – or if you hit a point where you decide you don't need them anymore – I'll be waiting for you. Even if that takes weeks or months. Even if it takes years.'

He left Noah's bedroom and, moments later, I heard the front door close and his car start.

* * *

I spent that first night in a B&B but my parents insisted I stay with them and, unable to think of a reason not to, I moved back into my old bedroom at Derwent Rise. A week after walking out on Flynn, I woke up on my forty-sixth birthday to a moment of clarity. I needed to leave Willowdale and start afresh somewhere new. A place that didn't remind me of everything I'd lost. A place where I didn't see sympathy in the eyes of everyone I met. A place where I didn't feel guilty all the time that I wasn't strong enough to support the people around me who were also hurting because they'd lost a grandson, nephew, cousin, friend.

It was a Wednesday so Flynn would be on site working on one of our long-term projects. I prepared a short handwritten letter, told my parents I was going for a drive, went to Darrowby's to collect a bundle of cardboard removals boxes, then parked on the drive at The Bothy.

I felt strangely calm as I packed up my belongings and loaded them into my car. The door to Noah's bedroom was closed and I paused on the landing, staring at it for several minutes, but I didn't go in.

Back downstairs, I placed my goodbye letter on the worktop by the kettle. My stomach churned as I read it.

Flynn
*   We both know we can't go on like this. The day Noah died,*

something died inside me too and I need a fresh start. My solicitor will be in touch about dissolving our business partner-ship and our marriage. The last 6 months have been hell so let's not prolong it. Please go along with it for both of our sakes.

Mel

Tears burned my eyes. It sounded so cold but that was how I felt at that moment. Cold, distant, detached. With a shaky sigh, I walked out of the kitchen, locked the front door and posted my key back through the letterbox. It was over.

23

PRESENT DAY

Over the years, I'd often wondered what might have happened if Flynn had ignored my plea and fought to save our marriage. That thought was front and centre right now as I gazed out of my bedroom window back at Willowdale Hall, my eyes resting on the boat house in the distance. Hubert Cranleigh had made some whopping mistakes and so had I and we'd both hurt people badly.

I dug in my jeans pocket for the piece of paper Flynn had given me outside The White Willow earlier. An email address and mobile phone number were written on it but nothing else. Should I agree to talk or was it too late? What was it he'd said. *Clear the air?* What did that mean? It could be anything from agreeing to say hello if our paths crossed to a deep and meaningful dissection of everything that had happened in the past. I wasn't sure which I wanted it to be but, with Mum's news earlier, I wasn't capable of the latter at the moment.

There was still no update from my parents but Dad had said they would need space to process things whatever the news. I needed to get on with some work so I went over to my desk, placed Flynn's contact details and my phone down on it and cracked on with my first task for the day.

A couple of hours later, Dad rang.

'It's not cancer. They said it's a fibroadenoma. It's not as common in women of your mum's age as someone younger, but it happens. They don't really know what causes it.'

'Does it need treatment?'

'No. It should gradually go down and will eventually disappear.'

That was fantastic news, but Dad had presented the information in an almost monotone voice. I'd have put it down to tiredness after what had to have been a trying week, but something told me to question it.

'You don't sound as positive as I'd have expected. Is there something else?'

He sighed and I could imagine the scene – him looking across at Mum for her permission to say more.

'Your mum had a funny turn while we were at the hospital.'

'What sort of funny turn?'

'Out of breath, heart racing. It could have been any number of things including a panic attack, but we're going back to the doctor next week for some tests.'

'Is Mum okay now?'

'Yes. She's relaxing on the sofa reading and she says you're not to worry about her. We think it's best if we have a quiet weekend as we're both feeling drained after the holiday then rushing around this week, but that doesn't mean we don't want to see you. How about Monday or Tuesday?'

Tuesday worked better for me so I suggested I pick up something for lunch so neither of them had to go to any trouble. I hoped Mum's funny turn really was down to a combination of fatigue and worry and nothing more concerning. For now, I'd do my best not to overthink it and focus on the relief that she didn't have breast cancer to contend with.

Placing my phone back down on my desk, my fingers brushed against Flynn's contact details. We did need to talk but one ghost at a time was enough for me. I knew Georgia was working on Saturday but we'd all agreed to skip family lunch on Sunday as Keira and Regan weren't around. Hopefully she hadn't filled her diary.

TO GEORGIA

You know you said you'd come with me to The Bothy whenever I'm ready? Would Sunday work for you? x

FROM GEORGIA

I'm all yours, whatever time suits. Maybe combine it with a walk in Whinlatter Forest and a drink and cake in the café? x

TO GEORGIA

Sounds perfect. I'll pick you up at ten x

24

———

March had arrived with a warm, sunny weekend filled with the promise of spring. I picked up Georgia on Sunday morning as planned. It felt a bit cheeky parking outside The Bothy or even elsewhere in the close, so we parked at a wide point on the approaching farm track.

'Ready for this?' Georgia asked as we exited the car.

'I think so. I'm glad you're with me.'

We wandered up the lane and paused at the opening of Whinlatter Close to take it in. The trees and shrubs had grown significantly since I left. In the front garden of The Stables ahead of us were flowerbeds where there'd previously just been lawn, and solar panels had been added to the roof of The Byre.

'Going any further?' Georgia asked.

I nodded and set off walking. The Bothy was at the top of the close and we paused by the green in front of it, gazing up at the enormous blossom tree which I'd planted when it was a sapling.

The new owners of The Bothy had painted the front door a petrol-blue colour. It was nice but I preferred the natural wood look we'd opted for.

'How does it feel?' Georgia asked, slipping her arm through mine.

'Strange but not scary like I expected.'

I felt a bit silly, having got myself so worked up about being back here, but now I felt very detached from the place. Maybe time was a great healer after all.

There were lots of cards displayed across the window ledge in the lounge of The Bothy so the current owners clearly had something to celebrate. My stomach flipped as I had a vision of that same window ledge covered in sympathy cards. I averted my gaze and focused on The Byre. There was a *for sale* sign in the garden with a red *sold* sign angled across it. When I'd searched online to see if The Bothy had been sold, I'd spotted that The Stables – Jan and Colin's house – had changed hands three years back but there'd been no indication of The Byre selling. Helen and Guy had presumably remained here and were in the process of moving now.

There was a car in their double drive and a ladder propped up against the front of the house, but no sign of anyone. Not that I wanted to bump into them. We never spoke again after the funeral. I had no idea whether Jessie had told them about me hounding her but, for the remaining months I'd lived here, we hadn't even made eye contact if we passed in our cars.

'We should probably go,' I said. If Helen or Guy appeared, I couldn't imagine they'd be pleased to see me.

At that moment, the front door of The Byre opened and a young man – probably in his mid-twenties – stepped out, holding a bucket of soapy water.

He looked across at Georgia and me. 'Are you all right there?' he asked. His voice was cheerful but the frown suggested concern at a couple of strangers staring at the houses.

'We're not casing the joint,' I joked. 'I used to live in The Bothy but I moved out of the area. I was just having a nostalgic moment.'

He put the bucket down. 'How long ago was that?'

'It'll be seven years ago in June.'

'In that case, you'll know my wife. Wait a second.'

He went back inside and Georgia and I crossed the road, stopping at the end of the drive. Moments later, a heavily pregnant woman stepped out of the house and her face fell when she saw me.

I gasped, recognising the young girl in the woman before me. 'Jessie?'

Watching her cradle her arms protectively over her stomach, I felt terrible. I'd treated her so badly after Noah died. I'd had no right to speak to her that way. What had I been thinking? Even though they hadn't been together when he died, I knew that Noah had meant the world to Jessie. She'd been grieving and must have been terrified having some deranged woman banging on her door every time she was home alone.

'I'm not here to cause any trouble,' I reassured her. 'I didn't know you still lived here. I was just here to... Oh, it doesn't matter. Jessie, I'm so sorry. I was in a horrendously dark place back then and you were one of several people who got the brunt of it. I should never have treated you like that. It was very wrong of me.'

She didn't respond for a moment and I thought she was going to order me off her land – which I'd have absolutely deserved – but she broke into a smile.

'I've just boiled the kettle. Would you both like a drink? I owe you an apology too.'

The man returned with a window wiper and Jessie did the introductions – Tom, married for nearly two years, first baby due at the end of the month.

'This is Mel and her sister, Georgia,' Jessie told Tom. 'Mel's Noah's mum.'

I didn't miss the raise of Tom's eyebrows when she added that part so he was presumably aware of our history.

'I'll leave you to catch up,' he said. 'These windows won't clean themselves.'

Jessie led us through to the lounge while she made the drinks. There were partly packed boxes strewn everywhere and I felt for her having a house move to contend with while heavily pregnant.

'You couldn't have timed it better,' Jessie said, reappearing and handing us mugs of tea shortly after. 'I was just about to take a break.'

'Do your parents still live here?' I asked tentatively, as I couldn't imagine Helen and Guy being nearly as welcoming as Jessie.

'No. They moved to the Dales – Grassington – three years ago and Tom and I bought this place from them. We thought it'd be the perfect family home but Tom's parents aren't local and, four months into my pregnancy, reality hit us as to how hard it would be without either set of parents close by. So we're moving to the Dales too.'

'And your brother?' I asked.

'Living and working in Blackpool. And Jan and Colin from The Stables moved to Devon a few years back, so it's all change here when we move out.'

'You said your baby's due later this month?' Georgia asked. 'My grandson is due on the 24th.'

'Aw, congratulations! Mine's a girl, due on the 20th so just under three weeks to go, although I wish I was resting rather than packing. The house sold in three days so we should have been settled in our new place by now but the chain fell apart. We found a new buyer quickly but they can't move until May, which is frustrating but these things happen. Anyway, enough about me. I heard you'd moved to Newcastle, Mel. Are you just visiting or are you back for good?'

'Back for good. I'm working on a project at Willowdale Hall.'

I told her more about it and was touched that she remembered how much I'd loved the place, and she shared a little about her life since I'd left – her job as a nurse and that Tom was a radiologist she'd met at the hospital. I noticed the way her face lit up and her eyes shone as she spoke about her husband. I'd wondered whether, if Noah had lived, he and Jessie would still be together but it felt as though she'd found the life and the person she was always destined to be with. And I was okay with that.

'We'd better leave you to get on with the packing,' I said when we reached the end of our drinks.

She screwed up her face in the direction of the boxes. 'I suppose they're not going to pack themselves. Before you go, I wanted to apologise for what I said about you not giving enough attention to Noah. I was upset and I think I might have exaggerated. He *did* have moments where he felt like that but I did with my parents too. I think it's a teenage thing – we want to be wanted but we also want to be let loose and I'm dreading trying to find that balance when this one's a teen.'

I smiled at her as she cradled her bump. 'I'm sure you'll be a great mum. You always had a nurturing side.'

She smiled back at me. 'I hope that what I said didn't make things worse. You and Flynn...' Her cheeks flushed. 'When you split up, I wondered if—'

'It was nothing you said,' I told her. 'Flynn and I dealt with our grief very differently and we couldn't find a way to do it together.'

There was no need for Jessie to take any blame. Granted, what she said had been the trigger for the start of the end, but I'd been so wound up about everything back then that, if it hadn't been that, it would have been something else. The relief on Jessie's face made me think she'd been carrying that guilt around for all these years and, for me, it was a relief to be able to say sorry for how I'd treated her too – something I reiterated strongly before we said goodbye.

'Well, that was unexpected,' Georgia said as we walked out of the close to return to the car. 'How did it feel to see Jessie married and pregnant?'

'Surprisingly okay. She looked happy, didn't she?'

'She did.'

'You know when I came over for your birthday, do you remember me going outside with a coughing fit? That wasn't the reason. I had a moment looking across at Keira and Johnnie, expecting their second baby, and it struck me that it could have been Noah and Jessie.'

'Aw, Mel. Why didn't you say anything?'

'Because it was your birthday and I was being silly.'

She placed her hand firmly on my arm to stop me walking and stood facing me. 'That wasn't silly at all. That was grief knocking on your door. You'll never forget Noah – none of us will – and moments like that are bound to creep up on you, often when you least expect them to. But do you know what you can do when they do?'

'What?'

'Talk to me.'

She drew me into a hug and we stood there in the lane for several minutes, holding each other tightly. Tears pricked my eyes but I blinked them back. I didn't want to cry. If I did, I felt sure that the tears would never stop.

* * *

A little later, we parked in Whinlatter Forest and set off along one of the shorter walking trails.

'Has visiting The Bothy helped lay some ghosts to rest?' Georgia asked.

I pondered on that for a moment before shaking my head. 'It's brought a few things back. I was awful to Jessie. I'm so ashamed thinking about it now. I kept hounding her for information until she snapped and told me something I didn't want to hear.'

'Hounding? I thought you only saw her the once after you'd discovered it was drugs.'

Shame swept through me. 'I wish. I only told you about that time, but there were others…'

As we continued along the path, I shared what I'd said and done and what it pushed Jessie to reveal.

'The thought of Noah feeling invisible was like an arrow through my heart,' I said. 'If that was how he felt, then perhaps he'd turned to drugs to fill some void inside which I'd created.'

'No, Mel. You can't blame yourself.'

'Can't I? I'm a workaholic. I always have been. Flynn wasn't a workaholic like me, but he was a grafter and he was ambitious so he was happy to put the hours in. The hard work reaped financial rewards and Noah got the benefit of those, but was having the latest iPhone really as important to him as having my time?'

'You *did* give him time. I can't believe you'd ever question that.'

'I don't think it was enough. Jessie said we didn't involve him in the dream house and she was right. We shut him out. It wasn't intentional but it happened. We never once asked him for his opinion. What sort of message did that send him?'

Georgia stopped walking, grabbed the tops of my arms and turned me to face her. 'Stop right there! I refuse to let you do this to yourself. Noah was a confident kid who had a great relationship with you and with Flynn. If he'd wanted to be involved in the house, he could have shoved himself in there and demanded to be included.'

She released my arms, but she wasn't finished. 'And don't forget the dream house was exactly that – a dream. You hadn't found a plot of land for it and you knew that, when you did, the plan would need to change to fit the space and the environment. If Noah had still been living at home at that point, of course you'd have involved him but it wasn't real and Noah would have known that.'

'Fair point, but it wasn't just the house. I think he might have tried to talk to me about other things and, you know me – if it's subtle, I'm oblivious.'

'I know that about you, but Noah knew it too. We all did. Family standing joke.'

'I was his mum. I should have known he was feeling pushed out.'

We set off walking once more.

'Do you know what the hardest job in the world is?' Georgia asked. 'Parenthood. I reckon that, because he was eighteen and because you were his mum, you'd probably have been the last to know what was going on with him. In the main, kids turn to their friends first. Maybe he did turn to Jessie and maybe he did share some stuff and maybe some of it was about feeling left out but you'll never know for sure. You're blaming yourself for something a scared, grieving teenager said – something she's just admitted she over-exaggerated – but the only one who knows what really went on is Noah and he's not here to explain. You drove yourself up the wall trying to find answers last time and did you get them?'

'No.'

'So don't go down that road again because the answers weren't available back then and they certainly aren't going to be now. And please stop blaming yourself. Jessie's admitted to exaggerating how things were. Maybe you can blame yourself for making her snap, but you can't blame yourself for whatever Noah was or wasn't feeling. Promise me.'

'I promise.' But I wasn't confident it was a promise I could uphold. Jessie might have apologised and claimed she'd made a bigger thing of it than it was but I'd had seven years to think about her words and she'd been right. I hadn't done it consciously and I certainly hadn't done it when he was young and dependent on me but, when Noah hit his teens and became increasingly independent, spending more time in his room or with his friends, I'd prioritised work. I'd thought he enjoyed his freedom – no embarrassing mum always wanting to know what he was doing – but I hadn't been there for him when he'd really needed me and that was hard to come to terms with.

25

In equal measure, I was looking forward to and dreading Tuesday lunchtime with my parents. I still felt ashamed for storming round there and having a go at them on Friday. Even if Mum hadn't had a health scare to contend with that week, it had been the wrong approach to take. I wished I'd paused to think that through, but being impulsive in my personal life was one of my faults that hadn't improved with time, no matter how self-aware I was about it.

I drove into Willowdale first thing for some freshly baked bread from the bakery, picked up the rest of our lunch treats from a deli in Keswick, then returned to the hall for a couple of hours of work.

Georgia messaged me shortly before I left for Derwent Rise to wish me luck. I hoped I wouldn't need it.

It was a little awkward at first. Dad welcomed me at the door but he looked frazzled. I dropped the bags off in the kitchen before going through to the lounge to say hello to Mum. I looked from Mum to Dad and back again. There was tension in the air, as though I'd arrived in the middle of an argument, and I hoped our time together would ease rather than exacerbate it.

'How are you feeling?' I asked Mum. She was sitting in her usual spot on the sofa with her feet raised on the recliner.

'Tired. I think a combination of a week away and last week's shenanigans have well and truly taken it out of me.'

'If you need to rest, we can take a raincheck,' I said.

'Have you two been in cahoots?' She looked from me to Dad, eyebrows raised. Evidently that's what the argument had been about.

'No, but you *do* need to rest,' Dad said.

'And I've been doing that all morning and will continue to do so all afternoon just like I did all weekend so please let it go and make me the cup of tea you promised me fifteen minutes ago.'

'I thought I...' Dad shook his head. 'No, I put the kettle on but then the post arrived and I forgot. Cup of tea coming right up. Do you want one, Mel?'

'I'd love a coffee.'

'He's driving me mad,' Mum said as soon as Dad left the room. 'I know it's only because he cares but I can't even scratch my nose without him telling me to relax.'

'Are you in pain?'

'I am today. I'm on the strongest painkillers I'm allowed but they don't always hit the spot. What gets me the most is how erratic it is. Sometimes I can feel fine and, at other times, I can barely move. I thought I'd be in agony when we were away, especially after a long journey in the car, but I had the best week I've had in ages. I was okay most of last week too, then I woke up on Saturday feeling like I'd done several rounds in a boxing ring and that hasn't improved since.'

'Is there anything they can do for it?'

'Possibly an injection in my spine, which sounds grim, but

there's no guarantee it'll work. I'm on the waiting list but I'm undecided about going ahead with it.'

Dad returned to the lounge with drinks and the pair of them told me more about Mum's back and how significantly it had deteriorated across the past twelve months or so. Dad was officially Mum's carer and they'd had various alterations made to the house including having their en suite turned into a wet room so there was more space for Dad to assist Mum.

'When my hair needs washing, it's like a surreal visit to the hairdresser's,' Mum said. 'Your dad's there in his swimming trunks and my pink flowery shower cap while I sit in the middle of the room on a plastic chair getting shampooed. You should see him.' She laughed lightly. 'Maybe you shouldn't. There are certain things you can't un-see.'

The atmosphere had definitely lightened and it was good to see Mum laughing about her predicament.

'Is there anything I can do to help?' I asked.

Mum shook her head. 'We're fine. Your dad's doing a great job.'

I made a mental note to check with Dad privately that he was managing okay as, if he was finding caring for Mum a challenge, I couldn't imagine him giving her any indication of that.

'The mobility scooter on holiday was a game-changer,' Dad said. 'Your mum was worried she was going to miss out on valuable time with Astrid and it was the only solution that made sense.'

'I should have accepted I needed one sooner,' Mum admitted. 'After all those years of trekking miles up fells and across the countryside, it's been difficult to admit that I need help walking. On holiday, it struck me that I either hopped on a scooter or I spent most of the holiday on my own. After I got used to the controls, I found it liberating so we decided to get one. Finding the lump delayed that a bit but we're going scooter shopping tomorrow.' She rolled her eyes at Dad and added, 'If I'm not in too much pain and ordered to relax.'

Dad and I went into the kitchen to prepare lunch and he told me they'd decided to change the car too, trading theirs in for a vehicle with more space for the scooter and in which the seats were higher, making it easier for Mum to get in and out.

After we ate, it was time to address the main reason for me coming – the move to Newcastle and my subsequent absenteeism.

'I can't fully explain why I went,' I told them. 'I just woke up on my birthday with this overwhelming need to get away and try to start afresh and, once that idea took hold, I couldn't shake it. As for why I stayed away for so long, I'm still trying to work that one out myself.'

'We understood you leaving after everything you've been through,' Mum said. 'We even understood you staying away but it hurt that you rarely came back and a phone call from you was once in a blue moon.'

'And it's not as though we didn't call you,' Dad added. 'I dread to think how many conversations we had with your voicemail.'

I let them get it all out in the open – how they stopped leaving messages because they were worried they were exacerbating my problems by staying in touch when I so clearly wanted space. They'd understood me holidaying over Christmas and New Year for the first few years and still understood why I'd want to escape for the anniversary of Noah's death over New Year, but that they found it hurtful that I still avoided the family every Christmas. Everything they said was fair and I appreciated that they delivered it in a non-accusatory way; simply a sharing of how they'd felt in the past and right now.

'We've missed you, Mel,' Mum said, 'and I'm sure you don't

need us to tell you there's a Noah-shaped hole in our lives. We often speculate on what he might be doing now.'

I nodded. 'I do too. Sometimes it's heartwarming, but most of the time it's heartbreaking.'

We sat in silence for a couple of minutes. I'd already admitted that I was working things through but it felt too vague. If I was going to build bridges and move things forward with my parents, I needed to be as honest with them as they'd been with me.

'I wasn't doing so great in Newcastle.'

I told them that I hated my flat, admitted that I hadn't made any friends in Newcastle and, cringing, shared Graeme's proposal disaster.

'The only thing that has kept me going is work so I flung myself into that more than ever before. I think I was scared that, if I stopped working, I'd be forced to reflect on everything that had gone wrong and it might just break me for good.'

'Are you doing any better now that you're back in Willowdale?' Dad asked.

'I'm taking it a day at a time.' I told them about visiting The Bothy with Georgia, our conversation with Jessie and my unexpected encounters with Flynn.

'I *will* talk to him at some point. I'm just not quite ready yet. I've discovered that Mark still sees him regularly, which isn't really surprising considering how close they were. But it struck me that you were really close to him too. Have you stayed in touch?'

'He sends us Christmas and birthday cards,' Mum said. 'We send them to him too. We see him around from time to time so we always stop and say hello.'

'He brought a gift round for your mum's eightieth,' Dad added. 'June would have liked to invite him to her party but...'

'But you didn't because of me,' I said when he didn't finish the sentence. How bad did I feel? While I hadn't told anyone they couldn't see Flynn, my insistence that I didn't want to hear anything about him didn't convey a message of support for any of my family to keep him as part of their lives.

'We've missed Flynn.' Mum's eyes sparkled with tears. 'It was incredibly hard losing all three of you like that.'

The lump in my throat was back and I nodded. 'I'm sorry. I needed to get away and I wasn't thinking about the impact on everyone else. If I could go back, I'd do it all differently.'

'Does that mean you'd be okay now if we were to see more of Flynn?' she asked.

'I never said you couldn't. I just don't want to hear about it. Sorry if that sounds harsh.'

'You must have missed him too,' Mum said.

I had, but I wasn't going to admit that. I knew how Mum's mind worked. She'd have us walking up the aisle again if I did and that was never going to happen. The most Flynn and I could ever hope for was a lack of discomfort if we found ourselves in the same place at the same time. So I ignored the statement and suggested another round of drinks.

I could have shared a lot more – things I hadn't even told Georgia yet – but it would have been too much for them. I didn't want them worrying about me. All they needed to know was that things were still tough but that I was coping.

Overall, it felt like a successful visit. I suspected they'd held back on their hurt, but I'd held back on mine too. We agreed we'd all work harder at staying in touch and that a great starting point would be a regular Tuesday lunch – a chance to spend some time with them on my own when we could properly talk.

I said goodbye around mid-afternoon and got into the car. I'd intended to go back to the hall to work but, as I reached the bottom of the drive, it suddenly popped into my head that I should have bought a ream of printer paper when I'd been to town this morning but had been so distracted by the wonderful choices at the deli that I'd completely forgotten. I might as well go back into town and get the paper now.

As I drove into Keswick, I felt a lot lighter. There'd been some uncomfortable moments with Mum and Dad but they'd been necessary to find a way forward, which hopefully we had done. I was fortunate to have such understanding parents.

I picked up a ream of paper and was returning to the car when a jumper in a boutique window caught my eye. It was just a plain crew-neck but the material looked so soft and the colour – duck-egg blue – was gorgeous. I looked down at my chocolate-brown wool jumper under which I was wearing a plain black T-shirt before returning my gaze to the mannequin. In my short time in Willowdale so far, I felt as though some colour was returning to my world. Perhaps it was time for it to return to my wardrobe. I nipped into the boutique and made the purchase. Newcastle hadn't been my fresh start after all, but it felt like Willowdale was.

26

The rest of that week and the next two flew past. Oliver and Rosie loved the plans I drew up for the conversion of Willowdale Hall. The ground floor of the west wing would be their private living quarters and most of the rest of the hall would be divided into luxury self-catering holiday apartments sleeping from two to six guests. I'd initiated a conversation about keeping the former ballroom and another of the larger spaces as function rooms for events. I knew an events manager at a similar-sized venue to Willowdale Hall which I'd worked on previously and she'd emailed me some income projections. Oliver and Rosie agreed it was a no brainer for bringing in an additional income stream while retaining the beauty of those larger rooms which were really too grand to use as apartments.

I'd settled into a routine which wasn't all about work. It was such a novelty having a social life again and a better work/life balance. Family-wise, I had lunch with my parents every Tuesday, the wider family Sunday lunches and I usually met up with Georgia on my own one lunchtime or evening. I was really enjoying being back around my family again and, every time we got together, I felt less like an outsider. There were still references to things I'd missed but at least I knew what was going on with everyone right now. I'd definitely made good progress in healing the rift with my parents and felt like I was more present in Georgia's life. My sister had put in all the effort before and now it felt more equal – something which she'd noticed and had remarked on herself.

My old morning routine had been to make a coffee then crack on with work no matter how early I'd risen. Now I joined Emma at Casa Alpaca a couple of mornings a week to chat while I helped her clean up and prepare for the day ahead and sometimes I took a coffee break with her and Killian, who was also really lovely. I helped Rosie muck out the horses another couple of mornings, and walked the dogs with Alice on the other days. I joined Alice, Rosie and Emma at Horseshoe Cottage for lunch on a Wednesday and, on Thursday evenings, I walked down to the quiz with Rosie and spent an hour with her, Autumn and Dane before breaking off into our separate teams. I loved how Oliver and Rosie's family had accepted me as though I was one of them, and really appreciated how welcoming their friends had been too. They'd all said how much they enjoyed my company and it made me realise how much I'd missed human interaction.

I didn't see as much of Oliver as the others with him travelling to Penrith most days for work and staying over at his house there for a couple of nights. Although Rosie never complained, I sensed that she'd rather he was home more often. I'd walked the dogs with Alice one morning and she'd mentioned Oliver's commute so I'd taken the opportunity to ask whether he'd considered leaving the surgery to work full-time at the estate.

'No. He loves his job too much,' Alice had told me. 'While he's 100 per cent behind it and keen to be involved, the hall conversion was always Rosie's passion. But he *would* rather work closer to home. He's put out feelers but, unfortunately, there aren't any openings locally.'

Alice reckoned that Oliver and Rosie would manage the best they could for now but things would come to a head when they were much further into the project and it either became too much for Rosie to handle alongside running the stables or she found out she was pregnant. Alice swiftly changed the subject and I wondered if she'd shared something with me that she wasn't meant to. Rosie hadn't mentioned anything about trying for a baby, although there was no reason for her to share something so personal when we'd only met a couple of months ago.

Of everyone new that I'd met, I felt closest to Emma. We'd talked about going out for a drink one Friday or Saturday night but it hadn't happened yet and I hadn't pushed her for a date. Establishing a new business took time and, on top of that, she was in a fairly new relationship and needed time to see her large family who lived in and around Ambleside and her best friend near Carlisle. I was confident we'd put a date in the diary eventually as Emma didn't strike me as someone who made false promises.

Last Saturday, I'd booked Georgia and me onto an official alpaca walk. Even though I'd spent a fair bit of time around the Magnificent Seven, I asked Emma to give us the full customer experience as though I'd never met the herd and knew nothing about alpacas. Her knowledge was exemplary and the passion she had for the animals oozed from her and made me feel really proud of my new friend.

Mum loved animals and Georgia and I thought she might like to meet the herd. The route wasn't wheelchair or scooter friendly but Emma offered meet and greet experiences where customers could pet and feed the alpacas at Casa Alpaca. Georgia had a day off today so we'd booked Mum and Dad and ourselves onto one of those. Dad was able to drive his car right up to the gate so Mum only had a short distance to walk to the benches.

'You'll have a chance to feed and stroke all of the Magnificent Seven,' Emma told us after she'd run through the safety briefing, 'but we'll do it in two sittings. First up are Barbara, Camella, Jolene and Maud.'

For me, the most special part of the meet and greet was watching Mum's face. She was a little tentative at first but it didn't take her long to settle into it and stroke the alpacas with confidence. I took several photos and some video footage to share with them later. Dad was in his element too and every smile and burst of laughter filled me with happiness.

We all went to The White Willow afterwards for lunch and, for the first time since Noah died, I wasn't aware of any distance between my parents and me as they equally involved Georgia and me in the conversation.

'You know Gayle Atherton?' Mum said to me after we'd finished eating.

'I don't think so.'

'You must do. She's the one who went to Machu Picchu for her sixtieth birthday. Her cousin's that skinny man from that crime drama we used to like but got bored with in the third series.'

Mum was prone to conversations like this, convinced I knew people in the village who I might have once said hello to when I was nine. I had no clue who Gayle Atherton was – or the crime series, for that matter – but it was easier to go along with it.

'What about her?' I asked.

'Her granddaughter's off to university this year to study counselling and it got me thinking about what you'd said a few weeks ago about struggling with things. You're welcome to talk to your dad and me about anything you want, but I was wondering whether speaking to a professional might help. Unless you've already tried that.'

'I haven't, but I don't think I need help. Coming back here has been a good move.'

I appreciated that they cared but it was amazing how much stronger I felt in just five weeks. Being back home, being close to nature and surrounded by the people who loved me was doing wonders for me. With hindsight, it probably would have been a good idea to get some professional help when I moved to Newcastle and it became apparent that it wasn't going to give me the fresh start I'd hoped for. Then again, I'd had my head buried in the sand like Georgia said, refusing to admit that things were worse there than they had been in Willowdale. Seeing a counsellor had never entered my mind then. If it had, maybe I'd have returned sooner but I was here now and my life was getting back on track so perhaps I was exactly where I was meant to be when I was meant to be. It was a comforting thought.

27

I'd told Rosie I'd join her in the riding stables on Monday morning but the sound of the rain battering against the windows woke me up before my alarm clock sounded and I was very tempted to wriggle further under the duvet and stay there. Rosie wouldn't have minded me being a no-show. She'd made it clear that she loved my company and appreciated the help but there was never any obligation to turn up, even if I'd said I would. That didn't sit well with me. A promise was a promise and it wasn't like a bit of rain was going to do me any damage.

I wrapped up in my waterproof and reached for a golf brolly in a holder by the front door but changed my mind on hearing the wind outside. An umbrella would be turned inside out in no time.

It was a trudge across the estate to the stables at the far side. The quickest route was along one of the forest tracks but it would be very muddy and I wasn't convinced that a short cut through the woods in high winds was the best idea. As I hastened along the path at the edge of the woods, avoiding the puddles, I wondered if this was the type of weather that triggered Alice's PTSD. I hoped she was okay today.

'Good morning!' Rosie called cheerfully. 'You decided to brave the weather.'

'It's wild out there. I was sorely tempted to hide indoors.'

'Me too. I don't mind the rain but I don't like it when it's windy too.'

We discussed what I could do to help her that morning and I set about working.

'I was thinking about your mum on the way down,' I said when we took a break a little later. 'Is this the type of rain that can trigger an episode for her?'

'Exactly this. It wasn't windy that night but it was this sort of torrential rain. I used to feel so on edge any time it was like this. Mam hasn't had an episode since she left Applevale Lodge but it doesn't mean she won't, so I stopped by the cottage first thing this morning. She was up and she was okay. My dad tends to stay over when heavy rain's forecast and it really helps having him there. He's such a calming presence.'

The phrase jolted me. My mum used to say that about Flynn, that he made the perfect partner for me because he was the sunshine to my storm, able to calm me when the fire inside me burned out of control. It was true, but that was because Flynn had a gift for helping me see that whatever I'd got het up about didn't really matter in the great scheme of things. Until that time when it did.

Rosie and I returned to our work and my phone buzzed with a message.

FROM GEORGIA

Johnnie just rang. Keira's gone into labour and
it's advancing fast. They're on their way to the
hospital now. Keira's fine, taking it all in her
stride x

It was Keira's due date today and, although Astrid had been two weeks late, it hadn't followed that Arlo would be the same. My stomach tightened and a feeling of melancholy cloaked me. I knew why – because it was Monday and Noah had been born on a Monday. It angered me that it bothered me, just like it had angered me when I'd reacted badly to the news that my niece was expecting a boy. What had I just been saying to Mum on Friday about not needing any professional help? Maybe I did because having a negative reaction to my great-nephew being born on the same day of the week as my son wasn't rational.

'Anything else you need help with?' I asked Rosie when I'd completed the tasks she'd given me.

'No, you can head off now. I'd come with you but I'm going to check on Mam again.'

'Say hi from me and say hi to Autumn when you see her later.' The riding stables were closed on a Monday but Rosie gave Autumn a riding lesson. She'd offered me lessons too but I'd never fancied riding. I thought horses were beautiful creatures and I was thoroughly enjoying being around them, but heaving myself into a saddle and riding one held no appeal.

'What a numpty I am! Nearly forgot to say! We're skipping the ride cos of the weather and wondered if you'd like to join us for lunch at The White Willow.'

If she'd asked me before I got Georgia's message, I'd have said an enthusiastic yes but now I knew I wouldn't be good company so better to dip out than bring them both down.

'I'd have loved to but Keira's gone into labour. I want to get ahead with a couple of my other projects so I can take time out to meet the new baby.'

'Aw, how lovely. I hope everything goes well and I'll see you back at the house later.'

I pulled my waterproof back on, waved goodbye and left the stables, my mood as dark as the stormy skies overhead.

* * *

Back at the hall, I hung up my wet clothes to dry and warmed up in the shower. When I settled down to work I couldn't concentrate so I went downstairs, made a coffee and took it into the library. I'd fallen in love with this room and was so glad we were going to preserve it. With the fire lit, I curled up on one of the sofas with my favourite architecture book.

It was mid-afternoon when a message came through on the family WhatsApp.

FROM JOHNNIE

Arlo Nathaniel Randall is here! Born at 1.19 p.m. weighing 8lb 1oz. Everything went smoothly and Keira and Arlo should be home this evening. We'd love to introduce him to you all but it would be great if you could give us a couple of days to get settled in first.

The same weight as Noah! What were the odds? Different time of day, though. Noah had been a teatime baby. Johnnie's message was accompanied by a photo of Keira with Arlo snuggled against her and my breath caught. It was exactly like the photo I'd had when Noah was born. In fact, I could easily be looking at myself. Georgia and I looked very similar and Keira looked just like her mum so, by default, bore a strong likeness to me.

I really didn't want to get upset. This was a happy moment and Arlo was *not* Noah. Keira was *not* me. These were two very separate things, but that didn't stop a few tears escaping. I tensed when I heard the sound of dog paws skidding on the floor outside. I hadn't heard Rosie arrive home, although the front door was so far away and the walls so solid that I never did. She pushed the door open and caught me wiping my cheeks.

'Are you okay?' she asked, her expression concerned.

'They're happy tears. My great-nephew has arrived.'

I passed Rosie my phone so she could see the photo.

'He's so cute. Gosh, Keira looks so like you in this photo.'

That released another tear, which I swiped away.

'Did I say the wrong thing?' Rosie asked, sitting down on the sofa beside me. She looked so genuinely concerned for me and it felt like the right time.

'They're not just happy tears,' I admitted. 'Yes, Keira does look the spit of me in this photo and it's an almost exact match for one I had when my son was born.'

'Your son? I didn't realise you had any children.'

'Just the one – Noah – but he died when he was eighteen from a drug overdose.' It still felt so alien saying those words – partly because I didn't usually tell new people and partly because I still couldn't believe my son had been a drug user.

'Oh, no! I'm so sorry.'

'His dad and I had no idea he was in with a bad crowd and had got into drugs. I wanted answers – someone to blame – and it drove a wedge between us. I lost my son but I also lost my husband soon after. We had such a good marriage, you know. Never thought we'd end up divorced.'

'That's a lot to handle all at once.'

'It was and the truth is I didn't handle it well at all. Anyway, Keira having a boy born on the same day of the week as Noah, weighing the same as him and looking like him in the photo has brought it all rushing back, which is why I'm in here reading instead of working.'

'Do you want to talk some more about it?' Rosie asked.

It was so kind of her to offer, but that was hardly a surprise as everything Rosie had done since I'd met her had been kind. She was such a lovely person – as were all her friends and family – and I'd held back on them, not sharing the most important things there were to know about me for fear they might look at me differently. But they weren't like that and opening up just now hadn't been nearly as hard as I'd anticipated. Any other day and I might have accepted her offer but I was feeling a little too fragile today.

I smiled at her gratefully. 'Thank you, and I might take you up on that one day, but I'd prefer a distraction today. Tell me something to cheer me up. Any more news about Autumn and Dane's books?'

'Nothing new since the contract was signed, but I do have some good news from Mam and Dad. He's moving in with her.'

'Aw, that's lovely news. At Horseshoe Cottage?'

'Yes. I don't think I could have wished for a better partner for her because he completely gets it. He's got this big house in Grasmere which he loves, but he loves Mam more. He knows that this is the place she feels happiest and safest so he's willing to sell up and downsize massively for her.'

'Sounds like true love.'

'As I understand it, it was true love from the moment they met and, if people hadn't interfered and lied, he'd never have left. He says they're magnets and they were pulled apart when they shouldn't have been but the connection was so strong that they were always going to be drawn back to each other. Isn't that sweet?'

I nodded my agreement, smiling at her. Magnets. Where had I heard that phrase recently? And then it came back to me. It was when Mum had asked me over the phone why I'd split up with Graeme. I'd said we'd wanted different things and she'd suggested that the 'thing' I wanted was Flynn and that he was my magnet.

Was he?

* * *

Later that evening, I was in bed reading when there was a knock on my door.

'Would you like some more good news?' Rosie asked when I called to her to come in.

'Always.'

'Autumn's just FaceTimed me. Dane asked her to marry him tonight.'

'Oh, wow! That's fantastic news.'

'Isn't it? I'm so pleased for them both. It's exactly two years today since she arrived in Willowdale to stay with me. Dane cycled past as she was driving into the village and he was capti-vated by her. Autumn coming here completely changed both of their lives so proposing on the anniversary was perfect.'

'That's so lovely. Did she have any idea he was going to ask her?'

'She hadn't a clue. The plan was always to get married at some point but they wanted to focus on securing a publishing deal first.'

After Rosie left, I picked up my book once more, but I didn't open it. Autumn and Dane were a great couple and I was so pleased for them. How lovely that Autumn hadn't seen it coming. Flynn's proposal had taken me by surprise too and he'd also gone for an anniversary – my twenty-fourth birthday and exactly a year since we met. We'd taken the day off work and planned a hike up nearby Blencathra if the weather was kind, which it was – blue skies and sunshine but not too hot. Blencathra, also known as Saddleback thanks to its shape, was one of the most northerly fells in the National Park and, with an elevation of 868 metres, was also one of the highest. We set off in the morning with a picnic lunch and were a good hour into our walk when Flynn spotted a Scrabble tile on the track. Amused to see that it was the letter 'M' for Mel, I slipped it into my pocket. A little later, we spotted another one – an 'R' this time. By the time we made it to the summit, I'd picked up six Scrabble tiles.

Flynn and I paused by the summit stone – an engraved stone ring on the ground – to admire the incredible views across nearby Keswick, Derwent Water and several other Cumbrian fells, and further afield to the Cheviots in Northumberland and the Southern Uplands of Scotland. Despite the beautiful weather, there was quite a breeze so we dropped down a little to a more sheltered point for our lunch.

'Can you spell anything with those Scrabble letters?' Flynn asked after we'd eaten.

I removed the tiles from my pocket and spread them across my left palm.

'I've got an M, R, E, L, another M and a Y. Ooh! I can spell my name.' I laid one of the Ms, the E and the L together on the ground. 'And the word "me" if I take the L away, but I think that's it. Not enough vowels for anything else.'

'What if you had four more letters?'

I looked up at him, my eyebrows knitted. What was he up to? 'That's very specific. Do you happen to have four more letters?'

'I might have. Close your eyes and put your other hand out.'

I did as instructed and felt him place some more tiles on my right palm.

'Open them.'

I glanced down at the letters. 'Another M, another R, an A and an E.'

'What can you spell now?'

'Arm,' I said.

'Anything else?'

Suddenly I saw it. If I moved the A and the R from my right hand to join the M, R and Y in my left hand... My heart was pounding as I looked up at Flynn.

'Show me,' he said.

With shaky hands, I formed the two words on the ground above my name to create a short but wonderful sentence.

MARRY ME MEL

When I looked up at him once more, he was holding out a ring box in front of him. Dipping one knee to the ground, he opened up the box and I laughed at the wooden Scrabble tile inside with a heart drawn onto it and the infinity symbol at the bottom right instead of a letter value.

'I love you, Mel. Always have and always will so, if you'll accept it, here's my heart which will be yours forever.'

I couldn't speak. Flynn had done several romantic things over the year we'd been together, but this eclipsed them all. Blinking back happy tears as I nodded, I removed the heart tile.

'There's something else that belongs in this box.' He removed a ring from his pocket and held it out towards me. 'Will you marry me, Mel?'

I swear I floated back down Blencathra on cloud nine that afternoon. I asked Flynn whether he'd been worried about me sussing what he was doing before we made it to the summit but he'd laughed and pointed out my inability to notice anything subtle.

'Even if the tiles had spelt out *marry me* in order, I still don't think you'd have realised.'

He was very likely right about that. He'd been right about a lot of things and, when it counted, I hadn't wanted to listen. I'd walked away instead.

Sitting on my bed in Willowdale Hall twenty-nine years later, I felt overcome with emotion as I remembered that special day. I still had all of those Scrabble tiles in a velvet pouch in my jewellery box.

I scrambled out of bed and opened my desk drawer, removing the piece of paper Flynn had given me a little over three weeks ago. Should I arrange to meet him? What would I say if I did? Sorry seemed so inadequate. I shoved the paper back in the drawer, shaking my head. I was only thinking about it because I was feeling emotional right now and I might regret it later. There were far too many things I regretted which I'd done in the throes of heightened emotion. Best wait a bit longer.

28

By Thursday morning, the storm had well and truly blown over and spring had made a welcome reappearance. After a listless day on Monday, I'd absorbed myself in my work and hadn't actually left the hall. I should have had lunch with my parents on Tuesday but Mum had a doctor's appointment so they'd asked if we could take a raincheck. I hadn't helped Emma out and I'd even skipped Wednesday lunch at Horseshoe Cottage. But this morning, with the sun smiling through my window, I felt ready to escape the confines of my rooms and stretch my legs so I rang Alice to check it was okay to join her for a walk with Toffee and Chester.

'You're always welcome to join us,' she said, 'but, as we haven't been far over the last couple of days, I was planning to do Cat Bells.'

Cat Bells was the nearest fell to the estate and one of the most popular ones in the area. The three-and-a-half-mile return trip from base to summit could be completed within three hours, although experienced walkers could do it a lot quicker. Much as I loved the walk, I wasn't sure I could spare the time, but I glanced over to my desk and reprimanded myself. It was still early and, despite my lack of productivity on Monday, I'd more than made up for it over the last two days. I could afford the time and it would probably do me the world of good.

I arranged to meet Alice by the gates fifteen minutes later. Toffee and Chester were bouncing around excitedly, as if they knew that they were having a special walk today.

We left the estate grounds and wandered along the footpath in the direction of Cat Bells, avoiding the many puddles while the dogs ploughed straight through them. The change in weather had brought lots of other walkers out, many of whom had dogs, so we had a lot of stopping and starting as the dogs sniffed around each other.

'Such a beautiful morning,' I said, tilting my head back so the sun could kiss my cheeks.

'Gorgeous,' Alice agreed. 'It's great to be out. It's great to be able to be out. This time last year, I'd never have believed I could do this walk again.'

'What happened if you tried to leave the estate?'

'Panic attacks. I'd get all shaky, feeling sick and dizzy. Occasionally, I'd get so frustrated that I'd force myself to go out the gates and set off down this path. I'd spend what felt like forever at the entrance psyching myself up but the same thing happened every time I stepped beyond the gates – I'd barely make it any distance before I had to turn round and run back. The effort would take its toll and I'd end up barely able to leave my bedroom for the next few days. That's no way to live, so I stopped trying.'

'I'm so sorry you went through that. It must feel amazing to be able to explore now.'

'Gosh, it is. It's like someone pressed a pause button on my life and now they've pressed play again. I'm not completely recovered. The thought of going on holiday, even in this country, is still way down the line but every week I make a little more progress. Of course, there've been a few steps backwards here and there but that's part of the recovery journey and part of being human. We can easily be knocked off balance, but as long as we keep looking ahead instead of focusing on the past, we can get there.'

We'd reached the base of Cat Bells and set off up the incline in single file. I mulled over Alice's words as we ascended. What she'd said about a pause button really resonated with me. I'd definitely done that with my life and moving here had been about pressing play again, but I didn't feel like I was fully playing yet. I wasn't sure what needed to happen to feel like I was.

There were quite a few walkers on Cat Bells, some already making their descent, but it was nothing like the stream of people on a nice day during the school holidays. Most of the walkers we passed today were properly kitted out with sturdy walking boots or shoes and waterproofs but I'd seen it all over the years – shorts and T-shirts on a cold and rainy day, flimsy canvas shoes and even flip flops.

When we reached the summit, I reached out to place my hand on the trig point and laughed as Alice did exactly the same.

'Doesn't feel like you've made it to the top unless you touch it, does it?' she said.

Chester and Toffee walked round the trig point sniffing the base before flopping down on their bellies on one of the grassy areas.

I loved the views from the top of Cat Bells. At an elevation of 451 metres, it was one of the smaller Lakeland fells but the vista wasn't any the less spectacular for it. While Alice gave some water to the dogs, I stood with my hands on my hips, breathing in the fresh air and the beautiful surroundings.

Tomorrow, it would be exactly six weeks since I moved back

to Willowdale and I was feeling so much more at peace for being surrounded by nature instead of tall buildings and traffic noise. This had been the right move and one I should probably have made a long time ago, but I wasn't going to dwell on regrets. From now on, I was going to do what Alice had done and take control of my life. I wouldn't get derailed by the little things and, instead, would focus on the big picture of continuing to find peace and healing. That shouldn't be difficult when I was in a place I loved with people I loved doing a job I loved.

When I returned to Willowdale Hall and checked my messages, I found one from Keira to say that both sets of grandparents and great-grandparents had now met Arlo so she was ready to welcome all other visitors. I reminded myself of my resolve at the top of Cat Bells to focus on the big picture and not to be derailed by the little things and Arlo's arrival had been one of those little things that I'd already built up into something big when it hadn't needed to be. The best thing I could do to take control of my life right now was to see my new great-nephew today. I couldn't show up without a gift so I changed out of my walking boots and into a pair of trainers and headed straight into Keswick.

I'd bought Astrid a Jemima Puddle-Duck soft toy and Beatrix Potter's accompanying story when she was born so it made sense to keep that tradition going with *The Tale of Peter Rabbit* and a soft toy for Arlo. I also bought him a cute Peter Rabbit outfit, pushing aside thoughts of having dressed Noah as a baby in something similar. I placed the bags in my boot, planning to head straight to Keira and Johnnie's house, but an elderly couple at the car beside mine caught my attention.

'You admit I was right to suggest going down to the lake rather than straight home?' the man asked.

'If I admit it, will you promise not to do the smug grin?' the woman responded, her tone teasing.

'I promise.'

'Okay, I'll admit it. It looked especially beautiful with the sun on it.'

I'd been to the lake's edge several times in and around the estate but I hadn't come round to the east side since I returned to Willowdale and their conversation had just sold it to me. Locking the car, I set off on the short walk through Hope Park – a traditional park with flowerbeds and benches – then past Crow Park, which was a wide open space.

I didn't have the time or inclination to go for a long walk but a coffee overlooking Derwent Water, watching the activity on the beach, would be perfect. I nipped into Derwent View Café and bought a takeaway cappuccino and walked along Lake Road above the beach. It was always a lot busier here than on the Willowdale side of the lake because of its proximity to amenities – the town centre, the parks and the theatre. There was a large car park and the beach was the launch point for the lake cruises, a good place for launching kayaks and paddleboards, as well as being the starting point for the short walk to popular beauty spot, Friar's Crag. In the summer, it could be a challenge to find a free bench but I managed to secure one easily today and sat back, sipping my drink and watching the world go by.

Across the lake, I could see the estate, although the hall itself was hidden by the trees. Living there was such a dream and it would be strange moving out. Willowdale Hall was only ever meant to be temporary and I'd already stayed longer than anticipated.

A boat pulled up against one of the wooden jetties and several passengers disembarked. Last off were a man and woman. He stepped off easily but the woman seemed a little more hesitant, handing him her backpack and tucking her red hair behind her ears before accepting his hand. My breath caught as I recognised the man as Flynn and I leaned forward, watching them intently. On the beach, they paused, hugged for ages, then she leaned in and kissed him before they sauntered off the beach, arms round each other. She had to be his wife. I watched them disappear from sight, sadness enveloping me at seeing Flynn with someone else. I knew I had no right to feel that way – if anyone deserved happiness, it was him – but I couldn't help it. *You win some, you lose some.* And I'd lost big time when I'd walked away from Flynn.

I finished my coffee and sat for several more minutes drinking in the view across to Cat Bells, trying to shake my melancholy. I thought about how much I'd enjoyed my walk up the fell with Alice and the dogs this morning and how energised I'd felt at the top. I needed to hold onto that positive feeling and not allow myself to be brought down by seeing Flynn with his wife.

Returning to the car, I drove to Keira and Johnnie's house and, if there'd been any residual upset from seeing Flynn, it vanished there. Keira was buzzing, completely infatuated with her new baby boy and it was so sweet to see how taken Astrid clearly was with her brother. I couldn't feel down surrounded by so much happiness. Cuddling Arlo close, holding his tiny hand in mine was probably the best thing I could have done. He wasn't Noah and there was no reason for me to feel any differently about him than I had about Astrid. This morning, Alice had said something very wise: *We can easily be knocked off balance but as long as we keep looking ahead instead of focusing on the past, we can get there.* I'd been knocked off balance from the moment I knew Keira was having a boy simply because I was focusing on the past. From now on, I had to keep looking ahead.

I returned to Willowdale Hall a little later, determined to follow Alice's great example. Marching over to my desk, I removed the piece of paper containing Flynn's contact details and took it down to the kitchen to the recycling bin. Flynn had clearly found a way to heal and move on and there was no way I was going to open that wound for him by meeting up with him and raking over the past. Talking to him was not going to help me move forward – only I could do that. If we did bump into each other, I'd be polite and respectful because he deserved that, but there was no need for us to pre-empt that moment by meeting up. No need at all.

29

Another three weeks passed, taking me up to two months back in Willowdale. I felt really settled. I was loving my job, where I lived, and my social life. I was even enjoying the weekly quiz at The Hardy Herdwick despite my lack of general knowledge. Emma and I had managed a couple of nights out, which had been great fun, and I'd been to the theatre with Regan and Clarke, but I had two highlights each week – Tuesday lunches with my parents where we talked and laughed and felt like a united loving family once more and the time I spent with Alice, especially when we went walking with the dogs. Although we'd been through very different experiences, we trod a similar path towards healing. I deeply valued her counsel and told her so, and she shared with me how much she appreciated the different perspective I brought as a result of not knowing her when she was ill.

My living situation had been confirmed for the short-term future. Last week, Rosie had caught me curled up on the sofa in the library with my laptop on my knee, looking online at properties to buy and rent in the area and tutting at the lack of options.

'There really isn't any rush to move out,' she said. 'We both love having you here.'

'I love being here, but I can't stay forever. Although, if we shift the desk to the left a bit, what do you think about me moving my bed into that corner?'

'Maybe your drawing board in the opposite corner?' Rosie replied, laughing. 'Seriously, though, you're welcome to stay until we hit a point in the conversion where it's impractical. If I'm honest, I prefer knowing there's someone else in the hall on the nights Oliver isn't here. It's a big place to be rattling around in on my own.'

Rosie used to stay at Horseshoe Cottage during the nights Oliver worked away but when Xander moved in she'd decided it was time for her to fully leave home. I'd helped her move the rest of her belongings across and had hugged her when she became tearful. I remembered feeling that way when I moved out of Derwent Rise and into Flynn's flat shortly after we got engaged. Even though I was excited about the new chapter in my life, I was sad to leave my childhood home where I'd been so happy.

'Unless you'd prefer to separate work and non-work,' Rosie added.

I gave her a reassuring smile. 'Surprisingly, even though this is the first time I've lived and worked on the same site as a project, I've got a better work/life balance now than I've ever had before. So thank you for the offer. I'd love to stay longer.'

I was so grateful to Rosie and Oliver for their generosity. It'd be several months before work started on the hall conversion and, even then, I wouldn't need to move out immediately. When the time came, hopefully the market would have shifted and I'd find something suitable but I could relax and enjoy living in my favourite building in the meantime, still pinching myself from time to time that my childhood dream had come true.

Our usual family Sunday lunch had been cancelled today because Regan and Clarke had friends staying and Georgia and Mark had been away to a wedding. I'd still see some of my family today as Mum, Dad, Georgia, Mark and I had all been invited to The White Willow this evening for drinks and a buffet in celebration of Autumn and Dane's engagement.

After rifling through my wardrobe this morning for something suitable to wear and tutting at all the dark colours, I'd made the forty-minute drive to Carlisle. I hadn't been shopping there in maybe a decade so it was a trip down memory lane seeing which shops had opened and closed. I'd only intended on getting something for the party but returned to Willowdale Hall laden with bags of clothes and not a single black item among them. I'd even splashed out on a new coat – a vibrant green one – which made me feel so alive.

Rosie and Oliver had headed to The White Willow early to help set up so I walked there with Alice and Xander. I'd asked Dad if he'd like me to call at Derwent Rise on the way to help Mum with the walk but he'd said there was no need as she'd decided to ride her mobility scooter round.

I'd been in The White Willow maybe ten minutes when I spotted my parents arriving, Mum with one arm linked through Dad's and a sparkly purple walking stick in the other hand. As Dad settled her onto a chair, I crossed the room to greet them.

'Are you all right?' I asked Mum, concerned by how pale she looked.

'Tired and a bit out of sorts today. We had Astrid for a few hours this afternoon and it's taken it out of me. We'll probably not stay long.'

'How come you had Astrid?'

'Arlo had an unexplained rash and they needed to do an emergency dash to the hospital, but he's fine. It's gone now.'

I wished Keira had called on me to look after Astrid instead of Mum and Dad but they were probably panicking and didn't think. If it had been this afternoon, I'd have been back from Carlisle and could easily have helped. Next time I saw Keira, I'd make sure she knew I could always be called upon in an emergency.

Dad went to get some drinks so I sat down next to Mum.

'You look lovely this evening, Mel,' Mum said. 'That colour's stunning on you.'

I'd surprised myself with the bold choice of burnt orange but the satin wraparound blouse had called to me. I'd accompanied it with my best dark jeans and a pair of orange ankle boots with chunky heels.

'Thank you. It's not a colour I usually wear.'

'You don't usually wear colour full stop,' Mum said, 'but you used to. Before. I'm so happy to have seen you wearing more colours recently. You deserve to have colour back in your life.'

She took my hand and squeezed it as she held my gaze. I smiled back at her, tears pricking my eyes, knowing we weren't talking about my clothes anymore.

'It's taken a long time, but colour is definitely coming back,' I said. 'Thank you for helping it.'

She put her arms out and we hugged. What a fool I'd been to miss out on this but, as I'd promised myself, no regrets – just focusing on the here and now and a positive future.

When Dad returned, I chatted to them for a little longer but some of their friends appeared so I left them to it.

An hour or so later, Dad joined me and announced that they were heading home. He went outside to turn Mum's mobility scooter round while Georgia and I helped Mum into her coat. I picked up her walking stick and bag and we took an arm each to go outside.

'I'm so sorry for leaving early,' Mum said when we had her settled on the scooter with a blanket over her knees. Although it had been a gorgeous day, there was a chill in the air this evening which she'd feel even when travelling a short distance.

'It's been such a nice evening,' she said. 'They make a lovely couple.' She smiled at Georgia as she added, 'Nearly as lovely as you and Mark.'

Georgia laughed and hugged Mum goodnight. As I leaned in for a hug next, Mum tightened her hold on me and whispered in my ear, 'And nearly as lovely as you and Flynn were and still could be.'

My stomach flip-flopped at the suggestion. Had she really just said that?

'He's your magnet,' she whispered.

Magnets again? I wanted to ask her what she meant by that but I didn't want to detain her when she so clearly needed to get home for some rest. I'd ask her on Tuesday instead.

When Mum released me, she looked me deep in the eyes. 'Think about it, Mel.'

'Think about what?' Georgia asked.

'Whether she'd like to go into town for lunch on Tuesday for a change,' Mum said, super-speedy with her response. 'I'm off home to bed. You two girls look after each other. I'm so proud of you both, you know.'

'Have you been on the wine tonight?' Georgia quipped.

'Not touched a drop, but I've realised I don't tell you things like this often enough and now's as good a time as any. Both of you give me one more hug for the road.'

I was closest so I hugged her again, still feeling thrown by her comment about Flynn. 'I love you,' she whispered. 'I'm so glad you came home.'

'I love you too,' I whispered back. Another thing I couldn't remember her ever saying to me. Not that I didn't know it – we'd just never been a family who outwardly declared our love for each other.

She hugged Georgia too and I heard her whisper the same thing.

'Come on, June,' Dad said as a cold breeze ruffled Mum's hair and blanket. 'Let's get you home and warm.'

He hugged Georgia and me and we waved them off.

'Did she tell you she loved you?' Georgia asked.

'Yeah. I wasn't expecting that.'

'Me neither. Nice to hear, though.'

We returned inside just in time to catch Autumn and Dane each making a short speech. The pair of them looked so happy together and perfectly suited. I'd noticed earlier how good they were at working the room, making sure they spoke to all their guests, but how they'd glance across at each other every so often and smile that secret smile all couples seemed to share. Would I ever exchange a smile like that with someone special at some future point? Did I even want to? I had to acknowledge that I did, but I couldn't ever see it happening. There was far too much going on at the moment to even think about dating again. And, even if I did go on a date, could they ever compare to Flynn? I frowned. Flynn? Why was he in my head? Because Mum had mentioned him outside, of course! Why had she done that? If she and Dad had stayed in touch with him, they had to know he was married. Was she suggesting I should break up a happy marriage? My stomach lurched as it struck me that theirs might not be a happy marriage. Although they hadn't looked on the verge of a break-up when I'd seen them kissing on the beach the other week. And even if they were, Flynn and I could never go back. After how I'd treated him, there was no way on this earth he'd possibly want to.

If I ever felt ready to date again, I'd have to be really careful. The last thing I wanted to do was break someone's heart like I'd broken Graeme's. Poor man had never stood a chance with me. He wasn't Flynn. Simple as.

The party wrapped up at nine o'clock – no late night planned with it being a Sunday. Mum and Dad had missed the cutting of the cake so Autumn handed me a box containing a slice for each of them.

'I think Dad was a bit disappointed at leaving early,' Georgia said as she pulled her coat on. 'I'll ask if he wants a cuppa and some company with his cake. Fancy joining me?'

I'd arranged to walk back with Alice and Xander so I said goodnight to them and assured them that Mark would drop me back at the hall later.

Rather than knocking on the door at Derwent Rise and risking waking up Mum, Georgia let us in with the spare key she always had in her purse, and Mark, Georgia and I crept into the lounge.

'We come bearing cake,' Georgia said, passing Dad the take-away box as I closed the door behind us. 'And our company if you'd like it.'

He lifted the lid and smiled at the contents. 'I was just thinking I fancied something sweet but we don't have anything in the house, so this is perfect. And yes, please, to the company.'

'I take it Mum's in bed,' I said.

'Yes. She's not felt too good today but she was determined not to miss the party.'

Dad went into the kitchen with Georgia and returned with mugs of tea and his slice of cake on a plate.

'Is it just today that Mum's been feeling poorly?' I asked once we were all settled with our drinks.

'It's hard to say. She's in pain most days and she often tries to hide that from me as she says she doesn't want to bring me down. I can usually spot the days when she's suffering the most but it's hard to separate those from anything else going on. As I say, she was determined to get to the party but she could probably have done with resting more today.'

'It's so typical that we weren't around to have Astrid,' Georgia said. 'Sounds like the last thing she needed today.'

'Don't fret about it. It's one of those things and we could have said no but you know what your mum's like – any chance to spend some time with her great-grandchildren and she's in her element. Anyway, how was the wedding?'

I'd already heard about Mark and Georgia's weekend away while we were at The White Willow so, while they were recounting it to Dad, I zoned out and gazed around the room, smiling at the figurines we used to relocate. On one side of the room was a beautiful oak sideboard on top of which were twenty or so silver photo frames of assorted sizes and designs so I wandered over to look at them. Some photos had remained constant over the years including several wedding day photos – Mum and Dad's, Georgia and Mark's, Keira and Johnnie's – and graduation photos of Georgia and me, but others were regularly updated. There was a lovely one of Mum cutting the cake at her eightieth birthday party and another of Mum and Dad together that same day. I smiled as I picked up a frame containing a photo of Mum cuddling Astrid and Arlo. Aware that Georgia and Mark had finished telling Dad about the wedding, I turned round holding the frame.

'This must be hot off the press.'

'Taken about a week ago,' Dad said. 'I printed it off this morning and put it in the frame before your mum went to bed.'

'It's a great photo of them all. Mum's so photogenic.'

'That's because she's a beautiful woman.'

The passion and love with which he delivered that statement had me tearing up and I was grateful for the distraction of returning the frame to its home.

'Do you like the one of you?' Dad asked.

I frowned, confused, as the only photo I'd noticed of me was the graduation one and it was really old now. There used to be a wedding day one but that had long gone.

'Opposite end of the sideboard,' Dad said. 'Also hot off the press.'

I hadn't reached that side yet but soon spotted the hinged photo frame. On one side was a photo of Mum, Dad, Georgia and me alongside Maud and Jolene. I remembered Emma taking it on Mum's phone, telling us she was an expert in getting the best angle for the alpacas so that they looked like they were smiling. Sure enough, Maud and Jolene looked like they were grinning alongside us. On the other side was a candid photo of me with Charmaine. The wind had whipped up my hair and the white tuft on Charmaine's head. Emma – assuming she'd also taken this photo – had captured me laughing. Rosy-cheeked and sparkly-eyed, I barely recognised myself.

'Your mum loves both those photos,' Dad said, joining me. 'But she especially loves that one of you. She says it's the first time since we lost Noah that she's seen you laughing without guilt.'

'Without guilt?' I repeated.

'Yes. Allowing yourself a moment to live in the here and now instead of telling yourself you have no right to laugh after such a tragedy.'

I ran my fingers over the glass. No wonder I barely recognised myself. This photo looked more like the me before Noah died and seven years was a long time for that woman to have hidden herself away from the world. It was reassuring to know she was still in there somewhere and capable of reappearing.

'Would you mind sending me these two photos?' I asked.

'Will do, but I can nip up to my office and print you off copies now if you like.'

'That would be great, thanks.' I'd buy a frame for the one of the four of us and put it on my bookshelves, but it would be good to have the one of me on my desk as a reminder that I was allowed to laugh, to breathe, to live again. I glanced down at my blouse and smiled at the conversation I'd had with Mum earlier. *You deserve to have colour back in your life.*

After Georgia had seen the photos, she asked Dad to print copies for her too. Derwent Rise was a three-bedroom bungalow but, when Georgia and I were still at home, Dad had converted the sizeable attic into half office half storage, accessed via wooden steps. He disappeared upstairs to print the photos while I checked out the rest of the frames.

Mum had double photo frames for each of her grandchildren and great-grandchildren with a photo of them as a baby on one side and a recently taken one on the other. She used to jokingly refer to them as her 'first and last' photos but dropped that phrase after Noah died and his most recent photo literally was the last photo ever taken of him.

I picked up Noah's frame for a closer look. That last photo had been taken on Christmas Day when Flynn and I had invited the whole family over to The Bothy. It had been chaotic, loud and laughter-filled – exactly what a big family Christmas should be. I remembered Mum asking Noah if he'd wanted to remove the bright yellow paper party hat he'd got from his cracker before she took the photo. He'd laughed and said, *But how would you know it was taken on Christmas Day if I'm not wearing it?* before making his hat crooked and giving her his most dazzling smile. He'd been so happy and full of fun that day, I'd never have guessed that his personal life was out of control, and none of us could ever have imagined that, a week later, he'd be gone.

I put the frame back and was about to return to the sofa when a small frame caught my eye. Was that...? I lifted it up and my heart started racing.

'Mum's got a photo of Flynn,' I exclaimed.

'Must be an old one,' Georgia said.

'It isn't. She's in it and it looks recent.'

I handed the frame to Georgia who shook her head. 'I've not seen it before. Mark?'

Mark shrugged. 'Me neither, but you're right about it being recent. The beard was new last year.'

Georgia handed back the frame as Dad returned to the lounge and distributed the photos.

'Can I ask you about this?' I said, after thanking him. I held up the frame for him to see.

'Ah!' he said, grimacing. 'I forgot that was there.'

'When was it taken?'

He sat back down in his chair. 'Remember me saying he came round with a gift for your mum's eightieth? It was taken then. Does it bother you because I can put it in a drawer if it does?'

'No. Keep it out. It's right that he's still part of your lives.'

'If you ever want to know anything about Flynn...' Mark said.

I wished I could make them happy by saying yes but it would be too hard for me, too raw, to hear all about his wife and maybe even a new family. I meant it when I'd said it was right that Flynn was part of their lives, but he couldn't be part of mine, so I shook my head.

'Nothing's changed there. I'm completely fine with you all seeing him – including you, Georgia, if you want to – but I don't want to know any details. Sorry.'

The sad expressions were too much for me so I added, 'But I'll let you know if that changes.'

It wouldn't, but I felt as though I needed to give them a sliver of hope. They agreed not to give me any Flynn updates and the subject was thankfully changed.

A little later, the clock above the fireplace released a delightful ping as it did every hour and Georgia stretched.

'Ten o'clock,' she said. 'Our cue to head off to our beds.'

Dad said he'd poke his head round the bedroom door to see whether Mum was awake so we could say goodnight if she was. I'd carefully placed my photos in my handbag and pushed one arm into my coat sleeve when Dad's mournful cry of, 'No!' chilled me to the bone.

Georgia, Mark and I raced down the hall to my parents' bedroom and my heart shattered into a million pieces at the sight of my dad kneeling on the floor, cradling Mum's limp body against his. Her eyes were open, his were tightly closed, and he was repeating 'no' over and over again.

30

Georgia released a mournful wail and dropped to her knees beside Dad. I pressed my hand to my mouth, my heart pounding, goose bumps breaking out over my body.

'Call an ambulance,' Mark said, pressing his phone into my hand. 'Put it on speaker.'

Gulping, I dialled 999 while he calmly took control of the situation, encouraging Georgia and Dad to release Mum. As I ran through the details with the emergency call handler, the three of them lifted Mum off the bed and laid her on the floor so Mark could commence CPR. As a first aider on the Mountain Rescue Team, he knew what he was doing.

I felt so helpless as I hovered in the doorway holding the phone out in front of me. My eyes were fixed on Mum but my head was back in Noah's room as two paramedics checked his body for vital signs and looked up at me with sad expressions. One of them spoke to me but I'd been that shocked I hadn't heard any of the words as I'd sagged against Flynn.

This time, it was Georgia sagging against me. Feeling her

shaking, I slipped my arm round her waist. It would be fine. Mark knew what he was doing and the call handler had told us there was a first responder in the area who'd be with us in minutes.

'I'll go down to the bottom of the drive to watch for them,' I said, pressing Mark's phone into Georgia's hand. Every second was precious and I didn't want to risk the first responder driving past because they couldn't see the house names in the dark.

Minutes later, I spotted the marked car and guided the first responder onto the drive then into Mum and Dad's bedroom with his defibrillator, but it was already too late and no amount of shocking was going to restart Mum's heart.

'I'm very sorry,' he said as he closed Mum's eyes.

Georgia ran from the bedroom. Mark placed a reassuring hand on Dad's back before going after her. My heart broke for my dad, standing there staring down at his beloved wife, eyes wide, head shaking, no doubt wondering how he was ever going to cope without her. My heart broke for my lovely mum, taken from us far too soon. For my sister whose cries I could hear from the lounge. For her grandchildren who adored her, her great-grandchildren who wouldn't get a chance to know her. And for me and the lost years.

'I know it's a difficult time, but I need to ask some questions about June's medical history,' the paramedic said. He'd introduced himself when he arrived but I hadn't taken it in. As he packed his equipment away, I spotted the name Ben on his uniform.

'Is there somewhere you'd rather go to answer them?' Ben asked.

'I don't want to leave her,' Dad said, his voice shaky.

'I understand. Would you like me to help you lift June back onto the bed?'

Dad nodded and the pair of them lifted Mum. There was a

woollen blanket draped over the back of her dressing table chair so I placed that gently over her body. Dad sat down next to Mum and held her hand. I turned away, blinking back tears. I wanted to be strong for Dad just now. The tears could come later.

An ambulance arrived while Ben was asking questions so he broke off to have a conversation with the crew outside before bringing them through to the bedroom. Dad asked us if we could wait in the lounge while he answered some questions about Mum's medical history.

Mum's death, like Noah's, was classed as unexpected but, because of her age and whatever Dad had shared about her medical history, we were advised that there was no need for the police to attend and we were free to contact a funeral director. Trenham & Sons Funeral Directors had handled everything with dignity and respect when Noah passed so there was no question mark over using them again. Mark made the call and reported that they'd be with us within three-quarters of an hour. The ambulance crew and Ben waited until they arrived.

It was past midnight when Frankie Trenham and two of his sons left to take Mum to their chapel of rest. With Dad's permission, Georgia and Mark went back inside to put fresh linen on the bed and I stood on the doorstep with him watching one of Frankie's sons pull off the drive and out of sight.

'I can't believe that's June in there.' Dad's voice cracked mid-sentence, the later words coming out as a whisper.

I couldn't believe it either and I couldn't get any words out over the lump in my throat so I slipped my hand into his and we stood together staring into the darkness. How had the evening ended like this? Mum hadn't been feeling her best at the party but she'd still been laughing and joking. How could she have gone from that to being on her way to the chapel of rest?

'That must have been hard for you,' Dad said after a while.

'It was hard for all of us.'

'I mean after Noah.'

'Lots of difficult memories,' I admitted. 'Not something I ever wanted to go through again, but I'm glad I was there and you didn't have to face it alone. I'm so sorry, Dad.'

He sighed heavily. 'It feels like a bad dream. One minute, I have this sense that I'm hovering overhead watching it happening to someone else and the next minute it hits me that it's happening to me.'

It was cold on the doorstep but I sensed Dad needed to stay a little longer.

'She loved this view,' he said, eventually. 'Not that we can see far right now. I remember us coming to view the house. It was a beautiful spring day and June was heavily pregnant with you. We stood right here, facing out to the lake before we knocked and she said, *I don't care how dated it is inside or how much work needs doing, this is the place and we're going to be so happy here.*'

'And you were,' I said, squeezing his hand.

'We certainly were. I'm not sure how I feel about staying here long-term without her. She wanted me to, but I don't know if I can.'

'There's no rush to make any decisions like that, Dad. When the time's right for you, Georgia and I will be here to support you, whatever you decide.'

We went back inside and closed the door as Georgia and Mark appeared from the bedroom. Georgia's eyes and nose were red – something which always happened to her when she cried – so she'd clearly had another moment while she was away from Dad. I knew she'd jump into practical mode around him as the changing of the bedding had already shown.

'Mark needs to get home as he's got an early start at work tomorrow but I'd like to stay if that's okay with you, Dad.'

'Me too,' I said.

I thought he'd object, saying there was nothing we could do and we should go home and get some sleep, but he nodded slowly. 'The company would be appreciated.'

Before Mark left, we debated whether to tell Keira and Regan but it felt too late to ring them. The news could wait until the morning, especially as Keira and Johnnie were already facing disrupted sleep from Arlo's arrival and we didn't want to exacerbate that.

'I keep going over it all in my mind and I still think I should have checked on her earlier,' Dad said after Mark had gone.

'You can't think like that, Dad,' Georgia said. 'You heard what the paramedics said.'

Dad had berated himself earlier and the medical team had been full of reassurances that he mustn't beat himself up because it could just as easily have happened in the middle of the night when he was right beside her but asleep. They also said that, if it had been a cardiac arrest as suspected, she'd have been unconscious and not felt a thing. It was a small sliver of comfort in a dire situation.

'If it helps, I had the same thoughts when Noah died,' I said. 'I heard him coming home from the party. I'd been awake for a while and I thought about wishing him a happy new year and asking if he'd had a good time, but it was all warm and cosy under the duvet so I stayed where I was. The next day, I toyed with going in and waking him up but he hated it when I did that, especially when he'd been out till the early hours, so I left it. The thing is, if I had checked on him, what would have happened? The odds of me going into his room at the exact moment when he was in trouble were miniscule and, even if I had, could I have saved him? Could Flynn? If you had checked on Mum, you'd have likely found her asleep and left her in peace, or it would have already been too late. Please don't take on the blame for this because it can take you to some seriously dark places. Believe me, I know.'

'When did you stop blaming yourself?' Dad asked.

'Honestly? Just now when I said that.'

Dad's eyes widened. 'Oh, Mel. You've really blamed yourself for all these years?'

I nodded. 'For that and for so much more. I don't want to make this about me, but take it from someone who's been there that if you have medical professionals telling you there's nothing you could have done, then there really is nothing you could have done. Don't torment yourself thinking otherwise.'

The three of us stayed up talking for the next hour or so before Dad announced that he was flagging. He wasn't convinced he'd manage to sleep but he felt like he should try as the week ahead was going to be difficult with people to notify and arrangements to be made. Georgia and I said we'd help with as much as we could so he needn't worry about having everything to tackle on his own.

Georgia released a long sigh after we heard Dad's bedroom door close. 'That was horrific. I can't believe she's gone. Poor Dad. I don't...'

But her emotions prevented her from finishing the sentence. I rushed over to her and held her and stroked her hair as she cried. I wished I could cry too. I wanted to but the tears wouldn't come. Maybe it was the shock and it would catch up with me later when I was on my own.

It took a while for Georgia's tears to subside but, when they did, I fetched her a glass of water and a cold, damp flannel to place over her sore eyes.

'I've been thinking about what Mum said when they left the

party,' she said, removing the flannel from her eyes after a few minutes. 'She's never told me she loves me before. Do you think it's possible she somehow knew?'

'I was thinking the same thing myself. They never told me the outcome of any of her tests either – kept saying there was nothing conclusive – but I'm wondering if they were stalling for time. Did they tell you anything?'

'No – just kept saying Mum needed more tests. Makes me wonder if they'd discovered it was her heart that was the problem.'

'It's possible,' I said, nodding. 'When we were outside, Dad said he wasn't sure if he could stay here without Mum but that she wanted him to. They could have been having end-of-life conversations on the back of whatever they'd found out.'

'But why not tell us? They told us about the breast cancer scare.'

'Not at the time. I only found out because I turned up on appointment day. It's possible they'd never have said anything but I put them under pressure so it came out.'

Georgia sighed. 'You could be right, although why tell you about the funny turn at the hospital if they wanted to keep us in the dark?'

'Maybe they weren't expecting it to be anything serious. It's probably not helpful speculating. I'm sure it'll come out across the week.' I ran my hands down my face, feeling drained. 'I'm going to try for some sleep. There'll be a lot to do tomorrow.'

'Yeah, I should probably try too.'

We stood up and hugged each other once more before heading off to our former bedrooms. I sat on the edge of my bed, my head dipped. The last time I'd stayed in this room had been the night before I left for Newcastle. I never imagined that the next time I stayed would be the night my mum died. As a wave of deep sadness swept through me, I closed my eyes tightly, expecting the tears to fall, but they didn't. My eyes burned but they remained dry. I had to still be in shock. Maybe tomorrow.

31

Georgia joined me in the kitchen at half six the following morning as I was boiling the kettle.

'I've looked in on Dad,' she said. 'I woke up in this stupid panic that he'd have joined Mum, but he's sound asleep. I'm thinking we're best to leave him be.'

'I agree. It probably took him ages to settle so he might as well sleep while he can. How are you feeling?'

'I'm devastated, Mel.' Her voice cracked and tears tracked down her cheeks. 'I thought we'd have her for a lot longer. I remember when we were kids, someone living into their seventies was thought to have had a long life but, these days, eighty's no age.'

I wrapped my arms round her and stroked her back as she sobbed. Once again, my throat was tight and my eyes were burning, but I still couldn't seem to release any tears. What was wrong with me?

Dad joined us in the lounge shortly after eight, wearing his pyjamas and a dressing gown.

'Did you manage to get any sleep?' I asked.

'Yes, but I've no idea how. It took me forever to drift off.'

'Breakfast?' Georgia asked.

'I'm not hungry, but a cup of tea would be good.'

I wasn't going to tell Dad he should eat something. I'd hated people trying to force food down my throat after Noah died, as though I was a small child being told to eat their vegetables. Dad would eat when he was ready. I made a round of drinks while Georgia nipped outside to phone Regan, hoping to catch him before he set off to work.

'How did he take it?' I asked as she entered the kitchen through the back door.

'Shocked, upset, gutted he was away for the weekend and missed lunch with her but I reminded him he wouldn't have seen her anyway because she was skipping lunch for the engagement party. I think that helped ease the guilt.'

'Are you going to call Keira now?'

'It might be better face to face. Johnnie'll be at work already and I can't bear the thought of her being all upset while she's got a baby and a toddler to care for. But that means abandoning Dad.'

'Don't you worry about that. I'll let Rosie and Oliver know what's happening and I'll stay here.'

Georgia carried Dad's drink through to the lounge and told him she was going to see Keira but would be back later.

'Keira's not going to take it well,' Dad said, shaking his head when Georgia had left in his car. 'Your mum was close to all her grandchildren but, after Astrid was born, she formed an extra-special bond with Keira. When she was on maternity leave, she'd often pop round and June was looking forward to her doing the same with Arlo.'

I couldn't think of anything helpful to say to that, so I sipped on my tea. It was probably best for Dad if I remained silent, giving him a chance to say what he wanted when he wanted.

'She loved her family so much, you know,' he said after a while. 'She often said how lucky we were that everyone had settled round here and, even though you had your time in Newcastle, she never doubted that you'd return one day.' He smiled ruefully. 'Took a bit longer than we'd have hoped, but she was right.'

'If I'd have known this was going to happen—'

Dad raised his hand to stop me. 'Don't even go there. None of us can see into the future and you going down a tunnel of regrets isn't going to help anyone. The important thing is you did return and everything was right in the world again. She was so happy to have you back. Tuesday lunches with you were the highlight of her week.'

'Were they really?'

'They were. She loves... loved... Sunday lunch with the whole family but she could find it a bit exhausting having everyone together. She preferred spending time with you all individually, properly talking without all the distractions and interruptions.'

'I loved our Tuesday lunches too. I know things are going to be up in the air for the next couple of weeks but I think we should keep them going if that's okay with you.'

Dad's eyes clouded with tears and he nodded and gulped. 'I'd like that.'

* * *

By the time Georgia returned to Derwent Rise, it was late morning. Between us, Dad and I had made most of the phone calls to friends and relatives to let them know about Mum. A couple of their closest friends offered to phone other villagers which was helpful.

As anticipated, Keira had taken the news very badly, especially as she felt she'd had some part to play in it by getting Mum and Dad to care for Astrid yesterday. No matter what Georgia said, she couldn't seem to bring her round. Dad decided she needed to hear it from him so he and Georgia went to Keira's while I nipped back to Willowdale Hall to shower and change. Once I'd done that, I emptied the contents of my evening clutch bag onto my bed, intending to swap them into my regular bag. With everything that had happened, I'd completely forgotten about Dad printing those photos from our alpaca meet and greet. I studied the one of Mum with Georgia, Dad and me. She'd been in her element that day and this photo perfectly captured that.

Thinking about the photos reminded me of the one I'd spotted of Flynn with Mum. It struck me that he hadn't been on the list Dad and I had compiled of people to ring, but he'd want to know. It was possible that Dad hadn't added Flynn to the list for my sake and might have called him this morning but, if he hadn't, maybe Mark could do that. It wouldn't feel right coming from me. *Hi, it's me. You gave me your contact details for if and when I was ready to talk. Well, I've decided I don't want to talk but I thought you should know that my mum died last night.*

Flynn would presumably want to come to the funeral. That would make an already difficult day even harder but this was about my parents, not me. They'd loved him and he clearly still felt the same way about them to have stayed in touch. I kicked myself that I hadn't taken him up on his offer to talk after all. If I had, I wouldn't be in this predicament, but the truth was I hadn't and still didn't want to meet up with him. For me, that wound had never healed and I didn't want to deepen it. I didn't want to cause Flynn further damage either.

When I returned to Derwent Rise, Dad was on the phone. From what I could hear of the conversation, my guess was that it was someone from the village who'd heard the news third hand and wanted to pass on their condolences. I spotted Georgia in the back garden hanging out the load of washing I'd put on this morning in between phone calls so I indicated to Dad that I was going out to her. She had her back to the house and, as I approached, I realised she wasn't actually hanging anything up – just staring at the clothes she'd already put on the line.

'Georgia?' I said gently, not wanting to scare her by suddenly appearing by her side.

She turned round, tears streaming down her cheeks once more. 'Hanging up Mum's clothes,' she said, her voice breaking, 'knowing we won't...'

There was no need for her to finish that sentence. The cream top flapping in the wind in front of us was Mum's go-to top – one of her favourites which she said she could dress up or down and never seemed to age no matter how many times she washed it.

'It felt weird putting them in the machine,' I admitted, drawing her into a hug. 'But I didn't want to leave them in the basket for Dad to see to later.'

'You did the right thing. It's just... I can't believe she's gone.'

I hung up the last of the clothes while Georgia wiped her cheeks and blew her nose. What must she think of me for not crying? Hopefully she hadn't noticed.

'How's Dad been?' I asked.

'He's been on the phone most of the time. Putting on a brave face, I think.'

We went back inside just as Dad was ending his call.

'Anything you need us to do?' I asked.

Dad shook his head. 'You don't need to stay with me, you know. I appreciated your help with the calls and will appreciate it again when we have a date for the funeral, but I'm conscious I'm keeping you both from your jobs.'

'I'd booked today off with going away for the weekend,' Georgia said. 'So I'm free all day.'

'And I can be flexible with my hours,' I said. 'But if you do want some alone time, we don't want to crowd you.' I'd felt crowded when Noah died. I knew my family wanted to help and that they were grieving themselves but there were so many moments in the days following his death where I wanted to yell at them all to leave me alone because I couldn't stand the whispers, the concerned looks, the offers to make a cup of tea as though that could make things better.

Dad pondered for a moment. 'There's a couple of things I'd like to talk to you both about but how about some lunch first? Nothing fancy – just a tin of soup – then we can chat and you can have the rest of the afternoon free.'

Georgia and I agreed to his suggestion and soon had steaming bowls of spicy parsnip soup in front of us. It was one of my favourite flavours and it smelled delicious but I could only manage a few mouthfuls and even they were a struggle to force down. Georgia played with hers and Dad only managed about a third of his bowl.

'I thought I was hungry,' he said, 'but it seems none of us were. Leave the bowls – something to keep me busy later – and let's go through to the lounge for that talk.'

Georgia and I followed him and settled next to each other on the corner sofa while he sat back in the armchair, his hands steepled against his lips as though in silent prayer.

'We don't officially know the cause of death, but it's fair to assume it was a cardiac arrest. As you know, your mum had been having various tests and scans. We found out her heart wasn't doing so well and didn't want to say anything to you until we knew the specifics. We found out at the start of last week that it was coronary heart disease and she wanted a bit of time to come to terms with the news herself before telling you both. The plan was to let you know this week, but we were hit with the worst-case scenario before that could happen. I know that might anger or frustrate you but—'

'You don't have to justify yourself,' I interrupted. Dad was in enough pain and no way was I going to add to it. 'This was Mum's and your decision to make and I can completely understand wanting some time to process things first.'

'Me too,' Georgia agreed. 'No recriminations here.'

The tension left Dad's shoulders. 'Thank you. The other thing I wanted to say was that your mum and I have spent a lot of time over the past week talking about the wonderful life we've had together and what the future would look like for me without her in it if the worst happened. The reflection part was good but the future part was incredibly difficult because I'm really not inter-ested in a life without your mum in it. But that's the way the dice roll and I will find the strength somehow to do this without her.'

Georgia had started crying again and I took her hand in mine. There were still no tears from me, but I could barely breathe for the enormous lump blocking my throat. I didn't want Dad to have to face the future without the love of his life. I didn't want to face the future without my mum. I'd expected them both to be around for many more years and to have the chance to make them proud of me for finally getting my life back on track. It was too early to say how much of a setback Mum's death was going to be, but there'd definitely be a derailment. After my walk up Cat Bells with Alice, I'd sworn that the little things wouldn't derail me but this wasn't a little thing. This was huge.

'There are going to be a lot of tough days ahead,' Dad contin-ued, 'and, let's face it, nobody looks forward to a funeral. June has left detailed plans about what she wants, which I'll share with you once we secure a date. This is something we both did many years ago and, every so often, we've updated our wishes. I'm going to need your support and I'll be there for you in return but there'll be times when I just want to be alone and I hope you'll understand that. Some of those times, it'll be because I'm upset and I want to keep that private. I know there's nothing wrong with men showing their emotions but it's not how I was raised and, at my age, I'm not going to change. Other times, I'll want to be alone just to be alone. June was always the chatty one while I preferred to sit back and listen, so I know I'm going to find it hard being the centre of attention and having everyone asking if I'm okay and if I need anything. I know it's only because you care and I do appreciate that, but if I say I want to be alone, it's not code for me really wanting company but not wanting to say so. Does that make sense?'

'Perfect sense,' I said, having been in the same boat and knowing exactly where he was coming from. 'We won't crowd you. Just promise you'll say when you want some company, even if it's just to sit quietly while watching TV or reading a book.'

'I promise.'

Dad wanted some of that alone time now so we took our leave.

'Don't forget to bring the washing in,' Georgia said as Dad walked us to the door. 'As a heads-up, there's some of Mum's clothes out there.'

He nodded and hugged us both goodbye.

Dad had dropped Georgia off at her house after their visit to Keira so she had her car with her now. 'I know it's what he wants,' she said, opening her car door, 'but I feel bad about leaving him.'

'Me too, but I completely get everything he was saying. Everyone rallies around, wanting to take the pain away, but the truth is they can't. It's always there and sometimes you just need to be alone with it.'

Georgia looked as though she was going to ask me something, but her phone rang.

'It's Johnnie. I'd better get it.'

Although Georgia hadn't activated the speaker, she must have had the volume high as I could hear Johnnie.

'I'm so sorry to do this to you when you're with your dad, but Keira's been on the phone and she's in a right state with herself. Arlo and Astrid were crying too and I'd have gone home but we have a dog under sedation ready for an op and I'm the only one who can do it.'

'It's okay. I'm just leaving Dad's so I can drive to yours now and stay with her until you get home.'

They ended the conversation and Georgia gave me an apologetic shrug. 'Did you want to talk? Because it sounded like you did.'

'Gosh, no. I was just sharing an experience. You go and be with Keira.'

We hugged then both got into our cars and set off in opposite directions. As I drove along the drive at Willowdale Hall, I waved to Emma who was setting off with four of the alpacas and a group of women who all looked to be about Mum's age. Or the age Mum had been. That tennis ball in my throat was back and I knew there was no chance of me getting any work done this afternoon. I needed to be outdoors but not here. Much as I loved the estate, there were too many trees and I needed open space.

I parked outside the hall and ran inside to change into my walking gear. I shoved my woolly hat and waterproof in my small backpack along with a cereal bar, filled my metal bottle with water then drove out of the estate again. I knew exactly where I was heading – a lake which wasn't on the popular tourist trails and therefore more likely to be quiet. It was possible I'd see other walkers but not many and that was what I needed.

Loweswater, one of the smallest bodies of water in the Lake District, was approximately a mile long and half a mile wide and found to the far west of the National Park. Nestled in a wooded valley and surrounded by fells, it was known as *the peaceful lake* because it wasn't as close to amenities and therefore didn't attract so many visitors. Walkers could take a circular route round the lake but, for me, the beauty of any of the lakes was viewing them from above. The added bonus of looking down on Loweswater was seeing Crummock Water too – a body of water to which Loweswater was once joined.

I parked in a layby and set off along the track across a field. With each step, I felt like a tightly wound Jack-in-a-box desperate to spring from my confines. My pace quickened to a jog, to a run, to a sprint. My muscles cried out in protest at the unexpected exercise and I struggled to catch my breath but I kept running, praying I wouldn't slip or go over on my ankle. I could have taken a higher path but I stayed on the level and kept going until my lungs protested so strongly that I had to stop. Bending forwards with my hands on my thighs, I gulped at the air, trying to catch my breath. It didn't help still having that ball of emotion lodged in my throat. I needed a damn good cry but the tears still wouldn't come. Would shouting or screaming help instead? I straightened up and looked around me. I was about halfway along the lake, although some distance above it. A couple of hikers with a dog were on the higher path but the area was otherwise deserted. Except it wasn't. There were animals and wildlife everywhere – Herdwick sheep in the field which ran alongside the track I'd taken, cows in the field beyond that and I knew that the conifers by the lake were home to red squirrels. This was *the peaceful lake* and I had no right to disturb that, no matter how much pain I was feeling, no matter how badly I could do with that release right now.

When I finally got my breathing back under control, I sank down onto a grassy slope and drank from my water bottle. How many times had my parents walked along this path or the one above as they explored their beloved lakes and fells? I imagined them sitting on this very spot with their flasks of tea and a piece of Kendal Mint Cake, Dad trotting out his usual joke about it bearing no resemblance to any cake he'd ever eaten. It must have been so hard for them when they couldn't do their walks anymore. I knew from Georgia that Mum had encouraged Dad to go without her, but he hadn't been interested. Might he be interested in a few walks with me instead? I'd give it some time before I suggested it.

I reflected on the time I'd spent with Mum since I returned to Willowdale and Dad's comment about Tuesday afternoons being the highlight of her week. They'd been a highlight for me too. It was so unfair that she'd been taken away just as we'd got our relationship back on track. I'd missed out on so much by leaving and I'd assumed we'd have years left to make up for it. I needed to focus on being grateful for the time we did have instead of what we could have had if I hadn't fled. I focused on Alice's words once more – *We can easily be knocked off balance but as long as we keep looking ahead instead of focusing on the past, we can get there.* I needed to do that for me and I needed to help Dad find a way to carve out a future for himself without the love of his life by his side. And in the process, maybe I'd find a way to do that for myself without Mum and without the two other loves of my life. Maybe.

32

On Thursday morning I woke up feeling concerned about Dad. Across the week, I'd respected his desire to have space. I'd checked in with him over the phone on Tuesday morning and he'd told me that Regan and Clarke were visiting after work so asked if I could give him some space for the rest of the day. Georgia and Keira had visited him on Wednesday afternoon and I'd spent the day with him yesterday. The results from Mum's post-mortem had come through and confirmed what we'd all suspected – sudden cardiac arrest. How strange that my eighty-year-old mum and my eighteen-year-old son had both died from fatal heart attacks, albeit for very different reasons. Both left gaping holes behind them and a trail of broken hearts. Having Mum's cause of death confirmed meant we were able to sort a date for the funeral so Dad and I spent most of the yesterday phoning round to let people know the arrangements.

With all those visitors and so much to do, Dad had barely left the house and that wasn't good so I phoned him after I made my morning coffee and suggested a walk together today. He passed on my offer but phoned back within the hour to say he'd changed his mind and getting out into the fresh air would be very welcome. As he hadn't spent much time in the fells since Mum's back problems started, he didn't want to go anywhere too strenuous but, equally, he'd prefer somewhere there weren't hordes of people. That was going to be a challenge. It was Good Friday, sunny and mild so there'd be people everywhere, somewhat limiting our options. I ambitiously suggested Latrigg to the northeast of Keswick but, when we approached it, we could see a stream of people making their ascent or descent.

'Why don't we try the old railway?' I suggested. 'If it's just as busy, we can return to Willowdale and walk round the lake instead.'

The three-mile former railway line ran from Keswick to just outside the village of Threlkeld and was popular with walkers and cyclists as well as being pushchair and wheelchair friendly thanks to the smooth tarmac surface. Those wanting an extended circular walk could cross over the main road instead of turning off to the village and follow the route back into Keswick via Castlerigg Stone Circle. Dad and I decided to take the circular route but, if the popular stone circle was too busy, we could walk straight past it.

We were about halfway along the railway track when Dad announced that he'd spoken to Flynn this morning. My stomach lurched at the mention of his name and what I knew would be coming next.

'I've invited him to the funeral.'

I'd already found out from Georgia that Dad had rung Flynn on Monday, wanting the news to come directly from him.

'Is he coming?'

'Yes, but he isn't coming to the inn afterwards.'

'Because of me?'

He sighed. 'He said he doesn't want to cause any tension on an already difficult day.'

We continued on in silence and I tried to make myself say the words I was certain Dad wanted to hear – *I'll call him and let him know it's okay* – but I couldn't do it. This was hard enough without throwing a telephone conversation with Flynn into the mix.

'I was wondering if you could—' Dad started.

'I can't. I'm sorry. It's right that he comes to the funeral and I think he should come to the wake too but please don't ask me to tell him that myself.'

'Why won't you speak to him, Mel? I don't understand.'

That made two of us! 'It's complicated. And I know some people think that's a pathetic non-excuse but it's all I have. You can tell him he has my blessing to be there, but I'm not going to get in touch with him to give it myself.'

'I just think that, if you—'

'Dad!' The word came out a bit louder and harsher than I intended and I apologised. 'Can we drop the subject, please? You asked for space this week and I've respected that. Not talking about Flynn is my request and I'd appreciate if you respect that in return.'

'Okay,' he said. 'I'm not convinced that avoiding him is the right thing to do but I'll respect your wishes.'

'Good. Thank you.'

'If you ever do want to talk...'

'I appreciate the offer, but I'm fine and dandy.' I cringed inwardly. *Fine and dandy?* I couldn't remember the last time I'd used that old-fashioned phrase and, truth be told, I was anything but fine and dandy, but the last thing I was going to do was unleash it all on my dad with what he was going through right now.

We walked in silence for several minutes and I hated the tension between us. I needed a subject change.

'So, good news, Dougie's team are almost ready to start working on the boat house...'

It couldn't have been a better distraction. With Dad sharing my passion for history and old buildings, the conversation flowed all the way to the stone circle. We talked in more detail about the restoration of Willowdale Hall, the other projects I was working on now, and the various projects I'd worked on while I was living in Newcastle.

'It's looking busy,' I said as we reached the trail of cars parked on Castle Lane – the road running alongside the stone circle. 'Go in or go past?'

We paused by the first entrance and looked into the field where there were people wandering between the stones, taking in the views and posing for photos.

'I've seen it busier,' he said. 'Let's go in.'

Several children and a few adults were clambering onto the smaller stones and I sighed inwardly. There were signs at the entrance stating *no climbing* and it frustrated me when people ignored that, especially at a site which had been around since about 3000 BC and needed preserving. A cyclist had even propped his bike up against one of the taller stones.

'I know,' Dad murmured, catching me scowling. 'Drives me mad too. Don't look at it. Look at the view instead.'

We walked round the circle and stood at the far end of the field. Potentially one of the earliest of the 300-plus stone circles in Britain, the views from Castlerigg were second to none. Over-looking the Thirlmere Valley, the vista took in the fells of Helvellyn and High Seat.

'It's so beautiful,' I said.

'That's why I proposed to your mum here.'

My head shot round. 'You did? Why didn't I know that?'

He shrugged. 'I guess it never came up.'

'Would you tell me about it now? Only if it's not too painful.'

He smiled. 'That memory could never be painful.'

Dad had worked in the finance department for the water authority all his life, surviving through many changes over the years and finishing his career as finance director. I knew that my parents had met there but I realised I didn't know their story. When he'd mentioned in his speech at Mum's birthday that it had taken him eighteen months to ask her out, that had been news to me.

He told me that, when he was in his early twenties and Mum was in her late teens, she'd joined the typing pool and he'd thought she was the most beautiful woman he'd ever seen. He'd wanted to ask her out but she was really confident and popular and he was quiet and shy so he couldn't imagine she'd be interested in him. She often spoke to him but he thought she was just being nice. After a couple of drinks at the Christmas party eighteen months later, he braved asking her to dance and was stunned when she said yes. While they danced, she told him that, if he asked her on a date, the answer would be the same. So he did ask, she said yes, and then she proceeded to give him a lecture about what a tiresome eighteen months it had been making up reasons to visit the finance department and dropping subtle hints that she liked him. I smiled at the thought of her giving him what for. She'd never have asked him for a date outright – it hadn't been the done thing back then – and it tickled me that Dad had been as useless at noticing subtlety as I was.

'That sounds very much like Mum,' I said.

'She was everything I'd ever hoped for in a partner and a million things more. I knew early on that I wanted to spend the rest of my life with her and just needed to find the right time to ask her. I brought her here on the first day of spring, telling her it was to watch the sun set, but it was really to ask her to marry me. I knew how much she loved reading love stories so I wanted to do something romantic. I'd prepared a poem and everything but I was so nervous. I couldn't stop fidgeting and, just before the sun dipped out of sight, she turned to me and said, *For goodness' sake, Bruce, are you going to ask me to marry you or do I have to get down on bended knee myself?* Knowing it was going to be a yes gave me the confidence to do what I'd intended to do.'

'Aw, that's lovely. And I hadn't realised Mum was quite so feisty back then.'

'She's always been feisty – just like someone else I know.' He raised his eyebrows at me and I smiled.

'So what was the poem?'

'Oh, gosh, it was awful and *poem* was a stretch – more like a few rhyming lines. Let's see if I can remember it.' His lips moved as though reciting it. 'Got it!'

> *Spring is here, which brings new life*
> *The flowers are pushing through*
> *Please say yes to being my wife*
> *I'll never stop loving you*
> *Spring is here, a brand-new start*
> *The birds are in fine song*
> *To you, my dear, I give my heart*
> *I'll love you my whole life long.*

'Aw, Dad, that's beautiful.'

'And I did,' he whispered, his eyes clouding with tears. 'I loved her my whole life long. I just wish we'd had longer.'

I hugged him tightly and we stood there for several minutes in this place that I hadn't realised was quite so special to him. Other than that sticky moment regarding Flynn, it had been a lovely walk full of interesting conversations but one thing had concerned me – that Dad seemed on exceptionally good form for someone who'd lost his wife less than a week ago. But holding him now, it was clear that he was struggling just as much as the rest of us. He'd already shared that he was of the *stiff upper lip* generation so I hadn't expected him to break down in floods of tears in front of me, but it was comforting to see some emotion.

'Thanks for sharing that with me,' I said as we left the stone circle and set off down Castle Lane for the last stretch of our walk into Keswick. 'I know you won't like this question, but how are you *really* doing?'

'I'm fine.'

'Fine means a million different things. Define yours.'

He laughed at that. 'My fine is fine. I wish with all my heart that what happened on Sunday hadn't happened but I can't change it.'

That didn't really answer my question but I wasn't going to push him any further.

'I know what you're thinking,' he said after a while. 'But you can stop worrying about me. When you lose someone you love, I know how important it is to give way to your emotions instead of bottling it all up but, like I said to you and Georgia, I'm not the sort of person who'll do that in front of others. That's private but the important thing is that I've done it.'

I could feel his gaze on me and wondered if that was a dig at me about Mum or perhaps even about Noah. Or both. I had kept it all bottled up and it terrified me that one day soon the bottle might become too full and the cork would spring out. It would be like opening up one of those cans full of springy worms and them escaping everywhere. If I could just shed a few tears, maybe it would be enough, but they just wouldn't come. Maybe they would at the funeral next Friday. When they did, I just hoped that it would be a bit of seepage and not the uncorking of the bottle because I couldn't help thinking that, if and when the cork did come out, it would be carnage.

33

A week later, it was the final Friday in April and Mum's funeral. I woke up feeling a heaviness on my chest. As I got ready, back to black, sadness wrapped itself around me and clung on tight, but those tears still refused to fall.

After several warm and sunny days, it was overcast and cool with rain expected by late afternoon. The grey sky mirrored the sombre mood as a small group of us gathered at Derwent Rise to travel in a funeral limousine with Dad. Mum's wishes had been for a service at Willowdale Methodist Church, where she'd been a member of the congregation, and afterwards at North Lakes Crematorium near Penrith – the same place where Noah had been cremated.

The Reverend Avryl Palmer read out the eulogy she'd prepared following a discussion with Dad, Georgia and me earlier in the week. She'd included comments from Mum's grandchildren and closest friends. Many of them made me smile and some drew laughter, which took me back to Noah's funeral when I'd been furious with people for laughing when there was nothing remotely funny about my boy lying in a wooden box.

Laughter was comforting and it felt good to commemorate the strong, vivacious woman Mum had been, celebrating her life instead of just mourning her death.

Georgia and I sat either side of Dad. She cried throughout the service and I willed myself to shed a couple of tears to show I cared, but to no avail. Dad's eyes were watery but he held it together somehow.

Reverend Palmer announced that there'd be further prayers at the crematorium and all were welcome. As the organist played a mournful tune I didn't recognise, we filed out. I kept my head down, not wanting to catch anyone's eye, ashamed that I wasn't in bits like my sister.

Back in the limo, onto the crem, another song, more prayers, more tears from Georgia and dry eyes from me and an open invitation from Reverend Palmer to join the family back at Lakeside Inn.

As we led the mourners outside, I did look up this time and my eyes met Flynn's. He was in a row near the back wearing a charcoal-grey suit and black tie. His hair had been cut and his beard trimmed. He'd always been a very handsome man but it crossed my mind that he'd aged well and looked even better with streaks of grey in his hair and beard. He nodded at me, that small gesture conveying his sorrow. I nodded back to him in acceptance. I hadn't wanted to call him but I was going to need to speak to him at the pub and thank him for coming. It was the right thing to do.

* * *

'Who are you looking for?' Dad asked back at Lakeside Inn a bit later.

'Nobody. Just seeing who's here.'

Dad evidently didn't buy that. 'Flynn's not here. He came to see me yesterday and told me he'd be at the church and crem but not here.'

'Did he say why?'

Dad looked at me meaningfully. As if I hadn't already guessed that I was the reason.

'I told him you were fine with it,' he said, 'but he said he didn't want to encroach.'

I could fill in the missing words – *If you'd called him like I asked...* – and felt terrible. One of Mum and Dad's friends was hovering nearby, clearly eager to speak to him, so I went in search of Mark. Flynn *should* be here. I felt guilty about enough things in my life without adding this to the list. Mark was near the bar talking to Regan and Clarke so I apologised to the boys and pulled him to one side.

'Can you call Flynn but give me your phone?'

He looked puzzled but handed me his phone with Flynn's number on the screen. I pressed the call button as I slipped out of the bar into the quieter foyer.

'Hi, Mark,' Flynn said.

'It's not Mark, it's Mel.'

There was a pause – presumably a shocked one – before he spoke. 'Mel? Everything okay? Sorry, stupid question under the circumstances. I'm so sorry about your mum.'

'Thank you. Look, I know we haven't spoken yet and, well...' I sighed. 'This isn't about that. I thought you'd be at the wake and you're not and I know it's probably because we haven't spoken but you mean a lot to my parents and I know Dad really wants you here, so if there's any possibility at all that you can get here, it would be really appreciated.'

I hoped that my garbled speech had sounded more like a polite request than an order.

There was another pause. 'I can, but only if you're sure you're all right with me being there.'

'I'm sure.'

'Okay. Give me twenty minutes.'

I returned Mark's phone, got myself a drink and took it outside to where there were several metal tables and chairs in the garden overlooking the lake.

'Not escaping to The White Willow this time?' Georgia asked, joining me at my table moments later.

'Not this time, although it's very tempting. Flynn's on his way.'

'Oh!'

I told her about the conversation with Dad and my subsequent call.

'Will you be okay?' she asked.

'I'll have to be. Dad needs this and it's only fair that Flynn has a proper chance to say goodbye.'

'You've got this,' she said, squeezing my hand across the table.

'Do you think I'm a bad person?' I asked her.

'For not wanting Flynn to be here? Of course not!'

'No, not that. It's Mum. I haven't cried about her. I mean, I shed a few tears the night it happened but it wasn't much and there's been nothing since.'

'I think I might have shed enough for the pair of us,' she said. 'Not crying doesn't make you a bad person and it certainly doesn't mean you don't care. You already know that I cry at everything, but I work with someone who says she hasn't cried since she was little. We all handle our emotions differently.'

I smiled and thanked her but it was an unhelpful platitude – the sort of thing I'd have said to Georgia if our roles had been reversed in the hope of providing some comfort. It didn't bring me any because I knew I was an emotional person who used to cry all the time. Why not now?

'How did it feel seeing Flynn at the crem?' Georgia asked.

I thought for a moment. 'Surprisingly comforting, but then I got here and I was relieved when Dad said he wasn't coming. Not that that feeling lasted long. Guilt took over that it was my fault and I should have called him when Dad wanted me to. I feel like a walking contradiction.'

'Everything's bound to feel off-kilter just now. It does for me and I don't have as much going on as you. You've done the right thing calling Flynn and it's not like you need to talk for hours. He'll understand that this isn't the time or place.'

'Yeah. Hopefully a hello will be enough.' I took a sip of my drink. 'I still don't want to know anything about him in the meantime.'

She made a zipping motion across her lips and we sat in companionable silence, sipping on our glasses of wine. I kept thinking about Flynn not being here. I knew why he'd dipped out despite Dad giving him the message that it was okay with me. It was because he'd put the ball in my court by giving me his contact details and saying it was up to me to get in touch when and if I was ready. I hadn't been in touch which told him I wasn't in that place and he'd respected my wishes and given me space. Typical Flynn, kind as ever.

Keira appeared and asked Georgia if she could look after Astrid while she changed Arlo's nappy. I watched my sister in the role of doting grandparent and thought about how much Mum had loved being a grandparent and great-grandparent. I'd never get to do that. Mum had been Grandma and Georgia had chosen to be Nanna. What moniker would I have gone for if Noah had lived and had children? As that ball of emotion inside me grew with the question, I tried to shove it from my mind. I needed to remain strong because, any moment now, Flynn would arrive.

34

Astrid spilt her drink down her dress so Georgia took her inside to dry her off. While they were gone, various friends of my parents – many of whom I recognised from Mum's eightieth – approached me to express their condolences. This time, instead of the jokes about when I was coming home, they shared how delighted Mum had been to have me back, how much she'd loved spending time with me, how proud she was of me, and how excited she'd been about me working at my beloved Willowdale Hall.

While each comment reassured me that the bruises in our relationship had healed, they saddened me too. By the time I spotted Flynn in the distance walking across the car park towards the side entrance, I was feeling extremely emotional. I needed to gather myself together before I saw him, but there was nowhere for me to go. There was nowhere to hide in the garden, the mourners had pretty much taken over inside, The White Willow was open and serving customers, and Willowdale Marina would be busy too. The only place I could think of where people might not be was the bench under the giant willow tree on the village green.

I downed the rest of my drink, slipped my jacket on, grabbed my bag and hastened out of the garden and across the car park before Flynn could find me. My stomach sank as I spotted a woman sitting on the bench talking on her phone while a black pug sniffed the daffodils. I was about to re-think when she wandered off, still chatting, so I dashed across the road and plonked myself down on the bench before anyone else could appear. I needed five minutes, that was all. Maybe ten. I'd close my eyes and try to relax.

The sound of a car horn startled me and I opened my eyes with a jolt. How had I managed to nod off sitting upright on a bench? I blinked a few times and ran my hands through my hair, trying to reorientate myself, and that's when I saw him, standing on the opposite side of the road. He slowly, seemingly hesitantly, raised his hand in a gesture that felt like half-wave, half-peace offering.

I didn't want Flynn to cross the road and join me on the bench. We'd be too close together if he did and it was safer to maintain some distance. I picked up my bag, paused on the footpath for a couple of passing cyclists, then joined him, keeping several feet between us.

'Thanks for coming,' I said, trying to channel the professional businesswoman in me to keep things civil and emotion-free. Not easy when my heart was racing so fast and thoughts of how good he looked were swirling round my mind.

'Thanks for calling me.'

'I shouldn't have had to. My dad had already told you I was okay with you coming and I thought...' I broke off with a sigh. Why was I lecturing him when a *you're welcome* would have sufficed? I softened my voice. 'Sorry. Tough day.'

'It's okay. Your dad said you were there when he found her. That must have been so hard.'

I could tell from the concerned way he was looking at me that he didn't just mean finding Mum. Flynn was the one person who could truly understand how devastating it had been to go through something like that – twice in my case – and I suddenly wanted to share it with him.

'It was like Noah—' But my throat was so tight that no more words would come. Tears pooled in my eyes and, as they spilled down my cheeks, Flynn closed the gap between us, pulled me into his embrace and I didn't resist.

With his strong arms around me and his head resting against mine, I had the sensation of finally being home. I used to think that there was nothing that couldn't be resolved by one of Flynn's incredible hugs. Until the worst thing possible happened and I was so mad with the world that I couldn't bear for him to touch me because a hug was *not* going to make that better. It wasn't going to bring our son back. So many memories flooded back of being in Flynn's arms – everything from a welcoming *good morning* embrace to a comforting *it'll be all right* hug to a passionate *take me to bed* clinch.

He tightened his hold and I responded by doing the same, my heart beating faster, butterflies swirling in my stomach. So many emotions were bubbling close to the surface, joy one moment, desolation the next and I could feel that cork inching out of the bottle. With a gasp, I released Flynn and stepped back. Not here. I couldn't lose it here. If that cork broke free, years of grief would come pouring out and I couldn't do that to my dad, my family, Flynn. Being here right now was meant to be a celebration of Mum's life and an emotional breakdown from me wasn't on the agenda. I needed to reapply my *nothing-to-see-here* mask and take control.

'I need to make sure my dad's okay so thank you for coming,' I said, aware of how exceptionally formal I sounded. 'Get yourself a drink. Mingle.'

Flynn tilted his head to one side, a slight frown rumpling his forehead.

'Thanks for coming.'

'You've already said that.'

'Because I mean it. Dad'll be very grateful. You mean a lot to him.'

'And you?' he asked.

The butterflies went wild as he held my gaze, an intensity in his eyes. I chose to ignore the possibility that he was asking if he meant a lot to me too. We really didn't want to open that can of worms.

'I'm grateful too,' I responded before walking past him to return to the wake. When did walking away become my default mode for when things got tough? I didn't want to be that person but, right now, I didn't feel like I had much choice.

35

On Sunday, the usual suspects plus Auntie Sue gathered at Georgia and Mark's for a barbeque. The mild sunny weather was set to turn to rain by the end of the week so it made sense to make the most of it while we could.

Mum had been quite set in her ways about having a traditional roast dinner for Sunday lunch and I think it was easier on us all by making the first Sunday get-together since her death something different. Had we gone for the roast, there'd have been the formality of sitting around the dining table and being acutely aware that her usual chair was empty. Plus barbequing gave Dad a focus as he could never resist taking over as head chef.

After everyone finished eating, Dad proposed a toast to Mum and raised his glass towards the sky. 'I know you're looking down on us, June, and very likely tutting and rolling your eyes at the absence of the Sunday roast. We miss you and wish you were here.'

His toast led into an afternoon of sharing our favourite memories of Mum. There was a lot of laughter and some tears. Not from me, though. I kept telling myself I didn't need to be strong and keep it all in in front of my family, but I knew that wasn't the reason the tears stayed at bay. A lot of soul searching over the weekend had made me realise that I wasn't just grieving for Mum – I was also grieving for Noah and everything I'd lost when he died. After seven years and four months of not dealing with any of those feelings, I was terrified of what would happen when the cork on my bottle of emotions was finally released.

I drove Dad back to Derwent Rise later that afternoon and joined him inside for a coffee.

'It was really special hearing everyone's memories today,' Dad said when we sat down in the lounge with our drinks. 'If June was watching us, she'd have loved it too.'

'It was lovely how all our memories were so different.'

I glanced around the room, noticing that the carpet had been vacuumed, the surfaces polished and the cushions plumped. After Noah died, the last thing I'd felt like doing was cleaning, cooking or doing the laundry. If it hadn't been for Flynn, the house would have been in complete disarray. It was a relief that Dad wasn't letting everything slip like I had.

'How are you finding being here without Mum?'

He sighed heavily and shook his head. 'I keep thinking she's just in bed or the bathroom and there'll be a shout for help from her at any moment. I've called her name a few times and then I remember she's not here and it hits me all over again. It's going to take a long time to adjust.'

'Have you had any more thoughts about staying here?'

'I change my mind several times a day so I'm going to have to give it a lot of time. The last thing I want to do is rush to move out then regret it down the line.'

It was a hard relate to that.

'Sounds sensible,' I said. 'Can I ask why Mum was so keen for you to stay?'

'Because she loved this place so much. I told you that she looked at the view and wanted it no matter what it looked like inside. June was always practical and controlled about decisions – very much a head-over-heart woman – but on this occasion her heart took charge. We looked inside and it was a tip. All I could see was the hard work and expense, but June could see the vision. Complete role reversal for us. I grew to love the house but she was smitten from day one and I don't think she could bear the thought of anyone except us living here.'

'You will do what's right for you, though?' I said. 'Even if that does mean going against Mum's wishes.'

'I will. Don't you worry about me.'

'I can't help it.'

I gave him the silence he needed to steer the conversation where he wanted.

'This might seem like a strange thing to say,' he said after several minutes passed, 'but I'm glad it was June who went first. I'd rather it was me shouldering the pain of life without her than the other way round and, this way, she did get her wish to stay here until the end. If I'd gone first, she couldn't have stayed unless she had a live-in carer. She couldn't bear the thought of a stranger moving in with her so that wasn't an option. She'd therefore have had double the heartbreak of losing me and our home.'

'Flynn and I had a few conversations about what to do if something happened to one of us. He used to say he hoped he went first because...' I tailed off, not sure why I was sharing this with Dad.

'Go on,' he said, his voice and expression encouraging.

'He hoped he'd go first because he didn't think he'd be able to live without me.' He'd also said I was the strong one but, when it came to us being tested by death, albeit not our own, I'd been the weak one and he'd been the one who'd held it all together.

We sat in silence for a while again, sipping on our coffees.

'Do you believe Mum's looking down on us?' I asked. 'You're not a Christian.'

'I don't think you need to follow any sort of religion to believe in – or want to believe in – there being something after death. Is there such a thing as heaven? No idea. Is it more about that person's love being so strong that they leave an energy behind? Or is it simply that we don't want to let go so we like to think there's something which allows them to be with us even if they physically can't be?'

He tilted his head and his brow furrowed. 'You're not a Christian either. What did you believe after Noah passed?'

'I don't know. Something. I couldn't accept that that was it for him, especially when he died so young.' I tried to swallow that dratted ever-present lump in my throat. 'D'you know what I really wanted? I wanted him to haunt me – to come back as a ghost and tell me what happened or, if he couldn't speak, to somehow convey to me that he was okay.' My eyes were burning once more as I added in a small voice, 'But he never did.'

'I wish he had been able to bring you that peace.'

Several more minutes passed before Dad said, 'I'm sure your mum visited me the night we lost her.'

I sat forward, eyes wide. 'You saw her?'

'Not quite. You know that feeling when you're in bed and someone sits down at the other side and you feel the mattress dip? I woke up feeling that and I could smell her perfume really strongly. It wasn't on the bedding because Georgia and Mark had changed it for me. I strained my eyes, hoping to catch a glimpse of her but I couldn't see anything so I spoke to her, asked if she was okay, told her I missed her and was sorry I hadn't said goodbye. This sudden feeling of warmth flowed through me and I heard her voice saying, *But you told me you loved me and that's all I needed to hear.* Next I knew, it was morning and time to get up. I've no idea whether she really did speak or whether that was her voice in my head, but I slept so soundly those few hours and I'm convinced that was thanks to June.'

I pressed my hand to my throat, feeling quite overcome with emotion. How much peace might I have felt if something similar had happened to me?

'I'm so happy for you that you had that experience,' I said. 'Will you tell Georgia?'

'I don't know. What do you think?'

I'd always been vocal about my belief in ghosts. You don't work in as many historical buildings as I had without hearing stories and seeing a few unexplained things yourself. Georgia, on the other hand, was stoic in her belief that there was no such thing.

'It's a tricky one. It might comfort her but it could just as easily upset her a lot. Maybe play that one by ear but just say if you want me to sound her out about the idea.'

'Thanks. I'll have a think about it.'

'Did I tell you I've seen a ghost?'

I told him about a conversion project I'd worked on a couple of years ago in an abandoned former cotton mill in Northumberland. It was reputed to be haunted by a young boy and girl who'd tragically died in an industrial accident as well as the mother of the boy who roamed the building looking for her child.

'I felt something as soon as I entered the building. I didn't feel any danger – more of an overwhelming sense of sadness. I never saw the children but I saw the mum twice. She was wearing a black dress and wringing her hands as she looked left and right. The first time, it was brief and she was in the distance, but the second time she was closer and I swear she looked straight at me. We both stood there for ages and then she just disappeared.'

'Did your colleagues see anything?'

'Just me.'

'I wonder if you saw her because you'd lost your son too.'

I stared at Dad wide-eyed. 'I can't believe I never thought of that but it would make a lot of sense.'

That thought was still with me when I returned to Willowdale Hall a little later. Had our shared experience – our shared pain – of losing our sons somehow connected us? I loved that I'd seen a ghost and it felt even more special now because of that connection, although I'd rather Noah had visited me than some stranger from the past. He could have given me some answers.

I shook my head. Answers. Why did it keep coming back to that? Why did I keep torturing myself when there were no answers? I couldn't go down that road again. I'd made great progress since coming back to Willowdale and that was the route I needed to take. Let go, heal, move on.

36

Oliver and Rosie had been incredibly supportive, telling me to take as much time off as I needed, but I'd managed to keep on top of the Willowdale Hall project and my work for other clients by working flexibly around supporting Dad. On Monday morning, it was time to return to a routine. I went to Casa Alpaca first thing and helped Emma clean up and feed the herd. Being around the alpacas was so calming. As I stroked Maud's neck and she nuzzled against me, I pictured Mum and how happy she'd been during the meet and greet. What a blessing that I'd been able to arrange something so special for her before she left us.

Returning to the hall a little later, I showered and changed, then went to the kitchen to make some breakfast. Rosie was pacing up and down between the oven and the island unit, her phone pressed to her ear, and she did not look impressed. Feeling like I might be intruding, I backed away mouthing an apology but she indicated that I was fine to stay.

'While I do appreciate you calling me first thing this morning,' she said, her tone strong, 'it would have been far more helpful if you'd let me know a couple of weeks ago... Yes, I understand that, but look at it from my perspective. You're the one who set the timetable so I don't think it was an unreasonable assumption that those timescales worked for you... I don't think I sound angry at all...'

She glanced at me questioningly and I shook my head.

'What you can hear is frustration and disappointment... In that case, let's just forget the whole thing. I'll pay you for the materials and we'll call that the end... Yes, I do mean that... You're seriously asking me why? Because I'm not sure who you're used to working with but I'm used to working with professionals... You can interpret that however you choose. I just think... Hello? Hello?'

Rosie took her phone away from her ear and scowled at it. 'He hung up on me. How rude is that?'

'That didn't sound like a good phone call.'

'It wasn't.' She flicked the kettle on to boil. 'Urgh! I hate confrontations. Sorry to land you with this first thing but, if you hadn't already guessed, that was Dougie Standish. Apparently he's over-committed on his projects and has decided not to work on the boat house after all because it's not as profitable as some of his other work.'

My eyebrows shot up. 'He actually said that?'

'Yep. Can you believe the audacity? So I've sacked him. I'm sorry. I know that wasn't my decision to make but I can't bear people who give you the runaround then let you down at the eleventh hour like that. So it looks like there'll be a major delay on the boat house and probably everything else.'

She dropped a teabag into a mug and made herself a drink, slopping milk all over the work surface and missing the bin with the used teabag, sighing loudly as it splatted onto the floor.

'Oh, my God! I didn't offer you a drink, Mel. I'm so sorry.'

'I think your mind's elsewhere. You take a seat and I'll sort it.'

'He said he'd got another builder lined up to take over but they wouldn't be free immediately which is the point when the conversation took a bad turn. He said he'd email their details over but I doubt he will now.'

My stomach lurched. Dougie Standish knew Flynn. What if it was him he'd recommended? I tensed as Rosie scrolled on her phone.

'Oh! He has. Must have done it before I sacked him. Baz Bempton. Anyone you know?'

'No. Not come across him before.'

Rosie tutted, shaking her head. 'I can't imagine we'll find anyone else at this short notice so there's going to be a delay anyway. Should I get in touch with Baz? And what about Dougie? Should I apologise and reinstate him?'

Rosie was usually really calm but she looked fraught.

'Is everything okay?' I asked. 'You don't seem yourself this morning.'

'I'm nervous and it's putting me on edge. Oliver doesn't want to stop being a GP but he would prefer to be closer to home so he's been putting out feelers. One of the GPs in a practice in Keswick has unexpectedly decided to take early retirement so Oliver's got a telephone interview over lunch.'

'That's fantastic news. Is Oliver nervous too?'

'He's taking it in his stride but I've got myself into a bit of a state. I want him to get it so badly. No more commuting would mean more time together.'

'I'm sure he'll ace it.' I held up my crossed fingers. 'Forward me the email with this Baz Bempton's details and I'll do some digging before you call him. Wouldn't want to offer him the job and discover mid-build that Dougie's fed us a dud.'

I made some toast and took it up to my bedroom while I did some research. Half an hour later, I found Rosie in the library.

'Bad news. I don't think I've seen a builder with so many negative reviews and complaints. It's a no for the boat house and a hell no for the rest of the work because he has no experience of renovating historical buildings.'

'Argh! I should have known that somebody available at such short notice would be no good. I'll email Dougie and tell him not to send Baz round.' She released a heavy sigh and shook her head. 'So we're back to square one. Nobody for the boat house and nobody for the hall unless I grovel. I don't suppose you have any contacts from when you lived here before?'

Yes, and he was the best of the best. I thought about what Flynn had said outside The White Willow when he'd congratulated me on securing the Willowdale Hall project. *How many times did we fantasise about working on the hall together one day? It's amazing that one of us has had that dream come true.* Flynn deserved this opportunity to have his dream come true too. I looked at Rosie's eager expression and knew I was going to have to put my personal feelings aside. It was the least I could do after everything I'd put him through. Was still putting him through.

'There is someone, but it's been a lot of years and I don't know what he's trading as. I'll do a search and come back to you.'

The relief on her face told me I'd made the right decision. 'Thanks, Mel. You're a star.'

A quick search on Flynn Waters brought up stacks of results and my breath caught in my throat at his trading name: Ark Building & Restoration Ltd. I needed to pause for a moment to take in that lovely nod to our son.

On the website, I clicked on various photos of the projects Flynn had worked on over the past few years and was seriously impressed, not that I'd have expected anything but top work from him. I took a screenshot of his contact details and messaged them to Rosie.

I recommend Flynn Waters. He's an exceptional builder, highly experienced with old properties, and extremely professional. You should probably know that he's my ex-husband

I read the message back, deleted the last sentence and sent it. I didn't need to drag my personal life into this. Flynn and I had been an amazing team once and we could be again. It was purely business and I needed to put my own feelings aside for the sake of Rosie and Oliver who'd been so good to me. The fact that Flynn was my ex wouldn't affect anything.

Fingers crossed.

37

On Thursday morning, I stood by the window in the empty bedroom opposite mine. Being at the front of the house, it gave me a better view of the driveway so I could see Flynn arriving. My stomach was churning from a combination of seeing him again and playing over and over in my head all the difficult conversations we might have today.

Rosie had told me that Flynn had initially said he was backed up with work and regretted he couldn't help her, but when she'd mentioned that I'd specifically recommended him, he told her to give him an hour and he'd see what he could do. He rang back half an hour later and said the boat house shouldn't be a problem and he could probably get a team on it by the end of next week but he'd need to meet me and look around the hall before he could commit to the refurbishment. Today was the only day he was free this week to do that.

Rosie had riding lessons all day and Oliver was at work but, as I was project managing the whole build, it was me he needed to see anyway. If he was interested in taking on the project, he could meet Rosie and Oliver one evening.

I tried to imagine what his reaction had been to hearing Rosie saying I'd recommended him. It could be anything from *she's got a nerve, only considering me because she's desperate* through to thinking I finally wanted to talk and only felt comfortable doing that in a work setting.

It was a miserable day with grey skies, steady rain and a drop in temperature. I shivered and rubbed my hands up and down my arms in an attempt to warm up. A white van emerged from behind the trees and I released a long shuddery breath before making my way along the hall and down the stairs. How would he play this? Would he be completely professional and only talk business – quite likely after I walked away from him at Mum's wake – or would he try to steer the conversation towards something more personal again?

The doorbell rang, making my heart pound. Another deep breath and I opened the door. I knew I should smile and welcome him inside but all I could do was stare at him. He really did look better than he ever had but there was still that vulnerability in his eyes which had been so endearing outside The Hardy Herdwick the night we met when he clung on to Edgar the elephant. I wondered if he still had my soft toy. I'd left it behind in my haste to pack and hadn't felt like I could ask him to return it. No, of course he wouldn't have kept it. He'd likely donated or binned it when he'd moved house, if not before.

'Coffee?' I asked, registering that one of us was going to have to speak eventually.

'No, thanks. I've squeezed this in and I've not got a very big window so I could do with cracking on.'

Very business-like so I took his lead on that, pushing aside an unexpected sensation of disappointment.

'Of course. Come in and we'll go through the kitchen and out the back to the boat house.'

I was already wearing my coat and walking boots and had my hard hat in my hand, as did Flynn, so we were good to go. He followed me in silence down the hall through the east wing and into the kitchen where I unlocked the side door. Silence remained as we set off across the wet lawn. I couldn't bear it. I needed to apologise to him for so many things but where could I start? *Sorry I didn't call you when you gave me your number. Sorry for walking away at the wake. Sorry for walking away seven years ago. Sorry for everything I said and did.* The list went on and on and with every fresh reason to apologise, that ball of emotion flexed.

'This is the boat house,' I said a little pointlessly when we reached it. 'Rosie forwarded you the plans?'

'Yes. She said you've already had the materials delivered.'

'Some are round the other side and the rest are in a storage shed near the house. Dougie's team secured the roof so you're safe to go inside.'

He put his hard hat on and wandered round the perimeter before going inside where he removed a small notepad and scribbled some notes in it. When he'd got what he needed, he asked me to show him the rest of the materials so we crossed the garden towards the end of the west wing where the storage sheds were and I stood in the rain as he checked on the materials, scribbling more notes in his book.

I'd hoped he'd take the professional stance but now I wasn't so sure it was the best approach. It was too awkward and uncomfortable, as though we'd only just met and taken an instant dislike to each other.

'Got what you need?' I asked, fighting hard to keep my tone friendly when he emerged from the shed.

'I do. Shouldn't be a problem to get some lads onto it fairly quickly, but I'll confirm a date later.'

'That's great news. Thank you. What do you want to see in the hall?'

'All of it. Give me a tour from the attic to the cellar and talk me through the plans but not in too much detail. I don't have time at the moment. It's just to give me a feel for the size and scope at this point.'

I led him across the back of the house and in through the kitchen door where we ditched our hard hats and wet coats. Staircases to the attic and cellar were behind two separate doors beside the kitchen. Flynn suggested we start at the top and work our way down.

'Some of the floorboards need replacing so you need to be careful up here,' I said when we reached the top.

As I walked Flynn through the plans, I had to keep reminding myself not to get carried away with the detail. He'd made it clear that time was an issue and I didn't want to detain him longer than necessary for both our sakes. He scribbled in his notepad, shone his torch here and there and knocked on several walls as we toured the attic rooms before descending to the first floor.

'Most of the rooms in the west wing are empty now. Darrowby's cleared them and some pieces will get restored and returned with others going into an auction.' I pushed open my bedroom door. 'This is my luxury suite.'

'You live here?' Flynn looked surprised.

'Yeah. I assumed Mark would have told you.'

'Mark doesn't tell me anything about you.'

'Because you don't want to hear it,' I said, jokingly.

'No. Because he knows you don't want me to know anything.'

His voice was gentle with a tinge of sadness which was echoed in his eyes as he held my gaze. I hated how much I'd hurt him. He hadn't deserved any of it.

'So, erm... I use this room and there's a Jack-and-Jill bathroom between this and the final bedroom which I use as an office. I was going to rent somewhere but I was struggling to find anywhere suitable to live and work. Oliver and Rosie said I could stay here as long as was practical. It makes it easier although it does sometimes get lonely on my own in such a big room in a huge building and...'

I tailed off, no idea why I was telling Flynn this and especially letting him know I was on my own and occasionally lonely. What was I thinking?

The tour continued and I stayed succinct and focused on the building project only, but thoughts kept pushing into my head about how amazing Flynn was to agree to come here when it couldn't be easy for him to be around me. He could have said no to Rosie. Or he could have turned up and been arsey with me, demanding we talk before he'd even consider taking on the work. But that wasn't Flynn's style.

Eventually it was time to go down into the cellar. I opened the wooden door and flicked on the light at the top of the staircase to illuminate our way. There was a thicker and older door at the bottom, which I pushed open. Stepping into the cellar, I groped along the wall, trying to find the light switch. I eventually felt it in an illogical place round the corner and the lights flickered for a moment before settling into a dim yellow glow. Remembering what Oliver had said about the door being sticky, I turned to tell Flynn to prop it open.

'Can you just—'

But I was too late and the door had closed behind him.

'Can I just what?' Flynn asked.

'I was going to ask you to prop the door open. Oliver says it sticks.'

He grimaced before pressing down on the handle and

attempting to pull the door towards him, but it didn't budge. He tried again several times, but to no avail.

'You're winding me up, right?' I asked, grasping at straws as panic gripped me at the prospect of being locked in a cold, dark cellar with my ex-husband and all our demons.

'I wouldn't do that. Feel free to try.'

I did, rattling the handle with increasing desperation. This wasn't good. Not good at all.

38

'It'll be all right,' Flynn said, his voice calm and soothing. 'We'll look around then try the door again. So, what can you tell me about the cellar?'

'Very little. I haven't spent much time down here as it's not part of the refurbishment plan. No windows, so they can't use it for accommodation. I checked it over to make sure there's no damp or structural issues and it seemed sound to me. Dougie spent longer down here and he didn't have any concerns. It looks like it's been used for storage. Oliver and Rosie say they haven't a clue what's down here.'

As I spoke, the lights – a couple of rows of exposed bulbs stretching to the far end of the cellar – kept flickering. Flynn picked up a duster abandoned on top of a crate and used it to avoid burning his hand as he went along one row and back along the other testing the bulbs.

'They're all screwed in tightly,' he said, placing the duster back where he'd found it. 'We might lose the light, not that it's great anyway.'

He whipped out his torch and slowly walked down to the end of the cellar, shining it at the walls and ceiling. There was no point me trailing behind him so I decided to look in some of the boxes. The nearest ones to me were vintage timber shipping crates and, when I shone the torch on my phone into them, it appeared that six of them contained a mixture of glassware, crockery and ornaments, all carefully wrapped. I didn't delve too far as I didn't want to risk breaking anything. There could well be some beautiful and potentially valuable pieces in there but I'd need to take them upstairs for a proper look. Another shipping crate contained folded-up curtains and there was one with some lacework, possibly table runners and place settings.

Piled next to them were several cardboard boxes full of paper-work and old photos. I lifted out a black-and-white photo of a woman and a girl standing by the front door of the hall and flicked it over to see if anything was written on the back. *Agnes and Rebecca, 28 July 1913.* The date jumped out at me – exactly one year before World War I began. They'd have had no idea about the loss and destruction that lay ahead. I turned it back to the front, wondering who Agnes and Rebecca were and what had happened to them. I'd done some research into the owners of Willowdale Hall but those names weren't familiar, although they could easily have been extended family or friends.

For the first time this morning, I felt a moment of calm. A box like this was a dream find for me and I could easily lose myself for hours in the history. At the opposite side of the room there was an old chaise with some padding bursting out of a hole. I carried the box over to it and gave it a wobble to make sure there wasn't a leg missing, but it seemed to be secure. I couldn't see Flynn but I could see his torch beam at the far end of the cellar so I sat down with the box beside me and rummaged further. Inside, there were stacks more photos, postcards, letters, invitations to parties and menus.

It wasn't long before I felt the cold seeping in. At first, it was just my hands and I kept rubbing them together in an attempt to warm them but soon my whole body felt cold and I regretted abandoning my coat in the kitchen. I definitely needed it down here. The T-shirt I was wearing might be long-sleeved but it was only thin cotton and provided no protection. I wished I was wearing a fleece, but I hadn't opted for trapped-in-cellar-chic when I'd dressed this morning.

Flynn returned and tried the door again but, after several attempts from him and from me, there was no way it was going to open. He couldn't even try to barge it as it opened inwards.

I took my phone out, hoping to ring Rosie for help, but there was no reception, which didn't surprise me considering we were underground. Flynn had no signal either. We tried all over the cellar but there was nothing. Next step was to check for some tools or even just a knife to see if we could jimmy the lock. Flynn took one side of the cellar and I took the other. Each time I checked a box and found nothing helpful inside, panic built inside me. The lights continued to flicker and even intermittently went off for a second or two.

'I don't like this,' I admitted to Flynn.

'Don't panic. We'll find something in one of these boxes and be out of here in a jiffy.'

I wished I could share his optimism. Most of the boxes were filled with papers and more photos but I couldn't muster any excitement about the history inside them while we were trapped. As we reached the end of the cellar, the lights flickered on and off in quick succession followed by a pop, a buzz and darkness. I stayed rooted to the spot for a moment, waiting for them to come back on like earlier but they didn't.

'Looks like the lights have died,' Flynn said, flicking his torch back on.

I couldn't stand it. I had to get out of here. It wasn't that I was scared of the dark or anything like that. It was being trapped with Flynn which was too much for me. I raced back to the crates by the door and began frantically searching in the boxes again for something to help force open the door.

'You've already looked in there,' Flynn said, 'and so have I. Nothing is going to have magically appeared in any of the boxes since we looked. There's no tools or anything down here so there's no point searching again. You'll have to let it go.'

I stopped rummaging and stood upright, my heart pounding as those words took me back in time. He'd said the same thing when I'd tried to find out why Noah turned to drugs.

'Let it go?' I cried, blowing my fringe out of my eyes. 'That's your answer to everything, is it? Just let it go, walk away, forget about it.' The words came out too loud, too shrill.

'I've no idea what you're talking about.'

'Noah, of course!'

Flynn came closer and I could only just see his face in the torchlight but he looked bewildered. 'I'm not the one who walked away. You did that.'

'Because you didn't care.'

'About what?'

'About what happened to Noah. About me.'

'Is that what you think? Of course I cared!'

'Then why didn't you show it?' I put on a deep voice to mimic him, part-quoting, part-paraphrasing what he'd said at the time. '*Every question leads to more questions. Where's it going to end, Mel? You're going to have to let this one go.*'

'And you took that as me not caring?' He took a couple of steps closer so that there was only an arm's length between us.

'How could you think that? It was because I cared so deeply about you that I said those things. I could see how broken you were and how every avenue you went down made it worse instead of better. I wanted you to stop for your sake.'

'But I couldn't stop. I had to know what really happened to him and I needed you to understand that, but you didn't even try.' As I said the words, I knew they were unfair. He *had* tried to understand. He'd repeatedly asked me why it was so important to me and I hadn't been able to answer him.

He gently placed his hands on my shoulders. 'I'm sorry if that's how you felt. My intention was *never* to brush it aside. I only wanted to take the pain away.'

And now he was apologising when he'd done nothing wrong. My eyes burned, my throat felt like it was on fire and it worried me how close to becoming uncorked that bottle of emotion inside me felt. I needed to apologise. I knew that. But for some unknown reason, I shrugged his hands off me.

'I didn't need you to take the pain away. Nobody could do that.'

An agonising sob burst from me, scaring me. Flynn tried to pull me to him but I shoved at his chest with both my hands and suddenly the fire was back.

'What I needed was for you to support me.' Another shove. 'To find the answers with me, to understand that I had to know.'

The cork finally burst from the bottle.

'You let me down,' I cried, pounding my hands against his chest as tears coursed down my cheeks. 'You let me down.' Those final words were barely a whisper as the fire left my body and I sagged against him, my cries echoing around the dark cellar.

Flynn pulled me close and held me as years of pent-up frustration and grief poured out of me. I needed him right now too and he was here this time doing the best thing he could possibly do for me – holding me and letting it all pour out. Pain, guilt, grief. And even though I was laying it all on him, he wasn't to blame. I was. Flynn hadn't let me down. I'd let him down, let me down, let Noah down.

39

Flynn somehow managed to shuffle me across to the chaise, still holding me and stroking my hair – something he'd always do to soothe me anytime I was upset or feeling ill. With the energy expended from my outburst, the cold really took hold and I couldn't stop shivering. Flynn slipped off the zipped jacket he'd been wearing under his coat and helped me into it. Initially the warmth from his body transferred to me and hugged me but that soon faded and I was shivering again. He left me for a moment and returned with one of the curtains from the packing crates, wrapping it round me like a cloak.

'You look like one of three kings in a school nativity play,' he said, making me laugh.

Next minute I crumbled again as I thought of Noah as a young boy.

'Do you remember when Noah was a king and his crown came apart?' I asked.

'I'll never forget him standing in the middle of the stage demanding they stop the nativity until one of the teachers stapled it back together for him.'

'Completely upstaged the little girl playing Mary. What was her name?'

'Maddie Weston. I don't think she ever forgave him.'

There was a pause and I wiped my cheeks.

'Feeling any warmer?' Flynn asked.

'Much. You should grab one yourself.'

He disappeared and returned moments later wrapped in a matching curtain.

'What else do you remember about Noah?' I asked.

Whenever I thought about Noah, the first image that always popped into my head was the day I found him and, when I pushed that aside, my focus was invariably on the last six to eight months of his life, searching for signs that I'd missed. I rarely remembered him as an innocent young boy. I feared that the eighteen-year-old Noah who'd died of a drug overdose had eradicated those memories so it had been a special moment just now thinking about him in the nativity.

'I remember that phase where he was obsessed with space and aliens.'

I frowned at Flynn, not recalling it.

'He'd stayed over at your mum and dad's for the weekend and your dad decided they'd watch a few films from our childhood. He became obsessed with *E.T.* Made your poor dad watch it three or four times that weekend.'

'Oh, gosh, yes. Didn't he want a Speak & Spell for his birthday?'

'Yes! He wanted to communicate with the aliens so we indulged him and he lost interest in it within five minutes.'

We spent the next couple of hours sharing stories from Noah's childhood, most of which made us laugh, some of which were poignant. I'd refused to talk about Noah for so long and wondered why when I could feel the conversation doing me so much good. Every so often, Flynn got up, swished his curtain cloak, and ventured over to the door, but it remained stuck fast. All we could hope was that, when Rosie finished at the stables, she'd notice Flynn's van still parked by the hall and come searching for us.

Flynn's stomach rumbled loudly and I checked the time on my phone – 4.06 p.m. – meaning we'd not only missed lunch but teatime was rapidly approaching.

'I'm hungry too,' I admitted. I'd skipped breakfast because I'd been nervous about spending the morning with Flynn. 'And I'm really thirsty.'

'In that case, come with me,' he said, taking hold of my hand.

He led me a little way into the cellar and shone his torch behind a dressing room screen. I was expecting it to illuminate the wall but there was an arched opening to another room.

'Go inside,' he said.

I stepped through the archway and gasped at all the dust and cobweb-covered wine bottles resting in racks. There had to be hundreds of them.

Flynn reached for one, blew the dust away and read the label. 'Nineteen sixty-three. I hear that's a good vintage.'

'You can't be serious.'

'You said you're thirsty.'

'But that bottle could be worth a fortune.'

'Or it could be rank. Either way, I'm sure Rosie and Oliver wouldn't begrudge us one bottle after we've been stuck down here for over five hours. We just need something to open it with.'

There was a ledge between the racks with some dusty wine glasses on it, also covered in cobwebs, and I spotted a corkscrew hanging from a hook above it.

'Could that open the door?'

'Doubtful,' Flynn said, 'but I can try. Can I suggest we open the bottle first in case we break the corkscrew on the door and we can't get out but we can't have a drink either?'

'Okay.'

The corkscrew didn't work on the door but Flynn admitted it had been worth a try. He offered me the first drink so I took a tentative sip just in case it was rank, but it was actually delicious. I didn't drink red wine very often but, if I did, I liked it to be really smooth like this. I took a bigger glug and handed the bottle to Flynn.

We returned to the chaise, passing the wine back and forth. With no food to soak up the alcohol, it went straight to our heads and the conversation soon moved away from the happy childhood anecdotes to our split.

'Why was it so important to you to find out what happened?' Flynn asked after he returned from the wine cellar with a second bottle.

How many times had I asked myself that same question over the years?

'It didn't tally,' I said. 'Noah and drugs, I mean. Why? Since when? I needed answers.'

He was silent for a while and I took another glug.

'I think there's more to it than that,' he said, his voice gentle. 'Come on, Mel, just tell me.'

I shook my head, my heart pounding as I fixed my eyes on the floor. I wanted to tell him. I wanted to explain, but could I bear to say the words?

He gently raised my chin. 'Please, Mel. I know there's something.'

My lips trembled as my biggest fear threatened to overwhelm me. I thought I'd unleashed everything that had been building up inside me but it felt like there was more to come and another kind word from Flynn would break me again.

'Don't,' I whispered, tears trailing down my cheeks, but I could understand why he wouldn't want to leave it.

'Whatever it is, it made you run and stay away and it's still eating away at you, isn't it?' His voice was so tender, so encouraging. 'I'm right here and I'm listening.'

'It's my fault!' I cried, springing to my feet. 'It's my fault Noah died.'

'How?'

'Because I was too consumed by my work to notice that our son was spiralling.'

Flynn jumped up, shaking his head. 'No! You can't blame yourself for that.'

My cloak slipped to the floor as I raked my fingers into my hair, clutching a bunch in each hand. 'I can and I do. I should have known he'd lost touch with his friends, broken up with Jessie and was failing at college. There'd have been signs and I missed them all.'

Flynn gently eased my hands out of my hair and held them between his. 'So did I, but I'm not blaming myself.'

'But you weren't at home as often as me,' I cried, pulling my hands from his grasp and pacing up and down as I ranted. 'I worked there. I was in the house with him so often and I was completely oblivious to everything going on in his life. I should have picked up on something. I should have realised. My fault.'

I sank back down onto the chaise, my energy zapped, silent tears dripping onto my T-shirt. I'd finally said it. I'd said the words out loud that had haunted me for all these years.

Flynn sat down beside me and put his arm around me.

'Have I got this right?' he asked. 'You became fixated on finding the truth because you were trying to ease your own conscience?'

'Something like that.'

'I couldn't disagree more strongly. It wasn't your fault, Mel. You did nothing wrong. Noah was eighteen. He spent most of his time shut away in his room and he kept things from us, just like most teenagers. I don't blame you and you shouldn't blame yourself and do you know what? If Noah was here, he wouldn't blame you either.'

His voice cracked and he released a deep shuddery breath. I felt his pain at my revelation and slipped my hand into his.

'I should have been honest with you back then,' I said.

'What stopped you?'

'Fear that you'd agree with me.'

'Mel, I'd never—'

'I know that, but my head was such a mess. I couldn't think straight about anything.'

Flynn picked up the curtain and draped it back round me before passing me the bottle of wine. I took a glug and passed it back to him to do the same.

'Do you still want to know the truth?' he asked eventually.

'Yes!' I said without hesitation. 'Even though there's nothing I can do about it now, I still want to know who Noah's new friends were and who gave him the drugs. It wouldn't answer all my questions but it'd be something and it might help me find a way to shift the blame from me to them and to forgive myself.'

Silence settled on us again, the only sound being the slosh of the wine in the bottle as we intermittently passed it back and forth until Flynn announced we'd finished it and a third bottle probably wasn't a good idea. I agreed wholeheartedly. My head was so fuzzy.

'Why did it take you so long to sell The Bothy?' I asked, my words slurred. 'I thought it'd sell just like that.' I tried to accompany the word *that* with a click of my fingers but I couldn't coordinate the movement.

'I had three offers the day it went on the market,' Flynn responded, his words also slurring. 'Didn't put it up for sale straightaway cos I kept hoping you'd come back.'

My heart skipped. 'Even after we'd divorced?'

'For a long time after. Kept hoping you'd have the time and space you needed and then you'd return to me.'

'Sorry.'

'Me too.'

'So when did you give up hoping and start dating again?' I asked.

'I didn't. Part of me kept believing that, with enough water under the bridge, we'd eventually find our way back to each other because we were always meant to be together.'

I laughed out loud. 'Yeah, right. That's the truth!'

'It is!' He sounded affronted.

'I'll accept that you believe the always being together stuff. You always were romantic. But the never dating stuff? That's bull-shit! You're married!'

'Married? What makes you think that?'

'Erm, the wedding ring for a start.'

He held up his left hand. 'This ring?'

'Yep! Gotcha! Married man.'

'Take a closer look.' He thrust his hand towards me and shone his torch onto it.

'It's very nice,' I slurred, struggling to actually focus on the ring.

'Closer. I'd take it off so you can see the inscription, but I'm not sure it'll come off my finger now. I've worn it for that long.'

Shocked, I grabbed his hand. 'That's the ring I gave you!'

I ran my fingers over the platinum band but he took his hand from my grasp.

'What can I say? Hopeless romantic.'

I couldn't believe he was still wearing his wedding band after all this time. My engagement and wedding rings were safely tucked away in their original boxes but I placed my hand against my chest, feeling the eternity ring I always wore on a chain. Flynn had given me it after Noah was born, and I could remember his exact words: *I've heard being a parent can be both the most rewarding and the toughest thing ever. This is to remind you that, no matter how tough things get, my love for you will last for all eternity.* He'd had the infinity symbol engraved inside the band with N L for Noah Lucas within the two ovals and our initials either side. I was about to show him it, but I suddenly remembered what I'd seen on the beach.

'Not married, but you *are* seeing someone,' I said. 'Or you were.'

'I'm not and I wasn't.'

'I saw you kissing a woman.'

'When?'

'Just over a month ago – end of March. I was watching the boats and you got off one with a woman with red hair. You hugged and kissed on the beach.'

'That was Lynette. She's a friend.'

'Didn't look like a friend to me.'

'Well, she is. She's the sister of a friend who thought it would be a genius idea to set us up cos we were both divorcees. I wasn't interested but he wouldn't drop it so I reluctantly agreed to meet her for coffee. Turns out Lynette wasn't interested either cos, like me, she hadn't wanted the divorce. We became good friends and when you saw us, we'd just been to Lodore Falls to scatter her dog's ashes because it was one of their favourite places to go for walks. She *did* kiss me. On the cheek to say thanks for being there on a difficult day.'

I winced. How wrong had I got that? 'I'm sorry about your friend's dog. Is she okay?'

'Getting there.' He gave me a playful nudge. 'I can't believe you thought we were kissing properly. Lynette would find that hilarious.'

'It was the angle,' I muttered. 'Sorry.'

'So, what about you? Any relationships?'

I told him about Graeme and the disastrous proposal, but skirted round the reasons why it had ended. I should have known he'd question it.

'Was it because of me?' he asked when I didn't respond.

He sounded so hopeful and, even though the drink had elicited the truth about so many things from me today, I couldn't bring myself to tell Flynn the truth about this. This was a man who hadn't put our house on the market because he'd hoped I'd come back, who still wore his wedding ring because the vows he'd made were forever, and who'd just told me he hadn't given up hope of me returning. Much as my heart might be screaming to admit that he'd held tightly onto my heart all along and I still wore my eternity ring, I hadn't yet found my way through the rain. Until I did, I couldn't give him hope. The water under our bridge had been extremely turbulent. Could we ever recover from that even if we wanted to? I'd broken his heart so badly and he hadn't deserved it. I couldn't risk doing that to him again.

'Mel?' he prompted.

'We just weren't right for each other.'

I felt his leg tense against mine and then he moved away to the end of the chaise. I'd upset him and I hated doing that but it was necessary to protect him.

We sat in silence as the time ticked by. Shivering, I pulled the curtain more tightly around me. It wasn't just the cold I was battling with now – it was the desire to sleep. A bottle of wine on an empty stomach had definitely taken its toll and all I wanted to do was curl up under my duvet.

'What was that?' Flynn whispered, grabbing my arm. 'Did you hear a car?'

'Rosie?'

Dropping our curtains, we raced to the door and banged and yelled for help. After several excruciating minutes, a voice called my name.

'Yes! We're trapped in here.'

'Step back.'

Flynn and I shuffled away from the door and it opened moments later. Rosie and Georgia stared at us.

'What happened?' Georgia asked.

'Door wouldn't open.'

'Oh, my God! Come out.'

As I stumbled up the staircase, I was very aware of how drunk I was. Behind me, I heard Flynn apologising to Rosie for drinking some of her wine but she dismissed it as she apologised profusely for us getting trapped. All I could think about was how desperate I was for the toilet, followed by a pint of cold water and a mountain of toast.

When I returned from the bathroom, I found them in the kitchen. Flynn had a glass of water in one hand and was eating a banana.

'I'm so sorry,' Rosie said. 'Are you okay?'

Georgia rushed at me with a hug, preventing me from answering.

'Bit drunk,' I murmured. 'Why are you here?'

Between them, Rosie and Georgia explained how Rosie had been delayed at the stables talking to a parent so had rushed in late, quickly changed and checked my bedroom, office and the library for me but, finding both empty, had presumed I'd left for the quiz without her. She'd noticed Flynn's van was still parked on the drive and was surprised at that considering he'd said he couldn't stay long. When she got to the pub, Georgia had asked where I was and Rosie had said there was no sign of me but Flynn's van was still there so presumably we'd been in another room deep in conversation. Georgia told her that Flynn was my ex and we weren't on speaking terms so that wouldn't be the case and something had to be wrong if he was still there and there was no sign of us both. They both raced back to the hall and heard us banging and shouting as soon as they opened the front door.

'Thanks for coming back for us,' I said. 'I need some food and bed.'

'So do I,' Flynn said and his cheeks reddened as his eyes caught mine. 'My bed. Home.'

'You won't be able to drive if you've been drinking,' Georgia said. 'I'll drop you home.'

'Thanks. Now would be good, if that's okay with you.'

'Of course.' Georgia hugged me again. 'I'll speak to you soon.'

'I'm so sorry, Flynn,' Rosie said as she followed them out of the kitchen. 'I know you didn't have much time free today and…'

I couldn't hear anything else she said as they'd moved out of earshot. I knew Flynn would be gracious and accept her apology. It wouldn't put him off doing the work and he'd be able to laugh about it with her soon. What could put him off the project was having to work with me. He'd barely been able to look at me. I'd wanted to avoid hurting him again but I'd still screwed things up.

40

I woke up on Friday morning with a banging head but, when that wore off, I felt better than I had in a long time. I'd finally found a release for my grief. Being trapped in a cellar with Flynn had been far from ideal but it had triggered an outpouring that had been long overdue.

I hoped that Flynn would get in touch today, even if just to confirm that he would be going ahead with the projects. Or not. My stomach lurched at the thought of the latter. The day slipped past without a peep from him.

Oliver and Rosie went to Christian's house for their tea so I dined alone in the kitchen and took my book through the library afterwards. It was late when they arrived back so Oliver poked his head round the door to say goodnight before heading up to bed and Rosie told him she'd be up in ten minutes.

'Have you fully recovered from yesterday's ordeal?' she asked.

'Just about. I don't suppose you've heard anything from Flynn?'

'Not before we went out, but let me check my emails again.'

Rosie took her phone out. 'Oh! He's been in touch and... hang on...'

I watched her face intently as she scrolled down the message. If her expression darkened, it meant he'd pulled out and I'd be to blame. She looked up and smiled.

'Good news. He's happy to work on the boat house and the hall but he needs the weekend to study his work schedule. He'll come back to us by the end of Tuesday.'

'That's great news,' I said.

She shrugged. 'It is for the project, but is it for you? I had no idea he was your ex-husband. Will you be okay working with him?'

'I guarantee neither of us will let our baggage get in the way of doing a fantastic job.'

'I'm not worried about that. I'm worried about you.'

'Honestly, I'm fine. We used to run a business together and we worked together brilliantly. I'm sure there'll be some awkward moments but we'll get past them and I know he's the best person for the job. He loves Willowdale Hall nearly as much as I do so we're in good hands with him.'

'Okay. I feel reassured.'

'How did Oliver's interview go, by the way?' I asked.

'Really good. They'll let him know next week so don't uncross anything just yet.'

* * *

On Saturday morning, I was walking back to the hall after helping Emma when a text message arrived from an unregistered number.

FROM UNKNOWN

Hi Mel, it's Jessie. Hope you don't mind me getting in touch but I found your number on your website. I'd really like to talk to you. Any chance you're free to meet me at The White Willow at 11 this morning?

What could Jessie possibly want to see me for? Intrigued, I replied immediately to say I'd be there.

I did a couple of hours' work then set off on foot to meet Jessie. It was a bright day with only a few white clouds breaking up the blue sky. The sun filtering through the gaps in the trees warmed my face and arms and I felt a lightness in my step. Last night before settling down to sleep, I'd looked at the photos of Mum and the alpacas and finally cried over losing her. I'd even welled up this morning seeing Jolene and Maud being really cute together, looking like they were giving each other kisses. I hoped that, now that the cork was out and I'd released my tears, I wasn't going to find myself at the other extreme, crying over everything like Georgia did.

I arrived at The White Willow five minutes early and spotted Jessie seated at a window table, a pram beside her. She waved when she saw me and I couldn't resist peeking into the pram when I joined her.

'Aw, Jessie, she's gorgeous. What's her name?'

'Isla. She was ten days late so she'll be five weeks tomorrow.'

'Congratulations to you both.'

'Thank you, and thanks for meeting me at such short notice.'

'I was intrigued when I got your message.'

Kelly appeared, greeting us warmly, and we placed an order for hot drinks and scones.

'Seeing you outside The Byre was quite the surprise,' Jessie said when Kelly left. 'I'm really glad we got to talk, but I didn't tell you the whole truth and it's been niggling away at me ever since.'

Whatever she was about to reveal evidently made her nervous as she'd picked up the salt shaker and was twiddling with it rather than making eye contact with me.

'Go on,' I encouraged, my voice soft. 'You can tell me anything.'

She continued to twiddle with the salt. 'When Noah died, you wanted to know who he was hanging around with and who'd got him into drugs. I told you I didn't know – just that they were a bad crowd – but that's not true. I knew exactly who they were.'

My stomach lurched. After all these years, was I about to finally find out the answer?

She put the salt down and held my gaze. 'It was Trent. He's the one who got Noah into drugs.'

I clapped my hand across my mouth. I'd expected her to rattle off some names of kids I'd never heard of, not to name her brother.

'Trent? But I didn't think they were even in touch. I thought they'd drifted apart when Trent moved up to sixth form.'

'They had. Trent didn't like Noah and me being together – said he didn't want to be the third wheel. They'd never mixed at school anyway – different friendship groups – so they drifted apart naturally. Trent's mates were trouble. They got into drinking at an early age and started dabbling with drugs at college. One of them even did some dealing. When Noah started at sixth form, he didn't have anything to do with them at first but we went to a party towards the end of the first year and it was in this really rough house. I refused to stay, but Noah refused to leave. Trent turned up after I'd gone and that's where it all started, although I didn't know that until much later.'

'Did you know your brother was into drugs?'

'I'd heard Mum and Dad arguing about it and I hadn't believed it but then I saw him high and...' She shook her head. 'It was awful. At that point, Noah was a couple of terms into sixth form and I knew he'd had nothing to do with Trent so I didn't tell him about the drugs cos I didn't think he'd ever be at risk.'

Our drinks and scones arrived so we paused the conversation for a moment. I sipped on my cappuccino but my stomach was in knots so I left the scone untouched.

'Noah wasn't himself over the summer,' Jessie said. 'He kept cancelling on me and, when we did go out, he was often moody and distracted. He'd never mentioned my brother and he'd always said drugs were for losers so it never entered my head that they'd reconnected at that dodgy party and Noah had started doing drugs himself. I can't believe I was so blind to it.'

'That makes two of us. I hadn't a clue either. Was that when you found out? After the summer?'

'Later than that.' Tears pooled in her eyes. 'There was this Halloween party and I stupidly assumed everyone would be getting dressed up. I made a big effort and, when I turned up, nobody else was in costume and they were all laughing at me. And then I saw Trent and Noah together. They were both high and it suddenly all slotted into place.'

It was uncomfortable hearing it so I could only imagine how Jessie must have felt seeing her brother and boyfriend in that state.

'We split up shortly after that,' she said, her voice hoarse. 'When Noah died and you found out it was because of the drugs, I wanted to tell you what I knew, but Mum and Dad were scared of the repercussions for Trent and they asked me to stay quiet. I'm so sorry.'

The tears were flowing freely now and my heart broke for her to have gone through that at such a young age. I was furious with Helen and Guy for pressurising her to keep quiet. I understood they were trying to protect their son, but what about their daughter? What about Noah? No wonder they'd pulled away from me instead of supporting me. They'd made out that I was too forceful with my questions but what they'd really been doing was closing ranks.

As Jessie pulled a packet of tissues from Isla's changing bag, I experienced a moment of clarity. Alice had said that the boat house and the car couldn't be blamed for her accident. The blame lay with Hubert Cranleigh because he was the one who'd made the decision to drive drunk and to cover it up afterwards. In Noah's case, Trent and his dodgy mates had been key players but ultimately there was only one person to blame for Noah's death and it was the one person at whom, up until this moment, I hadn't pointed the finger. Talk about an epiphany! The only person truly responsible for Noah's death was Noah. He chose to take the drugs. He chose to do something risky and paid for it with the ultimate price. I could have done with a few minutes to let that sink in but that would be unfair to Jessie who was clearly distressed.

'You don't need to apologise,' I said. 'What happened to Noah wasn't your fault, or your parents' fault. It wasn't even Trent's. Noah could have said no. He could have walked away but he didn't.'

'I wish he had. And I'm sorry I didn't tell you sooner.'

'I understand why you didn't, but I can't tell you how much I appreciate finally knowing. Dare I ask what happened to Trent?'

'He'd already failed his A levels, lost his university place and had no direction. Noah's death tipped him over the edge. He lost the plot for a while, getting steadily more dependent on drink and drugs. He stole money from Mum and Dad to fund his habit. They stopped having money in the house so he began stealing from me and our grandparents. That was the last straw and they asked him to leave. They didn't want to but they hoped it would shock him into getting his life back together.'

'Did it?'

She shook her head. 'He couch surfed for a while but, after another friend was rushed to hospital from an overdose, which he survived, he finally woke up and questioned what the heck he was doing with his life. He turned up at The Byre begging for Mum and Dad's support to get things back on track. He's since been through rehab and is now training as a counsellor specialising in addiction.'

'Sounds like he's really turned his life around.'

'Took a while, but he got there eventually. I told him it was time you had the full story and he wanted to come with me and tell you himself, but I thought it might be a bit much. If you do want to hear it from him, I can arrange it.'

I thought for a moment. 'Is he sorry?'

'Oh, my God! Yes! He often says that he did some really bad stuff in his addiction years but his number one regret has always been getting Noah involved. If he could go back in time and change only one thing, that would be it.'

'That's good enough for me. It might be helpful for Trent to talk to me but, to be brutally honest, I don't think it'll benefit me. I've finally got some answers and it's time for me to let it go. Can you tell him I accept his apology and I don't blame him so he shouldn't blame himself? Tell him to channel that energy into his studies and supporting others in need.'

'Will do. It's such a weight lifted. I hate keeping secrets.' Jessie smiled at me as she wiped away the remnants of her tears. 'Thanks for being so understanding. Flynn said you would be.'

'Flynn?'

'He came to see me yesterday. Didn't he say?'

'No.'

Our conversation in the cellar swirled round my mind. *Do you still want to know the truth?* Flynn had asked, and I'd replied, *Yes! Even though there's nothing I can do about it now, I still want to know who Noah's new friends were and who gave him the drugs. It wouldn't answer all my questions but it'd be something and it might help me find a way to shift the blame from me to them and to forgive myself.*

Finding out the truth had helped me to shift the blame but not to where I'd expected.

'Wait a minute! How did Flynn know about Trent?'

'He found Noah's phone when he was moving house. There were photos and messages on it and he pieced it together. I don't know whether he confronted Mum and Dad with it at the time. They never said anything to me if he did. I suspect he didn't. They'd kicked Trent out by that point and I can't imagine Flynn would have wanted to add to the trauma they were already going through. He's too nice to do that.'

Yes, he was. What a gift he'd just given me. I'd told him I still wanted to know the truth and he'd made that happen. Since returning to Willowdale, I'd taken many steps forward in my journey to heal, and a few steps back too, but in the space of two days, Flynn had helped me take two enormous leaps forward. I'd never admitted out loud that I blamed myself and doing so in the cellar had allowed me to finally release my pent-up grief and now the confession he'd asked Jessie to make meant I finally knew what had happened and had accepted that Flynn was right about me not blaming myself.

There were a couple more steps I needed to take. The first was to let my family in. That was long overdue and didn't scare me. They'd understand. The second step was another leap and it terrified me but, if I didn't go for it, I'd never forgive myself and I knew the dark places blaming myself could take me. I couldn't do that again.

41

Even though it was barbeque weather on Sunday, we'd decided on a traditional roast at Derwent Rise. The combination of my outburst in the cellar on Thursday and hearing the truth from Jessie yesterday had helped me move forward more than I'd ever hoped possible and it definitely felt the right time to let my family in.

Trying to explain the past seven years to seven adults at the same time would have been pretty much impossible, especially with the distractions of a baby and a two-year-old. I'd therefore messaged Dad, Georgia and Mark last night to ask if the four of us could talk after the others left. I sent a further request to Georgia and Mark not to mention anything about me being trapped in the cellar as a lot of what I wanted to say to them privately was connected to that.

'Did Flynn say anything to you when you dropped him home?' I asked Georgia while we were chopping vegetables in Dad's kitchen.

'All I know is that your builder let you down, he was asked to take on the project instead, you got locked in the cellar and you found a wine stash.'

It didn't surprise me that Flynn had left it there. He'd always been the soul of discretion and would have seen it as my story to tell Georgia – not his.

We had a lovely lunch together and, when Regan, Clarke, Keira, Johnnie and the kids left, Georgia made a round of drinks and we settled in the lounge.

'I've got so much I want to explain,' I said. 'I've been thinking a lot about how to tell you this and I don't think there's a logical way so I thought I'd start with Mum's funeral. I don't know if any of you noticed but I didn't cry at the funeral, before or after and it wasn't because I wasn't upset. It was because I couldn't cry. The last time I'd had a proper cry was the day Noah died...'

I talked about the bottle of emotions steadily filling and pushing for a way out and how it took being locked in the cellar with Flynn to finally release them. I explained the desperate need to find someone to blame for Noah's death because I hadn't wanted to accept that I was to blame – something exacerbated by a young Jessie's suggestion that I'd made my son feel invisible. I told them what I'd only just admitted to myself this weekend – how I'd pushed Flynn away before he could do it to me when he realised what a terrible mother I'd been for being so involved in my work that I hadn't noticed my son's life spiralling out of control.

'I know now that it was the wrong thing to do,' I said, 'but my head was such a mess back then. I couldn't think straight about anything. Moving out wasn't enough, dissolving the business and getting divorced wasn't enough. Everywhere I went, I had memories of Noah and Flynn and they taunted me so I needed to be somewhere I didn't have memories and that's why I left.'

'And why you hardly ever came back,' Dad said.

'Exactly. It wasn't that I didn't want to see you all but it was just so hard. Every time I came here, I could see Noah and Flynn on the sofa, at the table, in the garden and all I could think about was how much I'd let them both down, what a failure I was and how much I hated myself. Again, I can look back at it and see how irrational it all was, but it didn't feel irrational at the time.'

I shared how lonely I'd felt in Newcastle but how every time I thought about returning to Willowdale, all the self-hate and anxieties resurfaced.

'I'm not sure how I'd have coped if it hadn't been for Georgia, Regan and Clarke being regular visitors. That was a lifeline for me. Even Graeme made a difference, although I'd never have got involved if I'd known he wanted more than I was capable of giving.'

They all knew the proposal story – or at least I assumed Georgia would have shared it with Mark – so there was no need to repeat that. I explained what had happened in the cellar with Flynn and finished off with my conversation with Jessie yesterday.

'So there you have it,' I said. 'I know that's a lot to take in and I'm sure you have questions.'

'I can't believe Trent was the one who got Noah into drugs,' Georgia said. 'Some friend he turned out to be. And I can't believe Flynn knew about it. Did he say anything to you, Mark?'

Mark shook his head. 'He probably thought I'd tell you and you'd tell Mel and it would tip her over the edge.'

'You're probably right there,' I agreed. 'I couldn't have handled the truth back then. Gosh, listen to me! I sound like Jack Nicholson in *A Few Good Men*.'

'You also sound a lot more positive,' Dad said.

'I feel it. I just wish it hadn't taken so long to get here.'

'Grief takes its own sweet time,' Dad said. 'Sounds like

yours has been waiting patiently outside until you were ready to let it in and I think you needed to be back here in Willowdale to do that. I don't think you could have done it in Newcastle.'

'No, I don't think I could.'

'Are you going to talk to Flynn about all this?' Mark asked.

'Yeah. I owe him that much.'

'I reckon he'll appreciate it. He doesn't say much, but I know he beats himself up for handling it badly.'

'There wasn't a good way he could have handled it. I was in such a mess that I think I'd have lashed out at him whatever he'd done because I couldn't lash out at the person I really wanted to – Noah – for making stupid choices and leaving us when he should have had his whole future ahead of him.'

Spending the afternoon getting it all out in the open was really therapeutic. I just wished Mum had still been around to hear me coming to terms with it all. When Georgia and Mark left, Dad asked me to stay a little longer. I hoped he hadn't taken my comment about the family visits to Newcastle being a lifeline as a dig because I hadn't meant it that way. But he had something else on his mind.

'What I'm going to tell you needs to stay between you and me because I don't want to go upsetting your sister,' he said when we settled back in the lounge.

'Okay. Go on.'

'When we were at the stone circle, I told you that it took me eighteen months to ask your mum out. I'd planned to ask her so many times but, every time we were together, something or someone got in the way. When we did finally start courting, we laughed about the false starts. June joked that we were like magnets – the attraction was there but we never quite got close enough for it to work and, once we finally connected, nothing was going to keep us apart. But it did. When you and Georgia were little, we split up.'

'You did? For how long?'

'Nearly six months.'

'Oh, my God! Why?'

'It all became too much. Parenting is hard and, even though it was obvious to me that June was an incredible mother, she didn't feel that way. Georgia had been an easy baby who got settled into a routine quickly – exactly what June had hoped for – but it was a different story with you. Nothing she'd done with Georgia worked with you and that messed with her head. Instead of seeing you as two different personalities who needed different things and adjusting her approach for you both, she kept trying the same thing over and over and blaming herself for doing it wrong. I tried to help her but everything I said or did inflamed her further – a bit like what you were saying about Flynn earlier and how he couldn't have got the approach right. I won't go into all the details – doesn't feel right when your mum's not here – but it got fraught and she asked me to leave. I didn't want to but I could see that she needed the space so I moved back in with my parents. It wasn't ideal but I wasn't worried. I knew we'd find our way back to each other because we were magnets.'

'Obviously you did, but how?'

'Time, patience and compromise.'

'Trust me to be the difficult baby,' I said, rolling my eyes.

Dad laughed. 'It was that feisty streak in you, showing itself from the very start. And if you're wondering why I'm telling you this, it's because your mum always believed that you and Flynn are magnets too and I'm inclined to agree. You needed more time than us and you'll need a lot more patience and compromise, but I really think you're meant to be. He still loves you, you know. I can tell. Just as I can tell you still love him.'

'Maybe, but it's not that simple.'

'It could be if you let it be.'

So now I finally understood what Mum had meant when she said Flynn was my magnet. Alice had said that people had interfered in her relationship with Xander but they'd been magnets and had pulled back towards each other eventually. Seeing them so happy together now, it was hard to believe they'd spent several decades apart. Could that second chance happen with Flynn and me? Was it really as simple as Dad believed – that love could conquer everything if you wanted it to? I hoped so because that was the final leap I wanted to take.

42

'Any news from Flynn?' I asked Rosie when I saw her in the kitchen the following morning.

Rosie checked her phone. 'Not yet, although it's a bank holiday so he might not come back to me till tomorrow. I'll let you know as soon as he does. And I hope you're not spending today working.'

I grimaced. That's exactly what I'd planned on doing.

She shook her head at me, smiling. 'You're a hopeless case. How about a compromise? Why don't I help you retrieve some of those boxes of photos and papers from the cellar and you can spend the day in the library going through them?'

'That would be amazing. Oliver doesn't mind?'

'He doesn't have the time to do it himself but he's interested in what's in there. He's got no problem with you going through it and pulling it into some semblance of order if you'd like that.'

'I would *love* that. You've just made my day.'

After carefully propping the cellar door open, we retrieved the first four boxes, figuring that would be more than enough to keep me out of mischief for the day. I hadn't got very far into box one when Rosie appeared.

'Email from Flynn. He's sending a team to crack on with the boat house. They'll be here a week today and he'll be here the Monday after to go through the plans for the hall properly. Slight delay but at least things are moving.'

Rosie left to meet Autumn at the stables for her riding lesson and I returned to the boxes but I'd only removed a handful of photos before I sat back on my heels with a sigh. Flynn really wouldn't be on site until a week on Monday? I'd have to wait a whole fortnight until I saw him again? That was too far away. I'd treated him terribly since I'd returned to Willowdale – ran out of the pub when he turned up, barely exchanged three words with him outside The White Willow, ignored his request to meet up and talk, refused to call him personally to let him know it was okay to come to every part of Mum's funeral, barely spoke to him when I begged him to come to the wake, but recommended him to my boss when Dougie let us down. That must have made him feel so used. And, worst of all, I'd unleashed all my frustration on him in the cellar and then I'd refused to admit that the reason things could never have worked with Graeme was because my feelings for Flynn had never changed. I was still just as deeply in love with him as I'd always been.

Last night, I'd realised something else – that a big part of the reason I'd never returned to Willowdale, despite that magnet pulling me back, was fear of Flynn rejecting me like I'd rejected him. I'd already lost Noah and could never have him back but I could pretend there was a possibility of having Flynn back as long as I didn't try and fail.

I wished I'd kept his contact details. I'd have messaged him right now if I had. Mark would give me them but I didn't want to drag him into it. I'd already made things difficult enough for my brother-in-law. This was something I had to do alone and I needed to do it now.

TO ARK BUILDING & RESTORATION LTD

Hi Flynn, Mel here. You kindly gave me your contact details for when/if I was ready to talk. I wasn't and I didn't think I ever would be so I didn't keep them but now I wish I had. If that offer to talk is still on the table while sober and not locked in a dark cellar, I'd really like to go for it. Name your time and place and I'll bend over backwards to be there

A few minutes later, a message came through with the question *Now?* and a postcode. Now? I guess there was no time like the present and it wouldn't give me time to overthink it – or at least no longer than the car journey. It also meant I had no time to fret over what to wear or whether to do my make-up. I needed to go as I was. I pinged off a reply.

TO ARK BUILDING & RESTORATION LTD

I'll be there shortly

Five minutes later, I was in my car and on my way, heading in the direction of Whinlatter Forest. The satnav took me off a side road and down a track flanked by tall conifers. At the end of the track, I slammed on the brakes and leaned forward, eyes wide, hardly able to believe what I was seeing. The location was new to me but the house was as familiar as my own face. He'd only gone and done it! He'd built our dream home.

I stayed where I was for several minutes, mouth open, hand clutching my eternity ring through my pale lemon T-shirt, taking in the stunning timber-and-glass home with steel and stone accents blending beautifully within its woodland setting. It had never entered my head that Flynn would have done this.

Realising he was standing in the doorway watching me, I pulled over beside his van and exited my car but I only managed a few paces before a wave of emotion washed over me and the tears began. I wasn't going to be able to get a sincere apology out or talk about the past if I started off with an emotional meltdown so I lifted my hand to my forehead to shield my eyes from the sun and subtly wiped at my cheeks at the same time. Being make-up free would serve me well as there'd be no mascara runs to give the game away.

Flynn joined me. 'Surprise!' he said, his voice hesitant, his forehead creased, as though unsure whether I'd see it as a good or bad surprise.

'You built our house,' I said, my voice coming out a little husky. I inwardly winced at the use of the word *our*. Yes, it was *our* design and *our* dream, but it had happened without me so it was Flynn's and I had no right to stake a claim on it.

'I did.'

'You found some land.'

'It was part of Angus's dad's farm. He died and it passed down to Angus and his brother. I asked if they had a pocket of land anywhere that they'd be willing to sell to me and they came up with this. Decades ago, it had become a dumping ground for knackered machinery and was no use to them so they gave me a good deal on the proviso I cleared it myself.'

'It's a beautiful spot.'

'It didn't look it back then. Do you want to see inside? Or we can go to the café in the forest if you'd prefer.'

'No! I'd love to see inside.' The exterior had already blown me away and there was no way I could leave without seeing the interior.

What Flynn had created was even more beautiful than I'd imagined. With us both being passionate about old properties, our challenge had always been to create something that didn't feel overtly modern. The use of wood and curves rather than metal and straight lines delivered a warm and cosy feel while floor-to-ceiling windows invited the outdoors in.

Flynn didn't say much as we moved around the rooms, letting the design speak for itself. I spotted various changes to our original design. Some were unfamiliar additions and others had been ideas I'd put forward which we'd ruled out due to cost. On the walls was a combination of artwork we'd chosen together for The Bothy and beautiful pieces Flynn must have sourced since, all of which were 100 per cent to our joint taste.

Even though Flynn wasn't a reader himself, he'd included a snug – the one room I'd been the most excited about – with a log burner, cosy armchairs and a window seat. Floor-to-ceiling shelves were filled with books, ornaments and family photos.

'I love this room,' I whispered.

When Flynn didn't respond, I wondered whether he'd even heard me. As I peered closer at the photos, tears pooled in my eyes once more. I'd assumed they'd just be photos of Flynn with Noah but I was in so many of them too.

'Willowdale Hall!' I exclaimed, spying a Lego replica on one of the shelves.

'It's not as good as yours.'

'It's brilliant. I can't believe you made this.'

'The room felt empty without it.'

There were so many memories in this one room and, although it drew tears, they were happy ones.

Flynn led me upstairs and into the bathroom and spare bedrooms before opening the door to the master suite. I was immediately drawn to the doors at the back of the room opening out onto a large balcony with views over the back garden and the woods beyond.

'That's an incredible view to kickstart the day,' I said, crouching down by the bed to see what the view would be on waking up. I grabbed the bedside cabinet to steady me as I rose. My fingers brushed against something soft and I turned to see what it was.

'Edgar,' I whispered, my heart pounding as I picked up the plush elephant. 'You kept him.'

I couldn't keep the tears at bay any longer. I sank onto the edge of the bed, cuddling Edgar to my chest as I wept. This time, my tears weren't fuelled by anger or frustration, but by regret at everything I'd missed out on because I'd been too ashamed to admit that I wasn't coping and needed help, by pushing away everyone who could have given me that help and support, by running away instead of facing my problems no matter how painful that would have been.

'I didn't mean to make you cry,' Flynn said, panic in his tone. 'Can I get you anything? Tissues? Water?'

I looked up at his kind face, so full of concern.

'A hug?' I suggested, knowing that I didn't really deserve one but wanting his comforting arms around me so badly.

I stood up with Edgar still in my hands, my eyes fixed on Flynn's, steeling myself for rejection, but he smiled and put his arms out.

Just like it had outside the Lakeside Inn the day we said goodbye to Mum, being held by Flynn felt like home. Every time he came home from work, he'd sought me out and I'd broken away from whatever I was doing to hug and kiss him. He'd found it strange that his parents never reconnected when one of them arrived home from work or shopping or a night out with friends, as though they'd barely noticed each other's absence and certainly hadn't missed each other. He'd never wanted us to be like that, never wanted me to doubt how much he missed me when we were apart.

When the tears stopped, I didn't want to let go of him, but I had to.

'Sorry about that,' I said, stepping away and sniffing. 'I've made your T-shirt soggy.'

He looked down at the wet patch. 'It'll soon dry. Are you okay?'

'Yeah. I was determined not to cry today after the cellar episode but I wasn't expecting this.'

'After I sent you the postcode, I wondered if it was the right thing to do without warning.'

'It was. If you'd said you were inviting me to your house, I'd probably have suggested somewhere neutral but I'm glad I've seen this. It's even better than I imagined. I think it might be your best work yet and that was already an incredibly high bar.'

'That means a lot to me. It's not quite perfect, but...' He tailed off and shrugged. 'You wanted to talk. Should we grab a coffee?'

I wanted to ask what would achieve perfection for him but he was already on his way down the stairs. It looked pretty damn perfect to me, but perhaps the imperfections were noticeable from living in the property – a room which could have been bigger, a window positioned differently, more built-in storage space and so on.

Flynn told me to make myself comfortable in the lounge, checked what I wanted to drink, and headed into the kitchen area. The main living space was open plan with a colour palette of warm woodland tones. I wandered round the room, looking more closely at the items he had on display. I was drawn towards a shelving unit with the most beautifully crafted ark I'd ever seen. Pairs of animals were lined up waiting to board while Noah and his wife waited on board to welcome them. We'd bought our Noah a colourful wooden ark when he was little and he'd loved playing with it. I'd thought the detail on that one had been beautiful but this one of Flynn's was next level.

'This is stunning,' I said as Flynn joined me and handed me a coffee. 'Where did you find it?'

'I commissioned it. It isn't just an ark. I don't want to make you cry again but there's no way of cushioning this. You see how Noah's crook is metal?'

'Oh, yeah,' I said, peering closer. 'It's sparkly too.'

'A jeweller made it with some of our Noah's ashes inside the metal. The rest are in a container at the bottom of the boat so they can be removed and scattered. I didn't want to do that without you so... I hope that was okay.'

Tears escaped once more. I'd often wondered what Flynn had done with Noah's ashes. I'd nearly taken them when I left. I'd actually picked up the urn but it hadn't felt right to take Noah away from his home and his dad without discussing it and I wasn't strong enough to have that discussion so I left them, trusting that Flynn would do the right thing. I could never have imagined such a beautiful tribute to our son.

'It's really special. Thank you for doing that.'

I wiped my cheeks and went to take a sip of my coffee but paused when I realised that the mug he'd given me was my favourite one.

'You kept it!' I exclaimed.

He shrugged, but didn't say anything. The air between us crackled and I wondered whether Flynn's heart was thumping as fast as mine. He was so close, I could easily touch his face, kiss his lips. And that wasn't going to help resolve anything.

'I guess we'd better have that talk,' I said, trying to pull myself together. 'Or I'm going to keep finding things to distract me.' Like Flynn.

We sat at either end of a large sofa. 'How was your head after our impromptu drinking session?' I asked, thinking the conversation could be heavy so opening it with humour might be good.

Flynn smiled. 'Not so good. Couldn't tell you the last time I drank red wine. Yours?'

'The same.' I bit my lip and shook my head. 'There's so much I need to explain and apologise for…'

Flynn had always been a good listener – one of the many things I loved about him. He knew how much the feisty part of me needed to vent before I could have a calm, considered conversation and, although I wasn't venting this morning, I was a tangle of emotions as I talked about all the things that had been going through my head back then and what I'd made sense of since returning to Willowdale. It was an edited version of what I'd told my family, missing out the part about how I felt about Flynn for now. I would tell him, despite the fear of rejection, but it was more important to get everything else out in the open. I wanted to focus on the future, but a future with Flynn would be impossible without addressing the past.

He shared how he'd felt about what happened and it was enlightening to hear it through his perspective. I was aware of how carefully he chose his words, suggesting we'd both made mistakes rather than heaping the blame on me. I really appreciated the sensitivity, but I was the one who'd left and I was taking ownership of that and a whole lot more.

'You're not shouldering all the blame,' Flynn said. 'I won't let you. We were a partnership and we both made mistakes. We could both have handled things differently, and it's only when you have time and space that you can see that.'

He was so kind and gracious but part of my healing was to accept responsibility for the part I'd played in the end of our marriage and, while Flynn hadn't been perfect, I'd caused the most damage. If he'd been the rain, I'd been the raging storm.

'Thanks for speaking to Jessie for me,' I said. 'I met up with her on Saturday. I hadn't seen that one coming.'

'Me neither. When I found out, I thought about letting you know but I was worried it might do further damage.'

'It might have done back then.'

'Has it helped now?'

'Massively.' I told him about our conversation and my epiphany that, while what had happened to Noah was the most terrible tragedy, it had been caused by our son making a dangerous choice and not by anybody else.

'I'm so relieved you've accepted that now,' Flynn said.

'I still feel I had a part to play. I don't know if I'll ever feel completely guilt-free but I'm in a better place now than I thought I could ever be.'

We'd covered a lot of ground and come to a natural pause in the conversation. Flynn asked if I wanted to join him for a spot of lunch – a smoked salmon salad which we ate in the back garden.

'I can't stop looking at the house,' I said as I placed my cutlery down after we'd eaten. 'Can I ask why you included the parts we'd dismissed? And why did you keep Edgar and my favourite mug?'

A pause. 'I had my reasons.'

I didn't miss the stiffness in his tone. He stacked my plate on top of his and rose from his seat but I placed my hand over his.

'It's okay if you don't want to tell me.'

'It's not that.' He sighed and sat back down, pushing the plates aside. 'It's just that I don't think you'll want to hear the answers.' He scratched his head – a tell-tale indicator that he was nervous – before fixing his eyes on mine.

'Try me,' I said, gently.

He clasped his hands behind his head and I prepared for a big announcement.

'Okay. I changed the house for the same reason I didn't sell The Bothy straightaway. I kept hoping that one day you'd come back and we'd live in our dream home together, like we'd always planned. I felt like I'd let you down in our marriage so there was no way I was going to let you down with our home. When you came back, I wanted you to be able to drink from your favourite mug.'

I placed my hand over my necklace, tears pricking my eyes.

'As for Edgar, they say elephants never forget so I kept him on your side of the bed to make sure I never forgot about us. Something horrendous happened and it broke us but there were twenty-two and a half years before that which were amazing and Edgar was there right from the very first moment. I hoped he'd be there for a second chance too because I never stopped loving you.'

I stared at him through watery eyes, stunned at the beautiful things he was saying and how romantic it all was.

He stiffened when I didn't respond and grabbed the plates as he stood up. 'I know that's a lot to take in but I've never lied to you and I never will.'

I sat there for a moment, letting it all sink in. If he could be that honest with me, I could be with him. I followed him inside where he was loading the dishwasher noisily.

'You have so many amazing qualities,' I said. 'You're always kind, calm and thoughtful, even towards those who don't necessarily deserve it.'

He continued loading the dishwasher, but quietly, and I could imagine him wondering where this was going.

'You're passionate, romantic, funny, honest... I could keep going if you want.'

He straightened up and leaned against the worktop, arms folded but expression open.

'I manage all those things at work. Well, maybe not the romance part...' I rolled my eyes at him and drew a smile at that. 'For some reason I struggle with several of those traits outside of work. Although my outburst in the cellar might suggest otherwise, I have got much better at being calm, but I'm still really struggling with honesty. It's not that I lie. It's more that I keep things in when they're hard. I've done that a lot since Noah died and it has to stop. In the cellar, you asked me why it ended with Graeme and I said we wanted different things. Truth. But with a major omission. The different thing I wanted was you.'

Flynn's eyes lit up for a moment but he didn't shift position and I knew I'd need to work hard to convince him.

I pointed towards his wedding band. 'There's a reason I had the infinity symbol engraved on your ring. It's because I knew my love for you would last forever and it has, but I didn't think there was any way you could possibly feel the same about me after how I behaved. I destroyed us. I didn't deserve a second chance.'

'You were ill.'

'I didn't know that at the time. I thought what I was doing was normal and everyone else was being weird. There's something else.' I reached into the neckline of my T-shirt and lifted out my eternity ring on its chain. 'You're not the only one who couldn't take your ring off. I've kept this one on a chain next to my heart all this time.'

He unfolded his arms, his expression tender.

'Since I got back I've been thinking a lot about us,' I said. 'I've thought about the big moments like when we met and your proposal on Blencathra, but also the little things that meant the world to me like how you hugged me tightly every time you came home, how you always waited up for me if I needed to work late, how you said goodnight to Edgar before we went to sleep.'

His cheeks coloured and he smiled ruefully. 'I probably shouldn't admit it, but I still do that.'

'Admit away. It's lovely because you're lovely. Mum asked me why I'd split up with Graeme and I fobbed her off with the same excuse I gave you – we wanted different things – but she called me out on it. She said the different thing I wanted was you because you were my magnet. I didn't know what she meant at the time but I know now that it's the person who draws you back because you were always meant to be with them. You *are* my magnet, Flynn. It's always been you but I'm scared. So scared. Saying we never stopped loving each other is the easy part. What if we try again but we've changed too much? What if we can't get over what happened in the past? What if—'

I stopped as Flynn gently placed his hands on my cheeks. 'What if you just shut up and let me kiss you?'

I nodded and closed my eyes as his lips brushed against mine, sending a pulse of excitement rushing through my whole body.

'What if you stop overthinking?' he added.

He kissed me again, slowly and softly.

'And what if we accept that we don't have the answers but we find them out together this time?' He brushed his thumbs across my cheeks. 'I know it's a lot and we've been apart a long time but I know my feelings for you are never going to change. I've always been and always will be in this forever.'

As I melted into his kiss, I knew why this place felt like home.

It wasn't because I'd designed it or because I recognised ornaments and paintings from The Bothy or because he'd made my coffee in my favourite mug. It was because Flynn was here. Beautiful as it was, we'd never needed this dream home – we'd just needed each other.

43

A week later it was time to break ground at the boat house. Flynn had rearranged his schedule to make sure he could be there on what was a special day for all of us. For Oliver and Rosie, it symbolised the start of an exciting new era for the beautiful estate through which they'd been reunited. For Alice, it represented a rise from the ashes and the power to take something broken and make it beautiful again. The words she'd said to me the first time I'd seen the boat house still resonated with me – *Even the things that seem the most broken can be fixed with enough time, love and will.* At the time she'd added, *A bit like me*, but it was my truth too.

Alice and I had taken another walk up Cat Bells with the dogs last week. We'd had a wonderful heart to heart in which I'd told her all about Noah and Flynn. I'd thanked her for sharing her experiences with me because what she'd been through and what she'd learned from it had helped me immensely. I'd reminded her what she'd said about the broken pieces and shared how returning to Willowdale had helped pull mine back together.

'I'll never be fully intact,' I told her. 'It's not possible without

Noah, but I now feel like there are enough pieces to restore me to the point where I can see the sunshine after the rain.'

Alice had smiled at me. 'I don't think anyone makes it through life in one piece, although there are certainly some of us who get a lot more broken and battered along the way than others. I don't think healing is about putting every single broken shard back together. Healing can be about creating a different version of you. Have you heard of kintsugi – the Japanese art of repairing broken pottery with gold? It's just like that. After the accident, there's a moment when the vase or the dish or whatever it is will look like a lost cause, beyond repair, but some time, patience and love can turn it into something more exquisite in its imperfections.' She laughed lightly. 'You need a bit of gold too, of course, but you see where I'm going with the analogy.'

'I do and it's perfect.'

When we'd returned from our walk, I'd gone online to find out more about kintsugi. I'd seen photos of repaired pots before, but I didn't know much about the concept. With a rough translation of *joining with gold*, kintsugi had been around for thousands of years and had become a part of a philosophy around embracing flaws and the fragility of life. It really was perfect for me. I'd needed time, patience and love to put me back together but the key ingredient – the gold – had been Flynn and my family. Without them, those broken pieces would have remained that way. They were the glue that made me whole.

'My lads are ready to break ground,' Flynn said, joining Oliver, Rosie, Alice, Xander, Emma, Christian, Killian and me. 'Ready?'

I glanced at my new friends. We were all more than ready for this. Flynn waved to the mini excavator operator then put his arm round my shoulders as the scoop lowered and dug into the ground.

'The start of our first project working together,' Flynn said, cuddling me to his side. 'Willowdale Hall, eh? Doesn't get better than that.'

'Worth the wait?' I asked.

He looked down at me, his smile dazzling. 'Absolutely.'

And I knew he didn't just mean the chance to work at Willowdale Hall. The first time I'd seen Flynn, I'd been enchanted by his dazzling smile and had wanted to be the person who made it appear. How wonderful that, after everything we'd been through, I could do that again.

He lightly kissed me before running over to join his crew. I glanced across at Alice who was also smiling as she watched the buckled doors being ripped off the back of the boat house. She turned to meet my eyes.

'Kintsugi,' I said to her.

'Kintsugi,' she repeated, nodding at me.

I wasn't going to tell Alice but, when the boat house was ready for its interior design work, a kintsugi vase would be taking pride of place. I was sure she'd love that.

We watched for another ten minutes or so before returning to our activities for the day. Rosie headed off to the stables to meet Autumn for her riding lesson, Alice and Xander took the dogs for a walk, Emma and Christian returned to Casa Alpaca to meet some customers, Killian disappeared to do some fencing repairs, and Oliver went into Keswick to sign some paperwork. He'd secured the job at the surgery and was currently working his notice, which was fantastic news for him and Rosie. The agreed sale of his Penrith house would also mean additional capital for the project so good news for all of us.

* * *

Over the weeks that followed, Flynn and I spent a lot of time together working on the plans for Willowdale Hall. It was a dream to be working with him once more and we'd both expressed surprise at how easily we'd slipped back into being colleagues, as though there'd never been a gap.

Conscious that a romantic relationship where we just slipped back into our old patterns might not be the best way forward, we made the time to go out on proper dates. We had nights out at new restaurants and pubs as well as revisiting some of the places we'd loved in times past. We took romantic walks and even hired some kayaks from Willowdale Marina one day for a paddle on the lake. I was extremely wobbly at first but it soon came back to me – just like being with Flynn. After so long apart, it had taken us several tentative kisses before we settled back into being together but practice makes perfect and we'd certainly got a lot of practice in.

Much as I loved going out with Flynn, my favourite moments were when we were at his house, Woodland Rest. I'd been so entranced by the house that I hadn't noticed the name on my first visit. It was ideal for Noah's resting place in his ark. One day we might scatter his ashes, just leaving a small part of him forever with us in the metal staff, but for now it felt right that he was where we were, reunited as a family at last. Flynn had kept his promise about Noah's belongings. He'd placed them in storage for all these years so we had those to sort through too, but not just yet. We'd do it when the time felt right.

It was spring bank holiday – the last Monday in May – and the area would be heaving with visitors so Flynn and I were spending a peaceful day together at Woodland Rest. We'd had the whole of the family round for a barbeque yesterday and I'd shed a few tears seeing how happy they all were to have Flynn back as part of the family and knowing how much it meant to Flynn to be back in the fold once more. When I'd first told everyone we were trying again, they'd been delighted. Georgia had cried and Dad had hugged me before saying *magnets*, looking heavenward and nodding, as though communicating to Mum that she'd been right all along.

We'd also been out for a meal with Flynn's parents and I was relieved that neither of them held any animosity towards me for abandoning their son. They'd divorced a few years back so I'd been surprised at the suggestion to meet them together, but Flynn had told me they were getting on better apart than they ever had done when they were married. It seemed that marriage hadn't worked for them but friendship did.

Today, the glass doors along the back of the house had been pulled back, creating a seamless living space between inside and out. I was sprawled on my back on the sofa reading and Flynn was just relaxing, a bottle of beer in his hand, listening to the birds singing outside. I became aware of being watched and placed my book down on my stomach, smiling at him.

'Can I help you?' I teased.

'Just thinking how good it is to have you here.'

'It's good to be here. Really good.'

He took a sip of his beer and I returned to my book, contentment flowing through me at how much I loved spending time in Woodland Rest. I thought about my tour of the house and how he'd mentioned it was *not quite perfect* but hadn't expanded on that. In the times I'd visited, he'd never mentioned what was wrong with the place and I hadn't noticed any issues myself. I laid my book down again and reminded him of what he'd said.

'What would make it perfect?' I asked. 'I haven't found anything wrong.'

'It was this close to perfect the day you first visited,' he said, holding his finger and thumb about an inch apart.

'Very close, then.'

'And now it's this close.' He moved his finger and thumb nearer, smiling at me. 'You being here right now has done that. I love this – just being with you doing nothing in particular.'

'Me too. So what would make it completely perfect?'

'If you were here all the time.'

I closed my book and sat up properly, my heart racing.

'Move in with me, Mel. I know we said we'd take it slowly but I'm not convinced that's what either of us really want. It's certainly not what Edgar wants.'

I laughed at the mention of the elephant. 'Keep talking,' I said, shuffling closer to him.

'You can't stay at Willowdale Hall for much longer and the truth is that this is *our* house. I built it to *our* plans and I built it for us. You talk about buildings breathing. Well, Woodland Rest only started breathing properly when you arrived. What do you think?'

I shuffled closer still. 'I think that sounds perfect. Yes! Absolutely yes!'

Flynn's lips met mine and I melted into his kiss. For years, a fire had burned inside me fuelled by anger and frustration, but now a fire burned fuelled by passion for this incredible man. When I'd left him, he'd said, *I hope you find the answers you need, Mel. And when you do – or if you hit a point where you decide you don't need them anymore – I'll be waiting for you. Even if that takes weeks or months. Even if it takes years*. It *had* taken years but he'd kept his promise and waited for me. Now I was here to stay and I'd forever be grateful that, just like my parents, Flynn and I were magnets. We'd been on a hell of a journey both together and apart, but we'd navigate the rest of our life together and I'd never let the storm tear us apart again.

EPILOGUE
THREE MONTHS LATER

'Thank you all for coming,' Rosie said, her gaze taking in the crowd gathered on the lawn out the back of Willowdale Hall. 'This is an exciting moment for Oliver and me and it's such an honour to see so many of you here today – friends, family, neighbours, colleagues. As you all know, I love Willowdale Hall and I believed it could become great again. It has a history of being a place of safety and of healing – a place of convalescence for officers injured in World War I and a school for evacuees from Tyneside during World War II. Inspired by that, Oliver and I had a vision to make this a place where people can escape and heal. Last September, the arrival of our wonderful Emma and her seven gorgeous alpacas signalled the start of that...'

She waved in Emma's direction and Emma put her hands in the air, smiling as the crowd applauded.

'Today we're celebrating the first phase in our accommodation, creating luxurious rooms where guests can find peace and escapism. The boat house behind me has had a few struggles and Oliver and I were going to have it dismantled but my amazing mam, Alice, convinced us to keep it. And then along came our exceptionally talented conservation architect, Mel, with a vision to take the broken pieces and turn it into something astonishingly beautiful.'

She paused for more applause and I smiled, cringing at being the centre of attention – even if only for a moment – but appreciative of Rosie's kind words.

'Thank you to Flynn and his team for their work and to Mel again for her beautiful interior design. We'd originally talked about getting the boat house ready for the summer season but, considering it's the last Friday in August, you can guess how that went. Mel came up with the genius idea of running a competition where people could nominate someone they know who's had a tough time and could really benefit from spending a weekend for two away from all their worries in a place designed for peace and healing. We were in tears going through the entries and our heart goes out to all the people who are facing challenges in their lives right now. No way could we just pick one winner as originally intended so we chose three. The first winners will be staying next weekend but we wanted to give you all the first glimpse. Are you ready?'

Oliver passed her a pair of scissors.

'We considered several names but, in the end, we settled for something simple which says exactly what it is. I'm delighted to declare The Boat House officially open!'

Rosie cut the turquoise ribbon to cheers and another round of applause, then invited the guests to look around. Alice and Xander were in the first group.

'There's something in the lounge I think you'll appreciate,' I told Alice before she stepped onto the wraparound terrace.

It had been such a delight to furnish The Boat House in

restful colours. I'd loved sourcing the furniture and fabrics but the most precious purchase for me had been the kintsugi vase in Alice's honour. I'd found one in shades of blue, grey and green to match the landscape but the green was also a nod to the green man who'd haunted her for so long. I'd particularly loved how one of the gold repairs ran right through the green section and was certain she'd see the relevance when she saw it.

The Boat House was small so the tours were quick. Alice and Xander reappeared shortly after and Alice rushed over to me, arms outstretched, and hugged me close.

'I saw it and I loved it. Thank you for doing that. I noticed the colour too. It's absolutely perfect.'

'No, not perfect,' I said, smiling at her. 'It's exquisitely flawed like you and me.'

We hugged again and I counted my blessings that I'd met this wonderful woman who'd taught me so much and whose friendship I would value forever.

One of the grand function rooms had doors out onto the garden so they'd been opened up. There was a bar and buffet set up in the room and chairs and tables both inside and out. All my family had been invited and I noticed Georgia in deep conversation with Rosie. It looked like they were scheming something because they kept looking in my direction and smiling.

'What are you two up to?' I asked, joining them.

'Ooh, you'll find out soon enough,' Georgia said, winking at me.

It was a wonderful evening and I basked in the compliments for the design of the building and the interior. I even had a few enquiries as to whether I could be commissioned for home interior design. It was flattering but that wasn't my job – it was simply something I happened to enjoy and occasionally got involved in if the client asked me. The conservation architecture would always be my number one passion. Actually, number two. My husband would forever be my number one.

Flynn and I hadn't wanted to make a fuss about remarrying last Friday but we couldn't leave out either of our families. We'd made so many new friends through Willowdale Hall who'd been part of our journey back to each other who we couldn't miss out either so we'd had a small ceremony with just Dad, Georgia, Mark and Flynn's parents in attendance but ended up having quite the party in The Hardy Herdwick afterwards. It seemed only fitting that we celebrated our second chance in the place where we'd first met.

'Your wedding gift finally arrived,' Alice said, taking me to one side. 'Have you got a minute?'

She led me through the function room and into the library. We'd said no gifts but most guests had ignored that.

'Apologies again that it didn't arrive on time,' she said, picking up a wrapped box.

'Should I have grabbed Flynn?' I asked, suddenly registering that a wedding gift would be for both of us.

'No, it's fine. It's obviously for both of you, but it's more for you and I think you'll be quite amused.'

I removed the wrapping paper, opened up the box and lifted out an object encased in two pieces of polystyrene. Removing one piece, I saw what Alice meant about me being amused.

'A kintsugi vase,' I said, laughing. I studied the stunning vase in pinks and reds with gold ribbons running through it. 'It's perfect.'

'No. It's exquisitely flawed,' she said, copying my statement from earlier. 'Just like you and me. Great minds, eh?'

I hugged her. 'Great minds indeed. Thank you for this. I love it. And I appreciate the colours too.'

'Now that you've got colour back in your life, it had to be done.'

I packed the vase away and we returned to the function room and it was then that I spotted what Rosie and Georgia had been up to. Arnie from The Hardy Herdwick was setting up a karaoke machine.

'Not a chance!' I said as Georgia grinned at me.

'It has to be done. And you know what we're singing, don't you?'

I grabbed a glass of wine from the bar. 'I'd better get a couple of these down me first.'

An hour later, Georgia and I picked up a microphone each as the opening bars to Zoë's 'Sunshine on a Rainy Day' sounded. I rolled my eyes at her but sang along to the first verse anyway, encouraging the guests to join in with the chorus. As we approached the end of the first chorus, Georgia handed her microphone to Flynn and he smiled as he took over singing.

During the instrumental break, I lowered my microphone.

'I thought "Ain't No Sunshine" was your song.'

Flynn lowered his microphone too. 'It was, but I might have overplayed it while you were away.'

Microphones raised once more, we finished the song with the help of the guests before retrieving our drinks and swiftly making our way outside before we were roped into singing anything else.

The sun was setting and The Boat House looked stunning against an orange-hued sky. Everyone was either in the function room or just outside so we headed down the lawn, along the wraparound terrace, and stopped on the deck.

'I really am so sorry I took your sunshine away,' I said.

'It was raining,' he replied, pulling me close. 'And now you've brought me the sunshine after the rain and all is good in the world again.'

As he kissed me slowly and tenderly, I felt as though my world had finally shifted back onto its axis, although not on the same axis as before. Flynn and I had eventually found our way through the storm and, although we'd emerged into the sunshine, we weren't back to where we'd started. We were now in a new and different world. This new world would always be tinged with sadness because Noah and Mum were missing from it. A world in which my dad was trying hard to adjust to life without the woman he loved, sometimes taking strides forward but frequently stumbling and occasionally falling. But this was also a world full of hope and second chances – the pot of gold at the end of the rainbow – and I would be forever grateful to the wonderful people in my life who'd helped me see that. This new world wasn't perfect but it was exquisite in its perfections, just like me, Alice, Dad, Flynn and everyone else I knew who'd overcome adversity or was battling to do so, facing one day at a time with courage and hope.

When we pulled apart, I turned to look back at Willowdale Hall and smiled as Emma's words came back to me from the day I met her – *We'll soon have you all relaxed and any wounds healed.* That's exactly what had happened. This beautiful place which I'd fallen in love with as a child really did have the power to heal and what a gift it was to be working here, married to Flynn again, business partners once more, playing my part in bringing the sunshine after the rain for Rosie and her family and all the guests who stayed here.

I ran my fingers along the necklace I was wearing – the delicate silver chain Noah had given me for my fortieth birthday – and I had a sudden vision of him and Mum hugging each other as Mum whispered to him, *I was right about your parents. Magnets. But I'm always right.*

Maybe not always but, on this occasion, she absolutely was.

* * *

MORE FROM JESSICA REDLAND

Another book from Jessica Redland, *Healing Hearts at Bumblebee Farm*, is available to order now here:
    https://mybook.to/HealingHeartsBackAd

ACKNOWLEDGEMENTS

Each time I start writing my acknowledgements, I can't quite believe that I've made it to the end of another novel. This is my twenty-sixth book, released into the world very close to the tenth anniversary of my first ever book coming out. My debut book was actually a novella which came out on 23 May 2015 (now reissued as *Making Wishes at Bay View*, combining the novella and a sequel) with my first full-length novel (now *New Beginnings at Seaside Blooms*) released eleven days later on 3 June. Back then, I had no idea if I'd make it but early indications weren't favourable. My publisher ceased trading and I spent a few years as an indie disaster with pretty much no sales. I hoped my luck would change but with each new release bombing, it was looking less and less likely. Then the incredible Boldwood Books was established, I submitted to them on day one, they said yes, and the rest is history. Yay!

In celebration of ten years as a published author, this book is dedicated to you, the reader. Whether this is the first book of mine you've read or whether you've read them all, I'm so grateful. Whether you've discovered my work recently or been with me right from the start, I cannot thank you enough. Whether you've found my books online, in a shop, or through a recommendation by a friend (real or virtual!), I'm so appreciative. Without you buying or borrowing my books via a subscription service or library, I couldn't keep writing them because there'd be no income and I'd need to return to a 'regular' job to pay the bills.

I hope you've enjoyed reading about Mel's struggle to find the sunshine after the rain. While Mel fought to find her happy ending, so did I. I knew this book would be the start of the construction work at Willowdale Hall and I knew it would tell the story of a builder and an architect who'd been torn apart after the tragic death of their son, but the scenes I'd imagined between them just didn't fit for the Mel and Flynn who arrived on the page. They were meant to be angry with each other – an enemies-to-lovers story – but they refused to play ball. Mel was broken and angry with herself and Flynn was calm and hopeful. *Cheers, guys, you've completely scuppered that idea!* And the locked-room scenario I'd imagined – being snowed in – didn't work for the time of year. *Argh!* But the story they ultimately told me is one I prefer, which unexpectedly intertwined with the story of another character from Willowdale Hall. I'm looking at you, Alice!

An enormous thank you has to go to my bestie, super-talented author Sharon Booth. I always thank her in my books because I honestly couldn't do this without her help. Sharon helped me with my Flynn and Mel problems and my locked-room scenario, suggesting I move it to the cellar and that the stress of the situation would have Mel finally pouring out her hurt and pounding her fists on Flynn's chest. Sharon, you star! THANK YOU!

Thank you also to my wonderful editor, Emily Ruston. This is the first book we've worked on as a pair. She edited my last release too but with the support of my outgoing editor, Nia. When we were discussing how broken Mel was, Emily mentioned the Japanese art of kintsugi which really came alive for me in the final chapters for both Mel and for Alice. Emily – I'm extremely grateful for how positive you are with your valuable suggestions for improvement.

I always undertake detailed research for my books. Thank

you to Carol, a funeral director, for a lengthy conversation guiding me through the process and answering copious questions about the role of the police, coroners, medical professionals and funeral directors. Thank you also to Dr Jemima for her medical insights and steering me right on some assumptions I'd wrongly made about GPs passing on cause of death details.

A huge thank you to Harriet Salisbury, Administrative Assistant at Newcastle Cathedral for answering a multitude of questions to ensure Mel's visit to this real place was accurately conveyed. Harriet even annotated a map for me to show where to find the candles and donation boxes, and checked the Newcastle FC fixtures to see whether there'd have been a game on the day Mel visited the cathedral, making the city busier with fans. Thank you also to Pamela Spearing, Margaret Stephenson and Sara Louise – all members of my lovely Facebook group, Redland's Readers (you're very welcome to join us) – for their help in understanding how Mel might aimlessly wander from the shops to the cathedral. Their local knowledge, a map trail from Sara Louise and photos from Margaret helped me realise that an aimless wander was unlikely to lead Mel to the cathedral so I changed the story to make her visit deliberate. I live too far from Newcastle to have checked this detail out myself and it's wonderful when readers can help like this.

I needed names for several properties in this book and again turned to the members of Redland's Readers for some ideas for the three properties in Whinlatter Close. Thank you to Jill Andrews for The Bothy, Alice Cary for The Byre and Karen Armstrong for The Stables. The names worked together brilliantly.

They say it takes a village to raise a child. Well, that's true of publishing a book too. As well as Emily who I've already mentioned, my village is Boldwood's fabulous head of marketing,

Claire Fenby, who is such a joy to work with on my campaigns, Issy Flynn, Megan Townsend (welcome back!), Wendy Neale, Ben Wilson and the rest of the production team, and our inspiring and wonderful CEO, Amanda Ridout.

Thanks to the superb work of my copy editor Cecily Blench and my proofreader Susan Sugden for knocking the manuscript into shape and to Lizzie Gardiner for another incredible cover design. Thank you to Rachel Gilbey for organising the blog tour and all the fabulous bloggers/reviewers who so generously give their time to review the book for me. You're all superstars.

Once again, the story has been brought to life on the audiobook by the vocal talents of Rebecca Norfolk. Thank you also to ISIS Audio for the recording and Ulverscroft for the distribution to libraries. And thank you to all the amazing librarians out there who champion romantic fiction – #respectromfic – and who have recommended my books to their users. What wonderful people you are!

Thanks as ever to my fabulous husband, Mark, and our daughter, Ashleigh, who I'm sure are sick to death of the words, 'Please don't disturb me today, I'm on a deadline' and take heed of the request. Well, some of the time!

Thank you to my parents who always send me a congratulations card for each new book release. Huge hugs go to my wonderful mum who, like June, is in terrible pain with her back and has mobility challenges as a consequence, and to my fabulous dad who is her carer. For anyone else in daily pain, I send you my empathy and best wishes. While there are a couple of similarities between my parents and Mel's, I must emphasise that Bruce and June are *not* inspired by my parents. This is a piece of fiction and they are both fictional characters with fictional relationships with their daughters.

Finally, thank you to the authors at Team Boldwood for the

support and championing and my longstanding writing support group, The Write Romantics. Special thank you hugs to Jo Bartlett, Jackie Ladbury and Sharon Booth with whom I had the most amazing and inspiring writing weekend last year. We laughed such a lot and I'll never forget the moment when Jo and I were chased by a particularly aggressive swan. Special (if a little scary) times!

Big hugs, Jessica xx

ABOUT THE AUTHOR

Jessica Redland is a million-copy bestseller, writing uplifting stories of love, friendship, family and community. Her Escape to the Lakes books transport readers to the stunning Lake District and her Hedgehog Hollow series takes them to the beautiful countryside of the Yorkshire Wolds.

Sign up to Jessica Redland's mailing list here for news, competitions and updates on future books.

Visit Jessica's website: www.jessicaredland.com

Follow Jessica on social media:

facebook.com/JessicaRedlandAuthor
x.com/JessicaRedland
instagram.com/JessicaRedlandAuthor
bookbub.com/authors/jessica-redland

ALSO BY JESSICA REDLAND

WHITSBOROUGH BAY

Welcome to Whitsborough Bay

Making Wishes at Bay View

New Beginnings at Seaside Blooms

Finding Hope at Lighthouse Cove

Coming Home to Seashell Cottage

Christmas on Castle Street Collection

Christmas Wishes at the Chocolate Shop

Christmas at Carly's Cupcakes

Starry Skies Over The Chocolate Pot Café

Christmas at the Cat Café

The Starfish Café

Snowflakes Over the Starfish Café

Spring Tides at the Starfish Café

Summer Nights at the Starfish Café

Standalones

All You Need is Love

The Secret to Happiness

YORKSHIRE WOLDS

Hedgehog Hollow

Finding Love at Hedgehog Hollow

New Arrivals at Hedgehog Hollow

Family Secrets at Hedgehog Hollow

A Wedding at Hedgehog Hollow

Chasing Dreams at Hedgehog Hollow

Christmas Miracles at Hedgehog Hollow

The Bumblebee Barn Collection

Healing Hearts at Bumblebee Barn

A New Dawn at Owl's Lodge

A Forever Home at Honey Bee Croft

THE LAKE DISTRICT

Escape to the Lakes

The Start of Something Wonderful

A Breath of Fresh Air

The Best is Yet to Come

Sunshine After the Rain

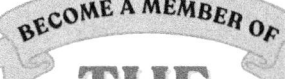
BECOME A MEMBER OF

THE SHELF CARE CLUB

The home of Boldwood's
book club reads.

Find uplifting reads,
sunny escapes, cosy romances,
family dramas and more!

Sign up to the newsletter
https://bit.ly/theshelfcareclub

Boldw♾️d

Boldwood Books is an award-winning fiction publishing company seeking out the best stories from around the world.

Find out more at www.boldwoodbooks.com

Join our reader community for brilliant books, competitions and offers!

Follow us
@BoldwoodBooks
@TheBoldBookClub

Sign up to our weekly deals newsletter

https://bit.ly/BoldwoodBNewsletter

Printed in Great Britain
by Amazon

62453329R00208